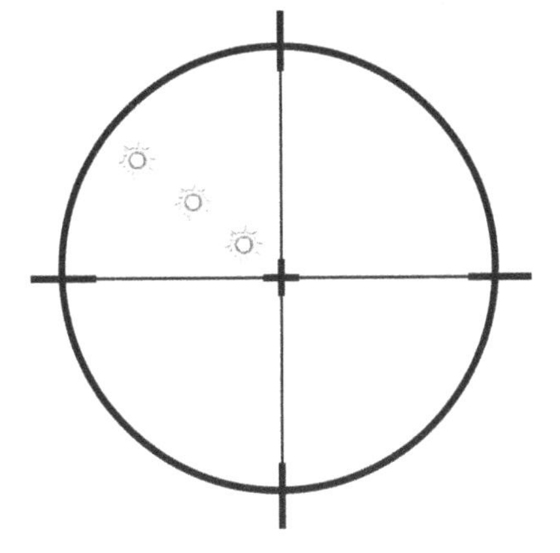

The Korean Connection

(a novel)

Other books by Dave Admire:

Terror in Paris

Samir's Revenge

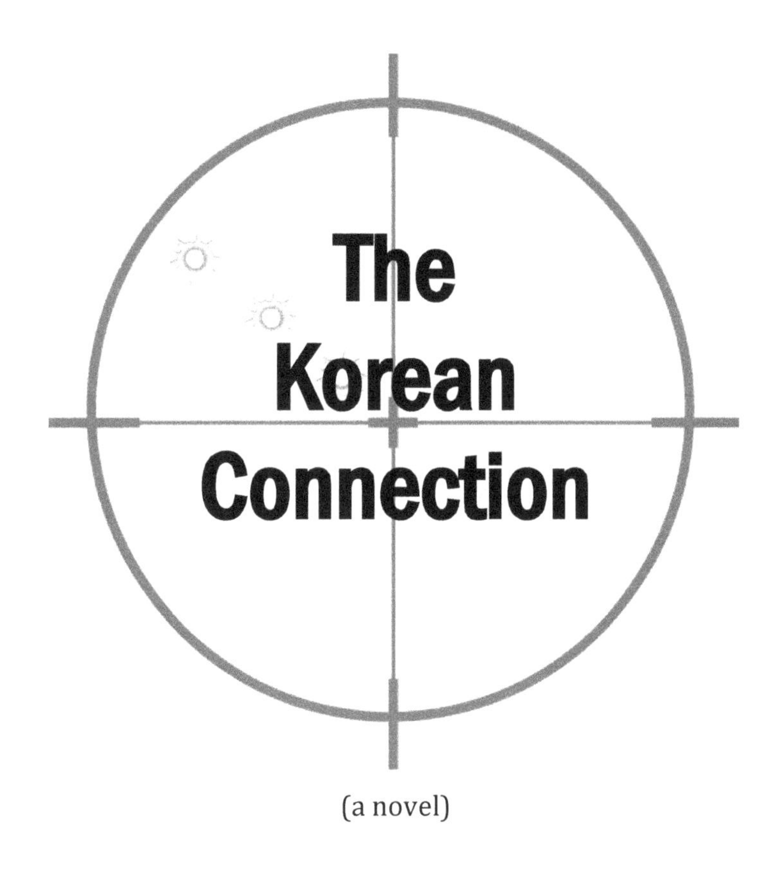

The Korean Connection

(a novel)

Dave Admire

Three Towers Press
Milwaukee, Wisconsin

Published by
Three Towers Press
An imprint of HenschelHAUS Publishing, Inc.
www.HenschelHAUSbooks.com

HenschelHAUS titles may be purchased in bulk for educational, business, fundraising, or promotional use. For information, please email info@henschelhausbooks.com

Hardcover ISBN: 978159598-982-6
Paperback ISBN:978159598-984-0

Library of Congress Control Number: 2023950994

Cover design by Ryan Allen, BigRDesign.com

Printed in the United States of America or other location.

This book is dedicated to my grandchildren Madelyn, Emma, Sophia, and Layla, who have brought and continue to bring joy to our lives.

Cast of Characters

Professors' Group
DJ Anderson, Sandy Anderson
Mac McDonald, Ann McDonald
Ty Smith, Leanne Smith
Derek, former student

US Government Group
John Bradford, US President
Layla Richards, Exec. Secretary
Renee, intern

National Security Advisors
Toni McCrae, Secretary of State
Kyle Taylor, Secretary of Defense
Brian Jenson, Secretary of Homeland Security
Julianne Simmons, Director of National National Intelligence
Eileen, Assistant
Brad Nelson, Chief of Staff
Bill Simpson, NSA

Military
Adm. Lara Williams, Vice Chair JCS
Gen. Pete Witkowski, Chair, JCS
Adm. David Miller, Cdr of US/IndoPac Com.
Adm. Wilson Turner, Cmd of USS *Reagan* fleet
Cdr. Jonas Hardy, CO of USS *Jackson*
Lt. Cdr Sam Hall, XO of USS *Jackson*
Cdr Jason Allen, CO of USS *Ohio*
Cdr. Jesse Carter, CO of USS *Georgia*
Capt. Shane Johnson, pilot
Lt. Donnie Sherman, co-pilot
Sgt. Jimmy O'Neil, loadmaster
Sgt. Wally Putnam, loadmaster
Maj. Jack Elliot

FBI
Ryan Tupper, Director
Sam Wyman, Director of Counterterrorism
Art Rheingold, Special Agent In Charge
Ross Hixson, agent
William Johnson, agent
Jim Franks, agent
John Wells, agent
Jim Driscoll, agent

Senate
Senator Kendricks
Phil Jackson, Chief of Staff
Linda Purcell, lobbyist
Ned Smith, RNC
Senator Bill Henry
Janice Peel, Director of Republican Women's Organization

Other Government Officials and Civilians
Dr. Madelyn O'Hare, Director CDC
Kyle Reese, interrogator
Karen Sommerfeld, Director of Public Health, Boston
Emma Miller, CEO of Mass General
Sophia Westfield, Mayor of Kansas City

North Koreans
Kim Jong Un, President
Chin-Sun, agent
Heather Lee, agent
Mr. Jin, Director of Nuclear Research
Kim Yo Jong, President's sister

French Government
Pierre Belcher, Director of Counterterrorism
Mael Couseau, Deputy Dir. Of Counterterrorism
Roger, informant

Terrorists
Ahmed
Kamil
Samir (deceased)
Salah (deceased)

Victims
Mike & Melanie Jacobson
Mark & Louise Mason, daughter Tiffany
Dr. Johnson

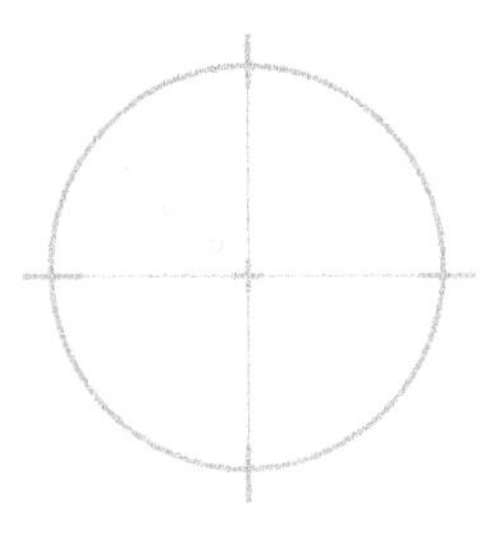

Chapter 1

The weather was a balmy 85° and the trade winds blew gently across the island of Maui. Chin-Sun was ensconced in a comfortable chair on the lanai of her room at the Napili Shores hotel. She held the binoculars to her eyes and scanned the far end of the beach of Napili Bay. On the table beside her were several photographs of three men, the men she was looking for. Chin-Sun had learned from Facebook that two of these men would be vacationing at the Mauian Hotel, located at the far end of the beach. She maintained surveillance for over an hour, but no one resembling the men in the photographs had ventured onto the beach.

Chin-Sun rose, stretched her arms over her head and walked into her room. Her eyes wandered over the room and took in the flowery comforter that lay on the bed. The room was unremarkable other than it was like most hotel rooms in Hawaii. Chin-Sun walked a few steps to the kitchen and boiled some water for tea. This is one of her true vices, to taste the fragrance of good tea. She returned to her chair on the lanai, picked up the binoculars and continued to search for the men.

Occasionally, Chin-Sun would put the binoculars down, rub her eyes and sit back to let the warm island breeze wash over her. As a high-ranking operative in the North Korean intelligence service, she had been to Hawaii many times. The passport and travel papers she carried identified her as a South Korean citizen who traveled to the US on business several times a year. Chin-Sun also had an office in Los Angeles for her import-export business.

The young woman had short black hair that framed her round face. At 30, wrinkles had not yet made an appearance and her face was smooth, her eyes bright. Many would call her beautiful. Chin-Sun still turned eyes when she entered a room. At five foot five and barely topping 100 pounds, she did not appear to be a threat to anyone. However, this North Korean agent had lengthy training in the physical arts and could defeat men much larger in size. Her voice was soft, with a singsong quality to it.

The North Korean agent's current operation began several months ago in Mexico City when she met with two Saudi men, Ahmed and Kamil, who had participated in terrorist attacks on Las Vegas, San Francisco, Seattle, and Paris. Those two men were the only survivors of the terrorist group involved in the attacks in America. Her government had directed her to meet with the two terrorists in Mexico City to begin discussions about a joint attack on the United States.

As a result of those discussions, she was in Maui to observe the two Americans who had interfered with the terrorist group's attack in Paris and in the US and to determine whether those men could possibly interfere with her country's plans to attack America.

Once again, she looked through the binoculars to see if anyone new had come to the beach. Her eyes darted from one person to another. Chin-Sun suddenly stopped to closely examine four new arrivals on the beach. The first couple was sitting on beach chairs in front of the Mauian Hotel. The man was wearing a multicolored swimsuit that was popular in Hawaii. His white hair matched the white beard that covered his face. The man seemed to be laughing with a woman seated next to him, who was wearing shorts and a Hawaiian print shirt. She had a trim figure with highlighted brown hair that fell to her shoulders. Both appeared to be in their early to mid-60s and seemed to enjoy each other's company. Another woman with short blond hair and wearing a Hawaiian coverup was seated in a chair next to them. In front of the three individuals stood a tanned man with short white hair and who seemed to be heavier than the others. In his hands was a tray containing four brown colored drinks. He handed a drink to each of the three people, then took a seat himself.

Chin-Sun picked up and examined the photos she had been given of the three men. She glanced from the photo of one man and compared it to the man with a white beard. After several glances, Chin-Sun believed she had found the two individuals she was looking for. At this distance, it was difficult to determine whether the second man matched one of the photos. Chin-Sun stood and headed for the door which led to the parking lot. Soon, she was driving toward the Mauian.

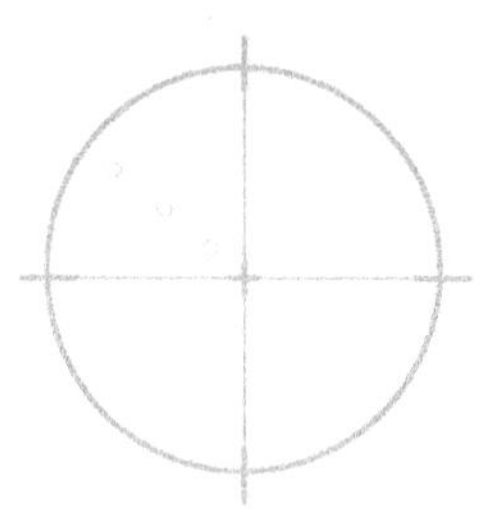

Chapter 2

As I sat down, Mac raised his glass and said, "Here's to Maui and peace and quiet." With that completed, he took a long drink and said, "Best damn Mai Tai I've ever had."

"Here! Here!" replied the two women as they sipped their drinks.

After taking a drink of my Mai Tai, I smiled at Mac and stated, "There are many more where these came from." We had arrived that afternoon after a long flight from Las Vegas. The drive from the Kahului Airport took an hour or so, but we were now happily enjoying the beach. A smile crossed my face as I looked out over the ocean at the islands of Lanai and Molokai. Clouds seemed to cover the mountains of both islands.

"Look at that!" I exclaimed pointing at the whale breaching several hundred yards away. "You don't see that every day."

"That's one of the things I love about this beach," smiled Sandy. "If you're here at the right time of year, you can see the whales breach quite often."

Sandy, my wife, and I had been coming to the Mauian for some 30 years now. It truly was one of our favorite places that drew us back almost every other year. Sandy and I have been blissfully married for as long as I can remember. She was just a few months younger than me, and we have had many incredible adventures over the years. We both enjoy traveling and had seen quite a bit of Europe. Neither of us had any great interest in traveling to Asia or

Africa. She turned and smiled at me which covered me with her love. I returned the gift.

I turned to look at Mac. "I'm surprised you're drinking the Mai Tai instead of one of your beers. You've reached a higher class than I expected." He did not respond but gave me the finger. "Mac, I think I'm wrong about you having reached a higher class."

"Listen, my friend, a good beer is in a class of its own which, I thought, you should know, but then again, maybe you shouldn't." Mac was a retired police officer who had many stories to tell. I expected that some of them were probably true but who knows. For a man in his sixties, Mac was in great shape and could handle himself in difficult situations. His wife, Ann, could do the same.

Mac had taught at our university before his retirement last year. He had joined me and our friend, Ty, when we took students to Paris on a study abroad trip. Unfortunately, we had been there but a short time before we became targets during a massive terrorist attack on Paris. The three of us survived these attacks, as did most of our students, because of good planning and a lot of simple luck. We also were fortunate to have survived a second terrorist attack the following year. The four of us had decided to come to Maui to get some desperately needed R&R.

Sandy interrupted my thoughts, "You had better be nice to each other or Ann and I may go to another island."

Ann stated, "I'm with you on that, or we can just take them out and drop them off in the ocean. I think they've seen better days so I'm not sure that they could swim back." The two women high-fived each other.

Mac replied, "What did we do to deserve such disrespect?"

Ann smiled sweetly at her husband and replied, "How long of a list would you like my dear?"

"Mac, you know, we will never win this argument. I suggest we retreat and talk about something else. What say you?"

"You're a gentleman and a scholar, DJ. I will follow you anywhere." With that, he finished his drink, held up his glass and said, "Are refills allowed?" I nodded at him, stood up and headed for my room so that all of us could refresh our drinks. When I returned, all their glasses were empty and waiting for the elixir I carried. Having a full kitchen in each room sure was handy.

A short time later, I stood, grabbed one of our noodles, a Styrofoam tube to sit on, and headed for the water. With my drink in one hand and the noodle in the other, I turned and asked, "Does anyone want to join me?" In response, both Ann and Mac grabbed their drinks and noodles and followed me into the water.

Sandy waved to me and said, "I'm going to enjoy the sun right here."

While sitting on the noodle in the ocean, I saw that Sandy was in a deep conversation with an Asian woman. It wasn't surprising since she made friends so easily. After an hour in the water, I told Ann and Mac I'd had enough and was getting out. Both waved to me indicating they intended to stay.

As I climbed the beach to where the chairs were, Sandy was still talking with the Asian woman. She introduced us and added, "Chin-Sun is visiting from South Korea." The Korean woman stood and bowed deeply to me while I put my hand forward to shake hers.

Chin-Sun placed her petite hand in mine and said, "I'm so pleased to meet you." Soon, the three of us were talking as if we had known each other for years. She told us that she was in Hawaii on business and would only be there for a few days.

Sandy asked "What business are you in?"

Chin-Sun replied, "Import - export. I have an office in Seoul and New York City." She lied to make it more difficult to find her. Soon our conversation turned to the beauty of the islands and how lucky we were to be able to enjoy them. Looking at me, she asked, "What is your background?"

I responded, "I retired as a judge and then started teaching at our university in the criminal justice department."

Chin-Sun looked at me quizzically and asked, "Is there a lot of crime in the city where you live? The reason I ask is that we hear that crime is a problem all over the United States. I mean, do you have to carry a gun for your own protection?"

"No, there's very little crime where we live. I do have a gun, but I don't usually carry it. Unlike our friends out there," I stated while pointing toward Mac and Ann. "He's a retired police officer and both of them always carry weapons."

Fifteen minutes later, Ann and Mac came trudging up the beach toward us, noodles and empty glasses in hand. Introductions were made all around and we continued our conversation. Mac didn't speak much, but rather watched Chin-Sun closely. After an hour, Chin-Sun stood and announced that she had to leave and meet a friend for dinner. As she walked away, Ann stated, "She was very pleasant. Will we see her again?"

Sandy responded, "I don't know. Just another friendly person on the beach. Perhaps we'll see her again."

Mac spoke up with a serious tone in his voice, "There's something strange about her. I don't like her."

"You're so damn suspicious of everyone," Ann stated. "There are many people you don't like and most of them you think are criminals."

I looked at Mac and saw that he was not joking. His eyes were hard and unforgiving. I knew Mac well enough to know that he had a sixth sense about people. I would talk to him about this.

Later, when we were alone, I asked Mac about his dislike for Chin-Sun.

Mac looked at me and said, "I am not sure I can put my finger on it, but something about her does not meet the smell test. All I can say is that my sixth sense tells me to be very wary of that woman."

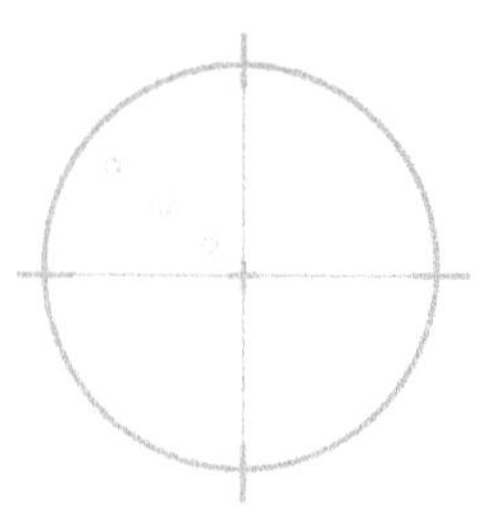

Chapter 3

Mael walked up to the door, knocked softly and waited until he heard a muted voice state, "Come in." Mael opened the door and saw the director, Pierre Belcher, seated at his desk shuffling through various papers. He glanced up, saw Mael and stated, "Have a seat Mael, I'll be with you in just a second." Pierre finished examining the papers set before him and smiled at Mael, his deputy director, and asked, "How have you been?"

"Good and you?"

"As good as can be expected," responded Pierre. As the Director of the Office of Counterterrorism in the French government, his responsibilities were large and varied. If one looked closely, it was easy to see the wrinkles that crawled across his forehead indicative of the stress he was continuously under. "Have you talked recently with your friend in the FBI?"

"Not since I last briefed you about the terrorist attacks in the US," responded Mael. "The forensics investigation at the professor's home did not turn up any new information. The FBI was able to determine that Samir, the leader of the terrorists who attacked Paris and the professors two years ago, was killed in the attack on the US during the fight with the professors last year. We were lucky enough to have sketches which came from a man who interacted with the terrorists. None of the bodies that the FBI found matched either of the two individuals that we had sketches of. So, it appears that either those two men were not involved in the recent attack, or they escaped."

Pierre remained silent for a moment before stating, "Have we made any progress in finding those two men?"

"No, they seem to have disappeared into thin air."

"Have you been able to identify the two remaining terrorists?"

Mael shook his head in the negative. "Neither the US nor ourselves have made any progress in either identifying or finding them. My guess is they have gone underground in order to avoid being found. If they're still in the terrorist business, we may not have any leads until the next attack, but we will keep looking for them."

The director stood and walked toward his espresso machine. He looked back at Mael, "Coffee?"

"No thanks, I've had my fill for today. Do you want me to check in with the FBI to see if they've come across anything new? I have asked my friend, Sam, to keep me informed of any new developments. Given the level of destruction resulting from the terrorist's attack last year, I expect he is swamped with other matters."

Pierre returned to his seat and sipped his strong espresso. "It might be a good idea for you to reach out to him. If those two terrorists are still active, they constitute a direct threat to both our country and theirs. You know, Mael, I have a funny feeling that these two attacks were not the end of the terrorists' efforts. It may be just the beginning. Let us hope that's not the case."

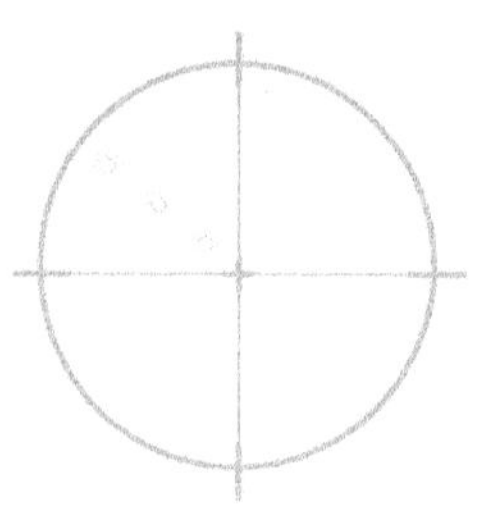

Chapter 4

Having left his apartment early that morning, Ahmed took a taxi to Charles de Gaulle airport leaving plenty of time to catch his flight. He headed to the ticket counter, checked in and walked to the screening area which led to his gate. With his new identification in hand, Ahmed passed through security without a problem. He was dressed like any other businessman in a dark suit, white shirt and light blue tie. As Ahmed walked to his gate, he stopped and bought a French magazine.

Ahmed visually examined all the passengers arriving at the gate area. None of those individuals seemed to be out of place and certainly took no interest in him. Since he was flying business class, he was one of the first passengers to board. Ahmed made himself comfortable, accepted the bottle of water from the flight attendant and continued to watch those who boarded the aircraft.

Within a short time, the plane's doors closed, and the aircraft was pushed away from the jetway as the flight attendants went through their safety briefing in both French and English. Moments later, the aircraft was hurtling down the runway and lifted into the air. Ahmed pushed the button that reclined his seat, closed his eyes and reviewed the hectic years and days leading up to today.

He, Kamil, Salah, and Samir had planned and led the devastating and successful attack on Paris two years ago. Unfortunately, Samir, the leader of the group had allowed his best friend, Salah, to lead the final attack against the American professors. During that attack, Salah had been killed which shook Samir to the very depths of his soul.

A year following the attack on Paris, Ahmed, Kamil and Samir had developed and carried out a plan to attack the United States. Part of the plan had included terrorist operations against Las Vegas, San Francisco and Seattle. Those plans were successful beyond their wildest dreams and had hurt America deeply. The final part of the plan was to target and kill the three American professors who had killed Salah and avenge his death.

The attack on the professors was well-planned but ended in abject failure even though each of the professors had been injured. Only he and Kamil survived that attack by hiding in the rocks. Ahmed saw the wife of a professor shoot and kill Samir. Kamil and Ahmed not only survived the attack on the professors, but also escaped to Mexico where their current operation was initiated.

Several hours later, the aircraft began its descent into the Dallas-Fort Worth airport. He exited the plane, went through customs, and walked to the next gate which would take him to his final destination. In short order, he was in the air again for the short flight to San Antonio.

After claiming his bag, Ahmed walked to the taxi stand and soon found himself heading into downtown San Antonio. The taxi pulled into the Omni Hotel on the River Walk where he paid the driver and walked to the registration desk. A young Hispanic woman, dressed in the uniform of the hotel, handled his reservation. He provided her with his French driver's license and a credit card. She gave him his room key and directed him to the elevator that would take him to the floor where his room was located.

Ahmed lay on the bed and stretched out. His current mission in San Antonio was to determine what potential sites in that city should be considered for their attack.

He was tired from the long flight from Paris and needed to get a good night's sleep so he could recon San Antonio tomorrow. He was scheduled to take a late flight the next evening to Philadelphia.

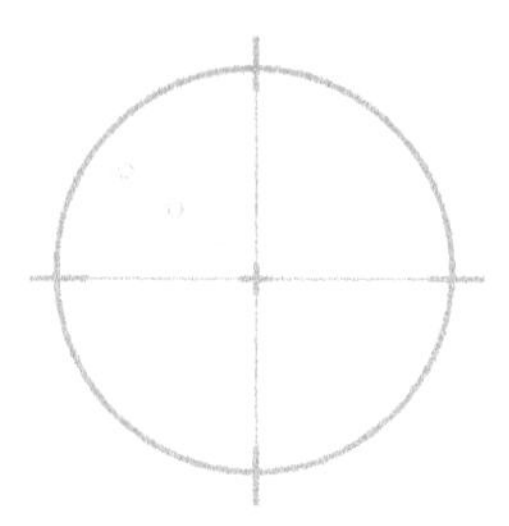

After resting for a few minutes, Ahmed left his room to find something to eat.

Chapter 5

Chin-Sun had returned to the beach in front of the Mauian the last two days. Her attempt to find the two men in order to put her plan into effect had been unsuccessful. After meeting DJ on the beach, she had determined that he was the second man that she was looking for. There was no doubt in her mind that he was one of the men pictured in the newspapers. Chin-Sun walked on the beach and came to a stop in front of the Mauian. She spread out her towel, sat down and waited for the four people to arrive.

Shortly before noon, she heard their familiar voices, but gave no indication she recognized them. They were behind her, getting situated for the afternoon. A few moments later, Sandy walked up in front of her and said, "Hi Chin-Sun. Did you decide to come down and get more time in the sun?"

She replied, "This beach is so beautiful; how can you not return. If I don't spend some time on the beach every day, I consider it a failed trip."

"Why don't you bring your things and sit with us?" Sandy asked.

"Sure, why not." Chin-Sun picked up her towel and followed Sandy up to where we were sitting. Once again, she spread out her towel and sat down facing us.

Ann smiled at Chin-Sun and asked, "Have you been working all this time, or have you been able to have some fun also?"

"I usually work through the early afternoon and then try to make some time for myself. In fact, yesterday, I had the best time."

I interrupted her, "What did you do that was so fun?"

"Well, I've always wanted to go deep sea fishing. One of my colleagues at the conference told me he had a friend who would take me out. I called the man, whose name is Rick, and was able to arrange an outing yesterday afternoon. We left the dock at about two and got back about eight. I was able to catch two large fish."

Mac spoke up, "What kind of fish were they?"

"I'm not really sure," she answered. "I'm sure he explained it to me, but with the excitement, I simply don't remember. Much to his chagrin, I said we should just release them."

"What kind of service did he provide besides taking you out?" I asked.

"Well, I showed up at the assigned dock in Maaleaa Harbor. Rick provided all the fishing gear, so I didn't have to worry about that. He had water and beer in a large cooler, and even brought snacks in case I got hungry. He was a nice guy and obviously knew where to find fish. It was a lot of fun, so I'll probably do it again when I return to the islands. I thought the cost was very reasonable. Rick charged me $300 for everything. Do you think that was a good deal?"

"It was a very reasonable deal," Mac replied and looked at the three of us and asked, "Is that something you guys would like to do?"

Sandy shook her head and replied, "I'm afraid I would get seasick, and that would be a downer for everybody."

Ann shook her head, smiled and said, "No interest on my part either."

I looked at Mac and said, "You might be able to talk me into it. I would not want you to go out on the big scary ocean all by yourself."

Mac dismissed me with a wave of his hand. Looking at Chin-Sun he asked, "Who is this guy and how do we get a hold of him?"

"His name is Rick and I have his number in my phone. Do you want me to call him?" she asked.

I responded first, "Sure."

She pulled out her phone and was shortly talking. "Hi Rick. This is Chin-Sun from yesterday. I met some people who might like to go fishing with you. Would you like to talk to them?" She listened and then handed the phone to Mac.

During his conversation with Rick, Mac made, with the approval of our wives, a reservation for the next morning at 9:00 AM. As Mac ended the call, he looked at me and said "$250 each. Not bad, I would say." I nodded my agreement.

Twenty minutes later, Chin-Sun rose to leave. "I have a date tonight and must go get ready. I wouldn't want to disappoint this cute Hawaiian gentleman."

"Well," Ann stated, "you guys are going to have fun tomorrow but what are you doing for us ladies tonight?"

I smiled at her and replied, "How about an extra strong Mai Tai?"

Sandy laughed. "My husband sure knows how to show a girl a good time. Go for it honey."

A few minutes later, I returned with four drinks. We all picked up our noodles and headed to the water with our drinks in hand and spent a pleasant hour floating in the ocean, talking and sipping Mai Tais. Mac and Ann finished their first and held up their empty glasses. I handed my drink and noodle to Sandy, took their glasses and headed to our condo.

Holding the newly made drinks, I walked down the beach and into the surf. It had gotten much rougher since I had left. The water was up to my knees when I observed a large wave coming in. I turned my back to it so the saltwater would not affect the drinks. The wave hit me with such force that it swept my legs out from under me, and I landed on my butt, but with the foresight to hold both drinks high in the air. Struggling to get up, I noticed that people on the beach were clapping for me. I took a bow and turned to rejoin my wife and friends when a second wave struck me causing me to fall once again. As I struggled to get up, the people on the beach were now standing and clapping. I bowed once again and headed into the ocean. One of the men on the beach said it was the best show he'd ever seen.

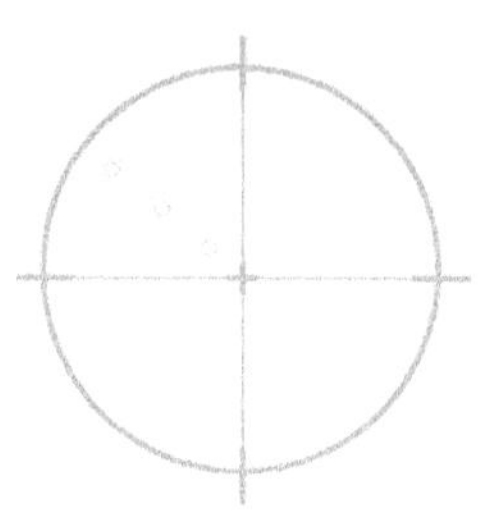

Chapter 6

Ty and his wife, Leanne, sat down for breakfast at the Claim Jumper in the Golden Nugget Hotel in Las Vegas. They had driven down the previous evening to enjoy a little gambling before leaving for a week in San Antonio. Ty smiled at Leanne and stated, "I forgot to ask, did you end up winning or losing last night?"

"I know you wish I would say that I lost so that you could tell me 'I told you so'," Leanne replied. "But the truth of the matter is, that I won $600 which will give us a little play money in San Antonio. Did you gamble at all?"

"No, but I did wander out onto Fremont Street and had fun watching the freaks out there. I can't believe what some people do to earn a buck. It did give me a chuckle or two, I must admit." After completing their breakfast, Ty obtained the check from the waitress, examined it and left enough money to cover the check and a tip.

Within the hour, Ty and Leanne were boarding the plane that would take them to San Antonio. When they arrived, they went to the baggage claim to collect their two bags and found transportation to the hotel. Before noon, the cab pulled up to the San Antonio Marriott Riverwalk, and soon they were walking in to register. There was a bit of a line since there were many guests trying to check out. Within one-half hour, Ty and Leanne had settled into their room. Ty asked, "What do you want to do first?"

"Let's walk over to the Alamo and check that out. I had some friends tell me they really enjoyed it. Are you hungry, Ty?"

"DJ told me the same thing. I'm good for an hour or two. Let's grab a quick lunch after we do the Alamo."

"That works for me."

It wasn't a long walk to the Alamo. Leanne and Ty went to the stand that had an audio tour and purchased two. For the next couple of hours, they walked around, stopping to listen when instructed by the audio tour. After the tour ended, Leanne went into the gift shop and Ty looked for a place to wait. Seeing a bench with a woman sitting there. Ty asked if he could sit with her, and she agreed. Soon her husband joined them, and in no time, they were talking like old friends. After Leanne returned, Ty introduced them to Linda and Gerry. The two couples decided to have lunch together, and they began walking toward the Riverwalk to search for a place to eat. When they reached the Riverwalk, they strolled along the walkway stopping to review each restaurant's menu.

Ahmed had spent the morning driving around the city to orient himself. Now he was seated at an outdoor restaurant waiting for his meal to be delivered. Something caught his eye across the narrow river. The Saudi observed four people, two men and two women. One man and one woman looked familiar to him. He brought his menu up so that only his eyes were showing. Looking over it at the four people, Ahmed saw them turn and begin slowly walking toward the next restaurant. He was shocked to see and immediately recognized the man and woman as one of the American professors and his wife.

The two couples stopped at the next restaurant, looked at the menu and entered the restaurant unaware that they were being watched.

Ahmed remained seated pondering what, if any, action he should take against these two people. He was sure the man was one of the professors they had tried to kill several months earlier.

The only reason they had attempted to kill the professors was Samir's need to avenge Salah's death. At the time of the last attack on the professors, he had this man in his sights. However, when he pulled the trigger, Ty had moved suddenly and was only struck in the hip. Another professor came to his aid and was also shot. Shortly after that, Samir had been killed and Ahmed and Kamil had to hide as FBI agents swarmed over the area. Now, that same man was before him.

Ahmed knew that Chin-Sun had flown to Hawaii where the other two professors were known to be vacationing. She was going to decide whether to kill them or simply leave them alone. Now, he had to make that same decision regarding Ty. When planning their last operation, he had indicated to Samir that any action against these professors could not interfere with their attacks on the United States. Samir, however, had wanted these men eliminated.

As he sat in the restaurant, Ahmed was not sure whether he should do anything regarding this man. Just then, Ty and Leanne and the other couple walked out of the restaurant and said their goodbyes. The couples headed in opposite directions. Ty and Leanne walked past his location, and he turned so as not be seen. Having paid his bill, he rose and began to follow them, still not sure what action he should take.

Ahmed saw them walk into the Marriott and he followed. He saw them enter the elevator alone and watched the elevator until it stopped at the fifth floor. From the newspaper articles he had read, he remembered their names were Leanne and Ty Smith. He took a seat in the lobby and tried to figure out how he could get the room number. Ahmed knew that if you asked at the registration desk, they would simply refuse to give it to him to assure their guests' privacy. Instead, he walked up to the desk and said that he wanted to leave a message for a business associate. They handed him a pad of paper and a pen, and he wrote that he would meet Leanne and Ty at 8:00 AM in the morning in the lobby. He folded the paper and handed it back to the clerk. Ahmed watched the clerk write on the paper, 508. Now, he had the room number.

Ahmed went outside, pulled out a cell phone and dialed Chin-Sun's number. The phone rang once and went directly to voicemail. He left a brief message asking if she wanted him to kill Ty. A few moments later, his phone rang, and he answered it. He recognized Chin-Sun's voice. She said, "I received your message. Do not do anything unless you're absolutely sure that you will be successful and not be caught."

"Well," he responded, "he is here with his wife, and I do not have a firearm of any kind. It will be difficult to kill him without killing his wife also. I can do it, I'm sure."

There was silence on the phone for several minutes then Chin-Sun responded, "I am not convinced that their deaths can occur without suspicion being cast on you. It is their lucky day. I will see you as planned."

As Ahmed was placing his phone in his pocket, the elevator doors opened, and Ty and Leanne walked out. As they walked by, Ahmed had brought a magazine up hiding his face. "Yes, Mr. Professor, you are very lucky today, he thought.

One hour later, Ahmed's phone rang. Answering it, he heard Chin-Sun say, "I've changed my mind. Get someone to kill them. Make it look like a robbery gone bad." She gave him the name and number of a local gang member and then hung up.

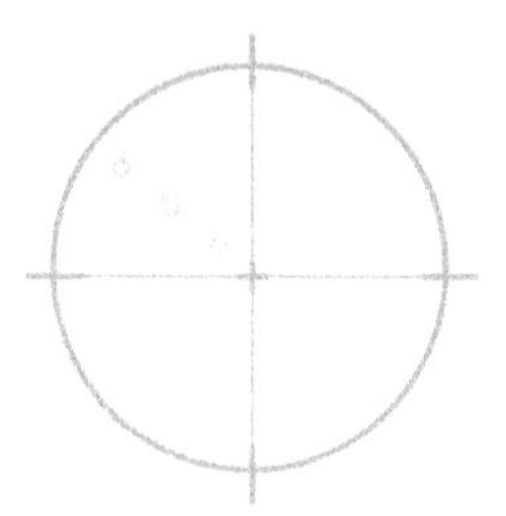

Chapter 7

The next morning, Mac and I drove to Maalaea Harbor to meet Rick, the skipper of the boat that was going to take us fishing. As we got to the dock, oddly, I did not see a sign that said "Rick's Fishing Tours," which I understood was the name of Rick's business. As we walked down the dock, we noticed a charter fishing boat tied up in an empty space. I saw a man sitting on the flybridge looking out over the ocean. I tried to get his attention by waving at him, but it took several seconds before he noticed me. "You don't happen to be Rick, are you?"

"I am he," he replied with a huge grin crossing his face. "Are you the two gents that Chin-Sun referred to me?"

I returned his smile and stated, "That be us."

"Come on board. Welcome to the best fishing tour boat in the islands."

Mac and I stepped aboard and shook hands with Rick. "My name is DJ, and this old guy is Mac. If you speak loudly enough, he should be able to hear everything you say."

Mac responded, "Don't worry about speaking loudly, I can hear just fine." Pointing at me, he continued, "He has been slipping deeper into dementia for some time now."

Rick looked at both of us, not sure which one to believe. He laughed again and said, "Well, this should be an interesting trip. Come on, I will show you around." He took the next 15 minutes showing us the flybridge, the lounge below, the head, and the fishing gear at the aft end of the boat. He also pointed out the cooler which contained water and beer. Seeing that we were carrying snorkel gear, Rick asked, "What are those for?"

Mac answered his question, "If the fish weren't biting, we hoped you might be able take us to a good snorkeling spot. Is that possible?"

"I don't see why not. I always aim to please." Rick laughed at his own response, and we joined in. "Why don't we fire this puppy up and be on our way. You can sit back and enjoy the sun. I have a special place where I believe you will get all the fishing you want."

Mac and I opened a beer, sat back and enjoyed the warm sun on our faces. I studied Rick for a few minutes as he was standing before the helm on the flybridge. He was wearing a Hawaiian swimsuit and a yellow T-shirt with a beer bottle advertisement on the front. He appeared to be a native Hawaiian with unruly, curly black hair. Rick seemed to be in his late 20s, solidly built and stood just under 6 feet tall. I could hear music coming from the flybridge and watched Rick bounce back and forth with the beat.

Mac was taking a long drink from his beer bottle when I asked, "What do you think of our captain?"

"Well, he seems friendly enough, I guess. Why do you ask?"

"I'm not sure. I thought his business was located at the dock in Maalaea Harbor. However, he was just tied up to the dock. I thought that it was kind of strange that there were no business signs on the dock or on his boat. It didn't bother you?"

Mac answered, "I thought it was a little odd, but who knows how he does his business. Maybe it's less expensive to not have a permanent presence on the dock. Oh well, does it really matter anyway?"

"Probably not." Mac and I continued to shoot the breeze as Rick took us to our fishing spot.

After a couple of hours, I realized we were now out of sight of land. Soon, the boat began to slow down and came to a stop.

Rick climbed down the stairs from the flybridge and turned to face us. He stopped at the bottom of the stairs, reached behind him and pulled out a small revolver. "Well, gents, I guess this is where the fishing ends."

Both Mac and I immediately jumped up. I heard Mac say, "What's this all about?"

"The Korean lady said she wanted you dead and she paid me $20,000 to take care of it for her. Nothing personal, you understand. Just a good business deal for me and an unfortunate one for you." Rick had a grin on his face that nearly stretched around his head.

Suddenly, Mac threw his beer in Rick's direction, and I followed suit. I immediately grabbed my snorkel bag and jumped overboard on the right side of the boat and Mac did the same on the left side. I dove as deeply as I could and heard Rick's gun firing. Following that, I heard Rick fire again, but since it sounded further away, I assumed he was shooting at Mac. I rose to the surface approximately 25 feet from the boat and saw Rick running to the flybridge. I took the mask from my snorkel bag and placed it on my head. I glanced in Mac's direction and saw him doing the same thing.

I looked back and saw Rick at the helm, starting the engine and pulling away. He circled back toward us and started firing once again. Diving down about 10 feet, I watched the boat go by me without any indication that Rick was still firing. As he pulled away, I came to the surface to catch my breath. I looked over toward Mac just in time to see him surface, but he kept his eyes on the boat.

Rick brought the boat to a stop approximately 50 feet from where we were treading water. He shouted at us, "There's always more than one way to skin a cat. I doubt that you old men could swim back to the islands, especially given the current that exists out here." As he climbed down the stairs to the rear of the boat, he opened a bucket and began tossing chum into the ocean. When he finished, he yelled, "I hope you enjoy the various types of sharks that we have around here." He smiled once again, climbed back onto the flybridge and waved at us as he pulled away.

Mac and I swam toward each other, and I asked, "Now what?"

Mac answered, "I don't know about you, but I want to get away from that chum. It won't take long for the sharks to appear!"

We reached into our snorkel bags, pulled out and put on our fins and snorkel. After adjusting our snorkels, we started swimming in the direction we believed the nearest island was located.

After swimming for half an hour, I reached out and grabbed Mac. My arms were aching as well as my legs. The adrenaline that had powered me through the first half-hour was fading away. Mac looked at me, wondering why I had stopped. I shoved my mask and snorkel back onto my head and Mac followed suit. "I need to rest a minute."

"Listen DJ, we haven't put enough distance between ourselves and the chum. This could turn dangerous awfully fast."

I stated, "I know. Why don't you keep going and I'll follow you in a minute or two."

"That's not going to work. We need to stick together. Let's rest here for a couple of minutes before we take off again."

I shook my head, and said, "What happens if a shark wanders by?"

"Then we take off swimming like hell."

"Mac, you stupid shit, you can't outswim a shark."

Mac smiled at me, "I don't have to outswim a shark—I just have to outswim you."

I rolled my eyes at him, "That only applies to bears, asshole."

"Oh, well, I thought it sounded pretty good anyway. Sharks or bears, what the hell is the difference?"

Changing the subject, I said, "You know the best way to fend off a shark attack?"

"Oh, this ought to be good. I can't wait to hear it."

"I heard this from a shark expert at the Maui aquarium years ago. He said that when a shark comes at you, you should immediately go into a fetal position and remain still."

Mac responded, "Oh, that's exactly what I'm going to do. I'm going to let him come over and take a bite out of me without trying to fight the shark off. I think the saltwater has gotten to you, DJ."

"Listen, Mac, if you go into a fetal position, you are like a big ball and the shark can't get its teeth around you. Think about it, it makes sense. Oh, holy shit." I said pointing over Mac's shoulder. Coming through the water was a dorsal fin that appeared to be attached to a fairly good-sized shark. "Let's do it, Mac," I said as I put my snorkel tube and mask back on.

Mac followed suit but grabbed me by the arm and said, "If it bites me, I'm going to kill you. No shit, DJ, you are a dead man."

"If it bites you, Mac, we're probably both dead men." We both moved into a fetal position and kept our eyes on the shark as it approached. It swam approximately three feet away with its unblinking eye watching us. You could see the stripes down the side of its eight-foot body. It swam slowly away. We lifted our heads out of the water and I said, "It looks like a tiger shark, one of the deadliest to humans."

"That's all I need to hear, asshole," Mac responded. "Oh shit, here it comes again." We both immediately tucked into a fetal position, and once again, kept our eyes on the shark as it came toward us and swam by. The shark circled us again and again, sometimes closing in toward us and we responded by going into a fetal position. After waiting a while and keeping a lookout for it or another shark, we started swimming with renewed energy toward an island that was a mere bump on the horizon.

After we had been swimming for a couple of hours, I pulled up to rest for a few minutes. Mac said, "I feel like have been burned to a crisp."

"Turn around so I can look at your back. You definitely have been burned pretty bad, Mac. Your skin is too white to be swimming around all day like this," I smiled at him. "You know, you really should be using some skin protection. At least a 50, I would think."

"You asshole, if my arms weren't so tired, I would try and drown you right here and now. Why don't you open your eyes and look at me?"

"My eyes are open; I can't see very well. I think it must be the saltwater. My mask is leaking."

"Let's keep going," Mac said, "I'm going to swim on my back, and hopefully it will cool off." We both set off again, belly up, heading to the island that hadn't gotten any closer. After we had been swimming for what seemed like hours, Mac pointed up in the air and said, "Now, what in the hell is that?"

I looked up in the direction that Mac was pointing, "I can't see for shit. What are you talking about?"

"I don't know, DJ. Looks like something's there. I'm not hallucinating, am I?"

"How the hell should I know, Mac? I can't see for shit either. You probably are hallucinating. Is it still there?"

Mac waited for a few minutes to respond, "I think so."

Lying there, I realized how totally exhausted I was. Continuing to float, I drifted off to sleep. It was the sleep of a dead man.

Suddenly, Mac jerked my arm, pointed to the sky again. "What is that, DJ?"

I opened and rubbed my eyes and tried to block the sun with my hand. Finally, I responded, "Well, it looks like one of those drones." It hovered over us for a long time.

"I wonder if it's going to land and take us home?" Mac asked.

"It could, I suppose, if it wanted to. It doesn't look very big though." The drone darted away. "It didn't like us very much. I'm going to get some sleep."

"DJ, it's back, but it's much noisier."

"Tell it to go home, I need to sleep." Just as I was about to nod off, I heard a loud splash not far from me. "What the hell's going on, Mac?"

"Damned if I know. I can't see anymore either. What the hell is going on?"

I couldn't see or hear Mac as I called out his name. The shark had come back and taken my best friend. I felt myself being tugged through the water and realized that my time had come also. Suddenly, I was pulled out of the water and placed on a hard surface. Water was being poured over my face and I was able to open my eyes. Smiling down on me was a young face encased in a helmet. The last thing I remembered hearing was someone say, "We got them. Let's head back."

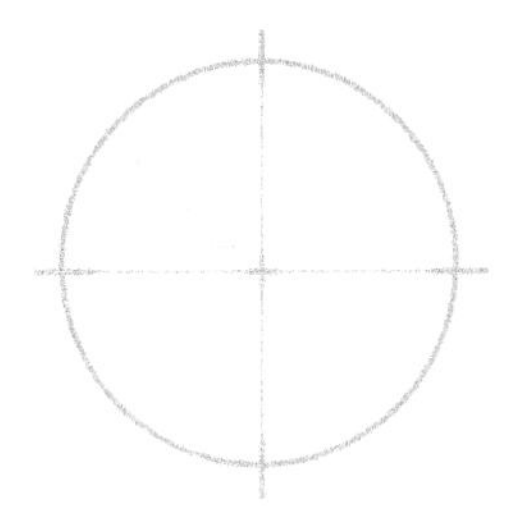

Chapter 8

Mael did not get back to his office until shortly after 5:00 PM. By the time he had checked his email and returned phone calls, it was nearing 6:30 PM. Mael picked up his phone and dialed Sam Wyman's number in Washington, DC. Sam was the Director of the FBI's Counterterrorism division. The phone rang several times and Mael thought that Sam could still be at lunch. He was about to hang up when Sam picked up the phone and said, "Wyman."

"Hi, Sam," Mael responded, "It's Mael. How are you doing?"

"Hey, Mael, I'm doing fine. You?"

"Doing well, thank you. I bet you're busier than hell."

"You have no idea," Sam responded, "but if anybody does have an idea what it's like, I'm sure that would be you. What's on your mind?"

Mael had learned that Sam was one that got directly to the point and did not mince words. "I wanted to check with you to see if you have any new information on the two terrorists that got away from you guys. I do not mean to be critical given the fact that we did not even come close to getting them. My boss wanted me to keep in close contact with you just to make sure we don't miss anything."

Sam responded, "I can't tell you how frustrating this job has become. These terrorists sneak into our country, cause incredible damage to our cities and then just disappear into thin air. No one on this side of the Atlantic has recognized the two men we believe escaped. Every police department in the country is on the lookout for them. Every border patrol agent knows what they look like from the sketches you provided, and yet, they simply disappeared. If my boss wasn't so understanding, I would have been fired a long time ago."

Mael spoke once again, "Are the politicians looking for scape-goats in your country too? They were certainly doing that in France. The man who ended up taking the fall for the attack on Paris was the prime minister. I will tell you one thing; I didn't shed a tear when he had to go. He continually tried to tell us how to do our job. Then, like a typical politician, he tried to shift the blame to us."

Sam answered, "We were pretty lucky in that regard. After the attack on Las Vegas, San Francisco, and Seattle, we were, as you know, able to kill all but two of the terrorists. The fact that we were able to kill most of them took the heat off of us. But if it happens again, there will be hell to pay."

Mael responded, "My boss wanted me to tell you that he believes the attacks in Paris and the US are just the beginning. He doesn't believe this thing is over and expects more attacks to come. How do your people look at this?"

"Most of us agree with your boss. We do have some individuals who believe that the terrorists have shot their wad. I think they've been smoking some bad weed." Sam could hear Mael chuckling over the phone. "In any event, Mael, we will leave no stone unturned in our search for those two. We are keeping our ears open hoping we hear something that will give us a lead. If anything comes up, you can be sure that I will contact you right away."

"Thanks, Sam. I will let you know also if we hear anything over here. Talk to you soon."

"Goodbye, Mael."

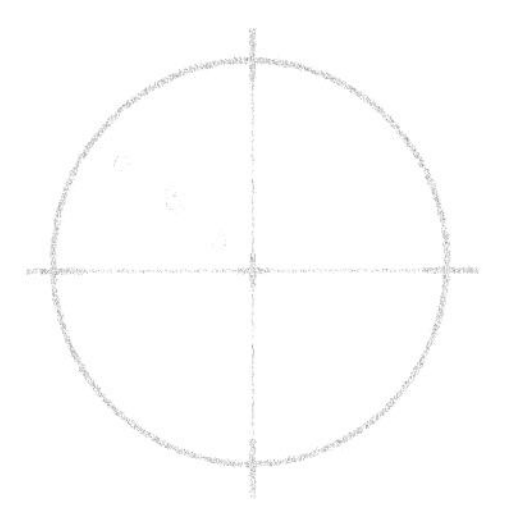

Chapter 9

It was 5:00 PM and Ann and Sandy were sitting on the lanai when the manager came hurrying up to them. They both looked up and saw the concern on his face. The manager spoke first, "I've just received a call from the hospital. They said both of your husbands are there and you should come right away."

"Are they okay?" both women asked at the same time.

"I was told they are in no danger. You do not need to worry about that. They did not tell me anything more than that."

"Thanks for letting us know," said Sandy. "Come on, Ann, we'll take my car." Both women grabbed their purses, locked the doors to the rooms and walked quickly to the car. Soon they were on the way to the hospital, which was about an hour away.

Through gritted teeth, Ann said, "Those bastards. If they did something stupid, I will make sure they're in the hospital for a week. You know how they feed off each other. Stupid is as stupid does."

"Ann, they could be hurt. Let's hope they're all right."

"Oh, I suppose you're right, but if it's something stupid, you'd better restrain me."

Sandy pulled up to the hospital, parked and the two of them walked, almost ran, for the entrance. At the front desk, Ann said, "We understand that our husbands have been brought here. Well?"

The receptionist looked at her and responded, "If you will tell me your last names, I can answer your question."

"I'm sorry," Ann replied, "I'm pretty upset. My husband's name is Mac McDonald, and her husband is DJ Anderson."

"Yes, they are here. You'll find them in room 116. Right down the hall to the nurse's station and turn to the left."

"Thank you so much," Sandy answered. Both women then hurried down the hall and soon were at room 116. When they entered, they observed Mac and DJ sitting up in their beds, each with an IV running into his arm.

Relieved to see that DJ was okay, Sandy stated, "What the hell is going on?"

Mac looked at me and said, "She's your wife. Why don't you answer."

I nodded and asked both women to sit down. Over the course of the next hour, I told them what had occurred. At various times during this conversation, Sandy would reply with such phrases as 'what' and 'that bitch,' and Ann said, 'no shit' and 'holy shit' and 'I'm going to kill that bitch.'

When I had finished, Sandy asked, "How are you guys feeling now?"

"Well," I responded, "except for a little dehydration, I think we're fine."

Mac moaned, "I'm burnt to a crisp. Look at my back." He turned so his wife could see his sunburn.

Ann started to laugh, "There's nothing wrong with you that a little aloe won't take care of. You are such a baby."

Mac replied, "You think I'm a baby. I bet we swam for several days and several hundred miles. You should've seen the shark that attacked us. It was 18 feet long if it was a foot."

I couldn't resist, but I had to poke some fun at Mac. "Aw, Mac, that was just a little fish. Why are you so upset?"

Mac pointed his finger at me, and said, "You just made number one on my asshole list. I probably won't be able to move for at least a week."

Ann slapped Mac on the back and said, "Come on, honey. Let's get going."

I'm not sure which was louder, Mac's cry of pain or our laughter.

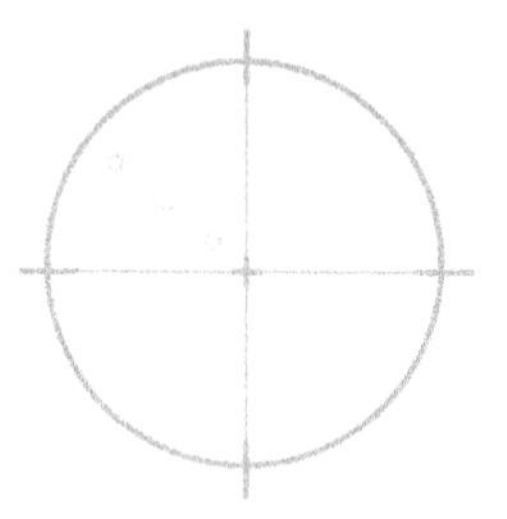

Chapter 10

The next morning, Sandy and I were sitting on the lanai talking about how lucky I was to be alive while trying to enjoy a good cup of Kona coffee. Mac and Ann, coffee cups in hand, walked up to the lanai and sat down. Mac was facing the ocean when I stated, "Mac, why don't you lean back and enjoy the view?"

"Shut up, DJ. You're still on my asshole list. You know my back is burnt and is killing me."

"Now, now dear," Ann stated sarcastically. "DJ is just giving you a bad time."

Mac responded, "I should've left him out there all alone when he wanted to rest and let someone else save him."

"If I hadn't told you to go into a fetal position, you'd probably be shark poop at this time."

Sandy pointed at both of us. "You both are lucky to be alive, so shut up." I could see that she was close to tears.

"You know, I've been thinking," I stated. "We should probably call Ty and warn him to be careful. It probably wouldn't hurt if we called Art Rheingold also. What do you think, Mac?"

"I usually get worried when you start thinking, DJ, but that's a good idea."

I picked up my phone, punched in Ty's number and waited for him to answer. After three rings, he answered and said laughing, "Why are you bothering me on my vacation, DJ?"

"Well, I have some news I thought you should know about. A woman from Korea paid someone to kill us." I proceeded to explain to Ty everything that had occurred in the last couple of days. "We have no clue as to why she took this action. It was just out of the blue. The police informed us this morning that she checked out of her hotel, but there's no indication that she has left Maui. There were, however, several women with Korean names that were on flights leaving yesterday. So, the bottom line is, we don't know if she's still here or not. However, if this is connected in any way to our confrontation with our Saudi friends, I wanted you to know about it so that you can take appropriate action to protect yourself and Leanne."

Ty responded, "Holy shit. Are you kidding me? We haven't seen anything suspicious here, but we will certainly keep our eyes open. We appreciate you letting us know. You have, what, about a week left in your vacation? Are you going home now or are you going to stay there?"

Since we were on speaker, I answered for the four of us. "We are not going to let that woman ruin our vacation! So, we plan to stay here and enjoy ourselves. Obviously, we will be on the lookout for anything unusual. As soon as we hang up, I will call Rheingold and let him know what happened."

"Sounds good, but keep in touch. If anything new comes up, please call us and we will do the same."

Hearing the call disconnect. I looked through my contacts and dialed Art Rheingold's number. Art was our contact at the local FBI office prior to and during last year's attack on us. "Hi, DJ. Why do I have the pleasure of this phone call? I thought our business was concluded when Samir was killed."

"Well, I have some information for you." I filled him in on all the events that had occurred. "What do you think, Art? Do you think this is connected to Samir's group?"

"Damn, DJ, I haven't the foggiest idea, but I will tell you this. I know of no one who has trouble follow them, like you and Mac do. I will call Sam Wyman and see if he has any knowledge of this woman or of any plans against you guys and will get back to you as soon as I can." Art hung up, and it was quiet.

Looking at Mac, I said, "Well, Mac, there's nothing we can do now. Why don't we go out in the ocean and play with the sharks?"

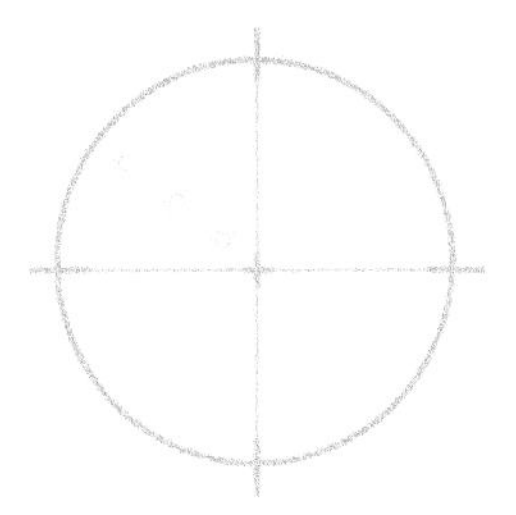

Chapter 11

Art Rheingold was sitting in his St. George office having just hung up from talking with DJ. He sat for a few moments contemplating what he had learned and trying to connect the dots between the terrorists and the Korean woman. As much as he tried, he could not find any connection that made sense. The question then became, should he call Wyman or not. He decided that it wouldn't hurt him to call, but it could hurt him if he failed to act.

He hit the numbers quickly and waited for Wyman to answer. It did not take long. "This is Wyman."

"Hi, Sam, it's Art Rheingold. Do you have a minute?"

"Sure, what's up?" Wyman continued to read the document displayed on this computer.

Art responded, "We've had an interesting development. I just received a call from DJ Anderson. He and McDonald are vacationing in Hawaii with their wives. On the beach, they met a Korean woman who seemed to take an interest in them and, making a long story short, told them of a fishing trip she had taken with a local tour guide. Our two professors then signed up for the same trip with the same tour operator. While out in the middle of the ocean, the tour guide pulled a gun on them and said the Korean woman wanted them killed. They jumped overboard and managed to escape without injuries except for a very bad sunburn."

"This sounds like a local matter rather than one for the FBI. Is there something there that should be of interest to us?"

"None that I can see," Rheingold answered. "Their position was that they had never met this woman and did not understand why she would pay someone to kill them. They further indicated they don't believe in coincidences and simply wondered whether we have any information about the terrorists and if there is a Korean connection."

"Art, while I understand their concern, there's nothing that has come across my desk that would lead me to believe that this is anything other than an unfortunate coincidence. I've not seen any report that would confirm that something was brewing that involved Korea. Obviously, that doesn't mean there is nothing happening, but we simply have not heard of it. I will get this information to my counterparts in other agencies to see if they have any information that could confirm that a connection exists. Other than that, I'm not sure what else can be done. Why don't you let them know of our conversation and what I indicated I would do?"

"I will do that. You know, if this is real and somehow this woman is connected to the terrorists, the professors are in a world of hurt. All because they tried to save themselves in Paris and then tried to avoid being killed in the US by terrorists. Now someone else is trying to take them out. Talk about bad luck! On another subject, have you made any progress in identifying who the terrorists were that got away?"

Sam answered, "Not really. The only reason we have for believing that anyone got away is from the professors. They looked at all the terrorists who were killed and did not recognize anyone but Samir. They raised the question about the two others who we had sketches of, at least one or more of them thought they saw those two at one time or another when they were attacked.

"I've talked to the French counterterrorism officials also, and they've made no progress in identifying these individuals either and indicated that there's been no sightings of those two men in

France. As they told me, it was like they disappeared into thin air. Maybe we should see if we can find any connection between those two who escaped and the Korean woman. If we could determine that, then I think the professors have a right to worry."

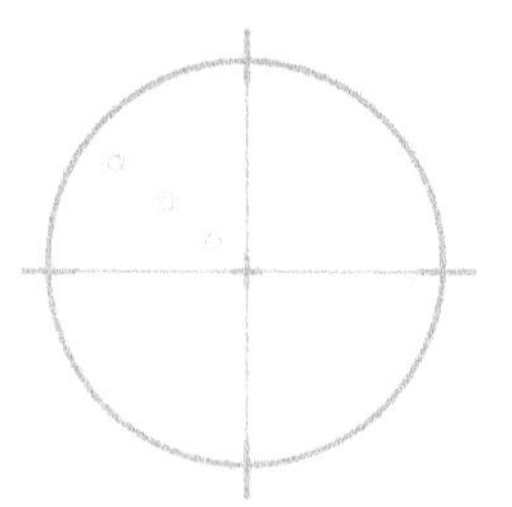

Chapter 12

Mac stood up and said, "Well, guys, I'll be taking off. I am going to find Rick and Chin-Sun so we can finish this business once and for all.

I responded, "Just a minute, Mac. I'll go with you."

Before I could stand up, Mac stated "No, DJ, you're going to stay here. I don't want to hurt your feelings, but, frankly, you would only get in my way. I don't want to have to worry about you getting hurt. I appreciate your willingness to go with me, but I think it's better if I go alone."

"Mac, how about I come with you?" said Ann.

"No, honey, this is a job for me and me alone." With that, Mac turned around and left. He drove to the police station and was soon standing in the chief's office. Chief Nane Kai, a native-born Hawaiian, pointed to a chair for Mac to sit on. Mac had met the chief previously at the hospital when he and another officer came to talk with them before starting their investigation.

Mac asked, "Where are you in the investigation, Chief?"

"We have been looking for both individuals but have found nothing as of yet. We also have a bit of a jurisdictional issue brewing between this office and the Coast Guard. They believe they have primary jurisdiction since your attempted murder occurred at sea. Our position is that the conspiracy to commit murder occurred in our jurisdiction. Since the press is already inquiring into this, I may allow the Coast Guard to lead this investigation. If they are unsuccessful, they can take the heat. I don't need it."

For a minute, Mac thought about what he'd been told. Finally, he said, "Chief, I'm going to be straight with you here. I intend to find these two regardless of which agency will be leading the investigation. I know this is a mess for you given the attempted murders of two tourists. I may, however, be able to help you out. If you will appoint me, say as a reserve officer, that will give me some cover and may become a positive for you if I find these people."

The chief pondered what Mac had said. If he let the Coast Guard have the lead in searching for these two people, it would give him cover if they did not find them. Also, if Mac found them, his office could take credit for solving this crime. It would also get this man out of his office. He agreed to Mac's suggestion and within a short period of time, the paperwork was completed, and Mac walked out as a new employee of the Maui Police Department.

Mac spent the next four days looking for Chin-Sun and Rick. However, on the second day, he was called into the chief's office and was informed that a body had been recovered floating off Kahului. The chief took him to the morgue to view the body to see if it could be identified. Mac confirmed that it was Rick. He told the chief, "It looks like Chin-Sun is taking care of loose ends."

Mac returned late on the fourth day and found us on the beach. His frustration boiled over as he walked toward us. "I've not been able to find that bitch. There is no information regarding her or her export - import company in New York or in any other place that I have looked. The feds have no information on the woman named Chin-Sun coming in or out of the country. Obviously, that means that the name she gave us is false. Everywhere I turn, I run into a brick wall. The chief had his officers check with their informants to see if they could learn anything, but they too are running into a brick wall." Mac then sat down in a chair next to us and remained still.

Finally, Ann stated, "Listen, honey, you'll find her. She is obviously not a true South Korean as she claims. If she is an agent of North Korea, she's been trained on how to avoid detection."

Mac looked at all of us and stated, "I may not have found her here, but I will find her. I promise you that!"

I, for one, did not doubt him.

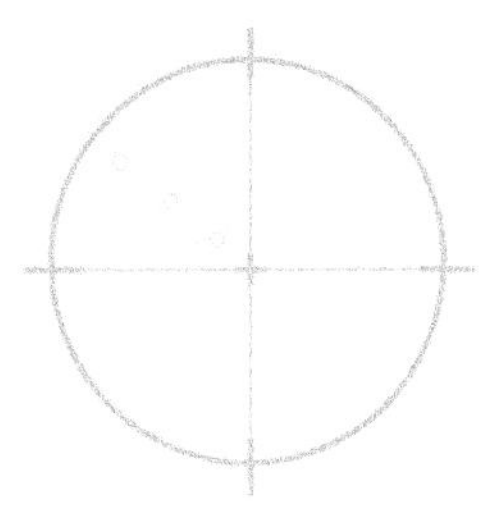

Chapter 13

Senator Kendricks was lying on his back looking at the ceiling when he rolled onto his side and gazed at the woman lying next to him. She was breathing softly, her breasts rising and falling with each breath. Kendricks could not take his eyes off her. She excited him in a way that his wife never had. He wondered if it was simply because she was Asian and knew things that his wife did not. Whatever it was, this woman pleased him greatly.

Kendricks was in a small hotel in Hanover, Virginia, which was halfway between Washington, DC and North Carolina. The senator had let Heather Lee select the location for their meetings because she had a perfect sense of style and discreteness. He glanced around the room, which was illuminated by the light of the approaching sunrise. It was not a large room and contained only a bed, a small table and a couch. They had spent many a cozy evening sitting on the couch watching old movies.

He had met Heather at a conference where he was one of the featured speakers. After his presentation, she approached him and asked to interview him for a blog she wrote. Heather explained that the blog and her podcast focused on US/Korean relations. The senator agreed and accompanied the young woman to a café, where they spoke for over an hour. Her questions were concise and to the point and led him to believe that she was somewhat of an expert on the topic of her blog.

When Kendricks spoke to her, he found himself enchanted with the beauty of the younger woman sitting across from him.

Heather's dark black hair tumbled to her shoulders easily, her face was unblemished, and her green eyes spoke to him. As they talked, she smiled, and her lips seemed to invite him in. As the senator made these observations, he realized he was reading in things that simply weren't there, but for a man having just turned 55, it was an exercise that made him smile.

As their interview was concluding, she asked if it would be appropriate to meet him again to show him the finished piece she was writing for the blog. Kendricks readily agreed and gave her the number to his personal cell phone. One week later, she contacted him and asked if they could meet.

When the two met for dinner, it took only a few minutes for him to review what she'd written and agreed that it was a correct rendition of their interview. For the next two hours, they spoke about many things. Heather had told him she was a second-generation Korean American and had grown up in a small town in southern Oregon. She explained that she obtained a degree in communications from the University of Utah. The young woman in her demure way informed him that she had worked for a lobbying firm whose main clients were Asian countries. Finally, Heather said that her blog was now the main source of her income.

Kendricks and Heather had met several times after that, and their relationship had finally become sexual. He looked at the clock on the table and saw that it was nearly 7:00 AM. Kendricks reached over and brushed the hair out of her face and gently kissed her on the cheek. Her eyes opened and she smiled at him. Heather reached up, pulled his head toward her and kissed him gently. "Good morning, love," she purred. Heather rolled on her side and pushed him on his back and then snuggled up to him. "Why do you have to leave so early?" she asked.

That is one of the things that attracted Kendricks to her. Heather never pushed him to do anything but always let him know that she wanted to be with him. Since he was a member of the Joint

Intelligence Committee, he had to return to Washington for a briefing that was scheduled for 1:00 PM that afternoon. "I have a meeting I must attend at 1:00 PM or I wouldn't have to leave. When can we get together again?" he asked.

"You're the one who has a busy schedule. Why don't you check it and give me a call? I can clear my schedule easier than you can. I hope you make it as soon as you can though." She slid off the bed and walked to the closet to get her robe. Heather saw his eyes follow her 5-foot, 6-inch body. She turned, faced him seductively with her hands on her hips and said, "Or you could stay, if you really wanted to."

"You drive me crazy when you act like that. You're lucky that I have a little free time before I must be on the road." He stood and walked over to her, picked her up in his arms and brought her back to bed.

An hour later, Kendricks was on the road driving his Lincoln MKX. As the countryside flew by, he smiled to himself. If other men knew, they would envy the position Kendricks was in. He had an attractive wife who loved being the wife of a United States senator. She simply did not care who his bedmate was at the time. Following the election of President Trump with his sexual escapades, his constituents were aware of and dismissed the various affairs that he had had.

The ability to attract women like Heather, Kendricks knew, may be the result of the office he held. In any event, he didn't care, but rather enjoyed the pleasures women gave him. The senator smiled as the miles continued to roll by.

Chapter 14

After kissing Kendricks goodbye, Heather crawled back into bed and pulled the covers up around her. There was a little time to relax before the 11:00 AM checkout. The senator was a nice enough guy, but not really her type. He is 25 years her senior, and she preferred men closer to her own age. But at 55, he kept himself in relatively good physical shape and gave her enough attention to keep her happy. She didn't care for his graying hair, but she would not tell him that. As a lover, he was energetic but not satisfying.

The reason she was with him had more to do with business than it did with the attraction. What she told the senator about herself was essentially true and would hold up if investigated. Her parents did live in southern Oregon, and had for some time been sleeper agents for North Korea, which made her a sleeper agent also. When she was 19, she traveled to Thailand for some specialized training including how to please men sexually. She was taught in the arts by several Thai women and completed an internship at a Thai brothel.

Heather got out of bed, walked into the bathroom and turned on the shower. Before stepping in, she stood before the full-length mirror and admired what she saw. Heather turned to her left to see if there were any flaws, saw none, and turned to the right to do the same thing. Heather stepped into the shower and proceeded to enjoy taking a few minutes for herself. When she finished, Heather dried off and wrapped the towel around her hair. The young woman proceeded to apply her makeup and retrieved the clothes she would wear from her overnight bag. After she dried her hair, Heather dressed and admired how her outfit accentuated her figure. She looked at the mirror once again and smiled.

Heather walked over to her bag, reached in and pulled out a burner phone. She dialed the number, heard the ring and waited for someone to answer. "Yes," the man answered.

"Did you get everything?" Heather responded.

"Yes, the video and audio are clear. You did very well." the man said with some regret that he was not on the video. "Where will you see him next?"

Heather answered, "I think I will suggest that we always come here. That should make your job easier instead of having to go to a new place every time."

"You know," the man said, "if you want, we could spend some time together, just you and me."

"Keep your mind on your work or I must inform your superior." Heather ended the call with a smile on her face.

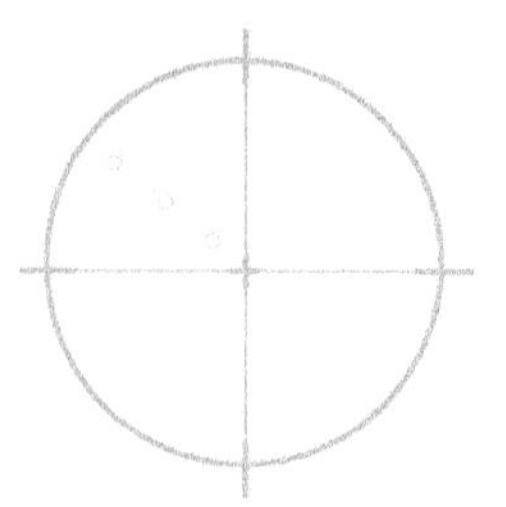

Chapter 15

The two gang members, Juan and Jesus, drove slowly into the hotel parking lot. They had discussed their plan several times making sure that each knew what they were going to do. The men had been given the room number where Ty and Leanne were registered.

As they walked into the hotel, the night clerk looked at them questioningly since it was 2:00 AM and said, "Can I help you?"

Jesus walked up to her and said, "We're here to visit some friends."

The clerk, Sharon, was in her early 20s and attending the University of Texas at San Antonio. To help pay for her studies, she worked part-time at the hotel during the graveyard shift. She reached for the telephone and stated, "I'll have security escort you to that room."

Before Sharon could say another word, Jesus pulled from his waistband a silenced handgun and fired two shots into her chest. Sharon fell to the floor without uttering a sound.

Jesus and Juan took the elevator to the floor where Ty and Leanne's room was located. They quietly walked down the hall and soon stood in front of Ty's room.

Inside the room, Ty was sitting on the bed turning over in his mind the conversation he had with DJ. It seemed to him that the attack on his friends was too coincidental for him not to be concerned. Then again, perhaps he was too concerned for no reason at all.

Suddenly, Ty heard what appeared to be someone trying to pick the lock to his room. He put his hand over Leanne's mouth and whispered, "Someone is trying to get into our room. Go into the bathroom."

Hearing the concern in Ty's voice, Leanne quickly and silently moved to the bathroom and closed the door.

Ty took his gun from the nightstand, turned on the lamp and moved behind the door waiting for it to open. He saw the doorknob begin to slowly turn and watched the door open quietly. Jesus and Juan quickly entered the room and were surprised to see that no one was in the bed.

Ty grabbed Juan around the neck, pushed his gun into Juan's back and said, "Both of you drop your guns!"

Jesus fired three shots at Ty but hit Juan in the chest. Ty was now holding the dead weight of Juan's body as a shield. Jesus fired two additional times but failed to hit Ty. Suddenly, the bathroom door opened. Standing there, totally nude, was Leanne who yelled, "Hey!"

Jesus turned for a moment and was stunned by what he saw. That moment of hesitation gave Ty the opportunity to fire four times at Jesus, who was struck by three of the four shots. Jesus was knocked back against the wall and slowly fell to the ground, still looking at Leanne.

Ty smiled at Leanne and stated, "Thanks for the interesting assist. Are you okay?"

Leanne ran toward him and threw her arms around his neck. "Yes, yes. Have you been shot?"

Ty responded, "I'm good. Why don't you get dressed? I'm going to call the police." Leanne grabbed her clothes and went into the bathroom to change while Ty made his call. Following that, he called DJ and told him what had happened.

Soon the police arrived and began their investigation. It did not take long before they found Sharon's body. It took several hours before the police left. Ty and Leanne were given another room. Sleep was hard to come by.

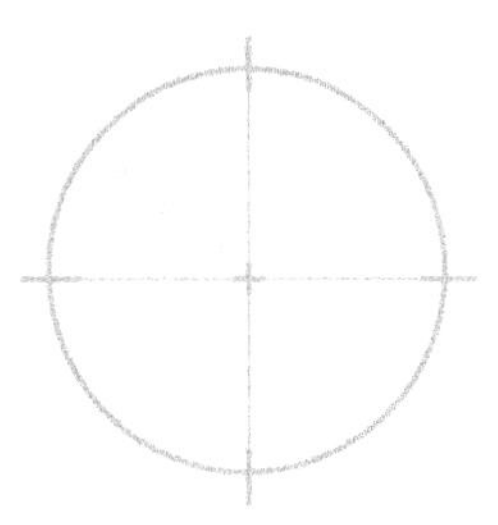

Chapter 16

As briefings went, this one wasn't as bad as many others I've had attended, Senator Kendricks thought. This briefing was given by Julianne Simmons, the Director of National Intelligence. Kendricks had known her for many years and had come to appreciate the dedication and intellect she brought to the job.

In the room were the Speaker and Minority Leader of the House, the Majority Leader and the Minority Leader of the Senate, and a few members of Congress who because of their interest or positions as committee chairman were allowed to be present. Simmons had gone through a list of countries whose importance to the United States could not be underestimated. She informed the individuals present of the status of the conflicts in the Ukraine, Afghanistan, Iraq and Syria. Furthermore, Simmons did provide additional background information regarding events in the Middle East and Asia. Her comments on Russia were no different than they were at the last meeting.

Kendricks believed that she was reaching the end of her presentation when she suddenly switched subjects. "I'm now passing out to you an update on the terrorist attack on our country, specifically the attacks on Las Vegas, San Francisco, and Seattle last year. The first section contains information on the total number killed and wounded that has been confirmed by us as of this date. The second section is a description of the damage that was caused and the estimated cost to repair it. The third and final section is compilation of actions that took place and resulted in the deaths of most of the terrorists. Information contained in sections one and two will be released to the press in the near future. However, the information in section three has certain classified information, which if released, could be harmful to the security of this country. Therefore, we invite you to read section three while you're here, but it must remain here. If you wish, you can take sections one and two to read at your leisure."

After passing out the updates, Simmons continued, "As most of you have read, most of the terrorists were killed when they attempted to eliminate three American couples. These individuals were the American professors who fought off the terrorists' attack in Paris two years ago. There were others involved including the professors' wives and a former student who was also involved in the Paris attack. As you will see when you read section three, we believe that two of the terrorist leaders got away. The professors had seen two of the terrorists' leaders during the attack and confirmed they were not among the dead.

"I'm bringing this to your attention because I was informed earlier today that a recent attempt was made on the lives of two of the professors. Evidently, while the professors were vacationing in Hawaii, they met a Korean woman on the beach. She arranged a fishing tour for them. During the tour, the tour guide pulled a gun on them and informed them that the Korean lady wanted them dead. They were able to get into the water without being shot and were left for dead. By luck, a Coast Guard helicopter rescued them several hours later."

Kendricks interrupted the director, "It seems to me that these professors are incredibly lucky. What is the chance that they could survive these three attacks?"

"Slim, I would say, Senator," Simmons responded. "However, what is of concern to us is whether there is any link between the terrorists who got away and this Korean woman. My analysts tell me that such a link is merely speculation at this point, but it is not one that we should discount. We are trying at this time to determine who the Korean woman is. The man in the tour boat was found dead in the ocean and we were unable to find any information about him.

"We believe it is more likely that this woman is a North Korean agent rather than a South Korean citizen. Given what we have seen from the crazy man in North Korea, we believe it is possible that he is behind this incident. If the Mideastern terrorists, who attacked the professors, are working with North Korea, that is something we must follow, and we will. Rest assured that if we learn anything further, we will inform this group of that information. Do you have any questions?"

Several of the people present asked questions about various issues that had been raised. After the meeting, Kendricks went up to Simmons and stated, "Are you sure the information about this Korean woman is well-founded? It seems a little slim to me."

"I understand what you're saying, Senator," replied Simmons, "You now know as much as I do. However, given the nature of the damages in the prior attack, I do not believe we can just dismiss these types of coincidences. In other words, there are no coincidences in this business. If we find nothing, we find nothing. We will have lost nothing except for some time and resources. However, if we do find something, we are a step ahead in deterring a potential attack in the future."

Kendricks responded, "I agree with what you're saying. We must look at these incidents closely. I appreciate how you're responding to what occurred in Maui."

Kendricks sat down, read section three and left the material on the table. He picked up sections one and two and headed for the door. It seemed to him that the director was tilting at windmills. He left the building thinking of Heather and wondering when they would get together again.

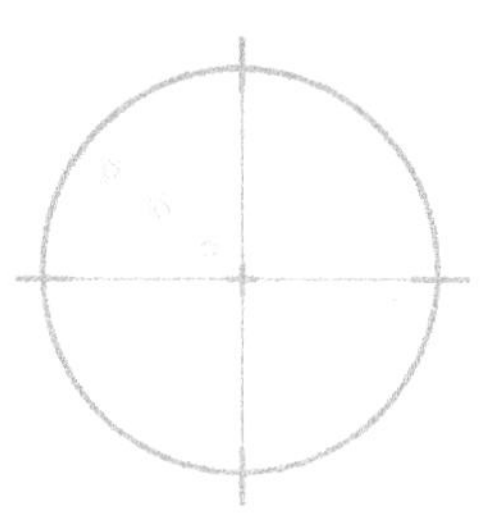

Chapter 17

The North Korean leader, Kim, was seated at his oversized desk as he waited for his next appointment. This is the date he had been waiting for. If the results he expected were positive, it would make him one of the most powerful men in the world.

Suddenly, there was a knock at the door. "Enter," he said with a harsh voice. He watched as two men entered, bowed to him and walked toward his desk. He motioned for them to sit down. "Well, what news have you for me. I trust that it is positive." Kim looked at both men with a hard stare, watching as the two men shifted uncomfortably in their chairs.

The man to his left was known to him simply as the "Doctor." He was dressed in an ill-fitting gray suit which matched the color of his hair. The Leader knew that the Doctor had come from a conference in China. "Well, Doctor, did you learn anything new in China?"

"Merely some technical matters that would not be of interest to you. However, the information I did receive merely confirmed that which I expected. The project we are working on is similar to one the Chinese are looking into."

"Does that help us in any way?" Kim asked.

"Only insofar that it confirms to me that we have accomplished something that even China has not been able to achieve. Frankly, I'm very excited that our accomplishments will bring great honor to you."

Looking at the second man, President Kim asked, "Do you agree with the Doctor?"

The second man, named Jin, was the director of the country's nuclear research program. He was dressed similarly to the Doctor, but his suit was black in color. "Yes, I do. I believe we're at the point that we can begin construction of ten devices and prepare them for distribution. Obviously, that is not within my jurisdiction. I'm confident that we can have the devices ready for distribution within a short time."

"I don't understand," Kim stated. "How can such complicated devices be ready for delivery in such a short time?"

The director smiled at the Leader and said, "I have such confidence in the Doctor and his work, that I ordered the construction of the devices some time ago. I know that you would want these devices available for use at the earliest possible moment. Therefore, I took the initiative to begin their construction early. I hope that meets with your approval?"

"Yes! Absolutely, it is approved. Have you given any thought as to how these devices can be transported without being discovered?"

Jin smiled and answered, "Yes. We knew that was a concern of everyone. My people have been designing and constructing a cylinder which will hold the virus. We will need ten of the cylinders to be shipped. I doubt if the US can discover one package, but if they do, the other nine should get through. As I said, you should be able to ship these devices within a short time."

Kim was smiling as he leaned back in his chair. He was prepared to bring America to its knees and to do his bidding. Nothing could stop him now.

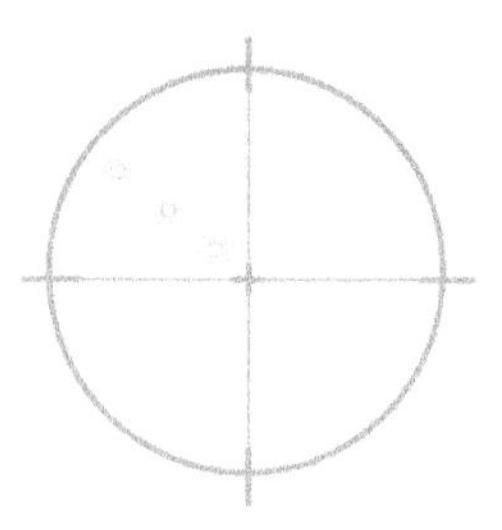

Chapter 18

Agent Ross Hixson was climbing the stairs which would lead him to the office suite of the Director of Counterterrorism. Hixson had been with the Bureau for just over seven years and had served in a variety of posts. He was wearing a dark suit, white shirt with a colorful paisley tie. Hixson belonged to a special division supervised by Sam Wyman. The purpose of this division was to ensure that people of power did not place themselves in positions where they could be compromised.

Shortly, Ross entered Sam Wyman's office suite and stopped at the receptionist's desk. "Hi Ginger, I have an appointment with the boss."

Ginger brought Wyman's schedule up on the computer and nodded to Hixson. "Yes, you're on his calendar." She picked up the phone and had a short conversation with Wyman. "He said he needs about five minutes before he can see you. Why don't you take a seat and I'll let you know when he's ready?"

Sitting down, he picked up a magazine off the table and began to peruse its contents. Finding nothing of interest, he returned the magazine to the table and began looking around the office. On the wall were pictures of the President and Vice President and some inexpensive art pieces. After a few minutes, Ginger's phone rang, she answered, and then motioned him to the door leading into Wyman's office.

Hixson opened the door, entered the office and saw Wyman sitting at his desk. Sam stood, reached across his desk and shook Hixson's hand. "How are you, Ross? I trust everything is going well."

"I can't complain," Hixson responded.

"Please take a seat. I understand you have some interesting results from snooping around. Why don't you tell me what you've learned?"

"As you know, we have a list of people we need to check up on and determine whether any are in danger of being compromised. Sen. Kendricks was assigned to me. I was able to access his calendar and found that he had been gone from his office for extended times. It was not possible to determine where he was going or who he was meeting with. I was able to follow him one time as he left his office by watching his car.

"He drove to a hotel halfway to North Carolina and went directly to a room without stopping at the registration desk. I accessed the hotel's computers and found only one name of interest, Heather Lee, who appeared to be the only occupant of that room. Since all the other rooms were occupied by couples, it appeared that he was probably visiting a young lady. As you know, that is something he does quite often."

"Were you able to confirm that he, in fact, was in that room?" asked Sam.

"No, I was not. However, the Senator did not leave that afternoon but stayed until the early morning. At 7:30 AM the next morning, Kendricks left the hotel alone. Shortly after 11:00 AM, I saw Ms. Lee exit the hotel, get into a car and head toward Washington.

"During the previous evening, I did a Google search on Ms. Lee, and found that she was of Korean descent, had her own blog on US/Korean relations and had previously worked for a lobbying firm. During that search, I was also able to obtain a photograph of Ms.

Lee. In reviewing her blog, I discovered that she interviewed the senator sometime before. It appears they knew each other.

"A few days later, I saw that the senator once again had an empty afternoon on his calendar. Rather than following him, I drove to the same hotel to see if he would show up. A few minutes after I arrived, I observed Ms. Lee arrive and enter the hotel. I was sitting in the lobby when she registered. She asked the clerk to send up a bottle of wine with two glasses. An hour later, who walks in, but Senator Kendricks."

Wyman looked at the agent and asked, "Were you able to determine whether he and Ms. Lee were together?"

"Not directly. However, I saw a young man carrying a bottle of wine and two wine glasses walk up and confer with the clerk. He headed for the elevator, and I followed. I saw him go to room 403 and knock on the door. The young man handed the wine and wineglasses to the person inside, the person said thank you and gave the man a tip. I recognized that voice. It was Senator Kendricks."

"Good work, Hixson," stated Wyman. "Have you discovered anything else about this woman that is of interest?"

"I've learned that she is a second-generation Korean American. Her parents moved here from South Korea many years ago and live in Oregon." Hixson further described her education and work experience to Wyman. "At this point, from my brief research, I'm not aware of anything out of the ordinary that would cause me concern. But as I said, I've not had time to fully explore her background."

Wyman looked at the young man and stated, "Well, it doesn't appear that we should be too concerned about Kendricks' affair with this woman. But to be absolutely certain, I want you to do more intensive background search and see what you can find." As he thought about this, he wondered whether Ms. Lee had any connection to the Korean woman in Maui. If that was the case, it would be troublesome. "I will send the photo of Ms. Lee to Art Rheingold and ask him to show it to the professors. I want you to get on this right away and find everything you can. When you've completed your work, come back and brief me. Understand?"

Hixson stood, looked at Wyman and said, "Absolutely. I will get back to you as soon as possible."

"Good, I look forward to seeing what you find," Wyman responded. Sam watched the agent leave his office and thought about what he had learned. He could care less who Kendricks took to bed, but his position on the intelligence committee caused him some concern. Kendricks wouldn't be the first man to whisper secrets to a foreign agent in the intimacy of the bedroom. He hoped Hixson would find enough information to clear Kendricks of any action that may compromise him or his country.

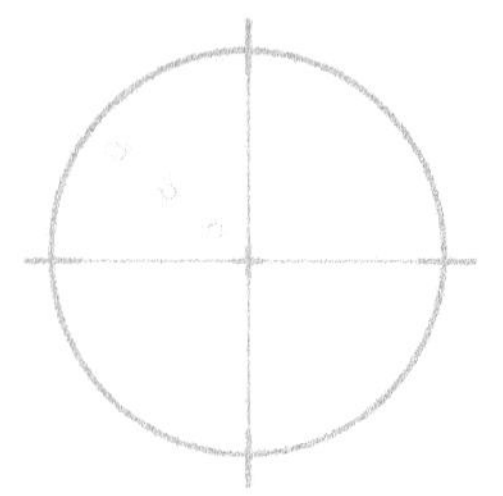

Chapter 19

It was a sad day when we had to leave beautiful Maui and return home. We took the red eye from Kahului to Los Angeles, and then a short hop to Las Vegas. We arrived early in the morning and had breakfast at a restaurant near the airport. Mac was driving his SUV, I sat in the front passenger seat, and our wives were in the backseat. I was still bothered by the run-in with the Korean woman. Even though we had discussed this before, I looked at Mac and asked, "Are you still concerned about Miss Chin-Sun? I wonder whether our dealings with her are over. What do you think?"

"I'm not sure, DJ. There must've been a reason why she wanted the guy to take us out fishing. I've never had any dealings with South Koreans and certainly not one that would require me to be killed. How about you?"

"I've never dealt with any Koreans as a lawyer and have not had any Koreans as a student. It's all quite baffling to me. The only thing I can think of is that she made a mistake in choosing us."

"If that's the case," Mac stated, "then I don't think we have anything to worry about. The question that bothers me is whether she is in any way connected with the terrorists we dealt with. Remember, two of the terrorist's leaders escaped when they attacked us at my ranch. Maybe we should call Rheingold and see if he has any new information that might connect her to the terrorist."

"Good idea." I took my phone and initiated the call to Rheingold. When he answered, I stated, "Hey, Art, it's DJ Anderson here."

"Hi, DJ. What's up?"

"Nothing you can't handle, I'm sure. Mac and I were wondering whether you were able to come up with anything about Chin-Sun?"

"Not much. We've not been able to make any connection between her and the Mideast terrorists that you dealt with. Why do you ask?"

"Well, it doesn't make any sense that she tried to kill us. Neither Mac nor I had any connections with Koreans previously. There would be no reason to do anything against us. It seems that there could be only two possibilities. One, she simply made a mistake at who she was targeting; or two, she had some connection to our terrorists' friends. By the way, did you make any progress in finding where the two that got away are at this point?"

"Neither we, nor the French, have been able to develop any leads on the two guys that got away. I think your assessment of the two possibilities is probably correct. I know of no other possibilities. We will continue to see if we can find a connection between the Korean woman and the terrorists."

"What have you been up to?" Art asked.

"We just flew in from Maui this morning."

Rheingold chuckled and stated, "And I'm supposed to feel sorry for you? I think not. We who have to work, do not take long vacations like you."

I responded quickly, "Only you would consider someone trying to kill you as a vacation. By the way, the white sandy beach we were on really is quite beautiful. You should try it someday."

"Asshole, I'll call you if we learn anything." Rheingold ended the conversation.

Mac interrupted my thoughts and said, "There's something sneaky going on in the backseat. Take a look."

Turning around, I saw that both women were smiling at me. Nothing seemed to be awry. I turned back and looked at Mac. "What are you talking about?" It was clear that Mac had seen something I had not. I was continually amazed at his powers of observation that he had developed as a police officer.

"They are drinking wine from a bottle which they continually try to hide."

Once again, I looked around and saw that the girls had silly grins on their faces. "Are you two drinking this early in the morning?"

With a funny grin on her face, Ann held up a bottle of wine and a plastic cup. Sandy giggled and then held up her own plastic cup. Sandy smiled at me and said, "We're just making the time pass faster."

"Uh huh," I responded as we continued down the road.

Sandy busted out laughing, followed by Ann.

"You know, Mac, sometimes it is hard to take these two anywhere."

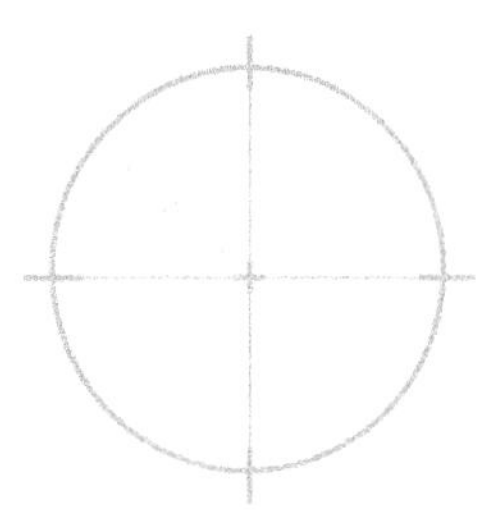

Chapter 20

The Doctor walked into his sparsely furnished office. His office, like others in the building, was painted a pale lime green. He had previously requested that his office be repainted in an off-white color. However, his superiors made it clear to him that he should simply work on his project, and that any additional requests for repainting would be dealt with harshly. Such was life in all of North Korea.

The man opened the top drawer of his desk, reached in, pulled out a bright red file and began perusing the latest reports received on the biological weapon they were developing. The Doctor had started his work several years ago when he had obtained several Ebola viruses. After suggesting to his superiors, that with time, funding and luck, it might be possible to develop an effective biological weapon to be used by his country. Since that conversation, he had spent his entire career trying to develop a weapon for which there would be no defense.

From his first samples of the Ebola virus, he had gone through several versions, each mutation of the one before. Each version had been labeled e1 through e15, the latest version. He had produced a vast quantity of the e15, which would be difficult to develop a preventable vaccine without his assistance. This latest version of the virus could be spread through airborne release and could also live for up to 24 hours on hard surfaces.

Because of the risk inherent in handling this extremely deadly strain of Ebola, the Doctor, along with his assistants, managed to develop a vaccine. This vaccine would protect those who developed and produced the strain, those who might handle it in transport and those who may release it into the air. Once inoculated with the vaccine, a person could come in contact with the virus without suffering the horrible effects it produced.

Almost as important as the virus itself, it was critical to develop a method for delivery. After much trial and error, his department had engineered a delivery system that was both simple and effective. It consisted of a small backpack that could also be carried over the shoulder. In the backpack, was a small cylinder much like those that carried oxygen for persons needing assistance breathing. It was designed to be used over and over and was easily refilled. The release mechanism was also simple in design, coming out of the backpack was an eighth-inch nozzle that directed the spray up and to the rear. This allowed the sprayed mist to linger in the air as people walked through it.

He smiled as he thought of this design. It was his intent that the bag with the small cylinder would be shipped through China to the US for sale as a pack and water bottle. That would allow the system to be transported to the US via normal shipping containers. The actual virus would be shipped in the same manner in large oxygen-tank-like cylinders to a warehouse or warehouses located throughout the United States. The small cylinders in the backpacks would be filled from these cylinders. It was very unlikely the port authorities would actually check to see if these cylinders did indeed contain oxygen.

The Doctor read the reports, leaned back in his chair, and pondered the deadly nature of the organism he had created. The Doctor had never felt concerned about his part in this deadly enterprise. He learned early in his life that one did not question the purposes of the communist leaders in his country. To do so, one would at least be imprisoned or executed. Any qualms of conscience would never overcome the reality of his own death.

Several people had been brought to his lab over the years from prison camps. These people were injected with the virus and became guinea pigs to determine if the vaccine they developed was effective. The people who had died before the effective vaccine was discovered numbered in the hundreds.

The Doctor, like the Nazis before him, understood that he was only following orders and could do no different. That was the thought that let him sleep at night.

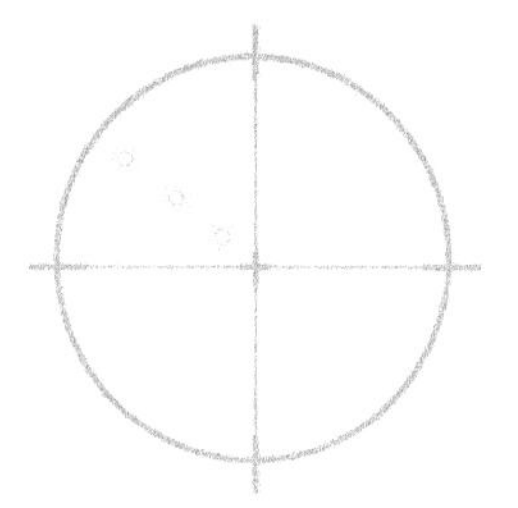

Chapter 21

Mael pulled into his normal parking spot, killed the motor and slowly got out of his vehicle. He was not sure if the director would still be in his office since it was early evening. He had tried calling Pierre both at his office and cell line but had received no answer. Mael knew that Pierre had many events that he was expected to attend in the evening hours, so he wasn't surprised when the phones had not been answered.

Even though he knew the guard well, Mael still was required to provide identification before entering the building. As was his normal practice, he took the stairs rather than the elevator. He entered the director's office suite and was soon standing before Pierre's office door. Mael knocked loudly and waited for an answer. There was no response from inside the office, so he used his key to open the door. Mael entered and looked around. Finding no one, he walked out of the office, locked the door and headed for his own office down the hall. Before Mael could open the door, his cell phone rang, and he could see that it was the director calling.

Hello," he answered.

Pierre responded, "I see you called."

"I did. I have some news which I think you will be interested in. Do you have time to meet tonight?" He knew Pierre would not talk business over an unsecured line.

"I'm just leaving a very boring party. I could be in the office within 20 minutes. Does that work for you?"

"It does. I will meet you in your office." Mael ended the call and walked into his own office to review some paperwork. After 20 minutes, he got up from his chair and headed for Pierre's office. The door to the office was open, he knocked lightly, and Pierre told him to enter.

"Well, Mael, what do you have for me?"

"We've come up with some information that leads me to believe that the two terrorists are alive and well and may be up to no good. Previously, I had asked all our agents to provide copies of the drawings of those two men to all their informants. Just recently, two of the informants provided new information to their handlers about these two men. They identified the men as Kamil and Ahmed. Supposedly, both men were in Paris within the last two weeks. The informants did not know but speculated that not only are they part of a terrorist group, but they were planning something new.

"One of these men indicated that he had overheard certain people talking and there was a mention made of some coordinated plan between them and North Korea. We have not been able to corroborate this information through other sources. Furthermore, this may simply be the ramblings of young men trying to impress their handlers. However, the reference to coordination between their group and North Korea is troubling."

Pierre took a moment before he responded. "Have your agents been able, in some way, to verify the credibility of these informants?"

"Not completely. I believe the information regarding the names is accurate, but I'm not sure, about the connection with the North Koreans. I asked my team to dig deeper and wider based on this information. Hopefully, something of value will come forth."

Pierre smiled at Mael, "Good work. I suggest you get this to the Americans as soon as you can."

Mael left Pierre's office fully intending to give this information to Sam with hopes that he might expand upon it.

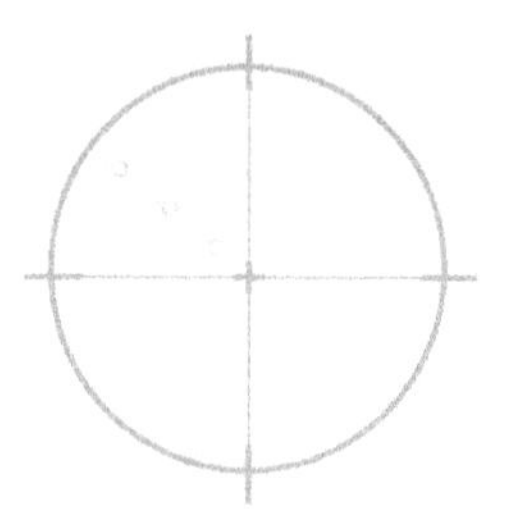

Chapter 22

Mael walked slowly back to his office as he considered what he would tell Sam. He walked to his door, unlocked it and entered his typical government office. Mael glanced around and chuckled to himself about the sparse furnishings he had acquired. He was not a man of "things" but one of "action." Mael sat down at his desk and looked up Sam's number. Soon the phone was ringing on the other end and a moment later, Sam answered.

"Hi, Sam," Mael stated, "I hope you're not too busy to have a short chat."

"For you, my friend, anytime. However, I have no information to give you at this point," Sam responded.

"I may have some information that may be of interest to you. Our informants have been hard at work and may have finally come upon something."

"Like what?" Sam asked.

"We believe that the two terrorists that got away after their attack on the professors have been in Paris within the last couple of weeks. Their names are Ahmed and Kamil. Evidently, they are part of a terrorist group, however, we do not know which one. Our informants indicated that they believed that a new attack was being planned. They had no information other than it was a plan.

"Interestingly, they heard some talk about a relationship with North Korea. I have no information other than that. It may help you to confirm that the attack on the two professors in Hawaii was a part of this plan. Why they would go after the professors, however, makes no sense to me."

Sam sat there for a few seconds pondering what he had heard. "You know, it doesn't make any sense to me either. It did not make any sense regarding their attacks on the professors in the US except for a potential revenge motive. What do you make of this information, Mael?"

"It appears to me that the North Koreans may very well be involved in a new attack. It will probably be against the US rather than France. Because this information is, at best, sketchy, it is hard to draw any firm conclusions. Only part of the information that we received has been verified. Obviously, I will have my informants continue to dig and see what they can find. Do you know of any reason why the North Koreans would actually attack the US given what the US's response would be?"

Again, Sam responded, "They have hated us for a long time, since we stopped their invasion of South Korea. There was kind of a lovefest with one of our prior presidents, which as you know, did nothing to ease tensions. That nut job in North Korea would probably really like nothing better than to attack us. If he had any sense at all, he would make sure that whatever attack was carried out could not be traced back to his country. It may very well be the reason Ahmed and Kamil may be involved. Do you have any additional information about these two guys?"

"Other than the information I've already given you; I really have nothing further to add. The names were given to our informants, but I'm not sure if it is second or third-hand information. We may be totally off base on this, but that is all we have to go on so far. I can assure you we will continue to find whatever information is out there. By the way, the drawings we have of those two missing Saudi terrorists led to this information. You know, those pictures, while they are good, are still pretty vague. The only people who can truly recognize them are your professors."

"You're right about that Mael. I will have the Bureau get in touch with them and let them know what's going on. From a practical standpoint, we may have to draft them into helping us catch these guys. I'm not sure how they'll feel about that."

Mael responded, "They seem to be stand-up guys. Don't you think they'll be willing to help you?"

"They've been through a lot recently. Samir tried to kill them in Paris and again where they lived. They may have had enough. We will contact them, and I will tell them they are needed once more. We just need help to identify the guys, not to go to war with them."

"Listen, Sam," stated Mael, "I must go. I'll be calling you again if we discover anything new."

"Thanks, Mael, we'll talk soon."

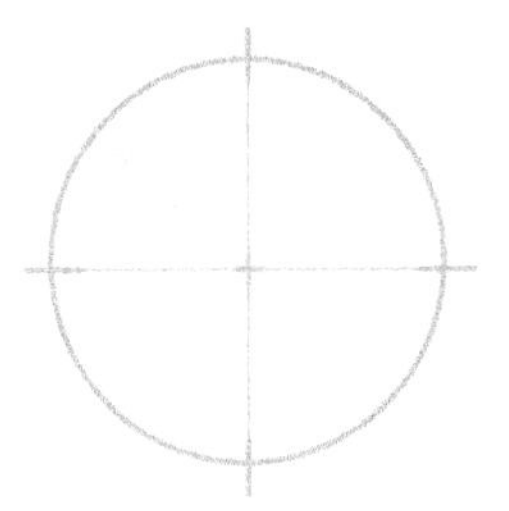

Chapter 23

After talking with Sam, Art Rheingold immediately called DJ and asked if he, Mac, and Ty could meet with him the next day. He had no idea how they would react to what he was going to propose.

The next morning, his phone rang, he picked it up and after listening said, "Please bring them to my office."

The door opened and in walked the three professors, each eyeing him suspiciously. He shook hands with each of them and asked them to take a seat. He smiled at them, which initiated the response he expected.

Mac spoke first, "Okay, you silly bastard. That smile of yours tells me we're in for a hard time. Just spit out what the bad news is."

"Well," Art responded, "I hate to tell you this, but we have learned that the two terrorists who got away during the attack on your home are within 100 miles of us and are coming with over 100 men."

"Holy shit!" yelled DJ.

Ty put his head in his hands and asked, "When did you find out and what are you going to do?"

Before anything further was said, Mac responded, "Wait just a minute, folks. Look at that slimy SOB. He still has that silly look on his face, and I truly believe that he is lying through his teeth."

I spoke next, "So he does, my friend, so he does."

Ty, who had jerked his head out of his hands and eyed Art closely. "Well, I'll be damned. He thinks that scaring us is funny as hell. Should we shoot him now or do we have to wait for a trial?"

Mac pulled out his firearm, pointed it the ceiling and stated, "Let's just shoot him now and be done with it. Justifiable homicide, no doubt about it!"

"Hold on fellows, can't we have a little fun among friends," Art stated quickly.

Looking at Art's bobbing adams apple. "This feels like fun to me. What do you guys think?"

Ty responded first, "How much jail time do you think we would get? If it's not too bad, let's go for it."

"Can't be more than a year or two. I mean he is an asshole. Nobody cares about assholes." DJ was smiling as he spoke.

Art looked questioningly at the three men seated before him. "You guys have a serious problem in taking a joke."

I chuckled and smiled at my two friends. "We really got him this time, didn't we?"

"It's way too easy to do this to him. I think kindergartners would be better at keeping their cool," stated Ty.

"You guys are truly assholes. I don't even know why I try to help you out," Art replied.

"It's because you love us, Art. Now, why are we wasting our time sitting here in your office?" DJ asked.

Art took a couple of deep breaths to calm down. When Mac had pulled out his weapon, it had shaken him. He knew full well that Mac would use deadly force when necessary "Well, guys, maybe we can start over with this little meeting. I have some new information for you about your Korean woman and the two terrorists. We received this information from the French. Evidently, the two terrorists are called Ahmed and Kamil. The French learned that they had been in Paris recently, and one of their informants discovered their names. Furthermore, the informants believe that there was some kind of relationship between the North Koreans and these two guys."

Mac looked at the two of us and simply said, "Well, I'll be damned. There was a reason behind that little swim we took with the sharks, DJ."

I looked at Art realizing how serious the situation had become. "Art, is this just a warning for us or do you have some additional information we should know?"

"Well, the French have raised the problem that we have. We have a drawing of the two men, and we know what their names are, as I said, Ahmed and Kamil. While the drawings of the men may be a good likeness of each of them, they are still relatively vague. The bottom line is, as we defend against any potential attack they may make, we may not be able to truly recognize them. As the French told us, you three are the only ones who actually saw these guys."

Ty asked, "And?"

"We may need your help in taking these guys down. We don't know yet, but we may need you."

I asked, "Just what would you want us to do?"

"I think the idea is that you three would be consultants to the Bureau to help identify Ahmed and Kamil. You will receive a per diem for your expenses and a daily rate of pay for your time. We haven't gone much beyond that because we simply do not know what's going on. We are trying to prepare ourselves for any eventuality."

I spoke up, "I'm not sure my wife would be really happy about me battling these guys again. I mean, I got injured in Paris, in my hometown and again in Maui. She will ask me what my life is worth, and I'm not sure your daily rate of pay will impress her."

"Yeah, I agree with what DJ is saying," stated Ty.

Mac was leaning back in his chair pondering this conversation. "Hey guys, it would look good on your resume. Consultants to the FBI."

I shook my head. "You and I are retired. Why in the hell would we care about our resumes? Certainly not for any job."

"I think it would be great fun to lie about all my experiences with the FBI when I'm having a beer at the bar." He smiled at us and then gave Art a big high-five.

I looked at Ty. "Stupid is as stupid does, I think."

"Oh, come on, DJ," replied Mac, "we will not be in any real danger since we are just there for ID purposes. Think how much fun we can have on the fed's dollar. It sounds like a pretty sweet deal to me."

"Let me run it by Sandy and see what she has to say. If she is okay with that, I'm okay with it. What about you Ty?"

"Well, I certainly can't let you two go and screw up the defense of our country alone. If our country is to be screwed, all three of us should be involved. Let me talk to Leanne."

As we stood to leave, Art once again shook each of our hands. "I look forward to hearing what you have to say. Wait a minute." Art placed a photo of a young Asian woman in front of them. "Do you recognize this woman?" Each of us shook our heads no. "She isn't the woman you met on Maui?"

"No," I responded. "Why?"

"Just wondering," said Art. As the three men left, Art put the picture of Heather Lee away.

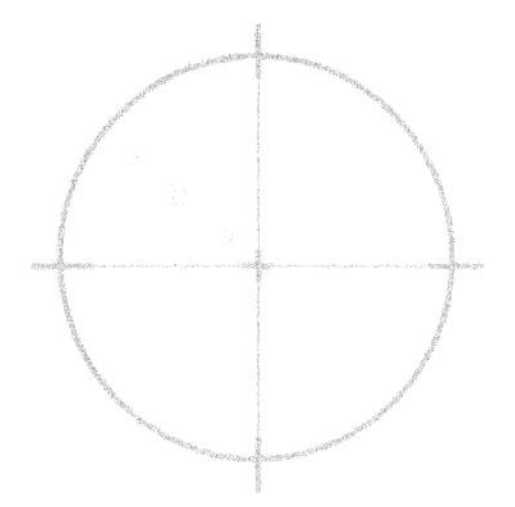

Chapter 24

After we left Art's office, it was decided that we all should meet to discuss Art's proposal at Mac's house at 8:00 PM. That gave us time to talk with our wives before we met.

Sandy and I had a brief discussion before we left for Mac's house. We decided not to discuss the proposal, but rather wait for everyone to be together. As we pulled up to Mac's house, we could see that Ty and Leanne were already there. Sandy and I got out of the car and walked up to the front door. Before I could ring the bell, Mac opened the door and bid us to enter. We followed him into the living room and saw that Ty and Leanne were seated on the couch and Ann was preparing drinks.

She looked up at us and said, "Hey, guys, how are ya?"

Sandy smiled at her and replied, "Given everything that's going down, I'm not really quite sure. How are you?"

"I'm quite good. It seems to me that we got the guys by the short hairs once again. Is that right, Mac?"

Mac smiled at her and replied, "You really should have been a comedian. I think you've missed your true calling."

Ann started laughing and walked over and handed Ty a beer and Leanne a glass of wine. Looking at Sandy and me, Ann stated, "What libations would you care for?"

Sandy answered, "I'll have a shot of tequila on the rocks and I'm sure DJ would like a beer." I nodded my agreement to Ann. With that, Sandy and I sat down and soon held our drinks in our hands. Ann came over and sat next to Sandy.

Mac picked up his previously opened beer, walked over and stood before us. He smiled and said, "Well, once again, we are meeting to talk about these damn terrorists." To make sure that we were all on the same page, Mac described our conversation with Art. "That's about the size of it." Looking at us, Mac stated, "DJ or Ty, do you have anything you'd like to add?" Both Ty and I shook our heads no. "Well, ladies, you now have the floor."

Leanne spoke first, "Have the three of you lost your mind? I mean, why would any of you want to get involved in this madness once again?" Ty started to speak, and Leanne stopped him with a vicious stare. "I'd like to hear one good reason why you should do this."

Mac looked at Ty and saw him raise his eyebrows. It was clear that Ty wanted someone else to address this matter. I started to speak when Mac waved his hand for me to stop. He knelt down in front of Leanne and talked slowly. "These two men are working with the Koreans and will work with the Koreans regardless of what we do. We do not know if taking aim at us is one of their goals. However, it seems to me that they mean our country no good. Our choices are simple. We do nothing and let the FBI handle it, and they probably will take care of it. However, there is this distinct possibility that they may not be able to stop whatever these people are doing without our assistance in identifying them. I think that's what this comes down to.

"From my perspective, I would rather help the feds with what seems to me to be at most an advisory role. I do not think that the risk of harm coming to us is very great. I'm not sure how I could live with myself if I chose to do nothing, and as a result, innocent people were killed or injured. That's how I see it."

Mac looked at me and I stated, "I, too, feel that the danger to us is minimal and the good we can do is great. As you know Leanne, I am not one who jumps at every chance to put myself in danger. However, I agree with everything Mac has told you."

With pleading eyes, Leanne turned to Sandy and said, "You are not going to agree with this are you? We have too much to lose. And we nearly lost our husbands three times in dealing with these terrorists."

Sandy had her hands together, twisting them nervously. "Leanne, I feel the same unease and nervousness that you do. I feel like my stomach is squeezing itself together. What has convinced me to go along with this proposal, is that until these two terrorists are dead, we may never live in peace." She looked up at Leanne and with a hard look and her voice rising stated, "This must be done. This madness must come to an end."

Ann stood up and with a smile on her face said, "Ahmed and Kamil need to have their balls shot off. Just like Samir, there will be no 72 virgins awaiting them." This comment brought a stream of laughter from everyone. "Leanne, these three men of ours are too stupid and inept to get themselves killed, no matter how hard they try. So, let's end this once and for all."

When Leanne quit laughing, she drained her glass of wine and stated, "Oh, hell, off with their balls and give me another drink. She looked at Ty and said, "You get hurt, and your balls are the next to go." Ty involuntarily grabbed his crotch, but managed to smile nonetheless.

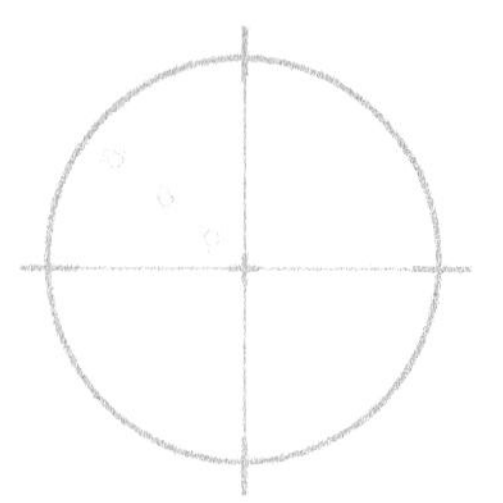

Chapter 25

Derek was sitting at his desk in his office at the FBI building pondering whether to go out for lunch or eat the two sandwiches he had made at home. He had received a call from a fellow agent, Pat, who inquired about going out for lunch.

Derek was a relatively new agent for the Bureau. After the show down with the terrorists at Mac's house, the President had let the Director of the FBI know that he felt Derek would be a fine addition to the Bureau. Derek had just completed his initial training and had been assigned to the Washington field office. His job so far had been shadowing other agents to get a feel for his responsibilities.

After receiving the call from Pat, Derek said he would get back to him as soon as he finished some paperwork. Derek reached for the phone to make his call when his phone suddenly rang. The person on the other end identified herself as the administrative assistant to Sam Wyman, Director of the Counterterrorism Division. She indicated the director wanted to speak with Derek sooner rather than later. Derek informed her that he would be right there.

As he walked to Sam's office, his mind scurried to every misstep he had made during his short time with the Bureau. As much as he tried, he could not, for the life of him, understand why the director would want to speak to him. He approached the director's door, swallowed hard and entered. Sitting at the desk was a young woman who appeared to be about 25. She looked up at him and stated, "Can I help you?"

Derek smiled at her, and gave her his name and replied, "I was called by the director's administrative assistant and was asked to come to see him."

She smiled at him again and asked him to take a seat on the sofa that fronted her desk. The young woman picked up the phone, pushed a button and stated that Derek was here to see the director. She listened for a moment and said, "You can go right in." She nodded toward the door that he was to enter.

Derek rose from the sofa, walked the short distance to the door, opened it and walked into the office. Sitting at another desk was an older woman, who introduced herself as Sophia, the director's administrative assistant. He walked over and shook the woman's hand. She stated "It will be a few minutes as he is on the phone. I will let you know when he is available."

Derek swallowed hard again and asked, "Do you know why the director wants to speak with me?"

Sophia could see that he was nervous and uneasy. She had seen the same look on many agents who were summoned to speak with the director. "I'm sorry, but I have no idea. However, I doubt that he's already planning your execution." She smiled and Derek laughed. At that moment, her phone rang, she listened and then said, "He's ready for you now."

Derek opened the thick wooden door and entered. He saw Sam seated behind his desk and walked toward him. Sam rose, came around his desk and shook Derek's hand. He led Derek to the seating area which had two sofas across from each other with a coffee table in between.

Sam asked, "Would you like some coffee, Derek?"

Derek declined Sam's offer and sat down on one of the sofas. Sam also took his seat, looked at Derek and stated, "I'm sure you're wondering why I asked you to come here." Sam smiled at Derek and said, "Most young agents who are called to this office appear a little green. However, the reason agents are called here has nothing necessarily to do with their job performance, as it is, a need for their expertise."

Derek responded, "I have not been an agent very long so I'm not sure what expertise I would bring to the table."

"For you, Derek, it's not your experience that I need but rather your relationship with certain people." Derek looked at Sam, clearly not understanding where this conversation was going. Sam continued, "Let me explain what I mean. I'm aware of the work you did with the professors fighting off terrorists in Paris and at home. I'm not sure if you know, but two of the terrorists you fought against, escaped being captured. Currently, there have been some unexplained occurrences that lead us to believe that those terrorists may be planning an additional attack on our country.

"First of all, Mac and DJ, were recently vacationing in Maui when they met a young Korean woman. She said she was from South Korea, but we are not sure that is correct. She had gone on a fishing trip and told the guys of her adventure catching some kind of fish in the waters off Maui. In any event, it sounded interesting, so Mac and DJ signed on for the same fishing expedition. When they were well out to sea, the charter captain tried to kill both of them. He told the guys it was at the Korean woman's request. Luckily, they jumped off the boat and spent hours in the ocean before being picked up by a Coast Guard helicopter. Also, the French informed us that these two terrorists, Ahmed and Kamil, might be planning a coordinated attack with some North Korean assets. We have not been able to confirm that information.

"We are taking this potential threat very seriously. Unfortunately, the only people who can identify these two terrorists are perhaps yourself and the three professors. We have asked them, and they have agreed to act as consultants to the Bureau in this matter. In essence, they will work with us to try and identify these two terrorists if we can find them. I would like you to be our liaison with Mac, DJ and Ty. Would you be willing to accept this assignment?"

"I'm not exactly sure what I would be doing," Derek answered. "Can you be more specific about what you would like me to do?"

Sam looked closely at Derek before responding, "You would have several responsibilities. First, you would be reporting directly to our agent in St. George. I think you've met Art Rheingold. You would be briefing him on any intelligence or information you may have. Second, if it is necessary for the professors to travel somewhere in hope of getting an ID on these terrorists, you would, of course, accompany them. They have been through a lot recently, and I was reluctant to place them in the field. However, if they can help us identify Ahmed or Kamil, we are willing to put them in harm's way. Third, it will be your job to keep them safe if that is at all possible. That's about it."

"How long would you expect this assignment to take?"

"Until the terrorist threat has been eliminated or proved to be false," Sam responded.

Derek stated, "Of course, I would be happy to take this assignment. I enjoyed working with those three men and eliminating this terrorist threat makes this assignment even better."

"I thought you would feel that way," Sam stated. "I want you to know, however, that we do not intend this assignment to be you babysitting these three men. We want to work with them, keep them safe, and hopefully identify the terrorists. I would like you to leave in the next 24 hours. If you need anything, all you have to do is ask."

Derek replied, "Just so you know, if the professors ever believed I was there to babysit them, I would probably end up buried somewhere on Mac's ranch."

"From what I've heard about these three guys, I understand why you would say that. Good luck."

Derek stood, shook Sam's hand and walked out of the office. Derek was a little heady as he left the office since these executive suites were kind of rarefied air for a new agent. He took out his cell phone and called Pat and told him he would not be able to make lunch.

As soon as Derek got back to his office, he started making arrangements to begin this assignment. Derek thought to himself, this was either going to be very boring or very exciting, but it was definitely going to be fun.

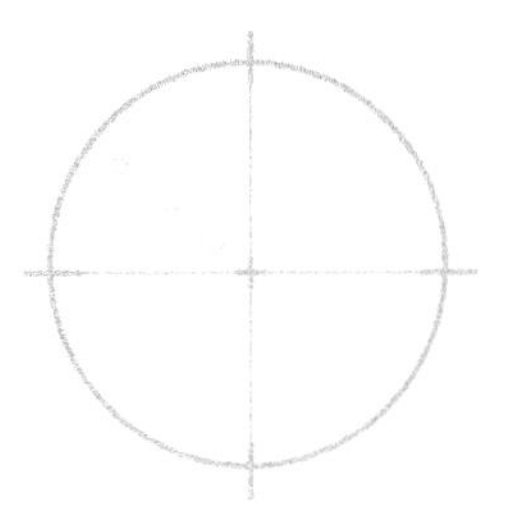

Chapter 26

Walking into his conference room, Kim saw the defense minister, the Chief of the General Staff and various other officers waiting for him. Everyone in the room jumped to attention as he walked in and waited for his order to be seated. He looked at each one of them before speaking. "I've called you here today to inform you of a very important operation that is about to begin. Up until now, you were not aware of the development of this operation as it did not involve the military. However, once this operation begins, you may be required to defend the nation against the United States."

Each of the men looked at each other wondering what was to come. Confused, the men sitting at the table expected they would have been included in the development of this operation, or at a minimum, have heard about it. Each of them waited for the President to tell them more.

Kim continued, "For the past several years, our scientists have been looking into the possibility of producing a biological weapon that could be used against the United States. Today, I'm here to tell you that they have succeeded. Our scientists have created a mutated Ebola virus. I am happy to tell you that the virus can stay in the air for some time and live on flat surfaces for even a longer time. Furthermore, they have developed a safe method to deliver this virus, in a manner which is undetectable. The virus will be in portable containers held in backpacks and will be sprayed into the air. A vaccine that will help protect our assets who will be spreading the virus has also been developed. In short, this plan involves shipping the virus to the United States in a way that is undetectable by their customs agents.

"We are working in conjunction with certain Saudis to do the actual spreading of the virus. Our only connection to them is through one of our agents. I trust that each of you understands that the Covid virus spread by the Chinese was not as effective as they hoped. I can tell you now, our operation will make the Chinese effort look like an amateur production. We can and will do better.

"Your part in the operation is simple. We must make sure that our armed forces are ready to respond to any overt act by the United States. I do not expect them to connect us to the spread of this virus, but if they do, we need to be ready militarily."

Kim looked around the table and saw faces that were as inscrutable as his. "Do you have any questions?" No one responded. "Good. As you know, this operation will be conducted under the utmost secrecy. You will not disclose it to any of the people under you. Your actions will simply be to keep us prepared. I will meet with each of you individually later to be briefed by you on the progress you've made."

As the men left the conference room, some had looks of deep concern, while others seem to embrace the opportunity to strike the United States.

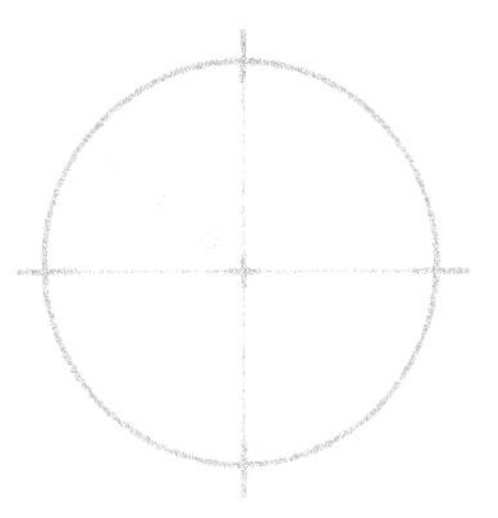

Chapter 27

Heather Lee was in her office when she heard her email alert. She opened the email, clicked on the new message, and saw that the message referred to a book Heather had read. This was a coded message from a friend of hers that indicated she should go to a specific chat room. It took just a moment to be in that room where she found an attachment waiting for her, which she opened. Heather was startled to see that it was from Kim himself.

The North Korean agent downloaded the encrypted message and ran it through another program that allowed her to read the message. As Heather began reading, she felt her throat tighten and her heart rate increase. Kim told her that the planned operation would begin shortly, and it was important that they have all the information Heather could gather as to the readiness of the United States government. Using another program, the message and the email were deleted.

Heather began to feel excitement surging through her body like a bolt of electricity. She knew the basics of the operation but only in the broadest sense. Because secrecy was tight, Heather knew only what her country wanted and needed, but not necessarily the actual details of the operation. Heather smiled to herself because she realized she was one of the few people in the world who knew the United States would be attacked in the deadliest way.

The young woman called Senator Kendricks on his private phone and arranged for the now-usual rendezvous. Hearing the excitement in his voice, she proposed meeting him once again.

Heather knew he wanted her, and that the unanswered question remained, how far would he go to get her? Early that afternoon, Lee had driven to their usual hotel in Hanover, Virginia. Before going to the hotel, she purchased his favorite wine and some new sex toys he would enjoy. Upon checking into the hotel, the young woman took a shower to freshen up, dressed in her sexiest negligee, put the wine on ice, and wrapped the small sex toys in a box. She knew that he liked to receive presents of any kind, and she was confident that these would excite him.

Heather lay down and soon was sound asleep. She began to dream of Senator Kendricks. Heather wondered if he truly loved her or merely used her body to meet his needs. It seemed she'd only been asleep a few minutes when Heather heard a loud knocking. Glancing at the clock on the bedstand, Heather realized she had been asleep for almost two hours. Heather saw that Kendricks was about to knock again when she opened the door. He stepped in, took her in his arms, and kissed her sweetly. He smiled at her, "What took you so long to answer the door?"

"I think I drifted off to sleep while waiting for you. In fact, I was dreaming about you." He took off his coat, hung it on the desk chair and sat on the bed. Heather walked over and sat in his lap, her arms around his neck. She smiled at him and began to softly kiss him. "I have a present for you," Heather murmured. "I think you'll like it."

"Well, let me see," he responded. He giggled in anticipation. "What is it?"

She stood up, walked into the bathroom and returned holding the present. Heather gave it to him and sat down on the bed beside him. Heather watched him open it with childlike glee. He pulled out the sex toys contained in the box and stated, "These will be fun to try today."

Heather stood up and pulled the senator to his feet. Slowly and very provocatively, she began to undress him. When he was standing before her, nude, Heather pushed him onto the bed. For the next hour, Heather pleased the senator with her body and the toys she had bought him.

As they lay exhausted in the bed, she began to plot out her next steps. Lee was resting easily in his arms with her leg and arm across his body. "Did anything exciting happen to you today?"

She heard a deep laugh come from within him. "Well," he said, "I think the last hour has been pretty exciting myself. What else did you have in mind?"

"Oh, nothing in particular. I just wanted to see how your day went." Heather lay quietly for a few moments before speaking again. "You know, my podcast is going very well. It might be time to have you as a guest once again. What do you think of that?"

Kendricks perked up upon hearing that. Like any politician, he liked to think that he carried a certain weight with the public. For the politician who desired higher office, it was incumbent upon him or her to be before the public's eye. Podcasts of national security issues certainly filled that bill. "I am sure that could be arranged."

Heather snuggled up to him even more in response to his comments. "Is there anything new that you would like to talk about since the last time you were on my podcast. I mean, it's probably not beneficial to repeat what they've heard before. You know, my listenership is over hundred thousand now, and, I think, your last appearance helped increase that number."

Kendricks liked the feel of her next to him. He had come to really enjoy his time with her and would seriously consider making things more permanent with her if he wasn't married. If she became unavailable to him, he would miss her dearly. "I'm sure I can come up with some new material. Is there anything in particular you would like me to discuss?"

"No, not really," she answered. "The regular news has covered Kim's firing of different missiles. There's really nothing new. Are there any other security threats that the US is aware of involving the North Koreans?"

"Well, there's an unconfirmed report that the North Koreans may be cooperating with Mideast terrorists, which could involve an attack on the US mainland. However, I cannot discuss that in public. You know what is interesting, though? The professors who were involved in the attacks out West have been hired as consultants by the FBI. Now, what is that all about?"

"I understand," Heather replied. She smiled at how easy it was to get him to reveal information. Thankful for the help he had provided, she snuggled even closer to the senator.

Without even realizing it, Senator Kendricks had crossed the line and put himself in jeopardy of a criminal indictment.

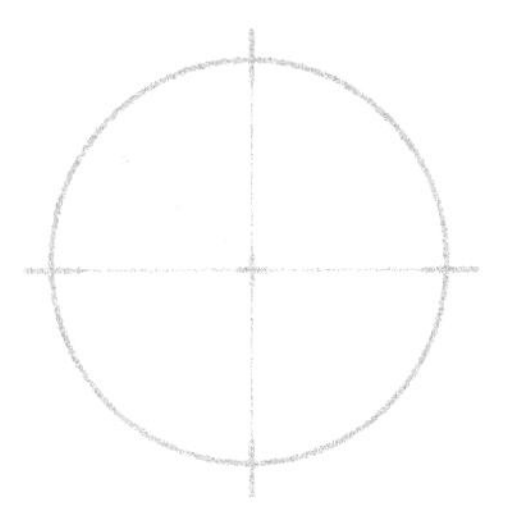

Chapter 28

I was sitting in my favorite chair reading the newspaper and drinking my first cup of coffee. Taking my last sip, I stood up, walked to the bedroom, and saw that Sandy was on her iPad. "I'm going to the store to get a prescription. Do we need anything else?"

She thought for a moment and responded, "No, I think we're good."

I smiled at her and said, "Be back in a few." I walked to the laundry room, opened the door to the garage, and saw that it was empty. Smiling at myself for forgetting that we had left both of our cars outside of the garage, I pushed the button which opened the garage door, walked out and got into my car. Reaching up to the visor, I pushed the button closing the garage door.

Before starting my car, I noticed the garbage can was still sitting at the curb. Exiting the vehicle, I walked to the garbage can and began to pull it up to the side of the house. I noticed what appeared to be string dangling from the exhaust pipe.

I grabbed the string and gave it a jerk. In response, a stick of dynamite fell onto the driveway. In shock, I stumbled backwards and fell right on my ass. Looking toward Sandy's car, I saw a string similarly situated. I crawled over and pulled out a stick of dynamite from that exhaust pipe.

My body was frozen in time as I glanced from one stick of dynamite to the other. Fear ran straight through me, and I began to shake realizing how close I came to meeting my maker. It was clear to me that when the tailpipe got hot, it would cause the dynamite to explode.

Hearing a door slam behind me, I saw my neighbor, Justin, walking down his steps. Laughing, he yelled to me, "What's the matter, old man? Can't you stand on your own two feet?" I crawled backwards away from the car and pointed at the dynamite. Justin came running over and saw the explosives on the driveway, "What the hell is that?"

I tried to stand but was unsuccessful. Justin helped pull me to my feet. "I was going to the store when I saw a string hanging out of my tailpipe. I pulled it out and it was that!" I started pointing at the dynamite. "I think someone is trying to kill me. It must be the terrorists." Justin and everyone else in town knew of my run-ins with the terrorists. "Justin, can you call the police for me. I must call Mac and Ty and warn them." I saw Justin pull out his cell phone and begin to dial.

I pulled out my cell phone and dialed Mac's number. As soon he answered the phone, I yelled, "Mac, where are you?"

"I'm sitting on the porch having my morning coffee. Why are you so excited?" I explained to him what I'd found. Mac replied, "I'll check my vehicles right now and call you back."

I responded, "Okay, I'll call Ty." Dialing Ty's number, my call went straight to voicemail, and I told Ty to call me because it was a matter of great importance. I then dialed Ty's wife, Leanne, who answered after the second ring. I explained to her what I found. "Did you drive your cars this morning?"

"No, we both walked to work. I'll talk to Ty, and we will go look at our cars. I'll call you when we know something."

My phone rang, I looked and saw that it was Mac. "Hey, did you find anything?"

"Yes, both of our cars had sticks of dynamite in their tailpipes. This is not good news, my friend."

"No shit, Dick Tracy. Is that all you can say, Mac?"

After calling Ty and receiving no answer, I called Leanne and she said they would go check their cars. "Can you call the police and have them come out and investigate?"

"The six of us need to get together again to decide what we're going to do. DJ, why don't we meet at your house around seven tonight?" Mac asked.

"Sounds good to me. When I hear from Ty, I'll let him know the plan."

I hung up and walked into the house to give this news to Sandy. To say that she did not take it well is an understatement. I didn't know she knew such words.

An hour later, Ty called and explained that when he and Leanne had walked back to the house to check their cars, they also found sticks of dynamite in the tailpipes. I told him the plan to meet at my house that evening; he said they would be there.

* * *

Later that afternoon, Derek heard the announcement that his plane was about to land. He placed the book he was reading into his briefcase. Derek's plane touched down softly and soon he was standing, waiting to exit the plane. He walked to the car rental booth, received his keys, and was on his way to the hotel that had been booked for him.

After unpacking, Derek decided to drive to DJ's house without first calling him. He knew that soon he would be bombarded with questions about his time as an agent. Derek decided to arrive there after dinner so that Sandy would not go to any trouble on his behalf. When he arrived at DJ's home, he saw that Mac and Ty were already there with their respective cars in the driveway. He walked up to the door and knocked loudly.

When I opened the door and saw Derek standing there, I turned and yelled to the others, "Guess who the wind blew in—our very own junior G-man." Everyone came out to greet Derek, shook his hand and clapped him on the back. "Well," I continued, "you're here at a very propitious time."

Derek smiled and said, "So, are you all done with dinner? I've been here for five minutes, and no one has offered me a drink. Where are your manners, DJ?"

Derek was dragged into the living room, pushed into a seat, and had a beer handed to him. Then we explained to him why we were gathered at my home that evening.

"Well, I guess I came at the right time. I've been detailed out here to watch over you feebleminded men and Ty also."

Both Mac and I started to object when Sandy said, "I always knew, Derek, that you were a good judge of a man's character." After we all finished laughing, she continued, "Derek, why are you really here?"

"Sam Wyman, the Bureau's Director of Counterterrorism ordered me to come and help you out. He explained that you are acting as consultants to the Bureau in an effort to ID Ahmed and Kamil. Obviously, I told him that it was a waste of the Bureau's money and the three of you would play a lot and work a little."

I started to object, but Mac said, "And there's something wrong with that?"

The rest of the evening, the seven of us discussed what options were available to us.

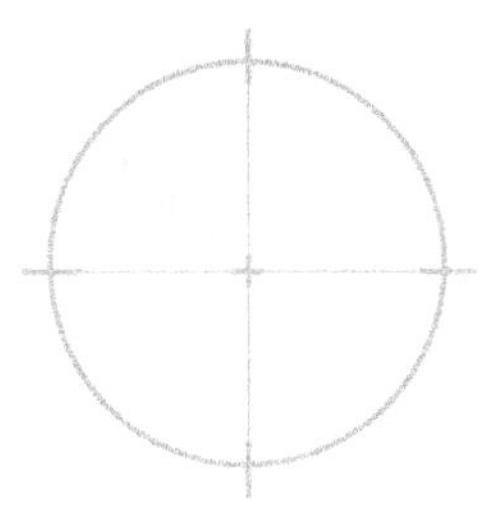

Chapter 29

The next morning, Derek's alarm went off at 7:00 AM. He awoke, stretched, and sat up in his bed. Derek planned to meet with Art to discuss his assignment. The information provided by the professors about the recent attempt on their lives made this meeting even more urgent.

After Derek showered and dressed, he drove to a nearby restaurant to have breakfast. When he finished eating his pancakes and a side of bacon, he called Art's cell phone. After the fifth ring, Art answered the phone. Derek stated, "Art, this is Derek. I was hoping that we might be able to get together this morning if you have some time."

"Hi Derek. Let me look at my calendar." After a few moments, Art continued, "I have some time at noon if that works for you?"

Derek answered, "That looks good. I'll see you in your office then." Derek terminated the call. He had picked up a paper on the way to the restaurant and began reading all the local stories. Since he had some time before his meeting, Derek drove to the local police station to talk to Chief Brian Martin, whom he had known since his school days as a criminal justice major. The young agent walked into the station, introduced himself to the receptionist, and asked to see the chief.

A few moments later, he was sitting in the chief's office talking about old times. Chief Martin said, "I know that the FBI doesn't come to my office to shoot the bull. So, Derek, why are you here?"

"I'm here to be the FBI's liaison to DJ, Mac and Ty."

Chief Martin knew the professors well since he had assisted them in fighting the terrorists some months before. He had been amazed at the fight that the three men and their wives had put up when the terrorists had attacked them. The chief had had no contact with them since the attack. "What the hell's going on that requires a liaison to the FBI?"

Derek responded, "The Bureau has received information that two terrorists who survived the attack here may be planning something new with the North Koreans. I don't know if you are aware, but Mac and DJ had an attempt on their lives when they were vacationing in Maui. Yesterday, each of the three men and their wives discovered a stick of dynamite stuck in the tailpipes of each of their cars."

The chief shook his head and looked at Derek, "I read the report on that. Is it starting all over again?"

"It certainly feels that way," Derek replied. "Well, the Bureau is concerned about a new potential attack; it is clear to us that the two terrorists who got away were only seen by me and the three professors. The professors have been hired as consultants to the FBI to help identify these two terrorists if they are found. I've been assigned to work with them and give whatever protection I can. However, you know those three guys would tell us they don't need protection, and frankly, that may very well be true. If they had any idea that part of my assignment was to protect them, Mac would probably shoot me and bury me on the ranch."

The chief started chuckling and replied, "I think you may very well be right about that. So, I suggest that liaison is the proper word to use."

Derek continued, "I thought we should share all the information we have with you, Chief. The Bureau wanted to make sure that you are kept up to date with the information we receive while I am here. We will keep you updated." With that, Derek stood, shook hands with the Chief and walked out the door.

Derek walked to his car, started the engine and headed for his meeting with Art. It did not take long for him to drive the 40 miles to the Bureau's office. He soon entered the building, opened the door to the FBI offices, and introduced himself to the receptionist. In minutes, he was sitting in front of Art Rheingold.

Derek had met Art after the attacks on the professors. He got down to business. "I'm sure Sam has informed you about my assignment here." Derek saw Art nod and he continued, "I met with the professors and their wives last night. Yesterday, they each found sticks of dynamite in their tailpipes. Obviously, someone is trying to kill them once again. Their main concern at this time is how the Bureau can help protect them. What are your thoughts on that?"

Art answered, "I'm not sure the Bureau is going to give them additional protection, but I'll run it up to Sam and see if he's willing to assign resources for the job. What are you planning to do now?"

"I'm just going to be hanging around with them until we need their help in the identification of the terrorists. Hopefully, that will not be too long. As much as I enjoy relaxing with these guys, sitting around is not how I thought my career with the Bureau would begin. Do you have any ideas for me?"

"Not really. This type of assignment takes a lot of patience as you wait for something to develop. If I have any jobs that can be done here, I may contact you and you can decide whether you want to do them or not." After discussing some potential jobs that may keep Derek busy, Art ended their meeting by stating, "That's about all I have. Why don't you contact me by phone every day and give me an update?" Art stood, shook Derek's hand and showed him the door.

Pondering what Art had told him, Derek headed back to his hotel.

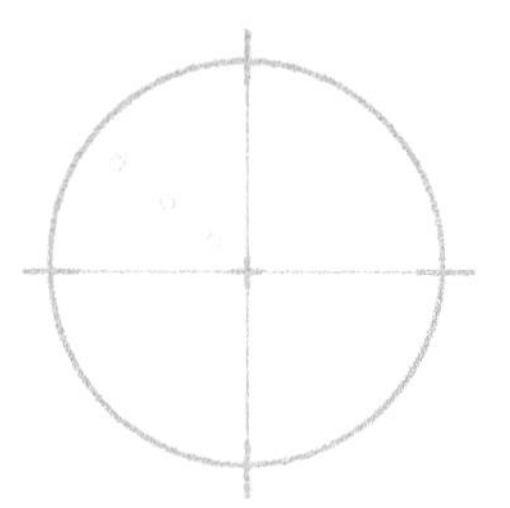

Chapter 30

Julianne Simmons, the Director of National Intelligence, had been meeting with her staff to discuss the North Korean situation. It had been a productive meeting and many of her staff gave her an abundance of questions to think about. She got up from her chair and poured a cup of coffee, her tenth cup that day. Simmons sat on the corner of her desk as she reviewed the meeting in her mind. Simmons knew she would soon have to brief the President about the potential connection between the terrorists and North Korea.

Simmons sat at her desk and looked at the stack of papers she needed to read. The hardest part of her job was to keep up with all the new intelligence coming into her office. As with all intelligence, there were no clear answers to the questions that lay before her. Often, information was fuzzy at best. Julianne understood, unlike most Americans, that intelligence was like a puzzle. You put as many pieces as you can on the table and then guess what holes still remain. Positive connections with one's allies are vital because they may have the one puzzle piece that you need.

Suddenly, the phone rang, startling her. She picked up the receiver. "Yes," she said to her assistant, Eileen, on the other end of the line.

Eileen had worked for her for many years. She was the keeper of the gate when it came to gaining access to Simmons. Eileen always seemed to know whom to put through and whom to put off.

Eileen stated, "Senator Kendricks is on the line for you."

"Thank you, Eileen." Simmons pushed the blinking light on her phone and said "Senator Kendricks, it's nice to hear from you. How is your day going?"

"Not too badly," he responded. "Some of the members of the Intelligence Committee and I have been talking about your office's future needs. I just wanted to check in with you and see if there's anything we could do for you."

"Well, as you well know, every bureaucrat in Washington could use some additional funding. To tell you the truth, though, I can't complain too much even about that. Is there anything in particular your committee is interested in?"

"Not really," Kendricks replied. "I think everyone wants to make sure we are doing whatever we can to assist in this country's fight against terrorism and some of the wayward countries we must deal with. I do have one concern that I would like to ask you about. The last time we spoke, you said you were getting some chatter of a potential problem with the North Koreans and others who may be helping them. Are you still concerned that this may become a problem for us?"

Simmons thought for a moment and then replied, "Yes, we're getting more and more rumblings that lead us to the impression that there may be something to the reports we are receiving. The French informed us that the cooperation between the terrorists and North Korea, may, in fact, be true. We're not sure, however, what type of attack may be in the works. You know, Senator Kendricks, this whole intelligence thing is a lot like smoke and mirrors. Sometimes you see something in clear light, then the next information you obtain makes your previous understanding inoperable."

Trying to hide his real reason for the inquiry, Kendricks asked, "Is there anything the committee can do for you regarding this threat?"

"Not at this time, but thank you for asking, Senator. I appreciate your keen interest in this matter, and you can be sure I will inform the committee when we have more solid information."

Senator Kendricks responded, "I can assure you that none of us wants to see another 9/11 on our watch, so, once again, if you need anything, please let me know. Thank you for taking my call. I know how incredibly busy you are and do not wish to waste your valuable time."

"Thank you very much for your concern, Senator. I look forward to talking with you in the future."

Simmons hung up and paused for a moment as she reviewed her conversation with Kendricks. Simmons had been approached by an FBI agent who indicated they had some concern about Senator Kendricks' relationship with a Korean woman and had asked her to inform them of any conversations she has with him about Korea. Simmons was very reluctant to comply with this request because of the potential fallout that could occur if her actions were discovered. It could appear that she was trying to hurt a United States senator. These are difficult times and sometimes even important people like senators don't necessarily do the right thing.

Simmons reached for her phone and called Agent Hixson. She told him about her conversation with the senator.

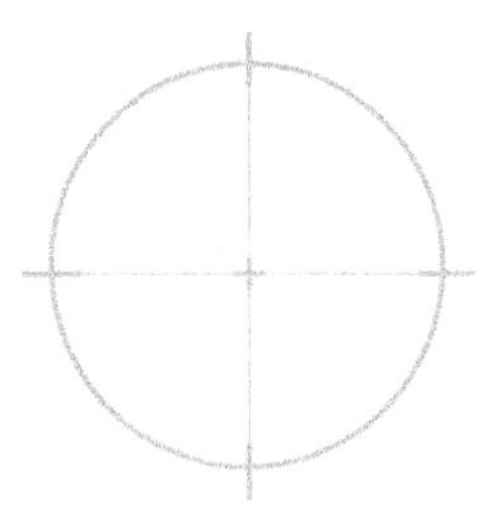

Chapter 31

Chin-Sun sat in her well-appointed office in downtown Los Angeles. While she was an agent for North Korea, she also operated a small import/export business dealing mostly in South Korean products. This business was optimal for her because it gave her credible reasons for traveling back and forth to South Korea. She only had one employee, her assistant, who also was an asset for the North Korean government.

Her assistant knocked lightly on the door, opened it, and walked into her office. "Mr. Song called and indicated he wanted to place the same order he did last month. Would you like me to arrange that for him?"

"I would appreciate it if you did that for me." The assistant turned around and left her office. This innocuous inquiry was a coded message to her that Mr. Song, who was her handler, wanted to meet with her at a playground at 4:00 PM that afternoon. She never held meetings in her office regarding her work for North Korea because of her fear that the federal government was listening to her conversations. The playground was ideal for this meeting because the loud noises of the children would hinder any attempts to hear her conversation with Mr. Song.

At the appointed time, Chin-Sun sat down on a park bench that was close enough to the playground to assure that her conversations could not be heard. She had worked closely with Mr. Song during the last two or three years and felt comfortable with him. Nevertheless, it was still important to maintain the security arrangements that both had agreed to. She trusted him as much as one can trust a fellow agent. Soon, she saw him approach. He was wearing a conservative business suit that fit his 5'8" height.

"May I share this bench with you?"

"Of course," she responded as she had in every previous meeting they had. They acted as if they did not know each other. "It is a beautiful day today, isn't it?" That was her code that it was safe for them to have their meeting.

He responded, "Yes, it is, but the smog is a little heavy." His coded answer indicated that they were free to talk. "I have instructions for you from our friends in Korea."

She raised her eyebrows but said nothing.

"With their shipments to begin shortly, they have become concerned over some information they had received recently. Evidently, there is some evidence that one of our competitors has new information." Chin -Sun understood that the competitor would be another North Korean asset. "Apparently, our friends from Paris have been discovered, but only certain educators can identify them. Those educators have been enlisted to point them out to individuals who would be bad for our business."

Chin-Sun looked at him closely to make sure she understood her directions. She asked, "Am I to go and take care of these educators?"

"Yes, that is exactly what they're asking."

"I am sure that our Parisian friends would like to see them once again. Are there any further instructions for me? If not, I will talk with our Parisian friends soon."

Song looked at her and stated, "Please keep me informed as to the status of these negotiations." He stood, bowed toward her and walked away.

Chin-Sun remained seated on the park bench for the next ten minutes or so. She stood and began walking away while trying to understand what may have caused these instructions to take action against the professors. It was, however, eminently clear that Kim wanted these individuals killed so they would not interfere with his plans. She would contact Ahmed and Kamil later that evening to discuss how they should proceed.

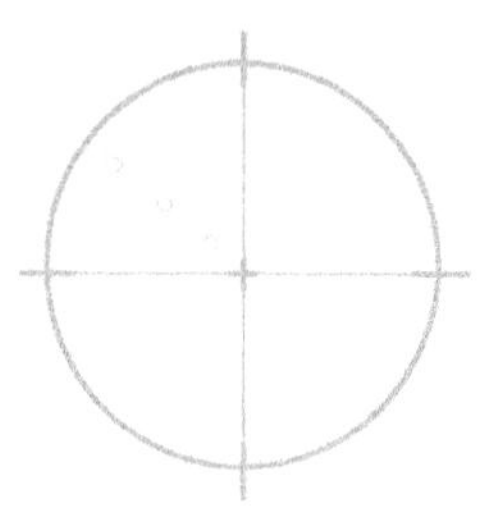

Chapter 32

Senator Kendricks sat down on the overstuffed sofa in his suite in a downtown Washington hotel. It was about time for his guests to arrive, and, for him, to begin the most important political discussion in his career. He had been thinking of, as many politicians do, running for president. It seemed to him that he was eminently qualified for the post, given his time in the Senate and his expertise on various national issues. The senator knew that any campaign for this office would be difficult at best, but he was willing to take on this difficult task not for himself, but for the country. Kendricks also knew that many politicians said and made the same commitments that he was about to make. However, he truly believed that this was his destiny.

There was a sharp knock at the door. Kendricks walked to and opened the door for the five individuals he'd asked to attend this meeting. The first man who entered was Phil Jackson, his Chief of Staff, an astute and experienced politician who knew his way around Washington. Following him was Linda Purcell, a lobbyist for the pharmaceutical industry, who would be his chief fundraiser. Next to enter was Ned Smith, a past chairman of the Republican National Committee. As such, he had tremendous contacts throughout the Republican Party. Of particular importance would be his ability to bring Republican operatives in each state to his candidacy. Following him was Senator Bill Henry, the current Chairman of the Senate Republican Campaign Committee. The final person to come into the room was Janice Peel, the executive director of the foremost Republican women's organization.

Prior to this meeting, Kendricks had talked with each of these individuals about his candidacy. Each of them had committed to supporting him. He began by stating, "I wanted to thank each of you for coming to this meeting. Hopefully, in the future, we will look back and see that this day was the beginning of a successful run for the presidency. As you know, I've been deeply concerned about the future course of our country. I think that the current president is leading us down the road that can only be described as disastrous for the country we love. I also believe that, at this time, I have the ability, experience and dedication to be a president that we can all be proud of. Because of your presence here today, I believe that you agree with me. I see this group as my inner circle of advisors—people who can and will get things done. I hope that today we can lay out a plan that we can follow which will result in a successful run for the presidency.

"The five of you have the required expertise that is needed by someone running for this office. As you know, Bill and I have been close for many years now. He will coordinate with each of you as we begin this campaign." Kendricks nodded at Purcell and stated, "I don't think there's a better fundraiser in the Republican Party than Linda. As we draw up our budget needs, she will be able to tell us whether the funds we are requesting can, in fact, be raised.

Smiling at Ned, Kendricks continued, "If there is anyone in this country who has more contacts within the Republican Party than Ned, I certainly don't know who they are. Senator Henry can lead us to others who supported Republican candidates in the past. And Janice can help us with a group of people the party has trouble attracting. I hope with her expertise, she will bring Republican women and independents to our cause. Does anyone have anything they would like to say?"

Bill spoke up. "Senator, I too, have talked with each of these individuals about your candidacy. I can tell you that they are as excited as I am to be in this quest. I suggest we begin over the next few hours to develop a plan that gives you the best chances of success in getting the Republican nomination for president."

Kendricks saw that each of the other individuals were nodding their heads in agreement. "Okay, then," he said, "let's get to work."

During the next several hours, the six people brainstormed a variety of ideas. Just after 8:00 PM, the group finished its basic plan, set forth each of their responsibilities, and established a timeline for each of the required actions. Kendricks thanked each of them for their help as the meeting ended and said goodbye as each one left.

He sat down on the sofa to review the plan for the election. However, his thoughts were interrupted by a light knocking at the door to the suite. He rose and walked to the door. Opening it, he found Heather Lee standing in the doorway. She smiled at him and said, "I saw the last of them leave a few minutes ago and thought you might like some company."

When she entered, he could detect the soft odor of her cologne as she passed by. He put his arms around her and kissed her lightly on the neck. "I cannot think of a better ending to this day than having you here." She snuggled into his arms, letting him know that she felt the same way.

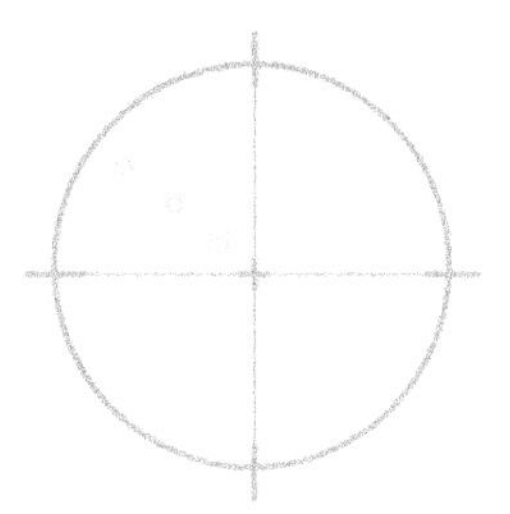

Chapter 33

Chin-Sun was trying to sleep on the plane before its arrival in Paris. She was not fully asleep but in that space between being awake and asleep. It had been a long flight and she was tired. The flight attendants announced a light breakfast would be served before landing. The lights in the plane came on, and she knew that the flight attendants would be rolling the carts down the aisle shortly.

Chin-Sun found that the breakfast sandwich did not appeal to her even though she was hungry. She did, however, accept some tea from the attendant. While slowly sipping on her beverage of choice, she once again looked around at the people on the plane. Chin-Sun always watched people to see if they had any undue interest in her. In her business, one could never be too safe. There had been a few times when Chin-Sun knew people were watching her, and she used the tactics she had been taught to lose them in the streets. Whenever that occurred, Chin-Sun always reported it to her handler so that he could take whatever action he deemed necessary. Being a foreign agent caused one to be always on guard even in the most innocuous situations. Too often, though, a statement or action from someone would cause her stomach to clench and her blood pressure to rise. Such was the life she chose for herself.

The flight attendants came through the cabin to pick up whatever garbage remained. Chin-Sun felt the clunk as the plane's landing gear was extended. She looked out the window and saw the small villages that dotted the landscape outside of Paris. She loved

Paris for many reasons. First, Chin-Sun felt safe, away from the prying eyes of the American anti-terrorism services. Second, she loved the Paris street scene with its outdoor cafés, bistros, and other food establishments. There simply was no place like her beloved Paris.

Chin-Sun quickly passed through customs and walked toward the line of people waiting for a taxi. When her turn arrived, she entered the taxi and gave the driver an address on the Île Saint-Louis. She kept her eyes closed, not wanting to engage in conversation with the driver. Soon, the vehicle came to a stop at the appointed location,

Chin-Sun paid the driver and exited onto the crowded street. Since she had given the driver the wrong address, Chin-Sun had to walk two blocks to her apartment. She took the lift to the third floor and walked down the short hallway until she stood in front of her door. With her key, Chin-Sun opened the door and entered the apartment. Like many Paris apartments, it was small but functional. She checked to see if anything was out of place and found nothing to cause her concern.

Chin-Sun had several hours before her meeting with Ahmed and Kamil. She took a quick shower to wash off the long plane ride. Entering the small bedroom, Chin-Sun lay down for a short nap. The agent awoke at 2:15 PM, refreshed and ready for her meeting. Taking her time, Chin-Sun walked to the Luxembourg Gardens. There were few people in the gardens since it was a weekday. She found a bench away from the traveled portion of the gardens and sat down to await the arrival of the two Mideastern men.

Chin-Sun continued to scan the park to see if anyone was paying attention to her. Finding none, she was relieved. Soon, Chin-Sun saw Ahmed and Kamil walking toward her. She took a small radio out of her purse, placed it beside her and turned it to her favorite station playing rock music. Chin-Sun knew that this simple gesture would obstruct people from hearing their conversation. The two men sat on the bench, smiled at her and proceeded to open books that each carried. Chin-Sun began her code to assure that they were safe to talk. "What book are you reading?" The man's answer would determine whether the meeting would continue.

Ahmed responded, "It's by Molière." That answer indicated they were safe to proceed.

"You both seem to be doing well. Do you have any concerns that the French may be onto you?"

Kamil answered, "We have no reason to believe that we are under suspicion. I think we can talk freely. You have new instructions for us?"

"Yes, I do. It will require that you return to the United States shortly. We have assets in the United States that tell us that the US security services believe an attack may be forthcoming. I'm not sure why, but your friends, the professors, are involved in some way. It will be necessary for you to kill them once and for all. Both you and I failed in our previous attempts. Next time, there will be no failure. Do you understand?" Both men nodded. "Have you thought how that might be accomplished?"

The two men looked at her and saw apprehension on her face. They both knew this woman of short stature had the power to cause them great troubles. Kamil looked at Ahmed, saw him nod and stated, "We need to tell you something that we've been involved in. The people in our group still feel the pain of the loss of Samir. They demanded that we take revenge on the professors. We contracted with someone to do this. That person placed dynamite in the tailpipes of their cars driven by the three professors and their wives. The intent, obviously, was to kill those six people. We have not heard whether that attempt was successful or not, but we expect a full report from the man we contracted with in the next few days. Hopefully, he was successful."

"Why did you not inform me of this action?" demanded Chin-Sun. Ahmed looked at her cold eyes, swallowed, and answered, "We did not think this involved your operation and did not believe that it would be of interest to you." The silence that followed seemed to last for hours. Ahmed continued, "Perhaps we were wrong."

"Let me tell you how wrong you truly were. If our operation is disrupted in any way, your lives will be forfeited. Is that clear enough?" She saw both men lower their eyes, avoiding hers, so she continued, "I suggest that it would not be in your best interest to attempt anything like this again without first clearing it with me. Is that understood?"

Ahmed answered, "Yes, we understand."

"Good," she stated. Chin-Sun stood, looked at the two men and spoke softly, "I think our operation will be successful, and each of you will be very rich men." She smiled at them and walked off.

Kamil spat out, "That bitch. Who does she think she's talking to? When this is over, we will need to eliminate her to ensure our safety."

Ahmed smiled. "That will be fun."

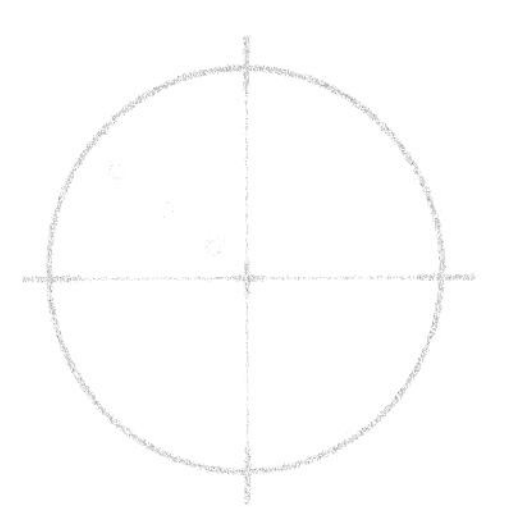

Chapter 34

Mael normally did not run informants. The handlers that reported to him did that work. However, he kept a few of his assets reporting directly to him. On this day, he was scheduled to meet with an asset code-named Roger. Because Mael was well known for working for the French government, he seldom, if ever, met with his assets in the open. That's why he was sitting in a well-to-do office of a French shell company. This office suite was small, having only a reception area that led into offices. Sitting at the receptionist's desk was a middle-aged woman who had worked for the French antiterrorism unit for some time.

The Frenchman arrived at this office early and was working on his laptop. There was a light knocking on his door to which he responded, "Come in." Standing in front of him was a janitor who stood about five feet tall and was dressed in the uniform of the building's maintenance team. "Roger, as always, it's good to see you again. Come in and sit down please." Mael watched the young man come forward and sit in the chair fronting his desk. "Are you concerned you were followed?"

"No," replied Roger. "None of my people come to these business buildings." Roger was of Lebanese descent and moved easily within the Paris' Arab community.

Mael leaned forward and passed an envelope across the desk. Roger picked it up and placed it in his pocket without looking at its contents. He knew that the sums contained in the envelope would be fair for the work he does for France.

"Do you have any news for me?" Mael asked.

"Yes, I do. I've been keeping my ears open for any information regarding the two terrorists who were involved in the attack on Paris and overheard something that you might be interested in. I was at a party in my neighborhood when I heard several men talking about joining a certain terrorist group. I was seated on the couch, and they were behind me. I did not dare turn to look at them because they would know I was too interested in the topic of their conversation. In any event, most of their conversation was of no consequence to us. There was, however, something they said that intrigued me."

"What was that?"

"Well, they were discussing two men who had asked if they would like to join a group to attack the Great Satan," he continued. "The men stated that they needed some men to go with them to the United States to kill three Americans who caused the death of their friend. The men at this meeting declined the invitation to go to America. In fact, they were concerned that there could be a price on their heads because of the information they now had."

Mael asked, "Did you hear anything else of interest?"

"No, not really. It was a short conversation and then the men talked about other matters."

"Do you know how many men were involved in this conversation?"

"I can't be sure, but from listening to the voices, I would guess there were three. When they quit talking, I heard them move off. I stood up to stretch but could not tell which of these people at the party had been talking."

Mael continued his questioning. "Do you think you could recognize their voices if you heard them again?"

"Maybe, maybe not. I would just have to see."

"Had you heard any of these voices prior to this party?"

"I don't think so."

Mael then asked, "How many people were at this party?"

"Oh, maybe 25 or so."

"Do you think you could ask the people who gave the party for the names of the people who were there? Remember, I do not want to put you in any personal danger."

"The guy who gave this party was someone I met at the club that I visit. He is not a close friend by any means. If I asked him that question, it would raise his suspicions, and I'm not sure where his loyalties lie."

Mael pushed a pad of paper over to Roger. "Would you write down the address where the party was held. Perhaps, I can obtain some additional information by surveilling that apartment." He watched Roger take the pad and pen and begin to write.

"You are doing well, Roger. Let's plan to meet again in a couple of weeks. You can make those arrangements with the woman outside. However, if something comes to your attention that you believe I should know immediately, you have the number where you can reach me." Mael got up, extended his hand to Roger and led him to the door. "I will see you soon."

Roger walked to the door, opened it, and was gone.

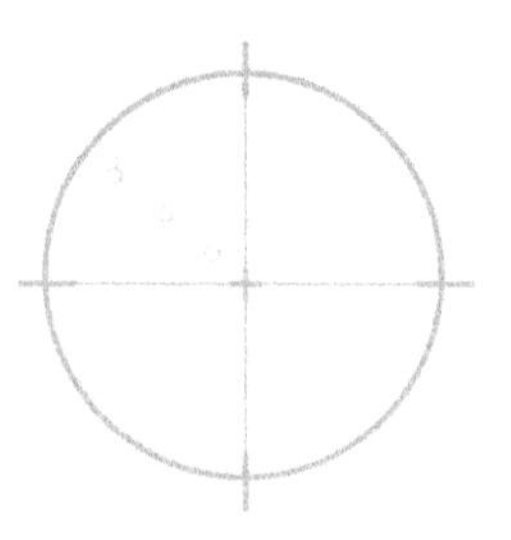

Chapter 35

Agent Hixson was sitting at his desk, his fingers interlocked, his elbows on his chair and his chin resting on his fingers. Hixson was staring at the computer screen trying to make sense of what he saw. He leaned back, stretched his arms and reached for the ceiling. Hixson could feel the familiar ache between his shoulder blades that came when he sat too long in front of the computer. The agent stood up and walked to the credenza that held his Keurig single-serve coffee maker. Hixson selected the pod that appealed to him, placed it in the machine, and waited for the cup to fill.

Since his conversation with Sam about Senator Kendricks, Hixson had scoured the internet for information on Heather Lee and learned that she was the daughter of first-generation Korean immigrants. She graduated from high school in the top ten percent of her class and received a scholarship to a well-known college. After finishing her degree, Lee had a few jobs in Washington, DC. Within the last year or so, he found that she had started her own podcast and blog about relations between the United States and both North and South Korea. There was nothing unusual about her education or career path that he could find.

However, there was something that bothered him about her. He could find no information about her or her parents' lives in South Korea before coming to the United States. Hixson had asked the State Department to inquire with their counterparts in South Korea and see what information they might have. What the agent had learned from that line of questioning was absolutely nothing. It was as if Heather and her family had not existed prior to entering the United States.

Since Hixson did not know what lengths the South Korean government went to in their investigation of Ms. Heather Lee, it was possible there were still records of her family and their activities in South Korea. Because that information was not readily available to him, he had a strong feeling that something was amiss. It was not out of the realm of possibility that Ms. Lee and her family were sleeper agents. If that was the case, Senator Kendricks could be passing information, intentionally or inadvertently, to the North Koreans.

While Hixson may have had his suspicions, he had no actual proof whether Ms. Lee and her family were actually sleeper agents. It appeared to Hixson that he had several options available to him. He could contact the FBI agent assigned to the South Korean embassy and ask if he would further investigate her family. Hixson could request additional resources from Sam to look at her background while in the United States. Also, it was possible that the court responsible for handling national security matters would authorize the secret search of her apartment, social media accounts, and cell phone records. Last, but not least, he could request that the court authorize a wiretap on her and Senator Kendricks' phones.

Hixson understood that would be a big ask, and one that would have to be cleared through the hierarchy of the Bureau. The FBI would be very reluctant to tap the phone of a sitting United States senator because of the potential problems that could come with that action. If it became public, that Senator Kendricks' phone had, indeed, been tapped, there would be a howl of protest from every politician in Washington, DC. The Bureau would have to carefully consider the risk when asking to tap the senator's phone.

Hixson picked up his phone and placed a call to the US Embassy in South Korea. Soon he was transferred to the Bureau's agent. Hixson explained his concern to the agent and requested that he do whatever he could to find information on Heather Lee's family history in South Korea. Next, Hixson drafted a memo to Sam requesting additional agents to investigate Heather and her family. He reread the memo quickly and then sent it on to Sam.

Within 20 minutes, he received Sam's answer. The director authorized three additional agents to help him determine whether or not Heather was a sleeper agent. Even with these additional resources, Hixson did not believe he could find the proof he was looking for without tapping the senator's phone, and more importantly, the hotel room that Kendricks sometimes shared with Heather.

Hixson looked at his watch and realized it was past 7:00 PM. He decided it was time to drive home to his wife and two small children. The agent picked up his briefcase, locked his door, and headed for the elevator. Since his wife dropped him off that morning, he was going to take a cab home. Hixson walked out of the building and waited at the curb for a cab. Within two minutes, a cab pulled over, he opened the door and sat down. The agent gave the driver the address he was to be taken to and took out a newspaper from his briefcase to read. Hixson did not notice that a car had followed him as he was driven home. Furthermore, he did not realize that his inquiries into Heather had garnered the attention of those assigned to protect her.

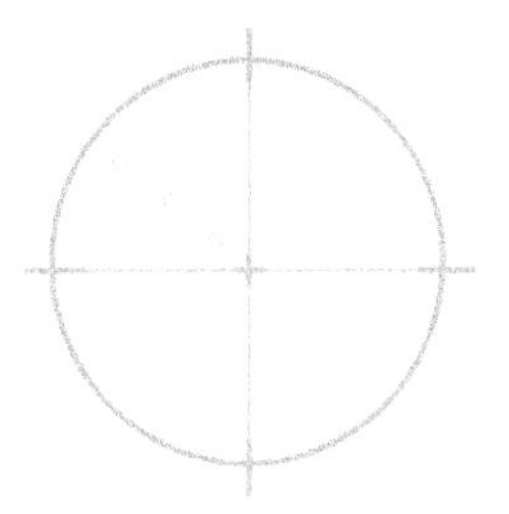

Chapter 36

Mael called Pierre on a secure line and informed him of the information he had received from Roger.

Pierre stated, "How accurate do you believe this is?"

Mael answered, "There's no way to verify either the accuracy of Roger's memory or the truth of what the men stated. I will tell you that Roger has been one of our best assets in the Mideast community. He has provided me with information that has led to the arrest of certain individuals who were either involved in or planning terrorist attacks. It seems to me that this information fits with the other information we've been able to piece together. However, as you well know, these may or may not be parts of the puzzle that we are trying to put together."

"I suggest that we pass this information onto the Americans as soon as possible. It's more important that we give them this information even if it's wrong rather than withhold information and find out it was correct. I assume you agree?"

"Yes, Pierre, I absolutely agree with your judgment. I will contact the FBI and pass it on immediately."

"Good, let me know what they say."

After terminating his call with Pierre, Mael dialed Sam's number. He heard the phone ring several times before going to voicemail. Mael asked Sam to call him as he had new information to pass on.

Several hours later, Mael sat in his apartment reading through a thick file of another potential terrorist attack. As he was reviewing the report of an agent concerning the agent's conversation with an asset in Marseilles, his personal cell phone rang. He answered it and heard Sam's voice.

"Sorry, Mael, for calling you so late, but I've been in one meeting after another all day. There seemed to be some urgency in your voice, so I took the chance to call you at this late hour."

"I'm glad you did, Sam. I have some information I think you'll find interesting. I met with one of my old informants today and he gave me some information I thought you should have." Mael proceeded to explain what Roger had brought to his attention. "So, what do you think, Sam?"

Sam thought about what he had heard before responding. "Well, it seems to me, that if this information is correct, the terrorists have once again targeted the three professors."

"That's how I look at it also," replied Mael.

"Poor bastards, they can't catch a break. I have one agent assigned to them already. I think I will need to authorize more resources for their protection. You indicated you are trying to determine who Ahmed and Kamil are. Did you have any luck in following up on that information?"

"No, not yet, but we are still looking at everything. Obviously, if I learn anything further, I'll get in touch with you immediately."

"Thanks, once again, Mael. I will keep in touch."

After hanging up, Sam placed a call to Art Rheingold. He briefed Art on the conversation with Mael. "Art, why don't you assign an agent to each of the professors. If you do so now, I will send some people out to replace your agents. We must do something to help these guys."

"Holy shit. You know, Sam, if we don't catch these guys once and for all, these professors are going to be killed. They can't be as lucky as they have been. I'm afraid for their lives."

"You and me both, Art. Unfortunately, I am afraid that the terrorist's effort to kill them exceeds our ability to protect them. Please let the professors know what we are going to do to keep them safe."

After hanging up, Sam leaned back in his chair, took off his glasses and rubbed his eyes. He was tired, bone tired. It's one thing for the professionals to be in this fight, but to expose non-combatants was very hard for him. Terrorists would target civilians randomly, but in this case, the professors were being sought out to avenge the death of Samir. Sam spoke softly to himself. "Damn, I don't know how much more these guys can take. This will be the fifth attack on them in two years. Damn."

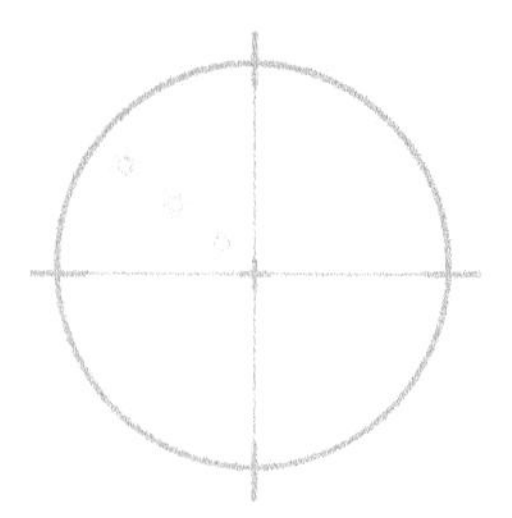

Chapter 37

Ahmed and Kamil prepared for landing and looked out their windows as the Boeing 777 began its initial descent. Their flight from Paris had been a long one and both of them needed to sleep. The two men were dressed in business suits that matched their cover stories of being sales reps for a French company. The plan they had put together was done hurriedly. Each man, however, believed it would be successful. There were gaps in the plan because they simply did not have sufficient information.

Before they left France, Ahmed contacted Chin-Sun and asked if they had any assets in the professors' town and were told there is a student at the university where one of the professors taught. The student had been directed to obtain as much information as he could about the professors, their residences and their movements, if possible. They would need this information to be able to determine how and when the professors could be eliminated. It was important that the professors be together when they killed them.

It was not long before the men felt the plane touch down and begin its journey along the taxiways to the terminal. Ahmed and Kamil quickly obtained their luggage and headed for the customs area. Each man went to a different line to pass through customs. Both men's experience with customs agents was similar. They informed the agent they were there on business and would be returning to France within the week. After their passports were stamped, the men headed to the car rental area. The two men got into their car and drove to their hotel.

Ahmed and Kamil checked in without any problem and soon were standing in their suite. Ahmed then called the student and asked him to meet them at the hotel the next day at noon. The student readily agreed and said he would be in the hotel lobby at the time indicated. Both men then went to the hotel restaurant for dinner. After placing their orders, Ahmed stated, "After our asset provides us with all the information he's discovered, we can finalize the steps we should take."

"Even though this hotel is a three-hour drive from the professors' town, staying here is our best option. It would just be our luck to stumble upon someone who recognized us from our previous attack. Hopefully, we can just get in, do the job and get out," stated Kamil.

"I agree," responded Ahmed. "I don't think we have any additional planning to do until we meet with our asset. The only thing left for us to do today is to eat and get a good night's sleep."

The next day, the men were dressed casually in slacks and polo shirts. At 11:45 AM, they took the elevator down to the first floor and walked toward the restaurant. Standing in front of the door was the student they were meeting. The student, dressed in jeans and a black T-shirt, stood around five-foot-nine. His black hair was of medium length and combed to the side above intense black eyes that matched his overall demeanor. They shook hands and entered the restaurant. Ahmed asked the hostess for a table for three away from other patrons. Once settled in their booth, a small, attractive waitress approached them. They gave her their orders and she smiled as she walked away.

Ahmed opened the conversation, "What information do you have for us?"

"I have the professors' addresses. Here they are. I also found out that two of the professors are retired, but the third is still at the university. It's easy to determine the schedule of the active professor. He is either in his office or teaching most of the time. Because the other two are retired, their schedules vary from day to day. There is simply no predictability where they will be or what they will be doing."

Kamil interrupted him and asked, "Are all three of them in their hometown at this time?"

"Yes, they are."

Ahmed then inquired, "Have you been able to find out whether the three of them get together at any regular time?"

"It seems that they have lunch together every Friday at a local café. It appears to be a standing date, for want of a better word. They typically arrive at about 1:00 PM. I discovered this information from another student and confirmed it by having lunch there last Friday. The three guys came in and sat at any table that was available. Their lunch lasted for about an hour and a half before they left."

"Did it appear that they were unusually attentive to their surroundings. I mean, were they checking to see if they were being watched or were concerned about the other people in the restaurant?" asked Ahmed.

"Not that I could ascertain. They seem to be three friends simply gathering together to eat and talk."

"Did you see anyone nearby that appeared to be watching over them?" asked Kamil.

The student answered, "Not that I saw. I haven't done this before, so it is possible that I could have missed someone."

"On another subject," asked Kamil, "were you able to obtain the weapons we asked for?"

"In the United States, it is not difficult to obtain weapons. I have those in my car."

Ahmed stated, "Good. After lunch, we will place them in our car. You have done well, and Allah will be pleased."

"Thank you. I've also brought with me a map of the city and where the restaurant is. I have also drawn a plan of the restaurant itself. I hope that will be of assistance."

The three men finished their meals, paid the bill and walked outside. Ahmed shook the young man's hand and said, "I will leave you here. Kamil will take you to your car and will direct you to where our car is parked. You can then place the weapons in our car. Good luck. I don't think we'll need to see you again, but if the need arises, I will contact you." Ahmed then walked back into the hotel toward the elevator, and Kamil accompanied the young man to his vehicle.

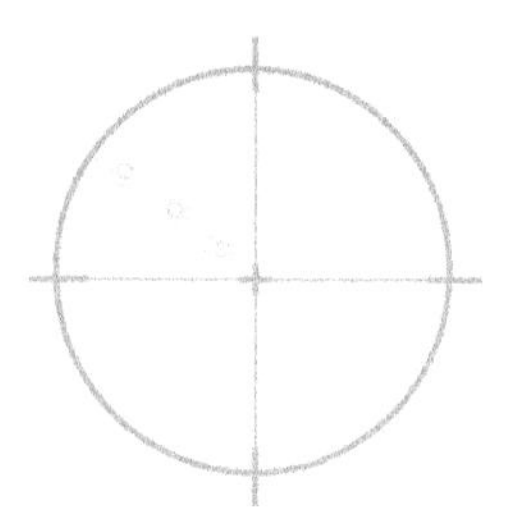

Chapter 38

Agent Hixson was reading several reports he'd received about Heather Lee. The first report from the Bureau's agent in South Korea described a lengthy and thorough process in trying to discover additional information about Heather. The final paragraph of the report indicated that he could find absolutely no information on her.

Hixson reread the report one more time. It indicated that the agent had requested help from the South Korean law enforcement agents that he knew. Furthermore, the agent had gone to a Korean library to ask for help in determining whether Ms. Lee had actually existed. He had also contacted various educational administrators to seek their assistance in obtaining the information he needed. Finally, the agent had contacted his informants and asked them if they could find any information on her. All of these efforts produced no significant information of any kind.

The second report he read was a compilation of all the information that the three FBI agents assigned to him had developed. One agent, a computer expert, had scoured the Internet looking for articles or other matters about Heather. The only intelligence he was able to develop was basically related to her podcast, blog, and information about where she had been employed. The other two agents had put feet on the ground in Lee's hometown. They talked with her neighbors, school officials, and her teachers. Finally, they had gone to the university she attended and talked with her professors. This work produced little or no new information.

The three agents also speculated that both Heather and her family could very well be sleeper agents. They based their guesses on the fact that they were unable to determine where her family lived prior to settling in their current hometown. The family seemed to be very tightlipped and did not share information with their neighbors or friends about their background. Other friends noted this lack of information, but they believed it was a cultural difference and left it at that.

When he completed reading and digesting these reports, Agent Hixson felt he needed to discuss these matters with Sam. He picked up his phone, dialed Sam's office and asked the receptionist for an appointment. She told him to hold on. A short time later she came back and said that Sam was available at 4:00 PM. Hixson told her that he would be there at that time.

At about 3:45 PM, Hixson picked up his file and headed out the door. A short time later, he entered the offices of the Bureau's top officials. Soon after 4:00 PM, Agent Hixson was directed to Sam's office. After shaking hands with him, Hixson sat down. Sam asked, "What do you have for me?"

The agent laid out all that he had discovered since their last meeting. He handed the various reports to Sam to read. Minutes later, Sam took off his glasses and placed them on his desk. He asked, "What is your take on all this information?"

Hixson answered, "There's nothing really concrete about Ms. Lee except that there is very little information about her or her family. While there could be numerous reasons why this is so, none are apparent to me. I think there are sufficient questions about her that lead me to believe that she may very well be a sleeper agent. That combined with the fact that she and Senator Kendricks are having an affair raises the question whether he has been compromised and is giving classified information to her."

Sam listened to that answer carefully and thought about it. Finally, he asked, "What would you recommend as the course of action we should take?"

"I believe we have a variety of options available to us. First, we can get a warrant to tap her and her family's phones. That may lead to the answers we need. We can also tap the phones of the hotel where she and Senator Kendricks meet. They are usually in the same room, so we only have to tap that one. We would also place a bug in the room. Finally, we could tap Senator Kendricks' phone. That would be the most drastic course of action we would take. Other than that, I have no other recommendations. I do not believe that any more computer searches or agents on the ground will turn up anything of significance."

"You do, I hope, understand the potential political problems the Bureau would have by tapping the phones of Senator Kendricks?"

"I certainly do, sir. Frankly, that is not a decision I would want to make." Hixson smiled at Sam and stated, "I guess that's why you make the big money."

Sam laughed and shook his head. "I think this is the course of action we will take. First of all, I'll authorize you to obtain warrants to tap Lee and her family's phones. Also, you can obtain a warrant for the hotel room they stay in. Those I could justify based on the potential that she's a sleeper agent. However, I'm not going to tap the senator's phone without more information. Any questions?"

"No, I'm good," replied agent Hixson. "I will ask the court for a warrant as soon as I get back to my office."

Hixson walked out of Sam's office and returned to his own where he prepared the necessary paperwork to obtain the warrants. He walked out of the building heading for the courthouse.

He had not walked more than six feet from the building when several shots rang out. Three of those shots struck Agent Hixson. He did not see the car that sped away. FBI security personnel arrived within 30 seconds. It was obvious to them that the agent was dead.

The news of Hixson's death came to Sam's attention almost immediately and he ordered that Hixson's briefcase be secured and brought to him right away. The connection between the young agent's death and his inquiries into Ms. Lee did not seem to be a coincidence. Furthermore, Sam now believed that he had sufficient information to request a warrant to tap Senator Kendricks' phone. He called in additional agents, showed them Hixson's files, and authorized them to attain the warrants necessary to initiate the taps and bug. When the agents left, Sam placed his hands on his head and felt the tears begin to flow.

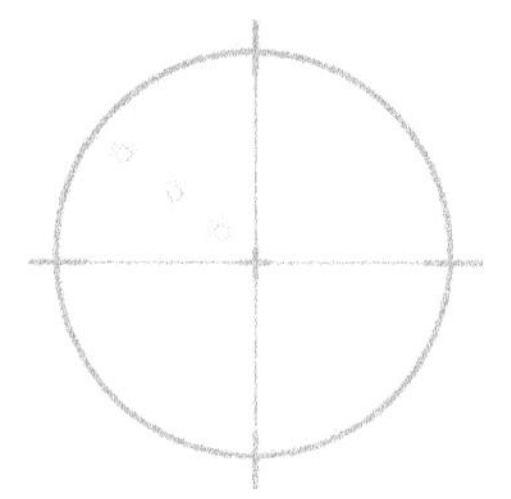

Chapter 39

It was Friday and a beautiful day outside. The sun was shining, the blue sky was unmarred by clouds, and a gentle breeze was blowing from the south. I arrived at one of our favorite restaurants a few minutes late and saw Mac, Ty, and Derek sitting at a table midway between the front and back door. I sat in the chair whose back faced the rear door. Across from me was Derek. Mac was seated to my left and Ty to my right.

As I sat down, Mac piped up, "Late again, as usual. Just like a lawyer—never on time."

"Oh, shut up," I replied, "You have become such a fussy old man in your old age."

Before Mac could respond, Ty said, "Can't we just order? I could be spending quality time with my beautiful wife rather than just sitting here with the old and decrepit."

"Now, now, gentlemen," said Derek. "I agree with Ty. We should just eat. Now, Mac, would you like me to have your food ground up so that it doesn't disrupt that delicate stomach of yours? And DJ, would you like your normal prune juice with your meal?"

"You certainly know and understand these two," stated Ty, who was laughing heartily. I responded by giving each of them the finger.

Mac, however, took offense as he leaned back in his chair eyeing both of them. "I take umbrage at what both of you have said. However, our junior G-man can say what he wants. Obviously, we don't believe anything he says due to his tender age and lack of experience. And you, Ty, should leave and go home to your wife." By this time, all of us were laughing.

Derek followed with, "Art is sending an agent to be with each of you. They should be here within the hour."

Mac responded, "Just make sure they don't get in my way."

The waitress came to take our orders. I was having a cheeseburger, Derek a chef salad, Ty a BLT, and Mac ordered chili. I looked at the other two men and stated, "Poor Ann, she will suffer tonight. I can just see him, walking around, blowing in the wind. I understand that his gas expulsions have been deemed a biological weapon by the Defense Department."

Mac looked at me, smiled and said, "Silly boy, I don't need chili to achieve that designation. In fact, the President himself called me and asked if I would join the Air Force. Evidently, they wanted me to fly over certain enemy territory and let fly. I'm still pondering that."

"My friend," Derek replied, "I think the Bureau could use your magnificent gifts."

"You tell your boss that I'm ready to serve my country as often as I can."

By this time, everybody around us was laughing at our conversation. A large, heavyset man sitting at a table next to ours said, "You all are truly full of it. No offense meant."

Mac smiled and waved his hand, "None taken."

Then a young student entered the front door and walked past us. I smiled at him, and he nodded his head. Derek stated "That was strange. He walked right out the back door."

I responded, "Aw, he's probably taking a shortcut."

* * *

After leaving the restaurant, the student called both Ahmed and Kamil, and informed them where the professors were seated in the restaurant. Following a brief discussion, it was agreed that Kamil would come in the front door and Ahmed would enter through the back door. When they were in place, Kamil called Ahmed and said, "Let's go and get them once and for all."

Each man rushed into the restaurant, one through the front door and the other through the back, with their 9mm pistols drawn. Everyone in the restaurant looked up. Both men started firing at once, aiming at the professors' table. A cacophony of shots echoed across the walls. I heard a man behind me scream and then felt what seemed like a baseball bat hitting me in the back, knocking me into the table and then onto the floor. I saw that Ty had also fallen to the floor, pulled his weapon from under his shirt and fired once. The gun fell from Ty's hand, and he slumped to the floor.

Derek likewise pulled his weapon and started shooting in the direction of the front door. I struggled to pull my 9mm from its holster but was unable to because of the difficult position I had landed in after hitting the floor. The firing seemed to go on for hours and the screams of people in the restaurant came from each and every part of the establishment.

The gunfire suddenly stopped, but the screams continued. Mac jumped over me and advanced toward the back door. He yelled, "Derek, I have the back door, you take the front."

"Got it," Derek yelled.

I couldn't get up, and realized I'd been wounded. Funny, I felt no pain, just the adrenaline coursing through my veins. The heavyset man who talked to us earlier, knelt down beside me. "Are you alright?" He asked.

"I think I have been hit in the back. Do you know if anyone else was hurt."

He looked around and stated, "At least three or four others. It's just so chaotic right now".

A few moments later, two policemen entered with their weapons drawn. The waitress quickly told them what had happened. As they started to head out the back door, she yelled at them, "Two other men, who were sitting here, chased after the shooters with their weapons drawn. Don't shoot them."

The medics arrived and began to triage those who had been shot. One woman and one man had been killed and two other men had been wounded. Soon, the restaurant was filled with policemen talking to witnesses and doctors trying to see if they could help. Ty was the first of those wounded to be taken away in an ambulance. There was so much blood flowing from his head. I was afraid that he was dead.

As I was waiting my turn to be examined, Derek and Mac came back into the restaurant. The policemen stopped them initially, but the waitress explained they had been patrons at the time of the shooting. Mac knelt beside me since I was now sitting uncomfortably against the wall.

"How are you doing?"

"Okay, for a guy who has been shot." The pain in my back was now intense. I waved the medic over and asked, "Can you give me something for the pain?"

"Soon," he responded.

"Asshole!" I replied.

Mac smiled at me and stated, "Such a baby. One little shot in the back of your shoulder and you're crying from the pain. You need to grow up and be a big boy." I tried to hit him, but he leaned back and started laughing. "You'll be okay. The medic is talking to the doctor now. I bet you will get your painkillers shortly. Where is Ty?"

"They have already taken him to the hospital. He was shot in the head. At least that's what the guy told me. There was a lot of blood. I'm not sure what that means, but I am afraid he may be dead."

Mac called Leanne and told her what had happened. Upon hearing that Ty had been wounded and was being taken to the hospital, she said she would drive there. The medics loaded me onto a gurney, and I was on my way to the hospital. I later learned that Mac called Sandy and told her what had happened. He also called Ann and asked her to go be with Leanne at the hospital.

Both Mac and Derek had to spend hours explaining what had happened and the actions they took. I found out later that neither one of them had seen who had shot us when they left the restaurant. It seemed as if the bad guys were going to get away.

By the time Sandy reached the hospital, I was already in surgery. After the operation, she was told that they cleaned out the wound, but saw no serious damage. When I awoke from the anesthetic, I found her waiting for me in my room sitting next to my bed crying.

Mac was also in the room, watching. He smiled and said, "You don't need to be concerned Sandy. He's much too tough of an old bird to be killed by one bullet alone. DJ, the doctor said that you would be out of the hospital in no time, but you would be sore for a while but with no lingering damage."

I looked at him and said, "What's the word on Ty?" I saw his face cloud over.

He was taken into surgery before you, and evidently just got out. They said the bullet creased the top of his head. It opened the scalp, which led to a lot of bleeding. However, it did not enter the skull. They told me they were going to keep him for a while to make sure that he has no swelling in the brain. Other than having a massive headache, he will probably need a wig to look presentable."

"That's good," I said, "I was afraid we might have lost him. Did you recognize the people who were shooting?"

"I can't be sure," he replied, "but the guy I was firing at could have been one of the Paris terrorists. I just can't be sure."

Sandy stood up and walked over to Mac. "I think we should let him rest now," she said softly. And with that, I drifted off to sleep.

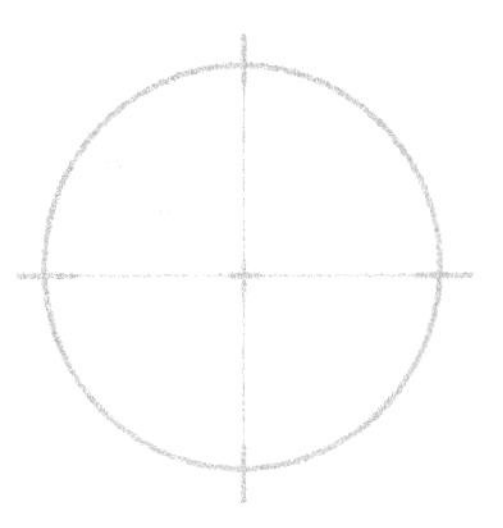

Chapter 40

The next morning, I was feeling much better. However, there was still significant pain where I had been shot the previous day. The doctor had prescribed sufficient pain medication so that I was, overall, comfortable. My doctor told me I had actually been shot in my shoulder. It still hurt, but the doctor had assured me that with time, I would have no long-lasting problems. Sandy had slept in the chair next to my bed during the night. Looking at her now, I could see she needed to get some rest.

She smiled at me. I said, "I think you need to go home and get some rest. You look tired. There's nothing you can do for me here, and I'm sure, the nurses will make sure that I have all that I need."

"I am a bit tired, but I think that Ann and Mac are coming by before noon. After they leave, I will head home and get some rest. Are you good with that?"

"Okay, I can live with that."

There was a soft knock on the door. I said, "Come on in."

Ann and Mac came through the door and stood at the foot of my bed. Mac smiled and said, "Well, I'll be damned! The dead has come back to life." Mac grunted as Ann gave him a sharp poke in the ribs. "Ann, darling, please don't do that. I might end up in the hospital and in the same room as DJ."

"Don't worry, Ann, I know that's just his way of saying 'I hope you feel better.' By the way, Mac, how was it that you avoided all the bullets that were flying around yesterday?"

"I know how to duck. You, on the other hand, have to stick your head up just to see what's going on. If you need further instruction on how to keep safe during a gunfight, I am more than happy to help you."

"It is beyond me that the two of you can joke about this matter as serious as it is," Sandy stated. "You both are lucky to be alive, once again."

Changing the subject, I said, "Why don't we go down to Ty's room and see how he's doing." Sandy and Mac helped me into a wheelchair, and we headed down the hall.

The door to Ty's room was open, so the four of us sauntered in, even though I was on wheels. Ty was sitting up in his bed, and Leanne was sitting next to him, holding his hand. Mac, as always, opened the conversation by saying, "Ty, when are you going to get out of bed and go back to work?"

"Who invited you into this room, asshole?"

Ann held up her hands and said, "For the rest of you, I will translate what was just said. Mac said, 'I've really been worried about you ,Ty. How are you feeling?' Ty answered, 'Not too bad, Mac, thanks for asking.' You just have to understand man speak."

There was another knock on the open door, Art and Derek entered and nodded to each of us. "Well, you don't look any worse than when I saw you a few days ago. By the way, when I told Sam what happened to you, he said the Bureau would send some flowers. I told him that would be a waste, but I'm sure your wives would appreciate the gesture."

I continued the conversation by stating, "Please, tell Sam that he should send us a good bottle of scotch. I promise that I will open it with care and drink as many toasts to him as I can."

Sandy's response was blunt and to the point. "Art, what are you finally going to do to make sure that our husbands are safe? You were late in getting agents here to protect them."

"Sandy, before we get into that, don't you think we should inquire as to how Ty is doing. I mean, he really hasn't opened his mouth since we've been here. I assume that indicates his injury is more severe than we were led to believe. Well, Ty, you have the floor," I said smiling.

"The doctor says that I am fine. They're going to watch me for a couple days to see if I have any swelling in the brain. I must say that I have a roaring headache. Other than that, everything is normal."

Mac spoke next with a smile on his face, "Ty, you never were much of a looker, but now with that bandage around your head, you are one ugly SOB."

After everyone finished laughing, including Ty, Mac became more serious. "The question is, I think, where do we go from here?"

Ann quieted everyone and said, "I've been thinking quite a bit about this. I have a proposal I want to put forward. If the terrorists believe that our guys are alive, they will continue to try and kill them. Why don't we let the terrorists believe that they were successful, and the three of you died during the shooting yesterday. If they believe you are out of the way, you would be free to do the work the Bureau has asked you to do."

"I like it," stated Sandy. "I know the editor of our local paper, and I am sure he would put in an article saying that you died. I also believe he could make sure that it went over the wire, which would go around the world."

Art spoke up and said, "I like it also. I think that Sam could get the French to run it in their papers as well. All in all, I think it would be more likely than not that the terrorists would see these articles. Ann, I like the way you think!"

After a long discussion, we all agreed that we should follow Ann's proposal and put it into effect. The next day, the following story went out over the AP:

> Yesterday, in what appears to be a random act of violence, several men and a woman were shot to death in a local café. Three of the men were the professors who escaped the terrorist attack in Paris two years ago and more recently at the home of one of the men. Their families have indicated that there will be no public funeral services, but only a private memorial service, later in the year. Once again, the ugly head of gun violence has showed itself in our country.

Within a week, Ty and I were released from the hospital. A few days later, we flew undetected to Washington to begin our work with the FBI.

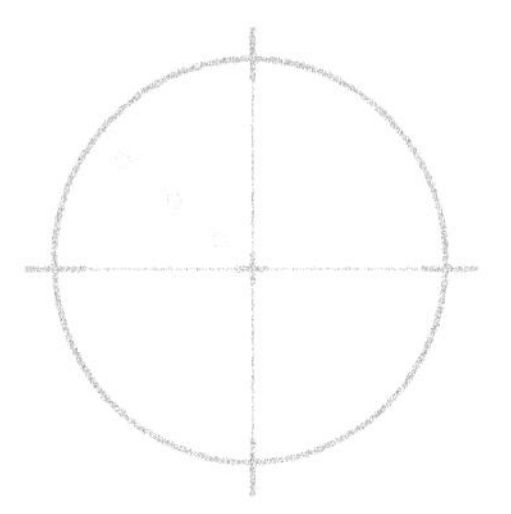

Chapter 41

After running from the restaurant, Ahmed and Kamil drove to the airport, where they took separate planes to Miami and Chicago. After Ahmed disembarked from his plane in Chicago, he purchased a burner phone from a kiosk in the airport. Scouring the various newspapers to determine whether the professors had been killed or not, he found a small paragraph in the AP feed which told him all he needed to know. Once he was in his rental car, he drove until he found an empty parking lot that would give him some privacy.

He dialed Chin-Sun's number and waited for her to answer. Then he heard her pick up and said, "Yes?"

"It's done. We were successful. I saw a story on the AP that indicated several people had been killed. Among them were the three professors. Would you like me to send you confirmation of that?"

"That's not necessary. I saw a similar story and knew then that your attack had been successful. Where are you and our friend currently."

"I am in Chicago," Ahmed answered, "Our friend is in Miami. Each of us is ready to proceed as planned. Do you know of any reason why we should not do that?"

"None whatsoever," Chin-Sun replied. "Our shipment has left Asia. When I have confirmation of its arrival, I will let you know. It is critical that we now determine where each spray should occur. I assume that, as you did in San Antonio, you will reconnoiter the cities assigned to you and will recommend to me a course of action. Tell me once again which cities each of you will be traveling to."

"I will be going to check out Boston, Philadelphia, Pittsburgh, Charlotte, and Chicago. Our friend will be visiting Tampa Bay, St. Louis, Kansas City, Minneapolis, and Miami."

Chin-Sun replied, "Do you believe that is possible?"

"Yes, we should be able to do that."

"It is important that you have prepared a route in each of the destinations for spraying. It is also important that you have arranged flights from one city to the next to be sure that you will be able to complete your task without interruption. I'm sure that you will make appropriate plans to leave the country."

Ahmed replied, "Yes, we will have the routes decided."

"I will inform you at a later time where you can pick up the material necessary for your work. It will also contain clear instructions on how to deliver the spray, and you'll also be given the vaccine to assure your safety. Since it will take several days before we see the outbreaks we expect to occur, you should have sufficient time to take your flight out of the country. Do you have any questions?"

"I do not. We will talk later."

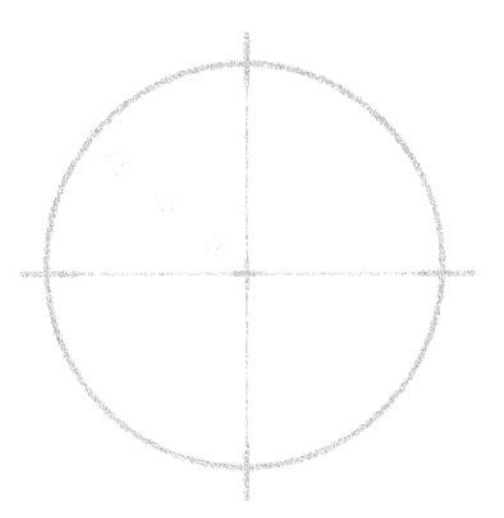

Chapter 42

Sam was sitting in his office working on the next fiscal year's budget. Of all the responsibilities that he had, trying to put together a budget was the worst. Not only was it boring, but in his business, the need for funds could shift very quickly. Sam looked at the computer screen once again and rubbed his eyes. Holding the position of Director of Counterterrorism was one he had always aspired to. Sam loved working in the field and did not ever think about the mundane administrative work his position would require.

Hearing the *ding* of his email alert, he realized that this would give him a few moments to avoid budget work. Sam opened his email and saw that he had received something from the NSA director. NSA was an acronym for the National Security Agency, the government agency that listened in to telephone conversations all over the world. This message was from Bill Simpson, the Agency Director. Sam opened the email, read it quickly and then clicked on the attachment.

In the email, Simpson had informed him that they had captured a phone call with male and female voices. The conversation was transcribed in the attachment. Simpson further indicated he was not sure if this was of interest to Sam but given Sam's previously shared communication about the potential for a terrorist attack, he felt he must send it on.

Sam read the transcript contained in the attachment. While there was nothing in the transcript that shouted out terrorism, when one read it with the background that Sam had; it was clear that something was afoot. The more he thought about that message, the more it seemed to him that this could be the target list for the terrorist's attack. Given the fact that the word *spray* had been used, it could be construed to be a means of transmitting a virus. Perhaps, maybe, coordination of government resources and cooperation between agencies has provided them with a clue on how to proceed.

Sam called his assistant and asked her to get Derek's number for him. Moments later, he was talking to Derek. "Derek, where are you now?"

"Sir, I am downstairs in my office. Do you need something from me?"

"Where are the professors?"

"In the cafeteria downstairs grabbing a bite to eat."

Sam continued, "Okay, I want you to gather them up and bring them to me."

"We'll be there in a few minutes." Derek hung the phone up wondering what was going on as he headed for the cafeteria.

Approximately 20 minutes later, Derek and the professors were ushered into Sam's office. Sam motioned them to the couches in his office, sat down himself, and said "Well, we may have a lead on where our terrorists are or may be." He handed copies of the transcript to the four men. "Please take some time and read this document. It's not long and doesn't have big words."

Mac looked at Sam and stated, "I guess the government is full of comedians."

The four men saw Sam chuckle. He then urged them to read the document.

When Ty finished reading, he looked at Sam. "I'm not sure why this is important. It just seems like a random conversation to me."

Sam looked at Mac and me and stated, "What is your take on this information."

Mac answered, "I agree with Ty. Why is this so important?"

Sam looked my way. "DJ?"

I kept studying the document for a few moments. "I'm not an expert on these things, but I think we may have a lead on the terrorists. We know that one party of the conversation was a woman and the other a man. The woman could be Chin-Sun and the man could be either one of the two terrorists. They talk about picking out various cities and determining routes in each one of them. But what strikes me the most unusual is they used the word *spray*. They may have given us a roadmap to where they are going. I don't know, maybe it's our first lead."

Mac asked, "Why are we concerned with spraying?"

I answered, "Mac, don't you remember during the Covid crisis, it was speculated that the Chinese sprayed the virus intentionally to infect people?"

Sam said, "Damn, DJ, you should have been a spy. Your interpretation of this transcript coincides with mine. If that is true, one of the men is in Chicago and one in Miami. Now, we just must figure out how to catch them.

He continued, "First, Derek, I want you to get copies of the drawings of the two men and send them to the directors of each of the airports in the cities mentioned. You can inform them that the FBI will be sending agents there immediately to watch for people coming from Chicago or Miami who look like the men in those drawings. Have my assistant help you with that.

"You guys," Sam said pointing at the three of us, "will go to different airports to help with this attempt to locate the terrorists. I will talk with our director and get him on board. We need sufficient resources to review all the videotapes of people from the flights arriving from those cities. He can also light a fire under any airport director who is not working diligently enough.

"I will be assigning an agent to accompany Ty and Mac. Derek, you will work with DJ. Those agents chosen will be here within the hour and the assistants in my office will arrange flights, hotels, and rental cars for you."

Sam looked at each one of us and said, "Let's hope we get lucky."

As we left Sam's office, Mac said, "This seems awfully thin to me. I wish there was more to go on."

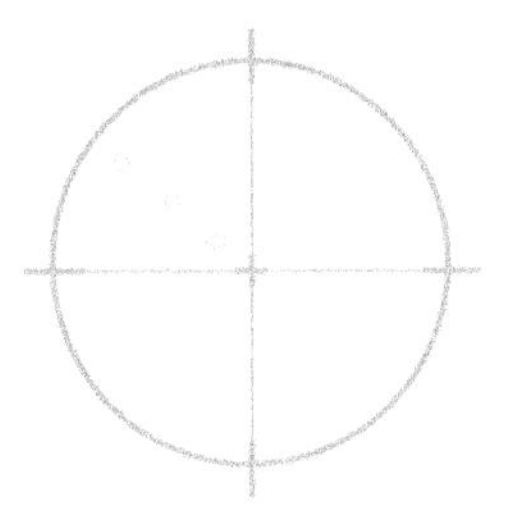

Chapter 43

Kim looked at the various men seated before him. He motioned for the Doctor to step forward, and asked, "Are you prepared to explain how the virus will be shipped and in what time frame?"

The Doctor felt the hard gaze of the Leader's eyes. He swallowed hard as he always did when standing before Kim. "Yes, sir, I am prepared to give you the information you have requested."

"Proceed."

The Doctor began, "All our dispersal backpacks with the small and empty cylinders have arrived at our sleeper assets living in the cities we have targeted to attack. The actual virus has been shipped through China to warehouses in those cities and should arrive shortly. We are confident these large cylinders holding the virus will not be found nor detected by the US customs service. I expect that all the shipments will reach their destination within a matter of days. I trust that I have answered your questions to your satisfaction."

Kim leaned back in his chair and with a smile on his face, responded, "You have done very well." The leader of North Korea leaned forward, looking at the military men seated before him and asked, "If the United States tries to blame us for these actions, are you prepared to defend our country accordingly?" He watched each of the military men nod that they were prepared. "He glanced at each one of them and stated, "I hope you are. Because if you are not, you will rue the day that you ever join the Armed Forces of North Korea. Do I make myself perfectly clear?"

"Very good, gentlemen. Let us move forward on this great adventure." Kim stood and strode out of the room.

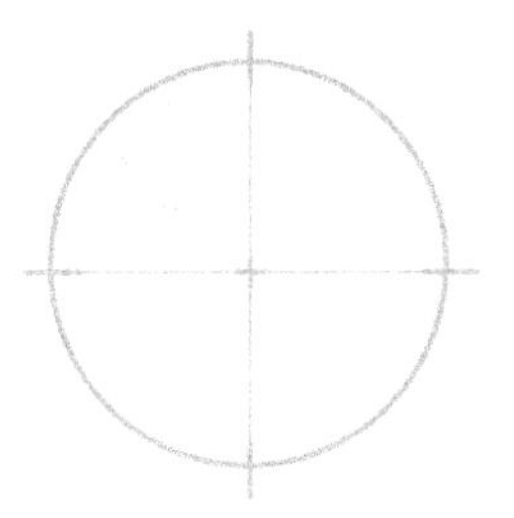

Chapter 44

When we sat down and reviewed the list of cities, we decided that we would go to the cities closest to Miami and Chicago. Ty and his agent were going to Tampa Bay; Mac and his agent were going to Minneapolis. I was going to Charlotte with Derek. Other FBI teams were stationed at the other cities with the drawings we had of the two terrorists. We were hoping there were no other terrorists involved since we would have no idea what they looked like.

Derek and I were in the control room at the Charlotte airport facing a wall full of video screens. Each of those screens were being broadcast from cameras aimed at each gate and adjacent broad passageways. As planes came in from Chicago or Miami, Derek and I would focus on the screens as the passengers would deplane. After watching for several hours, my eyes were bloodshot and weariness had settled in. It was difficult to keep my attention because I knew that I might be looking at the wrong gate or even the wrong airport. It was going to be a long day and night of surveillance.

Derek was a few feet away looking at the screens he was assigned to watch. For the first few hours, we kept up an animated conversation. However, at this point, our conversation had ceased, and we just kept going from screen to screen hoping we would catch a break.

A plane from Chicago was scheduled to deplane at gate 17. I found the screen showing that gate, sat down and watched people getting off. My eyes were drawn to a man who exited the plane and turned right. I got a good look at him and was shocked to see that it appeared to be Ahmed. I yelled to Derek to come over. It was important to get a second pair of eyes on the man. Derek took one look and said, "That's our guy!" We took off running toward the location. At the same time, Derek radioed the other agents stationed throughout the airport and airport security telling them where to go.

Derek and I arrived and found the man had been apprehended by airport security. In order not to cause problems within the airport, we took him to a conference room where we could interrogate him. I asked him, "What is your name?"

"Why are you holding me? I have done nothing wrong."

Derek showed him his FBI identification, and responded, "You are suspected of planning a terrorist attack in the United States. If convicted, you will spend the rest of your life in a small cell, and no one will know where you are. If you want some leniency. I suggest you start to cooperate."

I leaned over and whispered to Derek, "You are a natural for this shit."

The man answered, "I don't know what you're talking about. I've done nothing wrong. Please let me go."

Derek proceeded to read the man his rights and asked if he understood them. The man nodded yes. Derek said, "Let me explain why you're here." He pulled out the drawings that we had of Ahmed and Kamil and said, "This man, who we believe is you, is wanted for terrorist attacks in this country and in France. Now do you understand why you're here?"

The man pointed at the drawing and said, "That's not me. Just look!"

For the first time since we apprehended the man, I looked closely at his face. He certainly seemed to resemble Ahmed. I leaned closer and examined his face. Derek reached up and ran his finger against his forehead. Looking at his finger, the realization struck me that the man had make-up on, which made him appear to have darker skin. I reached up and tugged on his beard and saw that it pulled away from his face. I sat back and said, "You're wearing theater makeup. Is that correct?"

The man nodded his head in agreement.

"Why is that?"

The man responded, "I am an actor. This is part of the role I'm rehearsing for."

I had a sinking feeling that we had been duped. Derek looked at the man closely and said, "Explain yourself."

"I was approached by a man who told me about a movie they were going to make in the Miami area. They were looking for actors who could play certain roles. Part of my role required me to take this journey to Charlotte. They showed me the type of make-up they wanted me to use. I am supposed to return tomorrow."

Derek asked, "Can you tell me anymore about the man who approached you?"

"Not really. There was nothing unusual about him."

Once again, Derek showed him the drawings of the two men and asked, "Do either of these men resemble the man who talked with you."

Looking at the drawings again, the man responded, "Maybe. I am not sure."

Derek and I stepped out of the conference room and decided that this man was simply being used by Ahmed to keep us off his trail. I thought for a moment and then said, "We need to look at some more of the footage from gate 17 to see if Ahmed got off the plane."

Letting the false Ahmed go, Derek and I returned to the control room to view more video. About five minutes after the actor got off the plane, we saw Ahmed exit and turn left at the gate to leave the airport. By the time this was confirmed, we were sure he was far away. Derek issued an APB, but we did not have any strong feelings that we would find the terrorist.

While Derek called Sam, I called Mac to tell them what had occurred. After hearing my story, Mac responded, "Well, I'll be damned, the sneaky SOB. He suspected we might be watching the airports."

"It seems so," I agreed. "I'm going to call Ty to see if he has any news?"

"This consulting gig is so boring. I am going to have a drink. We will talk later."

After signing off, I called Ty. Soon he answered and said, "Hey, DJ, I was just getting ready to call you. We had something interesting happen here." He proceeded to describe a situation similar to ours. "What do you think about that?"

I explained what happened to us. "I will schedule a conference call with Sam for the morning."

After ending the call, I sent Mac and Ty a text telling them we would talk with Sam in the morning.

Derek and I headed to our hotel. Like Mac, we went to the bar to have a drink.

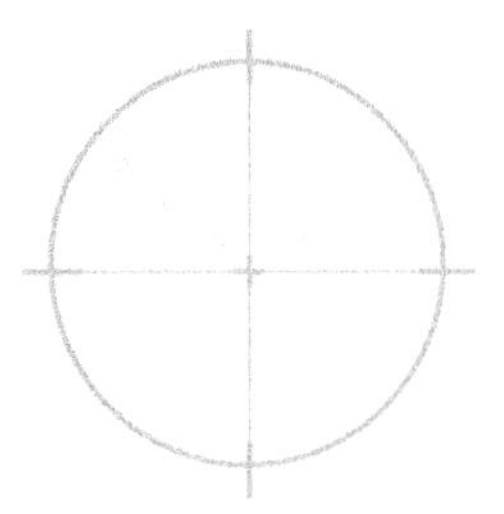

Chapter 45

Ahmed picked up his rental car and drove to a small, inexpensive hotel. Once he was settled, he placed a call to Kamil. It rang several times before Kamil answered. "Well, brother, are you safe?"

"Yes, I think so. I had an interesting time in Tampa Bay, however. My double exited the plane before me as we planned. I left the jetway and saw that he was surrounded by several security officers. I immediately turned in the opposite direction and made my way out of the airport. From my perspective, we made the right decision to have doubles. Did you have any problems?"

"My experience was similar to yours. Like you, my double was surrounded by what appeared to be security people. I did not spend a lot of time watching, but rather, left as soon as I could. I did not know how long it would take before the FBI realized they had a double instead of the real thing. However, it seems to me, it has changed how we are going to do our business. My suggestion would be that we drive our rental cars to target cities and stay away from airports. What are your thoughts?"

Kamil responded, "It appears that somehow, the government has determined where we are going to strike. We were lucky to get away this time. I doubt if they'll follow a body double again. Because of that, I think our only option is to drive from city to city. That will limit the number of cities we can spray. Perhaps we should talk to Chin-Sun to see what her wishes are."

"I agree, my brother. I will call her and get back to you. Talk to you soon." Ahmed dialed Chin-Sun's number.

When Chin-Sun's phone rang, she saw the call was from Ahmed's burner phone, and she answered, "Hello, Ahmed. Is there something we need to talk about?"

He explained what had occurred at both the Tampa Bay and Charlotte airports.

She responded, "You were wise to take the precautions you did. I did not think they would get onto us so fast. What do you think?"

"Well, Kamil and I believe it would risk our operation if we were to fly to the next scheduled airports. We believe that the safest means would be to drive to each city and conduct the necessary reconnaissance. We still must decide whether we would fly or drive to the city's when we are doing the actual spraying."

"I understand your concerns. I think that the course we should take would be the one that assures you will not be captured. How long do you think your initial reconnaissance of the cities will take?"

Ahmed responded, "If we were to drive to each of the cities, I expect it would take one to two weeks, and one to two weeks when the actual attacks occur. Obviously, we would not want to have the symptoms of the virus showing prior to our leaving the country. What is the expected incubation period for this virus?"

"The information I have been given indicates that the incubation period is two to four days and another five to seven days before symptoms appear, but who knows for sure. Given that fact, I believe that it may be necessary to reduce the number of cities that we attack so that no outbreaks occur until after you leave the country. Do you agree with that?"

"Yes," Ahmed answered, "That would be my recommendation also. Which cities would you like us to delete from the list if need be?"

Chin-Sun thought for a moment before responding. "I will leave that decision to you. I think that you know better, given that you're driving, you are familiar with the route you've chosen, and you know the time it will take to accomplish your task in each city. I would like you and Kamil to work on this. Any questions?"

"Not at this time."

"Good," she responded. "Please let me know when you'll be ready to initiate the attack." She disconnected the call and smiled as she felt the excitement coursing through her.

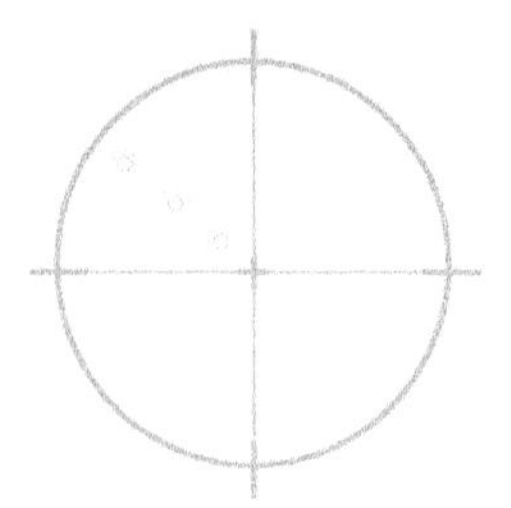

Chapter 46

In the morning, Derek and I called Sam, and he conferenced in both Ty and Mac. Ty and Derek gave a summary of what happened the previous day at the airports. When they finished, Sam spoke, "Well, gentlemen, does anyone have anything to add to what has been said?"

Ty responded, "Has there been any success in locating Ahmed and Kamil? Maybe we'll get lucky and find them."

"Not yet," Sam replied. "We will keep our agents looking at the other airports to determine if these guys fly to their next city. Frankly, I think that train has left the station. If they were smart enough to have doubles exiting the plane first, I'd be willing to bet they glanced back to see if it worked. Surely, they would've expected a call from their doubles to explain what happened to them. It's possible that these two men have abandoned their operation altogether. However, I doubt that. They have shown they are committed to their ideology.

"My guess is that they have decided to use different modes of transportation. There are three options we must look at. First, do we think they would use our train system to get where they need to go? Second, they could be using the bus system. Third, they could be using cars. I don't believe that one or two is an option for them. They would expect that we could have people watching the bus and train stations.

"That leads them to using cars they could either buy, rent, borrow, or steal. We will send out notifications with photos of the terrorists explaining what has happened to every new and used car lot and ask if they have sold a vehicle to either of the bad guys. The same will be done with all the car rental companies. The bad guys may be dumb enough to try to steal a car, but I doubt that for the simple reason that those thefts would be reported. If they have assets in this country who would be willing to loan them their vehicle, we will have no way of determining if that is occurring."

"Do you guys have any brilliant ideas? I could certainly use some."

"Sam, I think you've summarized the situation very succinctly," answered Ty.

"Where does that leave us?" I asked.

Mac responded, "Give me a second to chew on this." After a short period of silence, Mac spoke once again, "I think we have to shift gears on this. From the intercepted call, it appeared to me that these guys were checking out the cities just to determine how they should be attacked. Trying to catch them doing that is a fool's errand, I believe. Since we have no evidence that they were carrying the virus, then perhaps we should be looking for the virus rather than the men. What do you think, Sam?"

"Interesting idea, Mac. If we follow your train of thought, they will have to, at some time, pick up the virus. The most likely way to deliver this virus would be some means of releasing it into the air. That would require either a portable unit or a larger device containing the virus that would have been shipped here."

Ty interrupted, "If they had backpacks, for instance, they could return to the location where the virus was kept and reload. The other option would be that they had multiple backpacks at each location."

"That would be cumbersome at best," Mac stated. "I bet they would have a central location where the virus is located, which they could return to and reload before heading out to disseminate it."

Sam, who had been listening quietly, spoke up, "Mac, I think you're onto something. I believe we should change our focus of attack from finding the men to finding the virus. I will have Customs provide us with a report of every ship coming from the Far East. We will try to trace every package from any ships that are headed to our target cities. I want you and your agents to return to Washington as soon as you can. We need to organize how we receive this information, how we analyze it, and how we follow up on it. So, head on back to Washington and we will proceed with this plan."

After we hung up, Sam contemplated what was going on. He knew he could be entirely wrong on how to approach this because the virus might already be here. He decided to expand his request to Customs to cover a period of time over the last six months. Once again, Sam realized, he would need to have a lot of luck if he was going to capture these men before the virus was released.

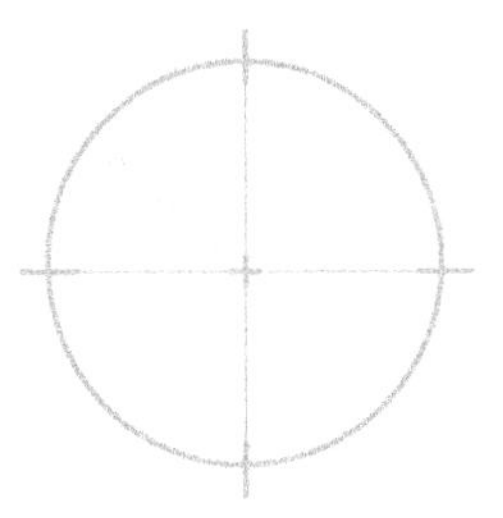

Chapter 47

Sam called the Speaker of the House and asked him to call a special meeting of the intelligence committee. Previously, he had talked with Julianne Simmons and informed her of what they had learned. It was important that the committee be kept informed of this potential attack. The Speaker readily agreed and set the meeting for the next morning at 9:00 AM.

Sam and Ms. Simmons arrived at the conference room a few minutes early. Already seated at the conference table was Senator Kendricks. He stood and greeted the two as they entered. He looked at both, and stated, "What's come up that has required this unscheduled meeting?"

Sam nodded to Ms. Simmons, and she answered, "Well, Senator, it appears we may be facing an imminent attack."

"From whom and how?"

"It looks like the two Mideastern terrorists who struck Las Vegas, San Francisco, and Seattle in the last year. As to how this will happen, we have not determined that yet."

"How serious of a threat do you believe this is?"

"We have been informed by the French that these two men, now known as Ahmed and Kamil, are in this country and are preparing to attack," replied Sam. "We nearly caught them a few days ago." Sam then proceeded to tell the senator about staking out the airports of the targeted cities. "You know, Senator, the information we received about these cities did not indicate they were being targeted. However, we referred to them as potential targets based on all the information we have received. That includes information from the French and those facts that we could determine on our own."

At that moment, several other members of the committee entered the room. Within ten minutes, all of the participants were present. Simmons began the meeting and presented the information to the committee she had previously given to Senator Kendricks. The meeting lasted over one hour. After everyone had left, Simmons and Sam continued to talk.

Sam rose, reached out and shook Simmons' hand. "Thanks for your help on this matter. Maybe it will help us prevent this attack."

As she turned to leave, Simmons looked back and said, "Well, the senator was certainly interested. No doubt about that." With that, she walked out the door, leaving Sam to wonder if Kendricks would be talking to Heather soon.

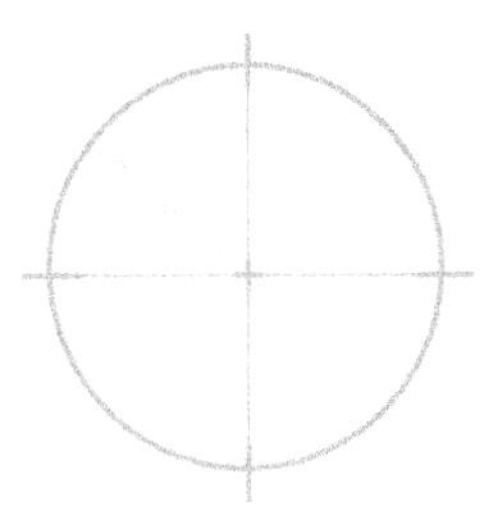

Chapter 48

Sam had just arrived back at his office after attending the intelligence committee meeting. As he sat at his desk, he was pondering the potential action that might be taken against Senator Kendricks. His phone rang, he picked it up and said, "Hello."

Mael stated, "Hey, Sam, it's Mael. Do you have a couple minutes that we can talk?"

"Of course. Do you have any information on our terrorists?"

"No, I do not. However, I have some associated information that I want to share with you. We have found and have taken into custody the financier of our terrorists."

"Well, that's most interesting," Sam replied. "What have you learned?"

Mael continued, "At this time, not a whole lot. This guy is not a diehard ideologue. We took him to a black site in Africa. We've just begun to squeeze him for information. The man's trying to remain strong, but that should not last long. He has told us that he provided funds for Ahmed and Kamil. While claiming he did not know what they were going to do in the United States, he continues to refuse to provide information about where he gets his money. I believe that with more pressure, he'll come clean.

"The man has been told that no one knows where he is and that if he is not more cooperative, he will simply disappear. The financier also indicated that he provided the funding for the terrorist attack in the US, but claimed he had no prior knowledge as to what was going to happen. He will crack pretty soon.

"Sam, can you hold on for a couple minutes. One of my men who has been interrogating him has just called."

"I'll hold," Sam answered.

Five minutes later, Mael resumed his conversation. "Well, Sam, just as I thought, the guy is starting to spill the beans. I'm sure he'll have a lot to say, but for your purposes, he did mention one important thing. He indicated that the funds that he received for Ahmed and Kamil's operation in the US came from a Russian. We did not get a name, but he said it was from a person in a high position. He also indicated it came through China."

"I'll be damned. Maybe it's Putin himself," Sam replied. "In any event, if the North Koreans are behind this potential attack in the US, there will be hell to pay. I'm not sure any explanation Kim would give would be accepted by the President. This attempt at taking lives is simply too serious to be swept under the rug. I am not sure what would happen if Putin were behind this."

"I understand," Mael offered. "Do you think that this information may help you deter a possible attack?"

"It may, once we combine it with all the other intelligence we've received." Sam then proceeded to review all the information they had. While he talked about Heather Lee, he did not bring Senator Kendricks into the conversation. Sometimes you share everything with your allies, and other times you withhold sensitive information.

Having completed their conversation, each of the men said their goodbyes and the conversation was terminated.

Sam called Derek and asked him to bring the three professors to his office. When they arrived, he explained the intelligence he'd received from Mael. "Gentlemen, we are making progress. Based on this information, I think we have to expand our Custom's search for any cargo coming from China."

Mac spoke first, "There must be thousands of containers coming from China into the US. How can we possibly cover all of those?"

Ty answered that question, "Remember, Mac, we will only be looking at those containers going to the targeted cities. I've been thinking about this. Many of those containers will be going directly to American businesses. I doubt that the North Koreans would send a virus to a company. My guess is that it will be sent to a storage warehouse where it will be held. That should also limit how many containers we must follow."

Sam ended the conversation by saying, "I like your idea, Ty. I'm also going to assign additional agents to assist in the analysis of the information we get. Let's hope our luck continues to hold."

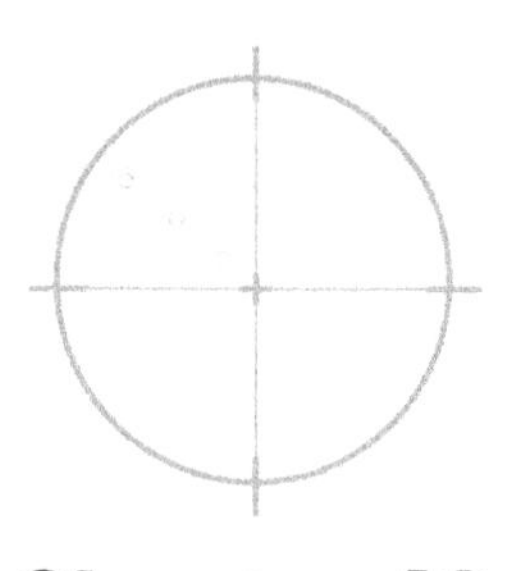

Chapter 49

Agent William Johnson had replaced Agent Hixson and was determined to avenge his predecessor's murder. The Bureau had placed additional resources at his disposal to help him achieve his goal. He had all the information available to him that Hixson was able to develop. On this day, Johnson was able to determine that Senator Kendricks would be gone from his office from midafternoon until midafternoon the next day. He was waiting at the hotel where Ms. Lee and Kendricks usually met. Previously, Johnson had had a team of agents place hearing devices in the room they used so that he could hear everything that was said between Kendricks and Heather.

Furthermore, he had an FBI SWAT team available nearby to arrest Ms. Lee should the circumstances warrant it. Johnson had arrived several hours early to see if Ms. Lee arrived. She did, in fact, arrive early. However, unexpectedly, Heather arrived with two other Korean gentlemen. The three of them walked into the hotel.

Within a few minutes, Heather walked into her room and Johnson heard her say, "Okay, the senator should be here by 4:00 PM. Do you have your recording equipment set up next door as usual?"

An unidentified male voice responded, "Yes, everything is ready to go. Are you sure you don't want me to spend some time here with you?"

"Get out before I report you to our superiors again!"

Johnson heard the man chuckle as he walked out and closed the door.

This was a new and unexpected wrinkle for Johnson. It was obvious that the Koreans were recording Kendricks' liaison with Heather. If they decided to arrest her today, he would also have to take down the two other gentlemen. Johnson called the leader of the SWAT team and explained what he had learned. The man replied that they would have a plan worked out to go after both rooms. The man explained that he had sufficient personnel available on his team to get the three people. Johnson sat down to await the arrival of Kendricks.

Just before 4:00 PM, Senator Kendricks drove up, parked, and walked into the hotel. A few moments later, Johnson heard a knock-on Heather's door. Heather opened the door, smiled and said, "Hello, my love. I'm so glad we have this time together."

The senator responded, "Yes, this time is so special to me. When did you arrive?"

"Oh, a couple of hours ago. I've just been sitting here pining away for you. Can you stay the night?"

"Yes, I've cleared my morning calendar, so staying here tonight will not be a problem." He took her in his arms, kissed her, and led her to the bed.

As their lovemaking progressed, Johnson became more and more uncomfortable listening to these private, intimate acts. Soon, the physical part, which was so embarrassing to Johnson, concluded. As he continued to listen, it became apparent that the two were resting in each other's arms. After some meaningless conversation, their talk turned toward business.

Heather stated, "I wanted to tell you that I've been getting emails from people who listen to my podcast asking when you're going to be on again. Evidently, you have become quite a hit with them. I'm not sure why, though." She was giggling as if it were a big joke.

"Are you trying to make me angry?" he asked.

"I'm trying to see if you can take a joke. Can you, my love? Or are you one of those Washington, DC, people who has no sense of humor?"

"Oh, shut up," he said, pulling her even closer to him. "I am sure the people listening to your podcast appreciate me, maybe more than you do."

"That's not funny," she replied.

"Now it appears that you are the one who doesn't have a sense of humor."

"Quiet. Let's talk about something else." Heather spent the next 20 minutes telling Kendricks about what had been going on with her podcast. As she spoke, she bubbled over with excitement. When she finally finished, she said, "You've been so patient listening to me talk about myself and my business. Let's talk about what's going on with you."

Johnson perked up, leaned forward and listened to Kendricks speak.

"It's been a busy week for me." Kendricks spent the next several minutes discussing issues he was working on. He also discussed his attempts to form a bipartisan group to reach agreement on pending legislation. He continued, "As you can see, nothing but real run-of-the-mill legislative business."

As she snuggled closer to him, she asked, "Anything new on the Korean front?"

"If you'll remember, we were concerned that North Koreans might be involved in a potential attack on our country. We now know that they are working with Mideastern terrorists and have discovered their names. It's interesting, the French have been able to help us quite a bit. Also, we have a good idea as to the cities that are being targeted for an attack. But, you know, all the information they get is a bunch of smoke and mirrors. Analysts have to figure out what the actual truth is and try to come up with a plan to prevent any attack. Anyway, it's mostly boring stuff." He rolled onto his side and began to kiss her again with passion. Heather responded with equal passion. She didn't need to remember what he said since it was all being recorded.

Johnson called the SWAT leader to inform him that they would arrest Ms. Lee and her compatriots the next morning after Kendricks left.

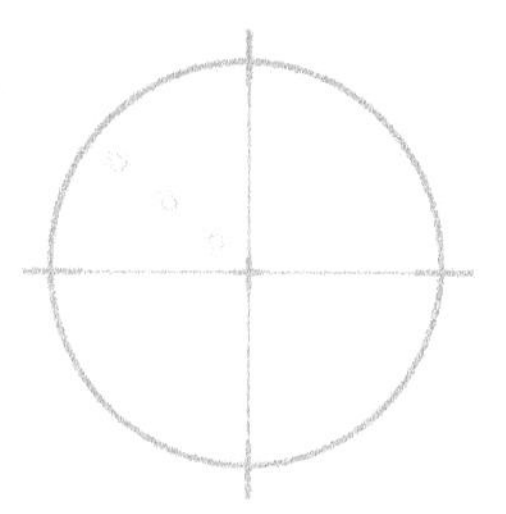

Chapter 50

The children's play area in Los Angeles was quiet with only one or two children on the park apparatus. Chin-Sun watched the children play for several minutes as she waited for Mr. Song. He had contacted her through the normal channels and had expressed the need to meet with her right away. A few moments later, she saw him wandering through the park toward her, carrying a small cooler. He bowed and once again asked if he could share the bench where she was sitting. She nodded her assent and waited for him to speak.

"Good morning, once again," he stated. She said nothing while waiting for him to continue. He looked around before he began. Seeing nothing that raised his concern, he stated, "I have exciting news. The shipments we have been waiting for have arrived. They have been sent to warehouses that have been selected in the target cities. What have you heard from our Saudi friends?"

Chin-Sun described the conversations she had had with the two men. She indicated that she expected to hear from them in the next day or so. At that time, she would have all the details of the proposed attacks. He listened carefully as she spoke, taking in all the information she provided. "I think we are ready," she said. "It appears to me that all the prerequisites for the attack are falling into place. Do you have any information that would cause me concern at this time?"

"We are still receiving inside information passed to us of the expectations and intentions of the counterterrorism services in this country. In fact, I am expecting a personal call tomorrow with the latest information on the US preparedness. Hopefully, that information will contain nothing of concern to us. Since our shipments have arrived at their warehouses, you can initiate the attacks.

"I have brought you this cooler. It contains the vaccine for you to give our Saudi friends. Once our Mideastern friends have begun the distribution phase, what are your plans? Since we have not been given the vaccine, I think it is wise for us to leave. How are you going to proceed?"

Chin-Sun asked, "Are you returning to our homeland?"

Song answered, "I expect not. If the US has any intelligence that our country has been involved in spreading the virus, I do not think Korea would be a safe place for anyone. That is why I have booked a direct flight from here to Amsterdam. Frankly, though, if the virus spreads quickly, there may be no place we can hide from it. What are your plans?"

"I plan to fly to Switzerland because I share your concern about the spread of the virus. Hopefully, at some point, the vaccine will be shared with us. Until we receive that, none of us are safe."

"Are the Saudis at all concerned that they are not receiving a true vaccine?" asked Song.

Chin-Sun replied, "It has never been raised by them as an issue. They will be shocked when they learn that the vaccine they are given lasts only one month. It should be enough to get them through their attacks on each city. Once they start to show symptoms of the virus, I would not want to be found by them. Clearly, they are the only ones that can connect us to the delivery of this virus. We would be stupid to allow them to live."

"I totally agree. Your planning of this operation has been masterful. President Kim is aware of your outstanding work, and I know you will receive rich rewards upon the successful completion of your operation." Song saw Chin-Sun lower her head slightly as she accepted his words of praise. "I must leave you now. If I learn anything further, we will meet again. Also, you may contact me at any time if you develop further information." Song stood and walked off.

Chin-Sun was unsure as to whether Song had or had not received the vaccine. She knew that she was not scheduled to receive the vaccine, which made all the talk of rewards meaningless. If she died as a result of the virus, it was just one more loose end that Kim had tied up.

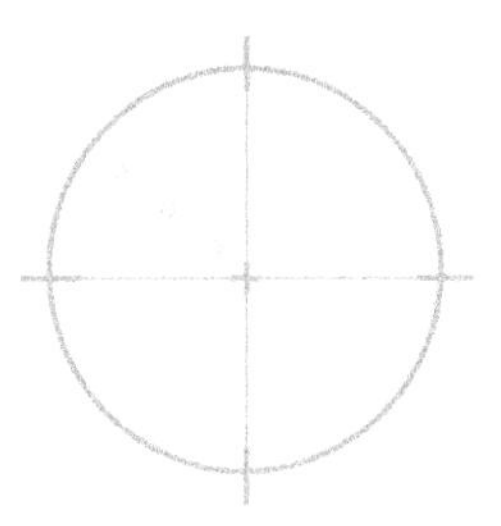

Chapter 51

Agent Johnson had enlisted another agent to listen to the sounds coming from Heather Lee's room. He did not want to have to listen to another session of their intimate coupling. That gave him time to ensure that an arrest warrant was issued for the two John Does in the room next to Heather's. Johnson also coordinated with the leader of the SWAT team on the plan to arrest Ms. Lee and her two compatriots.

It was about 9:00 AM when he once again took up listening to what was occurring in her room. It was quiet at first, but then he could hear them begin to wake up. He heard her order coffee for him and tea for her from room service. A few moments later, there was a knock on the door, and he could tell that the coffee and tea had arrived.

The next few minutes were consumed with small talk between Senator Kendricks and Heather. Johnson suddenly exclaimed to others in the van, "Oh, shit, here they go again." He switched on the sound so that the two other men in the vehicle could hear also. The three men listened to Senator Kendricks and Heather again consummate their friendship.

One of the men in the vehicle stated, "Boy, Senator Kendricks has a sweet deal. He's making it with a beautiful young Asian woman while we are sitting in this small van listening to their good time. There is something very wrong with that." Johnson and the other agent had to laugh in spite of themselves.

Shortly, they heard Kendricks invite Heather to join him in the shower. Twenty minutes later, the agents heard Kendricks getting dressed to leave.

The senator and Heather each made promises to the other that they would meet again in the near future. Johnson watched Kendricks leave the hotel, climb into his car, and drive off. Two FBI agents followed Kendricks as he headed back to Washington.

Johnson got on the radio to the SWAT team and stated, "Okay, gentlemen, now it's our turn. Let's execute the plan."

A total of eight agents were standing outside of Heather's room. Johnson and another agent were going to effectuate the arrest of Heather. The other six agents would assault the room containing Heather's two compatriots.

Johnson knocked on Lee's door and soon she answered, "Yes?"

Johnson replied, "Senator Kendricks asked me to deliver this gift to you."

"What is it?"

Johnson responded, "I don't know. It is gift wrapped. If you don't want to take it now, I can leave it at the front desk for you."

Suddenly the door opened to reveal Lee standing there in a robe. Johnson and the other agent quickly entered the room and pushed her onto the bed. Before she could even scream, Johnson had his hand over her mouth and stated, "I am from the FBI, and you are under arrest. If you say anything or scream, I will be forced to hurt you." At that point, Johnson heard the other team break into the next room.

The six agents entering the second room all had their weapons drawn. As they entered, the leader of the SWAT team yelled, "FBI, you are under arrest!" Before another word was said, the Koreans each pulled automatic weapons from holsters on their belts. After about 15 seconds, the gunfire was over. Both Koreans were dead, and three of the agents lay wounded or dying.

Johnson, who subdued and handcuffed Heather, rushed to the other room. He found one agent standing over the Koreans checking for life, and the two other agents kneeling next to the three agents who had fallen. One of the agents had been hit above his left eye and had died instantly. Another agent had been struck in the chest twice. He was alive only because he had been wearing body armor. The third agent was sitting on the floor holding his arm. He had been struck in the bicep of his right arm, and while in pain, would survive.

Johnson dialed 911 and told them they needed ambulances at the hotel. While waiting for them to arrive, he called Sam and reported what happened. Sam ordered a team of investigators to the hotel. Furthermore, he ordered Johnson to bring Lee to him. Johnson left immediately with Lee and a second agent.

Heather, with her hands cuffed behind her back, was screaming at Johnson as he put her into their vehicle and began the journey back to Washington. She was demanding a lawyer and wanted to talk to her parents. Johnson told her that would occur when they reached their destination. Even though he had told her several times to be quiet, she continued to scream and yell at the agents. Finally, Johnson reared back and slapped her across the face. He looked into her eyes and stated, “One of my agents has been killed and two others wounded because of you. If you continue to do this, I will simply shoot you and say you were trying to escape. Now, shut up!”

Heather looked at him with hatred in her eyes but said nothing more. When they arrived in Washington, she was taken directly to Sam’s office.

As they walked in, Heather began once again, “I want my lawyer and I want him now! You have no right to hold me without charges. I demand you let me go now!”

Sam eyed her closely and said, "Please sit down. I will explain to you what is going on."

Lee started to say something when Johnson grabbed her by the shoulders and shoved her into the chair. Standing behind her, he bent over and whispered, "I suggest you be quiet because he is not nearly as nice as I am."

After she settled down, Sam began, "You are under arrest for espionage, terrorism, and murder."

"I have not murdered anyone," she stated emphatically.

"That's true," Sam responded, "but your friends killed one of my agents. That makes you equally guilty."

"I want my attorney now. I know my rights."

"Well, in most circumstances, you would be right. But, as a terrorist, you are not afforded those rights. In fact, we are going to talk to you here for a while. If you're cooperative, you will stay here. If I hear that you have become uncooperative, you will be flown to Guantánamo immediately. As I'm sure you understand, we can hold you indefinitely at that location without trial. I can assure you that you will not see an attorney for many years. In fact, you will simply disappear from civilized society. It makes no difference to me which course you choose.

"You should know that we have audio recordings of you and Senator Kendricks. We have heard you elicit information regarding national security matters from him. While I am sure that you care about him..."

Heather shouted, "That bastard. I could care less what happens to him. He's never meant anything to me, and I screwed him only to get information."

Heather did not realize that this was being recorded for Senator Kendrick's listening.

Sam waved her off and said, "I'm done with her. Take her downstairs. If she gives you any trouble at all, I want to know about it."

As Heather was led out, Sam could hear her sobbing. She had just realized the situation she had put herself in.

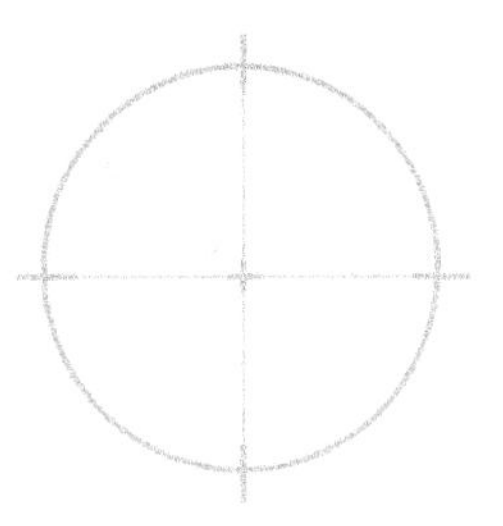

Chapter 52

President Kim was seated at his desk reviewing reports on the preparedness of his offensive missiles. He put the reports aside, convinced that his nation was prepared for any eventuality. He heard his email chirp and started reading the message concerning several students who had been arrested after a small protest. Kim thought for a moment and then answered the email, telling the person to eliminate these troublemakers.

There was a sharp rap on the door and his chief economic officer walked in. The man handed Kim the latest report on the state of their economy. He glanced at it quickly and saw that there was no change. Regardless of what actions Kim took, the news he received was always bad. He may have to find a new chief economic officer if the news is not better in the future.

Kim reached for his phone, dialed the number he knew by heart, and waited for the person to answer. A moment later, his mistress answered, "My love, how are you this morning?"

Her voice always warmed his heart and picked up his spirit. "As usual, the news has not been good. However, talking with you makes everything wonderful. What are your plans for the day?"

"I have no plans other than to please you. Would you like me to come to your home this afternoon?"

"It will depend on how my day goes. I will call you when I know my schedule. I can't wait to see you again."

She responded, "I await your call with great excitement." She clicked off the phone.

Again, there was a knock on Kim's door. He responded, "Come."

The door opened and the Doctor walked toward his desk. He said, "I have great news for you."

Kim responded, "Well, what is it?"

"I have been informed that all of our shipments of the virus have reached their destinations. We are ready to begin the attack."

Kim thought for a moment and then responded, "That is very good news indeed."

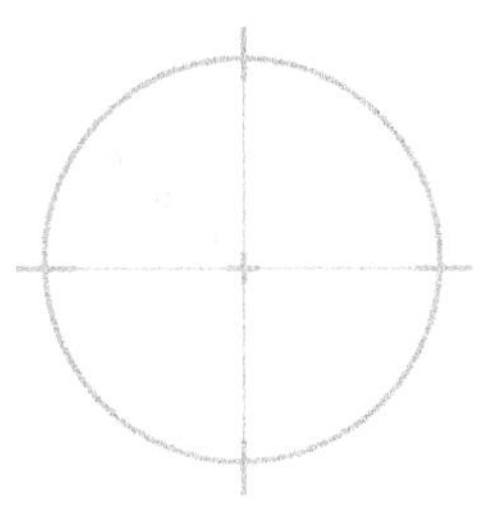

Chapter 53

There is a warehouse located in Alexandria, Virginia, which is used by the FBI when they need a large working space. The three professors were seated at one end of that warehouse. In front of them were long tables, some with computers and laptops. Also, there were at least 100 FBI agents working feverishly to determine which containers were being sent to the target cities.

At the far end of the warehouse, agents were working with port officials on the West Coast. They reviewed all the information they could develop on shipping containers arriving from China. Initially, Sam had ordered that all containers from Asia were to be checked. Since then, he had revised his order so that only those containers coming from China were to be looked into. He simply did not have the resources to do more. He hoped his decision was correct.

Once they gathered that information, it was sent to the second section of agents, whose job was to review, analyze, and then determine which containers were headed to the target cities. Then that information was sent to the third group of agents, whose responsibility it was to find where those containers went in each target city. The final section of agents forwarded that information to other agents in the target cities who were prepared to find and search those containers.

"It seems to me that this is taking a long time to get the information to the agents in the field," stated Mac.

Derek answered, "Don't you understand that we are talking about thousands and thousands of shipping containers. The trade we have with China is enormous. You can't just turn a switch and get the answer. This is long and tedious work to get the information we need."

"I know, I know," responded Mac, "but it is just so damned frustrating waiting here and realizing we may be late in finding the terrorist who will be spreading the virus. The sooner we are on our way, the better."

Ty interjected, "I'm with you on that Mac. But the only option we have is to wait and see if we get lucky."

The door behind them opened and Sam walked in. "What is the matter, guys? You look so downtrodden. What's up?"

Mac explained the conversation they were having. "Sam, this waiting is so damned frustrating. Is there something we can do to speed things up?"

Sam answered, "That is why I'm here. I wanted to talk to you about this matter. You sitting here on your ass is of no help to us. We need each of you to pick the city that you believe the terrorists will strike. I don't care how you make that determination. It can be based on Mac's famous gut feeling. Once you've made that determination, you need to get your butts out to that city and be ready to start searching for shipping containers. There will be other agents assigned to the other cities. So, where do each of you want to go?"

I answered, "I want to go to Philadelphia. I believe they may try to strike where our Constitution and Declaration of Independence were signed."

Ty spoke next, "I think I'll try Chicago because there are so many areas where you can spread the virus."

Mac was quiet for a moment before he spoke. "For some reason, I believe that these bastards will start with the smaller cities, I'm going to Minneapolis."

"Okay," Sam stated, "we need to get you on your way. The agent who accompanied you here will be with you on this trip also. If I determine that you are in the wrong city or cities, I will let you know. We need to be flexible enough to change when needed."

Sam turned and left the building.

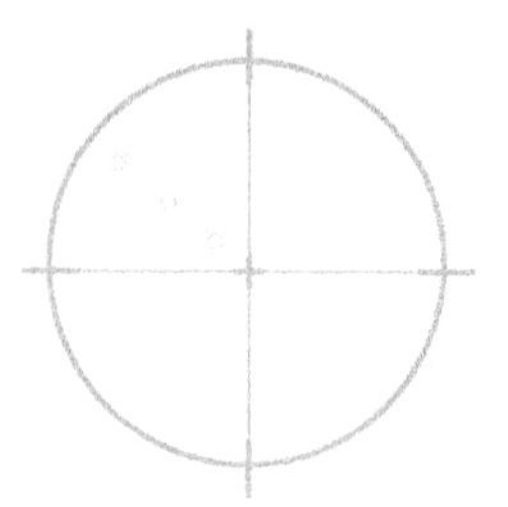

Chapter 54

It was a short flight from Washington to Philadelphia. Derek and I had speculated about whether I'd made the right choice in selecting Philadelphia. There was no way to tell if it was correct or not; we just had to wait and see if anyone showed up. We checked into our hotel on the outskirts of the city. Derek called the head agent stationed here who was waiting for word on which warehouse we should examine.

Derek and I decided we would have lunch before meeting up with the other agents. We went to a small café near the hotel and sat down in a booth. Derek ordered a chef salad, and I ordered a cheeseburger with everything on it. Just to be sure I wouldn't get hungry later, I asked for a side of fries also. I looked at Derek and stated, "What kind of sissy have you become, Derek? Here you have a small café, and they probably have the best burgers in town. And what are you eating, vegetables. I'm sorely disappointed in you, young man."

"DJ, you sound just like that Tyrannosaurus Rex buddy of yours, Mac. I had thought better of you."

"My friend, there is simply nothing finer in this land than a good hamburger. My doctor told me I needed to eat more greens. I asked him if he wanted me to get on my knees and forge in the grass. He didn't think that was nearly as funny as I did. Seriously, are you eating greens with a little protein on top?"

"DJ, the research is clear. People live longer if they eat less beef and more vegetables. I intend to live to a ripe old age."

"I'm 65 and have been eating hamburgers since I was five. Look at me, except for a little belly slipping over my belt, I'm in great shape. If you live to that ripe old age you talk about, it just means that someone will be changing your diaper for a longer period of time."

"DJ, do you have any idea what's in your intestines? I think you'd be shocked."

"Hell, Derek, I'm sure there are a couple of burgers from the 60s still floating around in there. But I'll tell you what. I'm sure they were good going down and they haven't bothered me since."

Derek looked at me and finally said," DJ, you are incorrigible, simply incorrigible."

"My mother thanks you, my father thanks you and I thank you. By the way, did you hear about the man who went to see his doctor. He told the doctor he wanted to live to a happy old age and wanted to make sure he was doing everything right. The doctor asked him if he smoked, and he replied that he never had. The doctor asked him if he drank, and he replied that he had never partaken of liquor. The doctor asked him if he had a happy sex life. The man replied that he wasn't married, and sex never meant anything to him anyway. Finally, the doctor looked at him and said, "Given your answers, why do you care how long you live?"

Derek laughed out loud, looked at me, and shook his head. Changing the subject, he said, "Why don't we go down and meet the other agents?"

I figured he wasn't susceptible to my changing his views on appropriate eating habits, so we finished our meal and headed to where the other agents were located.

When we walked into the downtown office, I counted ten agents waiting to be sent to warehouses that were thought to house a suspicious cargo container. They indicated that they had a hazmat team ready to take whatever action was necessary. I sat there for several hours, listening to the agents tell war stories about their time in the Bureau. Some were funny, some were unbelievable, and some were tragic.

About 5:00 PM, the agent in charge received a phone call indicating there was a certain shipping container that had been delivered to a warehouse a few miles away which needed to be checked. The twelve of us crammed into three cars and headed there as fast as we could. Upon arriving, the lead agent talked with the man in charge of the warehouse. He was not very cooperative because it was past the time for him to leave for home.

When the agent explained what he wanted, the man led us back into his office. He was able to track down the number of the container and where it was located. One agent had a tool to cut the lock off. It took him a few minutes to accomplish that. He swung the door open, and we saw that the container was fully packed. We had been told that we should be looking for a large cylinder like those that contained oxygen. The agents emptied the container rather quickly, but no cylinders were found. They tried to repack the container as it had been previously but were not very successful. The man from the warehouse wanted to leave so he told the agents he would repack it in the morning.

We thanked him and left the warehouse. It did not take long for us to realize that this search would be repeated time and time again. Only two or three agents were needed to respond to any shipping container that was called in.

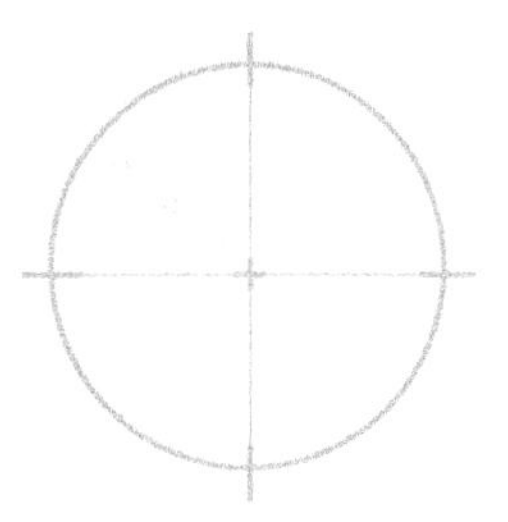

Chapter 55

Ann got into her new car, a white Toyota Land Cruiser, and headed out on a dirt road at the ranch until she reached the pavement of the street. After about ten minutes, she pulled up outside of Sandy's home, honked the horn, and waited with a smile on her face. She had a proposal for her two friends that she would explain at dinner. Sandy walked out and whistled at Ann's new car.

Leanne's house was a mere ten-minute drive from Sandy's and Ann made it in seven and half minutes. Leanne was sitting on the chair on her porch waiting for the two women to arrive. She heard Ann before she saw her, which prompted her to rise and walk to the street. She hopped into the back seat, and Ann was on her way.

"Hey, ladies, what sounds good to eat?" Ann asked. After much discussion, the three women decided to eat in a small bistro downtown. After they had been seated and ordered their drinks, Ann continued the conversation. "Well, I have a proposal for you. Our guys have been gone for a while now. I don't know about you, but I'm missing Mac. I think we should consider going to be with them. What say you?"

Sandy replied first, "I am missing my man too. I think that is an outstanding idea."

Leanne looked at the two of them and said, "I'm in, but aren't each of them in a different city? I mean, Ty is in Chicago. Where are your guys now?"

"DJ is in Philadelphia," answered Sandy. She looked at Ann and asked, "Mac is in Minneapolis, isn't he?" Ann nodded her agreement. The waitress appeared, took their order and left. "Ann, have you talked to Mac about your idea?"

"No, but what is he going to say? If he tells me no, I will ask him the name of his girlfriend in Minneapolis." All three women started laughing.

Leanne spoke next, "Ty will tell me it would be dangerous."

"DJ will say the same thing. We can tell our husbands if we don't come to see them, there must be some men here we can see." Leanne and Sandy high-fived each other.

Ann was quiet for a while before saying, "Just so you know, I will be bringing my weapon with me, and I suggest the two of you do the same."

Leanne looked at Ann and stated, "Do you really think we may need to use our weapons?"

"I think the chances are pretty small. However, I would not want to be without it if the need arose. Who knows, we may have to protect the guys from themselves and the bad guys," she said laughingly.

Sandy agreed. "I'm definitely going to bring mine too. I'd rather be safe than sorry."

Leanne looked at both of us and said, "Okay, I'll bring mine too, for no other reason than to make sure you two do not kill our husbands. As you know, I have told Ty that if he gets hurt, he may lose his balls. That's for me to do, not you two. I just want to make sure that we understand each other."

After Sandy finished laughing, she asked, "Let's call our guys tonight and tell them what the three of us are going to do. I think if they give us any trouble, we can use each other for support."

Soon, the women's meals came and there was no further talk about seeing their husbands. When Sandy got home, she called me at my hotel and told me that she had just come from dinner with Ann and Leanne. "I wish I could've been there like a fly on the wall. I may have learned something."

"I'm sure you would have." Sandy replied. "All we did was tell lies about our husbands which, by the way, was quite funny. Anyway, I have something I want to propose to you. In the next day or two, I intend to fly to Philadelphia so that I can be with you. Ann and Leanne are having the same conversation with their guys. If I hear any disagreement from you, I will have to check out the local boys here. Also, we will be coming armed."

From the tone of her voice, I knew there was not much I could do about changing her mind. Also, I missed her terribly. "Okay, you must agree to one condition. If you are in any danger at all, you must do what I tell you without argument. Can you agree to that?"

"Absolutely! I will make arrangements tonight and tell you tomorrow when you can pick me up at the airport."

"I can't wait to see you, babe." Our conversation ended shortly thereafter.

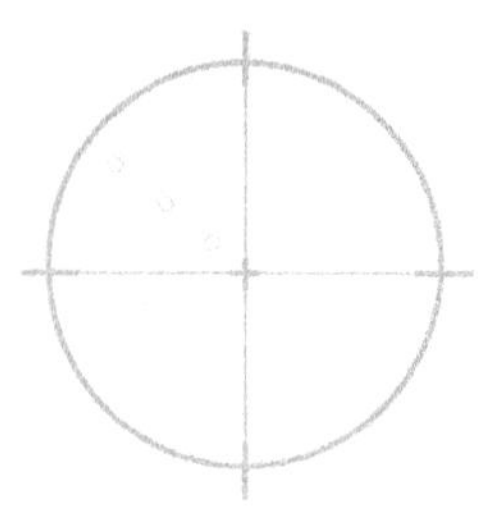

Chapter 56

Chin-Sun sat in a corner booth in the back waiting for Ahmed and Kamil. It was midafternoon so the small café had few patrons. She had chosen to meet the two in New York because of the diverse nature of the population. It was unlikely that either of them would stand out or draw attention to themselves. The day was overcast and the wind coming off the water would chill the unsuspecting. Chin-Sun had informed the two men that this would hopefully be their last meeting.

Sitting beside her was a small bag that held an even smaller cooler. It contained two small vials and four syringes. Within each vial was the vaccine for the two men. She intended to leave the bag with the men so that they could inject themselves in the privacy of their hotel room.

She looked up, saw the door open and recognized Ahmed and Kamil as they entered. They looked around the café and then headed toward where she was seated. Chin-Sun nodded to the two men, handed them the menu, and asked what they would like to eat. Ahmed smiled at her and said that they'd eaten earlier but would like some tea. She waved at the waitress, who came and took their drink order.

Getting down to business, Chin-Sun stated, "How have your reconnaissance efforts gone?"

Kamil answered, "We have examined each of the target cities and are prepared to move forward. Do you have a time for us to begin yet?"

"Yes, the deliveries have all been made. I have a list of addresses in each city where you can find the virus. I am also giving you a list of names and phone numbers in each city that you can call and get delivery of the backpacks containing the small empty cylinders.

"As to the start date, I suggest we begin as soon as possible. The longer we delay this attack, the more likely it is that our plans could be discovered. I suggest we aim for the day after tomorrow, but I will leave it up to you. That will give you sufficient time to reach your first target city, get the backpacks, and fill them in the warehouses. I presume that you have planned one day for each city. Is that correct?"

Ahmed nodded his agreement.

"It is important for both of you to keep in contact with each other during the next few days. It would be best if you contact one another after you have delivered the virus in the city you are in. I will be calling Ahmed every two or three days to check on your progress. Does this meet with your approval?"

Ahmed responded, "I don't see any problem with that."

Chin-Sun reached down and pulled the small bag up and placed it on the table. "In this bag is a small cooler. It contains a vial of the vaccine for each of you. It also has four syringes that you use to inject the vaccine. There are instructions that you need to follow for administering the vaccine. In essence, you will use one syringe to take half of the material in the vial and inject it before you begin the delivery process. There's another syringe that can be used with the remaining vaccine and should be injected one week after the initial injection. Following the processes described will keep you safe from the virus. You will need no further injections following the first two. I only have one cooler available to me, so I suggest that one of you buy an additional cooler or plan to meet up one week after the first injection. Do you have any questions?"

Kamil spoke first, "Are you sure that this vaccine will keep us safe from the virus? I'm concerned about that."

"The vaccine you will receive is the same one that I will inject into my body tomorrow. I've been assured by the highest authority that the vaccine will keep all of us safe. Other questions?"

Ahmed responded, "If I need to contact you, do I use the same phone number as always? I don't expect that I will need to call you, but I want to be sure I have the right number."

"Yes, I'll be using the same phone number." No other questions were asked of her by the two men. "Well, gentlemen, you are about to deal a devastating blow to this country. It has been my honor to work with you toward this goal." She reached across the table and shook each of the men's hands. "Good luck."

Chin-Sun watched the two men stand, walk to the door, and exit onto the street. She wondered how two seemingly intelligent men could believe that her country would leave them alive after they carried out their attacks.

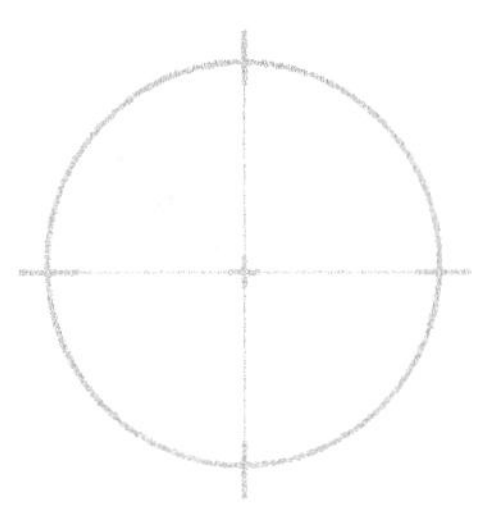

Chapter 57

It had been a long day in the Senate for Senator Kendricks. He had several committee meetings he had to attend plus several votes on the floor of the Senate. It was shortly after 6:00 PM, and he was ready to go home. As he was walking to his car, he was approached by two men in suits. The first man introduced himself as agent Jim Franks of the FBI. He also introduced agent John Wells. Both men produced their identification and showed those to the senator.

After looking at their badges, Senator Kendricks asked, "What can I do for you gentlemen?"

Agent Franks responded, "We were asked by Director Sam Wyman to come and speak with you. He would like you to allow us to take you to a meeting with him. At the conclusion of that meeting, we will take you back to your car. Is that agreeable with you?"

Kendricks thought for a moment and answered, "Gentlemen, I am very tired after a long day in this building. Could we not arrange a time for tomorrow or the next day?"

Franks looked at the senator and said, "The director stated that it was very important that he talk with you today and he hoped this would not be too great an inconvenience." Frank did not inform the senator that if he refused to come with them, they were going to arrest him on the spot.

Kendricks nodded and stated, "Then let's go. I know the director wouldn't approach me in this way unless it was important."

It was a short drive to the FBI building and Franks pulled his car into the underground parking lot. He led the senator to the elevators and then pushed the button to get to the floor where Sam's office was located. When the three men entered Sam's office suite, the assistant told him to go right in. As they entered Sam's office, Franks could see that the director was seated at his desk talking on the phone. Sam motioned for Kendricks to be seated before him. The two agents left the office.

Hanging up, Sam opened the conversation by stating, "Thank you, Senator, for joining me. Since it is the end of the day, I'm sure this is an inconvenience for you."

"I know you would not ask me here if it wasn't important. So, what's going on?"

"Senator, I'm going to be very frank with you. You will not like what you're about to hear." Sam watched Kendricks move forward in his chair with a look of concern on his face. "If you had not come here voluntarily, the agents were prepared to arrest you and bring you here."

"Arrest me? Surely, you're joking."

Sam noticed the Kendricks face had paled considerably. "I'm going to tell you why you would be arrested, but I want you to remain silent until I finished. Can you do that?"

The senator nodded his head in agreement.

"First and foremost, your mistress, Heather Lee, is an admitted North Korean agent. We have learned that each of the times you were in the hotel with her, you were video- and audio-taped by two other North Korean agents. Ms. Lee was arrested after the last time you were together. When the agents attempted to arrest the two other North Korean agents, one of my agents was killed, two others were wounded, and the North Koreans were killed.

"The courts authorized us to record the hotel room and both of your phones. Needless to say, we have you passing information to

Ms. Lee that we believe was communicated to the North Koreans. You knew from your briefings in the Senate that the US was facing a potential terrorist attack from North Korea.

"Would you like to say anything about what I have told you? I will have my agents read you your rights first."

Sam called his assistant and had the two agents return to his office. "Agent Franks, would you read the senator his constitutional rights please?" The agent did as he was requested and left the room. "Well, Senator, again, do you have anything you'd like to say?"

"I don't think so," stammered Kendricks. "What happens now?"

"I suggest that you not try to contact Ms. Lee because she is currently in federal custody at Guantánamo. Your case has been referred to the Attorney General for a decision on what charges should be filed. I think it's safe to say, Senator, your life has changed dramatically. This matter will be handled normally by the Justice Department, which means you will be called in to answer the charges. Since I've given you the courtesy of not arresting you, I suggest that you make no wild claims about this to the press. If you do, I'll have you arrested immediately. Do you understand?"

"Yes, I understand. I also appreciate the courtesy you have shown me by not arresting me at this time. I will have my lawyer contact the Justice Department so that I can answer these charges."

The senator stood and walked somewhat shakily to the door. As he left the office, the two agents took him back to his car. During that drive, no words were exchanged.

Kendricks drove home to an empty house. His wife was visiting some friends in New York. The senator walked to his desk and slowly sat down, trying to make sense of what had occurred. How could he have been so blind to the fact that Heather might have been an agent of North Korea. He was so wrapped up in her beauty and their love life that he had never even considered the possibility.

Kendricks realized that his senate career was over and certainly any hopes he had of becoming president. For a moment, Kendricks thought he should try to call Heather to see if this was simply a bad dream. The senator shook his head as he contemplated the fact that an FBI agent had been killed because of him.

His first instinct was to call his campaign group to seek their advice. What advice can someone give a man who has fallen for the oldest trick in the book—a young and exciting woman. When he reviewed his entire time with Heather, Kendricks realized he had been the target all along. The senator felt the bile rise in his throat as he thought of his guilt in this matter.

There was really no one he could talk to given what the FBI knew. His friends would shun him, as well they should. His fellow senators will stay as far away from him as they could. They did not want to be associated with his actions.

Finally, he picked up the phone and dialed his wife. Within two rings, she answered. Kendricks said, "You know, my dear, I have always loved you."

She responded, "And I love you also. Why are you telling me this?"

"Because I wanted to. Are you having a good time in New York?" His wife spent the next five minutes outlining what she had been doing since leaving Washington. "That sounds like fun."

"It certainly is and has been fun. I must run now dear; the girls are waiting for me."

After hanging up, he used a small key to open the side drawer of his desk. Kendricks pulled out a gray revolver. He had not used or shot the weapon for several years. He set the gun on the desk and opened the center drawer. Kendricks pulled out a piece of his senate stationery. He wrote "I have failed in my duty to my country. I'm so very sorry."

Kendricks picked up the weapon, placed the barrel in his mouth, and thought of Heather. Those were his last thoughts as he pulled the trigger.

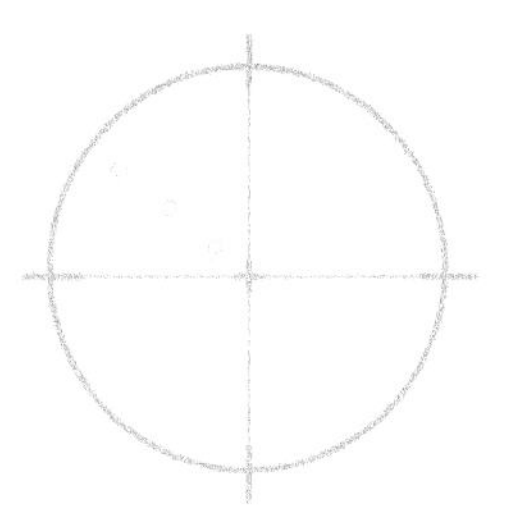

Chapter 58

After leaving their meeting with Chin-Sun, Ahmed and Kamil drove to their hotel in New York. On the way, they stopped and purchased an additional cooler for Ahmed. Once in the room, the men opened the cooler and saw the instructions for administering the vaccine. It appeared to be relatively straightforward to them. Ahmed took his vial and inserted the needle as instructed. He withdrew half of the liquid from the vial and held it up to look at it in the light.

Looking at Kamil, he said, "Well, I might as well do this." Ahmed held the syringe between his thumb and index finger and jabbed it into his arm. Slowly, he injected the contents. "I didn't feel the needle go in nor any pain when I injected the vaccine. I think I'm feeling better about our work with the virus."

Kamil followed the same protocol to inoculate himself from the virus. "I hope this works as she said it would. Otherwise, we're dead."

That evening, they made plans to begin their journey to their target cities. Ahmed was driving up to Boston and Kamil to St. Louis. The next morning, the two men ate a hearty breakfast in the hotel's restaurant. Afterwards, they headed back to the room, packed and checked out. Ahmed would reach Boston that afternoon, but Kamil would not reach St. Louis until late that night or the next morning.

The drive for Ahmed was easy and he checked into a hotel about 4:00 PM. He called his contact with the backpack and arranged to meet him at 7:00 PM. The exchange went smoothly, and Ahmed left to find the warehouse where the shipping container containing the cylinder with the virus was kept. The warehouse was located in a small industrial area that had several similar-looking buildings. Ahmed drove around the area to determine if the warehouse was being watched. He did not see anything initially, so he parked his vehicle three blocks away. Reaching the industrial area on foot, Ahmed made sure to stay in the shadows. He saw no cars or other vehicles that might have been used for surveillance, and carefully watched the warehouses near the one he wished to enter.

Unlike the other warehouses, someone was situated in a warehouse across the street from the warehouse where his cylinder was located. Lights shone through the windows of a second-floor office, and occasionally, he saw someone moving past the window.

At 10:00 PM, a car drove up and stopped near the door of the warehouse he was watching. A moment later, someone exited the warehouse and came around to the driver's side of the car. He watched the driver open the door and get out and the other man get in and drive off. Then the driver walked to the door, opened it and walked in. A few moments later, Ahmed saw the driver standing in the window of the upstairs office. He was holding what appeared to be binoculars to his eyes as he looked at Ahmed's warehouse. Obviously, the warehouse he needed to enter was under surveillance.

Ahmed continued walking through the shadows as he checked all the warehouses from which someone could observe his warehouse. He found no other evidence of surveillance.

At the back of his warehouse, Ahmed saw that there was a single window that could be accessed from the outside and could not be seen by the person surveilling his warehouse. He walked up to the window, pushed gently, and was relieved to find that the window was not locked. Ahmed climbed through the office window, closed it, and walked through the office to the floor of the warehouse. Ahmed made sure that no lights were turned on and he did not use the flashlight he carried. He searched the warehouse until he found the shipping container he was looking for. Ahmed took out a hammer he was carrying and pried the lock off of the shipping container. After moving several boxes and crates, he spotted the cylinder he was looking for.

Ahmed took off the backpack and attached it to the cylinder as he had been instructed and opened the valve to allow the virus to flow into the small cylinder in his backpack. When it was full, he disconnected the cylinder and separated it from the backpack. Ahmed placed the cylinder back in the container, repacked it, and closed it as best as he could.

After putting the backpack on, the Saudi could barely tell the difference in the weight of the backpack now that it contained the virus. He walked back to the office, opened the window, and crawled out. Ahmed shut the window but made sure that he could reopen it. Carefully, he made his way through the shadows and away from the warehouse. It took several minutes before he reached his car. Ahmed drove off heading for his hotel.

When he was safely in his room, Ahmed phoned Kamil and told him about the surveillance of his warehouse. He warned him to be extremely careful in approaching his warehouse in St. Louis. Kamil, who was still driving, promised he would take extra care when he looked for his warehouse the next evening.

The next morning, Kamil obtained his backpack from a sleeper asset and decided to drive toward the warehouse's location. As he drove around, Kamil was able to determine that the warehouse he was looking for was at the end of a long street surrounded by farmland. Kamil did not see any vehicles or individuals that concerned him.

Much later, about 2:00 AM the next morning, Kamil drove down the long dirt road that separated the farmland into two parcels. He parked and started making his way through the farm field to the warehouse, approximately one-quarter mile away. Kamil stumbled in the field as he felt his way toward the warehouse. When Kamil reached the warehouse, there were no lights or evidence that anyone was present. He picked the lock on the door and entered the building as quietly as possible. After searching for an hour, Kamil found the container that carried the cylinder he was looking for. Like Ahmed, Kamil filled his backpack as instructed.

Kamil realized that he would have to come back and refill his backpack, which would expose him to possible apprehension. Kamil decided that he would take the cylinder with him and eliminate the need to return to the warehouse.

After two hours of strenuous effort in the dark and dragging the cylinder through the field, Kamil reached his car. He laid the back seat of the SUV down and placed the cylinder in the back. He covered the cylinder with a blanket that he had brought with him from the hotel. Kamil turned the car around and drove back down the dirt road. Soon, he pulled into the parking lot of his hotel. Looking around and seeing that all the lights were off, Kamil carried the cylinder into his room. Exhausted, he fell into bed and was asleep moments later.

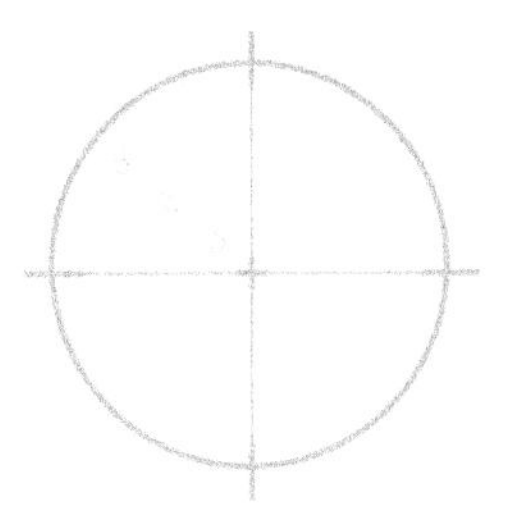

Chapter 59

Sam arrived at his office at 8:00 AM, an hour past his normal time. He walked over to the coffee machine and fixed his third cup of coffee of the day. On his desk was the latest edition of the *Washington Post*. His assistant always made sure that the *Post* was there for him to read when he started his day.

As he opened his paper, he saw a picture of Senator Kendricks on the front page. The story explained that the senator's top aide had gone to his house to discuss senate business and discovered the senator at his desk, a gun on the floor. The senator had been shot in the head. The story speculated that for some reason the senator had taken his own life. There was no evidence of foul play to be found in the home.

Wyman was a little surprised he'd not been informed of this event by the Washington FBI field office. Evidently, the Washington Metropolitan Police Department did not feel that this was a federal issue but rather a local one. It still seemed somewhat surprising that the FBI had not been notified. Perhaps they had been, but the news had not been forwarded to him.

Sam took a sip of his coffee and appreciated the full-bodied taste. He wondered if the national security people would be coming to talk to him. Given the fact that Kendricks was on the intelligence committee, it was likely he would be approached.

He thought about the senator, a rising star, who had fallen to earth. Because of the senator's powerful position, Sam understood the weakness certain men had for beautiful women. History was rife with the stories of good men having been led astray by beautiful and evil women. He did not feel sorry for Kendricks, who had made his own bed and he had decided how to end the scandal that surely was coming. Sam wondered whether Heather Lee had heard of Kendricks' death. She probably would get some satisfaction in it if she had.

He called his assistant and asked her to get an update on how the agency was coming with tracking down Chinese containers coming into the United States. Shortly, the man leading the effort, Jim Driscoll, called Sam. "Director, as you know, we are tracking a tremendous number of Chinese containers. We have found a good many of them, but I'm afraid there are many more that are unaccounted for. "

"Do you have any estimate as to when we will find all Chinese containers in the target cities?"

"Not at this time, sir. The number of shipping containers coming into this country from China makes our effort almost impossible. However, we shall try to find all of them."

Sam responded, "I appreciate all the efforts you've been making. Remember, we're talking about thousands, if not millions, of lives in the balance here. Keep up the good work. Call me if you have anything new." Sam hung up the phone and felt some fear in his heart. If these attacks go forward, he thought, our country will never be the same.

An hour later, the phone rang, and Sam answered it, "Hello."

Jim Driscoll responded, "Hello, Sam. It's Jim again."

"Do you have some new information for me?"

"Maybe. It may be nothing. We followed a shipment to St. Louis where it arrived a couple of days ago. Our agents went to the warehouse in question and talked to the security guard. He was leading them through the warehouse for inspection when they discovered a container that had been broken into. Something was obviously missing. The container was supposed to be carrying miscellaneous tools and equipment.

"After doing some additional investigation, the agents found a window that was unlocked. I should say that the warehouse was surrounded by farmland. The agents noticed footsteps and drag marks in the field. They followed the trail until it reached a dirt road. The trail ended there. As I said, it may be nothing more than some weed being snuck into the country. Anyway, I thought you would want to know in case you were able to tie it up with other information you may have."

"Thanks, Jim," responded Sam, "I will put additional agents on this to see what they can find." Sam knew that this information could be simply someone breaking into find something of value. However, the sinking feeling he felt in the pit of his stomach told him that this may have been the first cylinder they hoped to find. He ordered out an FBI criminal investigation team to St. Louis to see what they could find.

At this point, all he could do was wait and see what developed.

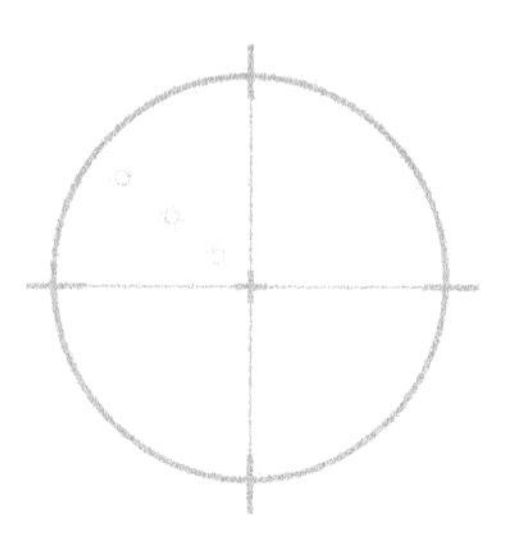

Chapter 60

Sandy's flight was scheduled to arrive at 6:15 PM at the Philadelphia airport. I made sure to arrive early. We agreed that I would meet her at baggage claim. I was sitting in a chair against the wall watching people coming toward their assigned baggage carousel. I saw Sandy before she saw me, so I stood and walked toward her. Soon, she waved at me and a few moments later, we were standing in front of one another. After a long embrace, I said, "Boy, have I missed you!"

She gave me a warm kiss and answered, "I've missed you too. Oh, there's my bag," she said pointing at a bag on the carousel.

I walked over, picked it up and said, "So, you didn't bring the big one, huh?" Sandy routinely packed more than I did, and it was a constant joke between us. As we headed toward where my rental car was parked, I asked, "How was your flight? Any problems?"

"It was great. I sat next to a most interesting fellow. He was a professor of botany at some college in the area. For the entire flight, we talked about plants. It was so interesting."

"Of that, I have no doubt. If I had been flying with you, I would've been able to catch up on my needed sleep," I said, winking at her. We arrived at the rental car, and I opened the door for her. "Let's go to the hotel and get you set up there. If you are hungry, we can grab a bite to eat later. How does that sound?"

"That works. I sure have missed you," she responded. "Have you made any progress in finding the terrorists?"

"Nothing yet. In fact, it's been extremely boring. I was talking to Mac yesterday and he said it reminded him of some of the stakeouts he was on early in his career. All we do is sit, wait, and watch. There are several warehouses around the city that have received many shipping containers from China. We must keep a 24/7 watch on each one. The Bureau has sent multiple agents to assist. Initially, we thought we needed two or three agents watching a warehouse at any given time. Now we just have one. That is except for me. Since I am not an agent, I am watching with Derek."

"Are you reconsidering working with the FBI on this?"

"No, not at all. It's just so damned frustrating. There are so many containers that could carry the virus. The number of people who could die is staggering. Derek told me that there is evidence that containers in Boston and St. Louis may have already been accessed. If there was a cylinder containing the virus, the terrorists may already be in the process of distributing it."

We arrived at our hotel and got Sandy settled. She decided she would like to have a bite to eat, so we headed for a diner I had been eating at regularly. After we entered, Sandy smiled saying, "Well, this certainly is a DJ type of diner. I presume that their number-one menu item is a hamburger."

"You know me too well." After she reviewed the limited menu, she stated, "I think I'll just have a salad with some grilled chicken on it. It takes a lot to screw up that order, but I will have to wait and see." The look she gave me indicated she did not have high hopes for this meal. In an effort to keep her off balance, I ordered spaghetti and meatballs.

"When am I going to see the warehouse?"

"What do you mean?" I asked.

"I want to see where you get to be so bored. I came to be with you, not to sit in the hotel room waiting for you to come back."

"It's not my call, but I doubt Derek will allow it."

Winking at me, she said, "Well, we will see about that. I will talk with him in the morning."

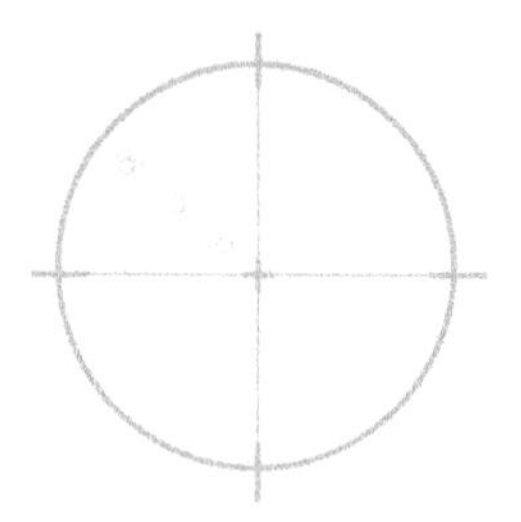

Chapter 61

Mael and Pierre were seated in a small bistro in central Paris awaiting their meal. They usually met once a week for lunch to catch up and to get out of the office. This bistro was a typical eating establishment in Paris. In this city, one was never rushed to finish your meal. To the contrary, it was expected that you would savor the meal and take the time that was required to do so.

The two men were discussing potential terrorist attacks in France as there was some concern that Marseilles and Lyons could be targets. Pierre had ordered additional agents to those cities who would assist the local officials in their investigation. While this was the normal protocol, it had never produced actionable results. He felt it was a waste of resources. However, political forces rarely made good use of resources to fight terrorism.

Pierre stated, "My greatest frustration in doing this job is the interference I receive from politicians. If they would simply let us do our jobs, we would be more effective. However, unfortunately, they seem to believe that they are better experts in stopping terrorism than we are."

Mael responded, "I am so thankful that I don't have to deal with those pressures. I do not have the patience to work with stupid people. I would probably simply shoot them and dump their bodies in the Seine."

Pierre smiled at him and responded, "That may be the very best way to deal with them."

As both men laughed, Mael's phone rang. He looked at Pierre, who indicated he should answer. "Hello." He listened for a few moments and then placed his hand over the phone and stated, "I need to take this call. I will go outside." Mael stood and walked out the door of the bistro.

He was outside for about ten minutes listening to the caller and asking questions. After hanging up, he returned to the table and sat down.

Pierre looked at him and stated, "Well?"

"That was one of my agents working in Lyon. He arrested an individual who they were led to believe knew about a potential attack in Lyon. The person denied any and all knowledge of an attack being planned in that city. However, he indicated that he had heard of an attack that was going to happen shortly in the United States. The man told our agent he heard that terrorists were going to use a deadly virus that can be spread through the air. That's all he really knew."

"Why don't you pass that information onto your FBI contact right now. There is no time to lose," Pierre said.

Mael pulled out his phone and dialed Sam's number. Sam answered groggily on the third ring. "Sam, Mael here. My boss wanted me to call you at this early hour and give you some information we just received. One of our agents was told by an informant that he had heard that your country would be attacked in the near future. The interesting part was that he indicated the attack involved a deadly virus spread through the air. I know this isn't much, but I want to give it to you as soon as I could."

"I appreciate your call. It confirms what we have suspected." Sam then brought Mael up to speed on what was happening in the

US. "We're trying to cover every container arriving from China, but the numbers are so large, I'm not sure we will be able to do it. Thanks for the information, Mael. I will talk to you later."

Sam then called the director of the Center for Disease Control and Prevention. He passed on the information he had received from Mael and described the results of their investigation. "I suggest you get ready because we may have a new pandemic to deal with."

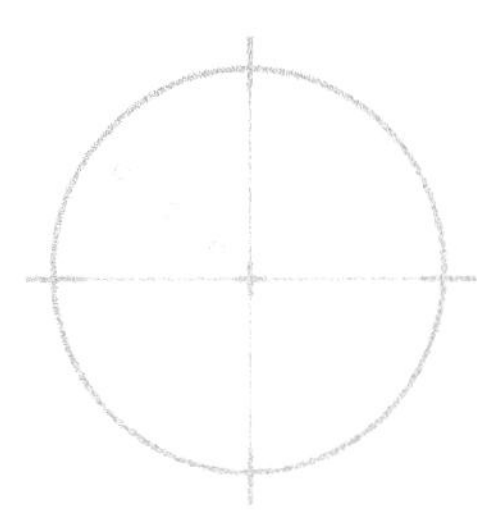

Chapter 62

Ahmed was in his Boston hotel room preparing for his first day delivering the virus. He wore gray slacks, a white shirt, and a dark blue blazer. Over his shoulder, Ahmed carried his backpack. His pants pocket held a device similar to a small garage door opener. To deliver the virus, all he had to do was press the button on the device. The spray could not be seen nor heard as he walked around.

Previously that day, Ahmed had purchased one of the final tickets for a concert at Symphony Hall. His research had shown him that this venue could seat over 2,500 people. Once his preparations were complete, he took a cab from his hotel to Symphony Hall. Upon entering the building, he went straight to the concert hall and walked in. The lobby was nearly full of people waiting to enjoy the concert. The terrorist smiled to himself, realizing that this could be the last concert they would ever listen to.

Pushing the button, Ahmed initiated the spray and began to walk down the aisle toward the stage. He turned and walked in front of the stage and back up the second aisle until he reached the door. He turned around and walked down the aisle until he found a row with few people seated in it. He walked through the row, continuing to spray the virus until he reached the far aisle. Walking up the aisle and out of the hall, Ahmed found the restrooms and walked into the men's room, spraying as he walked. Ahmed made sure that the surfaces around the sink received the spray as well.

Finishing, he walked to the entrance of the hall, stopped spraying and walked into the night air.

Ahmed hailed a cab to take him to the MGM Music Hall at Fenway. He had purchased a ticket for the evening event earlier in the day. He entered the concert venue and walked down one of the aisles. Ahmed knew he was getting close to running out of the virus, so he moved quickly, spreading it as far as he could. Once the device was empty, Ahmed left the hall and signaled for a cab to take him to his hotel.

Ahmed left Boston the next morning and drove to Pittsburgh, his next target. When Ahmed reached his room, he decided to call Kamil to see how he had progressed. Soon, Ahmed was speaking with Kamil. "How did your day go?"

Kamil answered, "Very well, I must admit. Tell me what you did."

"I delivered the virus to two concert venues. I ran out of the virus and came back to my hotel. Because my warehouse was under surveillance, I decided not to go back to reload, but rather move on to Pittsburgh. Where did you deliver the spray?"

"Well, I took a different approach than you did," replied Kamil. "As we discussed, I checked the various St. Louis concert venues here, but none had any events scheduled. I decided to take a different track and looked up and found three businesses I wanted to attack. I did so because they were full of children and their parents. The virus was delivered at the Sky Zone Trampoline Park, the Rock N Jump Trampoline Park, and a variety of Wonderland playgrounds. Each had many parents and children playing in them. I just walked round, distributing the spray as best I could. I was finished by 6:00 PM. Since I brought the cylinder with me, I reloaded and went to various theater complexes. In each movie, I walked down the aisles releasing the spray. I did two movie complexes, one with six screens and one with eight.

"At that point, I had run out of the virus. I then went out and had dinner, returned to my hotel, and now I'm talking to you."

Ahmed responded, "I think you did a great job. Have you noticed anyone watching you or trying to follow you?"

"No, not at all. How about you?"

"None other than the surveillance I found at the warehouse. I'm heading for Pittsburgh tomorrow. Where are you going?" Ahmed asked.

"My next target is Kansas City," Kamil responded. Soon thereafter, the telephone conversation concluded, and each man went to bed with no thought of the destruction they had wrought.

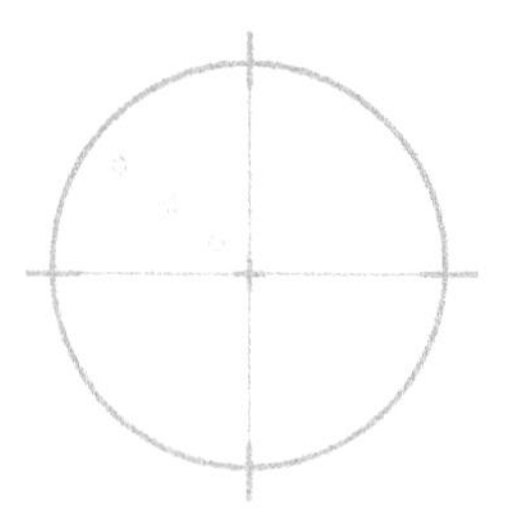

Chapter 63

Sam read the report from the NSA regarding the telephone conversations between Ahmed and Kamil. He called the agent supervising the discovery of and surveillance of the warehouses in Kansas City and informed him that a terrorist was headed to Kansas City the next day. Sam also sent a copy of the transcript of the phone conversations.

Sam asked, "Have you been told which warehouses and deliveries have been made in Kansas City?"

The agent answered, "I am up to date on the warehouses involved. However, I've also been told that there may very well be other warehouses that have not been discovered yet."

Sam replied, "We have been watching and trying to detect the terrorists. Now that the attack has started, that simply will not do. I want you to be prepared to search every warehouse and every container that has come from China. I will be going to court today to obtain an emergency search warrant for those containers. Once I have that, I want you to send your agents to check every warehouse that has shipping containers from China. Have your agents ready to proceed once I make my call giving you the OK. Do you understand?"

"Yes, I do. We will be prepared to initiate the search as soon as I hear from you."

Sam disconnected his call and immediately dialed the agent in charge in Pittsburgh. Sam informed him of the plan to search and told him to be ready to initiate the search when he called. The agent said he would be ready.

Immediately, Sam called the Justice Department and talked to the lawyer who routinely handled these types of search warrant requests. After laying out the scenario the country was facing in an affidavit, Sam and the lawyer, Kyle Benson, went to the court that had been designated to issue this type of search warrant. These courts had been established after 9/11.

Benson walked up to the court clerk and asked to see Judge Toni Pearson. Ten minutes later, Sam and Kyle were standing before her honor.

"Mr. Benson, what is it that brings you to my court today?"

"I have all of the information set forth in the affidavit in support of my requests for search warrants. May I hand it up to Your Honor?"

The judge responded, "Before I read it, can you give me an overall synopsis, please?"

"If I may, Your Honor, I would like to have the Director of Counterterrorism brief you."

The judge looked at Sam and stated, "Proceed."

Sam began at the beginning and left out no detail. When he finished, he stated, "The bottom line is, Your Honor, we are under attack by known terrorists attempting to initiate a pandemic of some type. We believe that attacks have already occurred in Boston and St. Louis. The next cities scheduled to be attacked are Pittsburgh and Kansas City. We have been watching the warehouses to determine possible locations for the virus. To save lives, we need to go in and search all containers coming from China in order to find the cylinders containing this virus. If you have any questions, I would be happy to answer them."

Judge Pearson took her time reading the affidavits before she responded. "Based on what I have before me, it is obvious that there is a clear and present danger confronting this country. At risk are the lives of thousands, if not millions, of people. In my opinion, there is probable cause to believe that the warehouses in question may contain the deadly virus. Therefore, I am signing the search warrants that you have requested. Good luck, gentlemen, and Godspeed."

Once out of the courthouse, Sam called the agents in Pittsburgh and Kansas City and told them to initiate the search. The real question, he knew, was whether they were in time or simply too late.

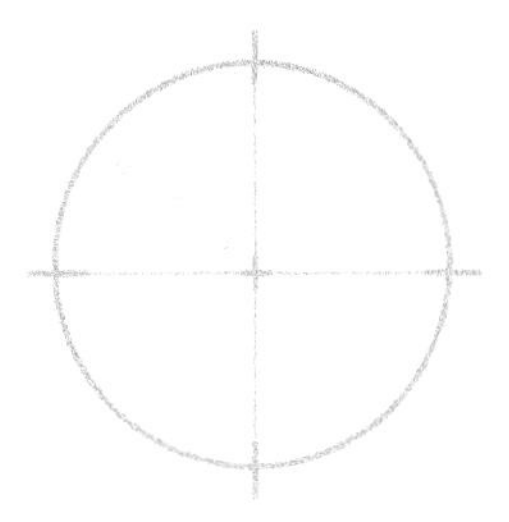

Chapter 64

After briefing FBI Director Ryan Tupper on potential or actual attacks that Sam was trying to prevent, Tupper indicated that they needed to brief the President, as soon as possible. He placed a call to the President's Chief of Staff to arrange for an urgent meeting as soon as his schedule permitted. The Chief of Staff stated that the President had a one-hour break at 2:00 PM. It was agreed that FBI Director Tupper and Director Wyman of Counter-terrorism, would attend. NSA Director Simpson, the Secretary of Homeland Security, Jensen, and Director O'Hare of the CDC would also be asked to be present at the meeting.

At exactly 2:00 PM, Sam, Ryan, and the three others were standing outside the Oval Office. Brad Nelson, the Chief of Staff, came out of the office and asked the five individuals to enter. The President was seated behind the Resolute desk, reviewing some papers. He stood, came over, and shook each of their hands and asked them to sit on two sofas that faced each other.

The President stated, "It's obviously unusual for the five of us to meet on such short notice like this. What problems are you bringing to me?"

Sam gave a rundown of all the events that he had been following. "That's about it, sir. We believe that it may be possible that this country is under attack by North Korean agents trying to spread a deadly virus and start a pandemic. We cannot say for sure that the attack has begun because we have neither caught the terrorists nor seen the results of their possible actions. We have additional agents searching for the virus. The problem is the time it takes to find and search the vast number of Chinese containers coming into this country. However, with the help of the NSA, recent information has revealed the potential targets. We also believe, based on intelligence we have developed, that the virus is an Ebola variant. That is all I can say at this point."

The President pointed at Director Simpson and asked, "Do you have any additional information about the situation before we talk about what we need to do?"

"Other than to say we are listening for more conversations that may help the FBI in finding these terrorists. Because of the seriousness of the situation, we have added additional resources to work on this matter."

The President looked at Dr. Madeline O'Hare, who stated, "I was warned by the FBI of the potential of this attack. As a result, we have placed resources in each of the target cities who can take possession of the virus if found. My people who work with this type of virus are ready to examine it and try to find a potential vaccine."

The President continued his questioning, "If people are infected with this virus, describe for me what I should expect to see in those individuals."

"If it is the Ebola virus, those infected might exhibit pain in various areas of the body. They may show dehydration, fatigue, fever, sweating, or chills. Victims may be coughing up blood, vomiting, suffering from diarrhea, have eye redness, headaches, or red spots on their skin. This virus is often deadly. If we have people exposed to it who spread it to others, we will be confronting a situation much worse than the Covid pandemic."

The President looked at each of the people before him and said, "What do you need from me?"

O'Hare stated, "Nothing at this point, sir, but if that virus spreads, we will need to be on a warlike footing to stop the spread."

The President stood and shook each of the individuals' hands and said, "Thank you for coming. Please keep me informed about everything you learn."

The directors left and the President resumed his seat at the Resolute desk. He understood the administration's response to this potential pandemic would define his presidency. He realized he would have to marshal the forces of the United States in a manner that had not been done before. The fact that this pandemic would be worse than the Covid pandemic was startling. If his people determined that President Kim was behind this attack, he would make that little prick pay.

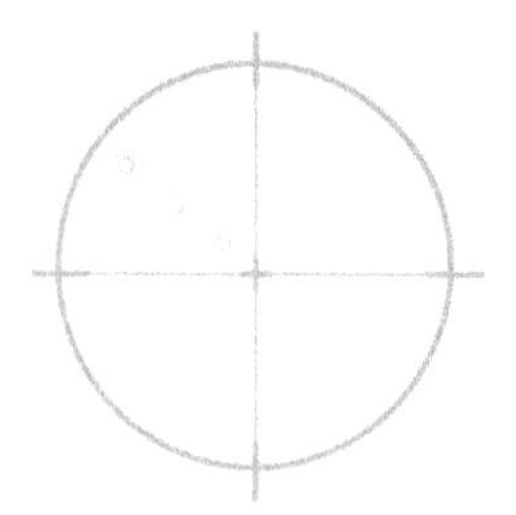

Chapter 65

At about 10:00 PM, Mike Jacobson led his wife to their car. He drove as quickly as possible to Massachusetts General Hospital. Jacobson parked, helped his wife out of the car, and they walked into the emergency room. It was very busy, which was nothing unusual for this hospital.

A triage nurse came up to him and asked what the problem was. He answered her, "It is my wife. Today, she started feeling ill. She has a fever and is very tired. We weren't too concerned until she began spitting up blood and her eyes became red and funny looking."

The nurse looked at the woman's eyes, and said in an urgent voice, "You need to come with me. Both of you need to come with me." She took them to the exam room and had the woman lie on the bed. "Can you tell me your name, please?"

"Yes, it's Melanie."

"Thank you, I'll be right back." The nurse went directly to the doctor in charge of the ER. "Doctor, I have a woman who has certain symptoms that are consistent with the Ebola virus." The entire ER staff had been given a quick training that morning as requested by the CDC. "What do you want me to do?"

"I want to see her before I decide what to do." The doctor walked back to where Melanie was lying. After a brief exam, the doctor stated, "We need to put her into an isolation room. Have her husband accompany her. Anyone dealing with her, or her husband, should, like us, be wearing protective clothing. Take some blood so we can determine if she has the virus. Call the CDC and report what we found. Let's hope this is not the beginning."

At the same time, a similar situation was developing in St. Louis some 1,100 miles away. In the emergency room at the St. Louis General Hospital, Mark and Louise Mason had brought their daughter, Tiffany, to be examined. She, like Melanie in Boston, was spitting up blood. Furthermore, she had a fever and various aches in her joints. The doctor who was examining her, Dr. Sam Johnson, immediately became concerned. Before their shift, they had received word from the CDC that the Ebola virus might show up. Dr. Johnson immediately ordered that Tiffany be placed in isolation along with her parents. He also began the process of determining whether she had the virus.

Dr. Johnson went to his office and immediately dialed the number for the CDC which had been given them during their training. He informed the CDC of his findings and his concern that this may very well be the Ebola virus. He was told by the CDC to isolate anyone who came in contact with Tiffany.

Moments later, Madelyne O'Hare, Director of the CDC, called Sam. "I hate to inform you of this, but we have cases in both Boston and St. Louis that may be Ebola. We have ordered everyone in contact with the victims to be isolated pending the results of blood tests of both individuals. If these people actually have the virus, we can say that the pandemic has begun. Obviously, your search for the terrorists and the virus is even more important."

Sam was stunned at how quickly the virus showed itself. "We will try to find the virus, wherever it is."

O'Hare shocked Sam even further when she stated, "God help us all."

Sam immediately called each of the lead agents in each of the target cities. He informed them of what he had learned. "The immediacy of the threat has been confirmed. Make sure your people understand what has happened and what we need to do. We stand at a crossroads—we can either stop the virus from being spread or begin burying its victims." *Or both*, he thought.

Later that day, Sam received a phone call from Dr. Johnson in St. Louis. "I've been asked by the director of the CDC to call you. We had a patient, a young girl, who came into our hospital earlier today. We confirmed that she had the Ebola virus. I am shocked to have to tell you this, but she died a few minutes ago. I've never seen a virus move so quickly or be so deadly."

After ending his call with Dr. Johnson, Sam began thinking of his own family. Would they stay out of the reach of the virus or would he have to watch them die a painful death. The hunt for the virus had suddenly become very personal to him.

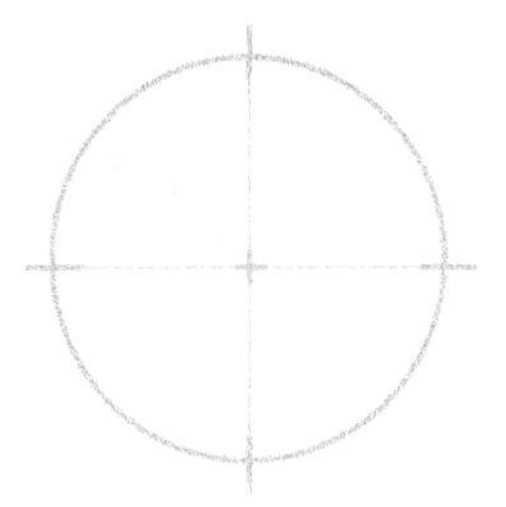

Chapter 66

At 7:30 AM, Sam walked into his office. Calling Mael was number one on his to-do list to let the Frenchman know what was happening. Sam dialed the number and on the fourth ring, Mael answered, "Sam, how are you?"

"Tolerable at best," Sam replied. "How are you, my friend?"

"I'm doing quite well, thank you very much. What is this 'tolerable' about?"

"Well, I wanted to give you a call and update you on what's happening here in the US. Thanks to you and others, we know that the terrorists in our country are named Ahmed and Kamil. From electronic intercepts, we know which cities have been targeted. So far, Boston and St. Louis have been attacked. The first victims have arrived at the hospitals. From blood tests, it has been determined that they were suffering from the Ebola virus. We are trying to figure out how the victims were exposed to the virus.

"At this point, I can tell you that the current numbers from the hospitals in Boston and St. Louis count more than 100 victims and we expect many more. Our first casualty who succumbed to the virus was a young girl. We have teams in place and searching at the other target cities."

"My God, Sam, what is your guess about the number of people who are at risk?"

"It's impossible to say, Mael. Our fear is that this could reach numbers higher than the Covid pandemic. I wanted to let you know how terribly serious this is. It will not take long before cases begin to appear outside of the United States. You may want to bring this to the attention of your superiors."

Both men were silent as they considered the possibilities.

"I will immediately inform my boss of this news. Is there any help that I can provide you?" asked Mael.

"There's nothing that I can think of at this time. We are continuing our search for the terrorists. The CDC is trying to track where all the people who have become ill have been in the last week. At least we gained some experience with contact tracing during Covid. It is simply a race to find those who are infected and those who were exposed to them.

"I believe our President will be addressing the nation in the next day or so to lay out what the country faces and what we need to do as individuals and as a country. But as you know, there are many people who don't want the government telling them what to do, regardless of whether it's in their best interests or not."

Mael stated, "I'm sure that France will begin to deny entrance to people coming into our country from the US, and I'm sure many other countries will follow suit. It may be a long time before international travel gets back to normal. Is there hope in finding a vaccine?"

"None currently. I'm sure that they are doing everything they can to find one. I have a meeting coming up, Mael, so I'm going to have to hang up. We will talk soon."

Mael said, "Good luck, Sam. Let me know if I can help."

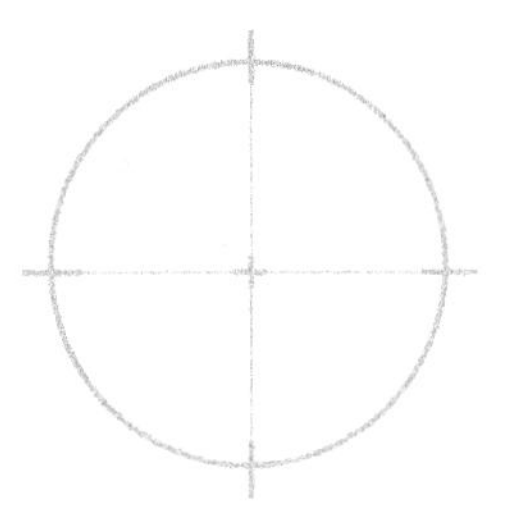

Chapter 67

Sandy and I were relaxing in our hotel room, having finished my shift for the day. Obviously, the Ebola virus was at the forefront of our minds, and we were talking about the risk of contagion if we stayed involved. We agreed we should call Mac and Ty to get the benefit of their views. I called Mac first and then conferenced in Ty.

I opened the conversation, "Hey, guys, I think that all six of us should talk about the Ebola virus found in St. Louis and Boston and decide what our next step should be."

Mac asked, "I'm not sure what you mean."

Sandy answered him, "Mac, I think the question is, should we continue helping the FBI or should we all return home. I mean, we may be in the crosshairs of the virus."

Leanne spoke next, "I've been wondering the same thing. I accompanied Ty to watch the warehouse he has been assigned to. To say it's been boring is an understatement, even though we've been spicing it up a bit. The fact that the virus is now here and spreading makes me wonder. I don't think the danger of being exposed by being near the warehouse is great, but we may very well be exposed to others who come in contact with the virus."

"Leanne, I've been wondering the same thing," said Sandy.

"Hold on a minute," stated Mac, "I don't see any real danger to us. All we are doing is looking for the terrorists. We are not going to be dealing with the virus. As long as we do that, I think we're safe."

"I agree with Mac," inserted Ty. "There's no need to panic about this. If it becomes dangerous, we head home."

"I think it's my turn to speak now," stated Ann. "I am as concerned as the rest of you about catching the virus. No one has told me anything that would make me think we are in danger of being infected. Also, no one has talked about the reason we are here in the first place. Our job is to identify and, if necessary, kill the bastards who are doing this. Frankly, we are probably the only six people in this country, plus Derek, who can do that."

Mac broke the tension when he said, "I know Ann, and when she sets her mind to something, I do not want to get into her way. As you know, she is armed and perfectly capable of putting terrorists away. That doesn't mean she wouldn't shoot me if I was inappropriate."

Ann smiled and looked at her husband, "Damn straight. Besides that, there are some terrorist balls that need to be shot off."

When I finished laughing, I said, "We would not want to get in the way of Ann shooting some poor guy's balls off." By this time, we were all laughing. "It seems to me, that we have agreed to continue doing what we're doing."

Sandy replied, "I'm in."

Leanne responded, "Okay, I can stick it out. We can always reconsider if necessary." Everyone agreed.

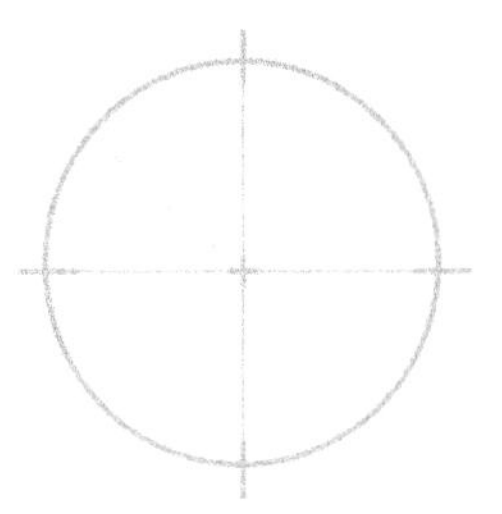

Chapter 68

Kamil drove out of St. Louis in the early afternoon heading for Kansas City, his next target. There was no need for him to leave any sooner since he planned to observe the next warehouse at dusk. As he was driving, Kamil made sure that he did not exceed the speed limit or violate any other laws that might draw attention to him.

Arriving at the hotel where he had reserved a room, Kamil was soon settled in. After he contacted his sleeper asset to receive his new backpack, he met the young man at a gas station close to his hotel. He then took the backpack back to his room to look it over. There seemed to be no problem with it, and he was sure it would operate as designed. Just in case, Kamil had brought the backpack he had received in St. Louis with him to Kansas City. If there had been a problem with the second backpack, the first had already proven its effectiveness. Now that he had two delivery systems, Kamil would fill both at the warehouse, which would save him from entering the warehouse twice.

In the early evening, Kamil drove to "his" warehouse and found a spot down the street that allowed him to observe the comings and goings from that building. For the better part of an hour, Kamil observed the warehouse with his binoculars and watched buildings nearby that could be used to observe the warehouse. He found nothing unusual that caused him any concern.

Once darkness had fallen, Kamil drove around the warehouse until he found a door at the back. Exiting his vehicle, he walked to the door and turned the knob. As expected, it was locked. Using the tools he carried, Kamil opened the door. Stepping inside, he listened to hear if anyone was present. Hearing nothing, Kamil began his search for the shipping container he had been told contained the cylinder he needed. After about two hours of looking, Kamil found the container and cut off the lock.

When he pulled open the heavy door, he saw that the container was crammed full of boxes and crates. He began to unload the container, placing the boxes in a haphazard manner around him. Finally, he found the cylinder he was looking for. It appeared to be undisturbed. Quickly, Kamil attached his backpack to the cylinder as he had been instructed and transferred the virus into the small cylinder in his backpack. He did the same with the second backpack.

As he was preparing to leave, Kamil once again looked at all the boxes he had removed from the container and made no attempt to replace them since he wouldn't be back after attacking his target that evening. Furthermore, Kamil would be leaving Kansas City for Minneapolis in the early morning.

Later that night, Kamil selected two theater complexes as his initial targets. Arriving at the first target, he walked to the ticket office and purchased one ticket to a movie. Proceeding to where the movie was being shown, he walked down the aisles, spraying as he had done in St. Louis. Kamil systematically moved into each theater showing different movies, spraying as he went. He left the first complex, drove to the second complex, and repeated the procedure. Kamil then drove to the Kansas City Power and Light District and for the next hour, he walked through several restaurants, bars, and various establishments, spraying the virus. Satisfied, Kamil drove back to his hotel, showered, and fell asleep, thankful that he had taken the vaccine.

* * *

Ahmed arrived in Pittsburgh in the early evening, checked into his hotel and had dinner. He met his sleeper asset, who delivered the second backpack to him in front of a local Target store. Ahmed then set out to search for the assigned Pittsburgh warehouse. With assistance of his GPS, Ahmed found the warehouse district he was looking for. However, the entrance was blocked by two police cars, barring entrance to the complex.

Ahmed drove around trying to find a location from which he could observe the warehouse and where he could park hidden from the police vehicles. The terrorist got out and walked through a large grove of trees across the street from the entrance to the warehouse district. He crawled to the edge of the trees and watched what was happening with his binoculars. Ahmed could see what he thought was the correct warehouse. Multiple police cars, vans, FBI vehicles, and hazmat trucks were parked in strategic locations. Within an hour, Ahmed saw two individuals wearing hazmat suits bringing a cylinder out of the warehouse. Handling the cylinder carefully, they placed it in a hazmat van, which drove off at a rapid clip.

Ahmed quietly returned to his vehicle, got in, and drove off. Stopping briefly at his hotel to retrieve his personal belongings, he got on the highway to Philadelphia. It was clear to him that Pittsburgh was no longer a valid target. What Ahmed did not understand, however, was how the cylinder had been found in the first place. Obviously, both he and Kamil would have to use extreme caution in the future. Ahmed knew this did not bode well for them.

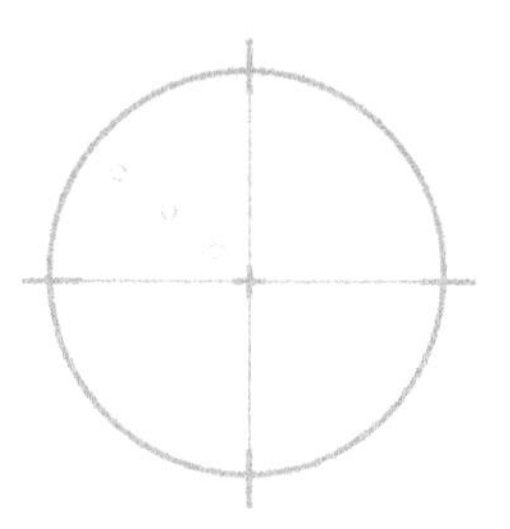

Chapter 69

President John Bradford was alone and seated in the residence dining room. His wife was still on the West Coast visiting elementary schools. He had talked with her just before he began his dinner, explained their current crisis and what he was going to say to the country. She promised she would watch his address and call him afterwards.

The President was dressed in a dark suit with a light blue tie. Since he was from Wyoming, he felt more comfortable wearing blue jeans and cowboy boots. And many times, that's what he wore in the Oval Office. However, the kind of address he was about to make to the nation required more formal attire.

Bradford had been in office for only two years. He was just getting comfortable in the job when this Ebola crisis began. Bradford had been the governor of Wyoming for eight years prior to being elected president. He, like many of the presidents before him, was faced with a divided country and a divided Congress. His first six months in office had been spent trying to get both Democrats and Republicans to work together for the good of the country. However, the mistrust that had been created between the two parties was so great that he had been unable to put together a consensus on how the country should move forward.

While the President wielded great power in certain areas, he lacked the authority to force the parties to work together. Bradford was convinced, however, that the country wanted the parties to put their differences aside and work for the common good. Perhaps, as time went on, he would earn the trust of both parties so that they could work together.

When Bradford had run for president, he had taken his message of cooperation to the people in every primary state and to the country as a whole. Everywhere he went, Bradford heard how disgusted the people were with Congress' inability to move the country forward. As a politician, the President also knew that he would have to keep fighting to achieve that goal of cooperation regardless of the opposition.

Tonight, President Bradford had several opportunities. First, he realized that the Ebola crisis and his reaction to it would define his presidency. Second, Bradford had the opportunity to establish himself as a vigorous leader. Finally, this could be the beginning of bringing the country together.

An aide walked into the dining room and told the President it was time to move to the Oval Office for his address to the nation. He rose and walked to a mirror. Bradford looked closely at how he appeared. This was not the time to have his appearance draw attention from the importance of his remarks. The President left the residence with his Secret Service detail and walked to the Oval Office.

He sat down, a microphone was attached to his lapel, and he completed a sound check. The President saw that his speech had been uploaded to the Teleprompter. As the director counted down from five to zero, Bradford looked directly at the camera and began to speak.

"My fellow Americans, I am here to discuss a grave crisis we are facing. A short while ago, our intelligence agencies learned that we might be facing a challenge that will test our resolve and dedication to this country. This will directly affect every man, woman, and child in the United States. This matter was brought to my attention by the Counterterrorism Office of the FBI. Initially, they told me that it was possible that this country would be attacked using a variant of the Ebola virus that is airborne and deadly.

"The FBI, along with help from our counterparts in France, learned that the Ebola virus may be in the process of being shipped to this country. There was no way at that time to confirm that the virus had been shipped or that an attack would occur.

"The FBI has informed me that they have confirmed, in fact, that this country is under attack. I'm going to show you drawings of the two men who are responsible for and are carrying out the attack."

The President paused while the images of the two men were shown. "If you see these individuals, please call your local FBI office immediately. We were able, by electronic surveillance, to determine the cities that would be attacked. Those cities are Chicago, Kansas City, Minneapolis, Charlotte, Tampa Bay, St. Louis, Pittsburgh, Philadelphia, Miami, and Boston. By identifying the cities, I am not prepared to tell you that each and every one will be attacked. That may very well depend on how you help us find these two men.

"I can now tell you, however, that we have confirmed that an attack has been carried out in St. Louis and Boston. We know this because we have citizens coming down with the virus. I can't go into detail what we are doing to confront this menace simply because I don't want to give anything away to the terrorists. The federal government has ramped up its efforts to provide assistance to these two cities and is prepared to do the same for any other cities that are attacked.

"I can assure you that the federal government has done everything in its power to be prepared for this situation and to hunt down these terrorists. I cannot stress enough how important it is for you to be on the lookout for these men and to inform the FBI should you see them.

"My advisors have informed me that the Ebola virus is far worse than the Coronavirus. Therefore, I have taken the following actions. First, I have directed the CDC to do everything in its power to develop a vaccine and any other means of stopping the spread of the virus as quickly as possible.

"Second, because it appears this virus is airborne, I have ordered that masks be worn at all times outside of your home. I know that some people find this contrary to what they believe are their rights, but the danger of this virus is so great that we must do everything in our power to stop its spread.

"Third, I have banned travel from this country to any other country.

"Fourth, every hospital and doctor will be informed as to the nature of this virus and the potential treatment for it.

"I have been advised by members of my administration, members of Congress, and members of the health profession to not tell you how serious this is. However, it is my firm belief that the people of this country can understand when they are confronted with a dangerous situation; and our people will face this crisis with incredible strength and perseverance. This country has faced many dangers in the past and we Americans have pulled together to defeat our foes. I believe we will do the same in this crisis. I will keep you advised of the current situation. You will receive both the good and the bad news because you deserve it. If we strive as one nation, we will come out the other end as a much stronger country with people dedicated to the common good.

"This attack is an act of war. To the people or nation that have been a part of this terroristic act, I promise you that we will find you and kill you. Our people deserve nothing less!

"Thank you, my friends, for listening tonight. I wish you Godspeed and may God bless the United States of America."

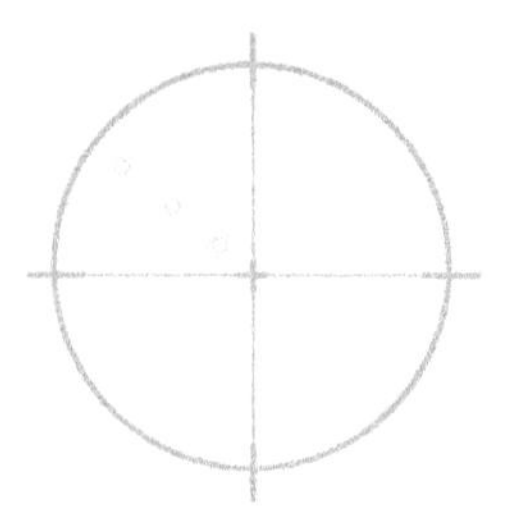

Chapter 70

Reactions to the President's speech came swiftly from various directions. In Congress, the support for the President was overwhelming. However, some Republicans objected to the mandate on wearing masks, and others blamed the President for the national crisis. Democrats were supportive of the President's actions by 100 percent. Part of this support was obviously because the President was a Democrat. However, Democrats had a long history of supporting a mask mandate dating back to the Coronavirus crisis.

On social media, the reaction was similar to that of Congress. Those who supported the President's position argued that the crisis was sufficiently severe to warrant the mask requirement. The contrary position was, once again, based on the violation of individual rights. Some people asked why this information had not been revealed previously. Others echoed the President's position that Americans could come together in times of crisis.

A snap poll of 1,000 Americans after the President's address indicated support for the President's position was 90 percent. A second poll taken shortly after the speech stated that the President's actions were correct by 94 percent. Bradford was buoyed by these expressions of support for his actions.

Further support arrived the next morning in the form of newspaper editorials. Most of the papers from across the country approved of his actions and recognized the leadership he exhibited. The talking heads on TV fell into a predictable position. Those who supported Democrats gave their support for the President's actions. Those who supported more conservative politics fell into two groups. First, those who recognized fact over ideology supported the President. The second group were more ideologically based. Their concern was beating Democrats, not sound public policy.

The White House, in determining support for the President's position, looked at the emails, telegrams, telephone calls, and letters addressing this issue. Like the polls taken after his speech, these indications of support or nonsupport ran heavily in favor of the President's actions.

Bradford was in the Oval Office when Brad Nelson, his Chief of Staff, entered. He brought with him a compilation of those indicators of support.

Nelson opened with, "Well, Mr. President, I think we can call your address last night a real success. Pretty much the whole country is lining up behind you."

The President responded, "The question is how long the support will last. It will erode, I think, if the number of deaths from the virus increases to a certain amount. The success of this administration lies in the hands of our law enforcement personnel. We must catch these terrorists quickly and find a vaccine that protects our people. Failing to do that, I will be a one-term president. Frankly, I'm not sure I should be rewarded with a second term. Have you heard anything further from the FBI?"

"I have not. They have promised that they will keep you advised of both their successes and failures."

"I want you to keep calling them every day so that they know we are paying close attention to their work. In fact, let's set up a daily meeting with the FBI."

"I'll get right on it, sir." Nelson rose and left the office.

The President pondered the situation. The potential number of deaths of those contracting the virus weighed heavily on him. At this point, there was nothing further for him to do. If Intel can confirm for him that North Korea's Kim was behind this, he then could act and take the necessary actions.

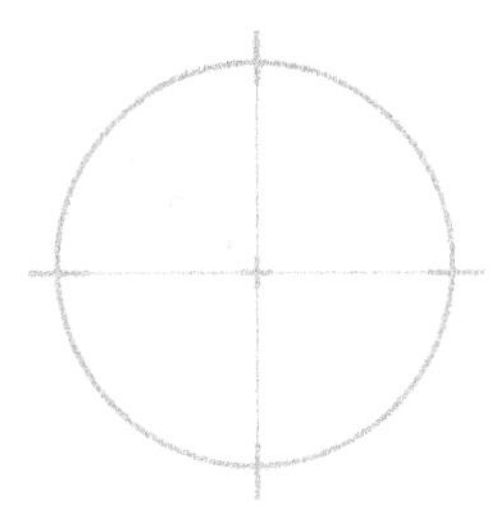

Chapter 71

Karen Sommerfeld, Boston's Director of Public Health, was in a staff meeting discussing the virus. Her secretary opened the door to the conference room and walked to her side. She whispered, "Emma Miller, CEO of Mass General, is on the phone. She needs to talk to you and said it's urgent."

Sommerfeld nodded to her and picked up the phone, "Hi, Emma. What bad news do you have for me?"

Miller, who had been CEO for the last seven years, answered, "Karen, I have not seen anything like this virus! The number of people coming into our emergency room has skyrocketed every hour. We have no more isolation rooms to safely keep these people. The deaths from this virus are coming fast and furious. It feels like I just put someone in a room and we're moving them to the morgue. It is critical for you to work with the other hospitals, and us, so that we can maximize our efforts in combating this virus. I assume we are getting assistance from the feds?"

"Not yet, but it has been promised. How quickly it will be here and in what form, I cannot say. Please put together a list of what you need, prioritized by importance. I will then have something to work with when I talk with the people at the CDC. That would be a big help for me."

"I will get that to you this afternoon. I'm not sure what you've heard, but in my discussions with the CEOs of the other hospitals here, we are all seeing the same thing. Hold on just a moment if you would please." Karen could hear mumbled voices coming over the phone. She waited patiently for Miller to return.

"I'm sorry for having to make you hold, Karen, but my staff just brought in the latest numbers on this virus. In the last 24 hours, we've had 120 come into the ER with Ebola-like symptoms. Of those, 75 have been admitted into the hospital. The rooms are full and new arrivals are in beds in the hallways. The people we are sending home are those that have relatively mild symptoms. The concern we have is that they may be passing the virus on to others by doing so. As you can see, we need help as quickly as you can get it to us. The longer we wait, the more people who are going to be affected. And, obviously, the more people who will die."

"My God," Karen responded. "The last time we talked, the number of patients was in single digits. And as I recall, it was just yesterday. Am I correct?"

"Yes, you're right. It is coming at us so fast I'm not sure we will ever be able to get in front of it."

"Okay, Emma. I will contact the CDC unless you already have. I assume they've been in touch with you. Is that correct?"

"Yes, they are talking to us about the number of people we are seeing. I am not sure they are in the loop as far as providing us with assistance with regard to additional beds, etc. I think they're handling just the medical aspect of this crisis, not the practical side, which has to be addressed immediately."

"I will also contact the CDC in any event. I will also find out who is on point in coordinating aid to us and others. Let's keep in touch, Emma. We must coordinate with each other."

Miller replied, "I will call you at least once a day to give you a status report. We'll talk later."

That same afternoon, a call came into the White House that asked to be directed to Brad Nelson, the Chief of Staff. After the operator confirmed that the caller was Sophia Westfield, Mayor of Kansas City, she put the call through.

Nelson's secretary answered the call. "Chief of Staff's office. How may I help you?"

"This is Sophia Westfield. I'm the Mayor of Kansas City. It's important that I talk to Brad."

"If you will hold on a minute, I will see if he's available."

A few minutes passed.

"Hi, Sophia. It's good to talk to you again. What can I do for you?"

"Hi, Brad, I'm not sure the director of the CDC has brought you up to date on what is happening here. The Ebola virus is running rampant! I just talked with the people at St. Luke's hospital, and they are pulling their hair out. The number of Ebola cases has shot up to the point that they do not have any room left in the hospital. I have checked with the other hospitals in Kansas City, and they are facing the same numbers. We have no rooms left and have begun placing patients in the hallways. The death rate is so high that our morgues are filled. Frankly, I'm concerned that many medical professionals will refuse to treat these individuals or terminate their employment. The death rate of this virus is so high that I cannot blame them. Simply put, we need your help, and we need it now."

"Sophia, I need you to do this for me. Can you provide me with a list of all the equipment or other needs you have? My job is to get it to you. I promise you I will light a fire under the responsible person's ass. I can tell you that the President has told me he wants no excuses from any federal employee for not getting the job done. If you feel anyone is failing to provide you with what you need, call me immediately. I cannot stress strongly enough that we want the federal government working at top speed and in cooperation with state and local governments."

"I can't tell you what a relief that is, Brad. I look forward to working with any and all parts of the federal government. The sooner, the better!"

"Also, Sophia, the President is considering coming to those cities that have been attacked. Do you think that would be helpful to your people?"

"Yes, no question about it. It will calm the nerves of our people to see that the President is here and making sure we get help."

"When this presidential trip is ready to fly, the Secret Service will be in contact with you. Feel free to call me at any time. We'll talk later."

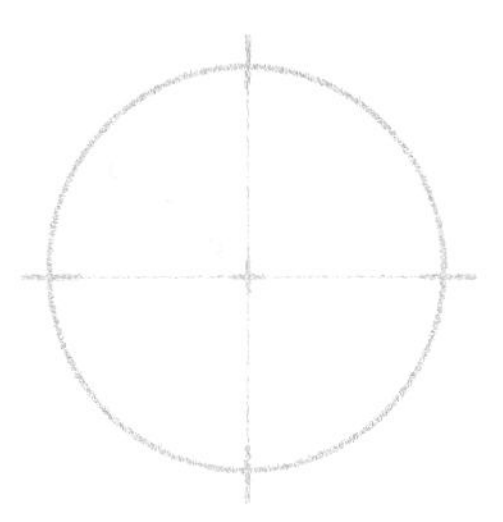

Chapter 72

The cell was nondescript with concrete walls covered by dark gray paint. It smelled slightly of old urine from previous tenants. Heather Lee sat in the corner of the cell with her knees pulled up toward her chest as she watched an ant crawl across the floor. She was dressed in an old orange jumpsuit that was two sizes too big for her. There were no windows in her cell, so she had no reference as to whether it was day or night. A single light bulb hung from the ceiling and burned all the time. Heather could not tell how long she had been there.

At odd times during the day, the slot at the bottom of the door would open and a plate of food would appear. Initially, she had rejected the food as unpalatable. However, when her hunger became too great, Heather ate the food ravenously. In the cell, there was a toilet and sink. Her bed consisted of a mattress on the floor and one blanket to keep her warm.

Heather had been trained in what to expect if captured. However, she never really considered that a true possibility. What Heather did expect was to be immediately interrogated about her connection with Senator Kendricks and how she obtained information from him. Heather held out hope that once he realized that she had been arrested, the senator would come to see her. Yet, he never appeared.

Suddenly, her cell door swung open, and a short, overweight man appeared. He watched her get up off the floor and said, "Ms. Lee, please come with me." The man led her down the hallway lined with cells until he reached a door at the end of the corridor. He opened it, bade her enter, and showed her a chair. She sat down and he pulled up a chair across the table from her. "Before we start, is there anything you'd like to ask me?"

"Yes, I have several questions. First, why am I being held here? Second, where am I? Third, I want an attorney—now! Fourth, when do I get to make a phone call?"

The man looked at her and responded, "First, you are being held on espionage and various terrorism crimes. Second, no one even knows this place exists and I'm certainly not going to tell you. Third, you will not be given an attorney at any time. Fourth, you will be making no phone calls. Do you have any other questions?"

"This is outrageous! How can an American citizen be held like this? I have certain constitutional rights that I want to exercise," Heather exclaimed.

"I understand what you're saying. You are not considered an American citizen because you are a terrorist. You have no constitutional rights so don't expect to exercise anything.

He continued in his high, nasal voice. "At this point, I want you to just listen to what I'm going to tell you so that you know what to expect. I'm going to ask you a series of questions and expect you to answer them truthfully. Failing to do so, well, I don't think you want to know what will happen. I will tell you this, however, if you do not answer my questions or if I believe you're lying, you will be sent to Guantánamo Bay. At that location, you will be waterboarded for over a period of two months. If at that time, you have not told us what we want to know, you will be sent to Morocco, where their treatment of you will be much less lenient than ours. In any event, I have no doubt that we will get the information we want from you sooner or later. You simply have to determine how much pain you are willing to take before you make a full explanation of your activities."

"You can't torture me! It's against the law." Fear coursed through Heather's body.

"The United States government does not consider waterboarding to be torture. What will happen to you in Morocco most certainly will be torture, but we will not be doing it. You see, there are all sorts of ways to get around these restrictions.

"Let me ask you a question. As you know, there is an attack on the US using the Ebola virus. It is proving to be very deadly. Do you think that there is anybody in America who cares what happens to you? I think not.

"Needless to say, Ms. Lee, you are in a very bad situation. How bad it gets or becomes is simply up to you. I'm going to take you back to your cell and give you some time to consider your situation. Come with me."

The man led her to her cell, opened the door, and allowed her to walk in. The sound of the door closing sent shivers up her spine. There was no question in her mind that these people would do whatever it took to have their questions answered. She sat down in the corner of the cell and began to ponder what she should do. After much thought, she decided she would deny any involvement in espionage or any other crimes and would delay them as much as she could by giving false answers.

A few hours later, her door opened, and the same small man motioned for her to come out. Once again, she followed him down the corridor and entered the room they had occupied before. This time, there were two additional men in the room. Both were large men standing over six foot five and weighing well over 200 pounds. She sat down and the small man sat down opposite her. He looked at her questioningly and then asked, "Have you had time to consider your situation?" He saw her nod her head up and down. "So, what is it going to be?"

"I committed no crimes. I have nothing to apologize for!"

"We assumed that would be your response," the man replied. The man stood, turned away, then quickly turned back slamming his hand on the table in front of her. Heather jumped out of her chair and fell over. One of the large men grabbed her by her shoulders, picked her up, and sat her down in the chair once again.

"I'm going to ask you a series of questions. If you are as smart as you are beautiful, I expect you to answer them truthfully. Why were you soliciting information from Senator Kendricks?"

"I wasn't. You can just ask him; he will tell you the truth."

"Senator Kendricks killed himself the day after you were arrested. That pretty much told us what we needed to know."

He watched Heather pale at the news of Senator Kendricks' death. "If you're expecting him to come to your rescue, that obviously isn't going to happen. Heather, you are on your own. No one knows where you are, nor will they. By the way, your other two North Korean compatriots were killed at the scene of your arrest. They did put up a fight, however, killing one agent and wounding others. Frankly, I'm amazed that you made it here alive. We don't take kindly to losing our own.

"I am going to ask you one more time. Why were you soliciting information from the senator?"

She glared at him with hate in her eyes. "Go to hell!"

"My guess is, Heather, that you will beat me there." The man nodded to the two other men, who came forward, picked her up by her upper arms, and walked out the door. They walked her down the hall and into another room. She saw that it contained a gurney, a table that had been raised at one end, and what appeared to be a hot tub.

One of the men said, "Take off your clothes."

One arm crossed her breast and the other covering her groin area. Heather shook her head no.

The man said quietly, "You have a choice, either you remove your clothes, or we will."

Knowing there was no choice, Heather slowly removed her clothes and was standing there in her nakedness. The two men came toward her and picked her up by each arm.

"What are you doing to me!" she screamed. The men did not answer but merely carried her to the tub and placed her in it. Heather screamed. The water was ice cold and soon her teeth were chattering.

One of the men asked her, "Are you ready to answer questions?"

"Never!" she yelled at them. After another 20 minutes, the men pulled her out of the tub and allowed her to dry herself off. The men led her to the gurney, picked her up, and laid her down. The two men gave her a warm blanket and watched her slowly warm up.

When it appeared to the two men that she was no longer suffering the effects of the chilling bath, they placed her on a table with her head slanting down. One of the men grabbed another blanket and placed it over her body, giving her some relief from her embarrassment. The men placed her hands and feet in restraints. Heather understood that she was going to be waterboarded. She did not know how long she could withstand that torture.

One of the men placed a towel over her face and begin pouring water on it so that victims believed they were drowning. One of the men drew the towel back and asked, "Are you prepared to answer questions?"

She tried to spit on them.

The dousing went on for what seemed like hours to her. Each time, she was waterboarded and then asked if she was going to answer questions. After the sixth waterboarding, she looked at one of the man, who saw that the hate had vanished from her eyes.

When he asked her the question, she nodded yes. The men undid the restraints on her wrists and legs. After giving her another towel to dry off, they handed her a coarse orange jumpsuit and allowed her to get dressed. They walked her back to the room where the small man was waiting.

He looked at her with pity in his eyes and stated, "Are you prepared to cooperate?"

"Yes. Yes, I am," she answered.

"I hope so," he replied.

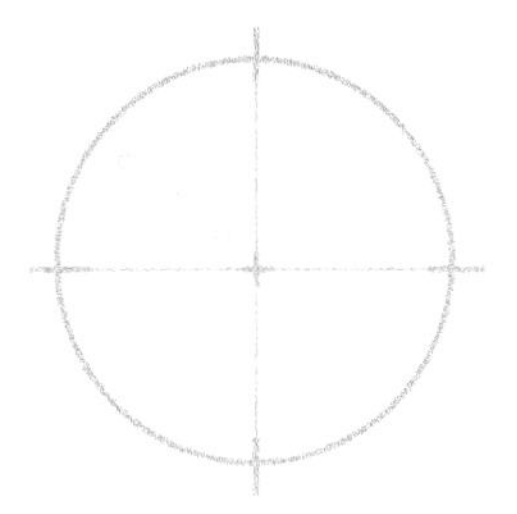

Chapter 73

The small man began in his high, nasal voice. "Well, let's try again. Do I have to tell you what will happen if you are not truthful?"

Heather whimpered and shook her head no.

"How long have you been meeting with Senator Kendricks?"

"I'm not sure exactly. It has been several months, but I don't recall exactly."

"Did you obtain information from him and pass it on to someone else?"

"Yes."

"Exactly what kind of information did you pass on?"

"Anything he told me, I passed on. But I was specifically requested to try and get information on North Korea and its relationship with America."

"Give me examples of the information you passed on?"

"He told me that the FBI was concerned about an attack from North Korea. He said he talked with a woman who briefed the committee he was on. This woman evidently told him about what was happening regarding North Korea attacking the United States. It was mostly about that."

The man continued questioning Heather about her relationship with the senator. Then the man changed the direction he was going. "What did you do with the information you received?"

"I really didn't need to tell anyone anything. The two men in the room next to me had videotaped and audiotaped everything that occurred. We had tapes of the senator explaining what he learned at the committee briefings. We also had videotape of him having sex with me, which we were going to use to blackmail him. I believe that information was forwarded to people in North Korea."

"Why do you believe that?"

Heather answered, "Because I received an email from the leader of North Korea saying that an attack would be forthcoming."

"Is that email on the computer we took from your house?"

"Yes, but you won't be able to get it and read it. I have a special program that deletes all my emails."

"Yes, I understand, but we have special people and programs that can find almost anything in a computer. What other people in the US work for North Korea that you have had contact with or know of?"

The man saw Heather hesitate and look at the floor.

"Must I remind you again what's in store for you if you do not answer these questions correctly and truthfully. I can assure you that as bad as you believe you were treated here, it can and will get immeasurably worse if you do not cooperate fully."

She looked at him and saw the determination in his eyes. There was no question in her mind as to the pain he could have inflicted upon her. "There was one person I was told I could contact if I got into a situation that I could not get out of. I was told this woman was a high-ranking operative of our country, North Korea. I mean my country is America, not North Korea."

The man handed her a pad and a pencil. "Please write down her name, phone number and address."

Heather wrote the name Chin-Sun, a phone number, and an address.

The man took the pad and pencil and said, "You have done well today, Heather. Your cooperation will benefit you in the future."

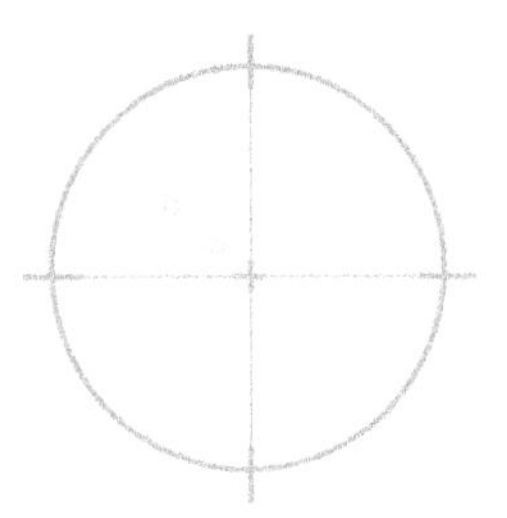

Chapter 74

Sandy and I spent a lovely evening having dinner at a local restaurant. As we walked out onto the street, I looked at my watch and realized we had about two hours before I began my shift watching the warehouse. My shift ran from 11:00 PM to 7:00 AM. As the two of us walked to our hotel, we talked about the events that occurred in Philadelphia. During our off time, we had been able to tour the various sites related to our country's heritage. It was fascinating to see where history had been made.

Switching to the present, Sandy asked, "Has the FBI made any progress in finding the virus here?"

"They have not found the cylinders with the virus yet. They have had agents checking all the warehouses where they believe shipments from China have been stored. Some agents checked my assigned warehouse a couple of days ago and found nothing. My question to them was, 'If you found nothing in my warehouse, why am I spending all night watching it?' They told me they didn't want to risk having missed the virus and not having the warehouse watched. So that means I get to continue reading the book I bought. Derek, however, is now watching a warehouse that has not been checked."

"Do you really think that no one will show up at the warehouse?"

"I think that if anyone was coming, they would have done it before now. So, I get to be paid for another day's work without having to do anything."

Sandy smiled at me and said with a sparkle in her eye, "If that's the case, is there any reason I shouldn't be able to accompany you and read my own book? Did you ask Derek if you could go to the warehouse?"

I answered, smiling, "Yes, he said it was up to me. I don't think he wanted to fight you over this. We decided previously that it would not be a good idea. I know that we have a different situation since our warehouse has been checked for the virus, but I'm not sure we should change."

Sandy's grin widened. "What could possibly happen? If, in the slim possibility, that someone showed up, I'm still in a different building and would not be in danger. Come on, big boy, let's do this." She once again gave me that sly smile.

I pondered the question for a few minutes and finally replied, "Okay, but only on the condition that you follow my directions and stay in the location where we watch from."

"You have my promise."

With that decided, we went up to our hotel room where I picked up my book and my weapon. Sandy pulled her weapon from under her pillow and when I looked at her questioningly, she responded, "Well, as Ann says, it's always best to be prepared." I thought for a moment and then nodded at her.

We arrived at our surveillance location and relieved the agent on watch. I sat down in front of three screens. The FBI had installed cameras watching the front and back doors and one inside the warehouse. Sandy sat down next to me, opened her book, and began to read. I did the same but made sure that I looked at the screens every few seconds. The inside of the warehouse was dark and it was difficult to see anything moving about. However, the front and back doors were lit with exit lights, which gave me a clearer view of those locations.

The hours of surveilling passed slowly, as they had since I arrived in Philadelphia. Sandy and I had quit reading and were talking. Something caught my eye on the screen showing the back door. I sat up, peered more closely at the screen, and saw a man dressed in black with a full mask covering his face. He was bent down, working on the lock. Suddenly, he stood up, opened the door and entered the warehouse.

The procedures we had agreed on required me to call the lead agent in Philadelphia and wait until backup agents arrived. I called the agent and informed him of what was going on. He told me to hold tight until he and the others arrived. I responded, "If this is one of the terrorists, he could be gone by the time you get here. I'm going down to the back door and see what I can discover."

The lead agent responded, "You will stay at your location until we arrive. Understand?"

I stated, "This is too important to be hung up on procedure. Just get here and back me up."

"DJ, you must wait for us. If you go in alone, there will be repercussions."

I answered him, "What are you going to do, fire me? I'll see you shortly."

As I stood up, I saw a very frightened look on Sandy's face. "Why don't you do what they tell you? This is too dangerous."

"It's probably only a burglar, but if it is the terrorists, we cannot let them get to the virus. I will make sure I'm safe, don't worry. You stay put."

Before she could object, I rushed down the stairs and outside, then ran to the side of the warehouse under surveillance. Slowly and silently, I made my way to the back. Peering around the corner of the warehouse, no one was in sight. Cautiously, I walked to the back door and listened but could hear nothing coming from inside the warehouse. Opening the door the intruder had used, I went inside as quietly as possible and let my eyes adjust to the darkness. After a short while, I walked down the aisle next to the outside wall and peered down each aisle as I came to it.

Reaching the third aisle, I looked around and saw nothing. However, hearing a door to a cargo container being opened, I drew my weapon, proceeded toward the sound, pulled my flashlight out, and held it next to my weapon. Drawing my breath in, I turned on the light, shattering the darkness. Standing before me, not 20 feet away, was Ahmed. He had taken off his mask and I recognized him immediately.

I shouted, "This is the FBI. You're under arrest."

As quick as a gazelle, he pulled out his pistol, fired a poorly aimed shot, and dived behind a shipping container. I immediately turned off the flashlight, fell to the ground and saw the flash of two shots that hit the container above me. Immediately, I rolled to the right side of the aisle.

Ahmed screamed at me, "Are you ready to die, FBI man?"

I was able to crawl behind another container that would protect me for the moment. I yelled, "Ahmed, it is your time to die."

"Ah, so you know me, FBI man. Prepare to die." He fired four additional shots at me. Fortunately, they didn't even come close. I leaned around the corner of the container and fired one shot toward where I believed he was. That brought no response.

As I was thinking about my next move, I heard Ahmed say, "You are too late, FBI man. I have the virus, and if need be, I will release it here. So, you see, you will die by my shooting you or even a more painful death, by the virus."

"I promise you, my friend, you will die also!" I knew the standoff could not last forever and slowly moved back to the outside wall. There, I decided to wait for the other agents. Twice more, Ahmed fired at me, and then I heard him running. It sounded like he was running for the back door. Luckily, I was closer than he was and ran toward the door. Kneeling, I turned the flashlight on and pointed it at the door. No one was there. Hearing something behind me, I turned and felt Ahmed kick me in the head. I saw stars for a moment, completely disoriented.

Ahmed turned on his flashlight and pointed it at me. He said, "Well, I'll be damned. You are one of the stupid professors from Paris. FBI, I don't think so. You're not going to cause me any further problems."

As he raised his pistol toward me, I asked, "Why are you trying to kill all these people with the Ebola virus?"

"Because I can," he smiled at me. I watched him raise his gun and point it at my head. My only thought was how much I regretted not waiting for the other agents.

A shot rang out, but I felt nothing. Opening my eyes, I saw Ahmed falling to the ground and holding his thigh. I looked behind me and saw Sandy standing there with her weapon raised. I ran over to Ahmed and kicked his weapon away. Because I had surprised him, he had not put on his backpack but was carrying it in his hand. I kicked the backpack across the floor and stepped back. My concern was coming in contact with the virus. Ahmed tried to stand, and I kicked him back down.

I looked at Sandy and said, "Wow, you were just in time. You missed hitting him center mass though."

Sandy rolled her eyes at me and stated, "I wasn't aiming at center mass; I was trying to shoot his balls off. I came pretty close, don't you think?"

Before I could respond, I heard the other agents in the warehouse. "Over here," I yelled. Moments later, four agents came running around the aisle.

"Is this one of the terrorists?" the lead agent asked."

"Yes, let me introduce you to Ahmed. I can give you a positive ID of him." Pointing behind me, I stated, "His backpack is over there."

As agents jerked Ahmed to his feet, he screamed and nearly collapsed. The agents searched him and found the device that would release the virus. A quick inspection showed that the device had not been activated to release the virus. With hate in his eyes and knowing that he had failed, Ahmed said, "She shot me. I need medical attention now."

The lead agent grabbed Ahmed by the shirt and said, "Shut up, asshole. If you're nice, I'll give you an aspirin at our office. If you're really nice, I will give you two."

The agent looked at me and said, "You're lucky you're not dead, and, by the way, you've seen your last days helping the FBI."

I responded, "If you had gotten here quicker, my wife would not have had to do your job." I gave the agent the finger, and Sandy and I walked out the door.

On the way back to our hotel, I called Sam and filled him in. "I can positively ID the terrorist as Ahmed. By the way, the lead agent here told me I was done working for the FBI. You will probably have that recommendation on your desk in the morning."

"Don't worry, DJ, you're still with us and always will be. One thing—tell your wife that I will arrange for her entry into the FBI Academy." He was still laughing when he hung up.

I also called Mac and Ty to tell them what happened. They both realized that their turn could come next.

Within minutes, Sandy, Ahmed, and I were each being washed down by a hazmat team to assure us that the virus had not been given to us. Sandy complained about the shapeless scrubs we were given to wear.

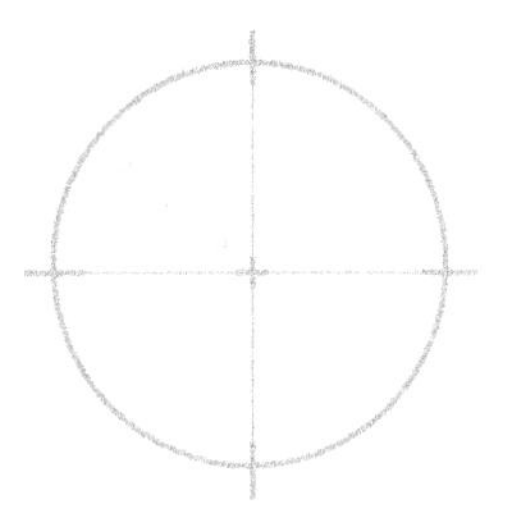

Chapter 75

Chin-Sun arrived home about 7:00 PM having completed a long day at the office. She went to her bedroom and changed into a comfortable silk robe. The North Korean agent immediately returned to her living room, sat down on the sofa, and clicked on the TV. Like everyone else in the country, Chin-Sun wanted to know the latest news about the Ebola outbreak. When ever a new city reported casualties, she smiled to herself and prayed that Ahmed and Kamil would continue their attacks.

As she watched, her doorbell rang. Chin-Sun walked to the door and looked through the peephole. She did not recognize the person outside and said, "Yes, can I do something for you?"

The man responded, "I have your pizza."

Chin-Sun answered, "I have not ordered a pizza."

The man stated, "I have the order right here." He read the address to her and held up the order so she could see it.

"You don't seem to understand, young man, I did not order a pizza. You should leave."

"Those dumb assholes at the store can't get anything right. Would you please take this pizza? If you don't, I must pay for it. This is the third time this week that this has happened."

"Okay. Just to help you out." She unlocked the door and began to open it when suddenly, the door was kicked in, knocking her to the ground. She looked up in fear and saw six men crowded into the room. All of them had their weapons drawn. Chin-Sun saw that each man had FBI stenciled on his jacket.

"What's going on here? Why are you doing this?" She attempted to stand and was jerked upwards by two agents.

"Chin-Sun, you are under arrest for espionage and other terrorist activities."

"What are you talking about?" she replied. "I've done nothing wrong. You must've made a mistake."

"You're going with us down to our office."

"Can I at least get dressed; all I have on is this robe."

The man replied, "How you are dressed is the least of your worries."

When they arrived at the FBI office, Chin-Sun was ushered into a conference room. Kyle Reese, the same man who had interrogated Heather Lee, was waiting for her. He looked at her, smiled and said, "Please be seated."

"Thank you."

"Let me tell you why you're here. You are being charged with attempted murder in Maui, espionage, and other terrorist activities."

Chin-Sun interrupted him and said, "I am innocent. I have done nothing wrong. You have the wrong person."

"Please don't interrupt," the man said. "Let me tell you why you're here. Previously, we sent a photo we took of you to the professors. You have been positively identified by them as the person who tried to kill them on Maui. For that crime alone, you could spend the rest of your life in prison. We've also learned of your involvement in espionage and certain terrorist activities. Heather Lee was arrested a short while ago. She is cooperating and has identified you as a high-ranking North Korean agent. I'm not going to go in to all that she has told us about you. But rest assured that you will be convicted of all crimes and potentially will be executed.

"But before we get to that unpleasantness, you should understand the following. You have two options before you. You can cooperate fully with us, and in return, we will inform the sentencing judge of your cooperation. Second, should you decide not to cooperate, you will be on a plane to Guantánamo Bay within the hour. As I'm sure you have heard, the United States believes that waterboarding is legal as an intensive interrogation tool. I would expect that after a few sessions on the board, you will be most cooperative. However, if that is not successful, you will be flown to Morocco, where they have more painful techniques available. Simply put, the choice is yours. Do you have any questions?"

"I want my lawyer. You cannot do this to me."

"You will not get an attorney. No one knows that you are here or in our custody. If asked, we will deny any knowledge of you. You are in a position I would never want to be in. You have 30 minutes to decide whether you're going to cooperate with us or not. That time starts now." Reese stood and walked out the door, leaving Chin-Sun to decide her fate.

Exactly one half hour later, the man opened the door and walked in. He looked at Chin-Sun with some sympathy and said, "Have you made up your mind?"

She looked at him with tears apparent in her eyes, and said, "Yes, I will cooperate."

"Good. Let's get to the meat of it. Who ordered this operation to start an Ebola pandemic in the United States?"

She looked at him and smiled, "Our leader, Kim. It was his idea, and as I understand, he has been working on this plan for several years."

The man stood, walked to the door, and left the room. Stepping into the hall, he took his cell phone from his pocket and dialed the number he had been given and waited for someone to answer.

Yes."

"Mr. President, it was Kim."

"Thank you."

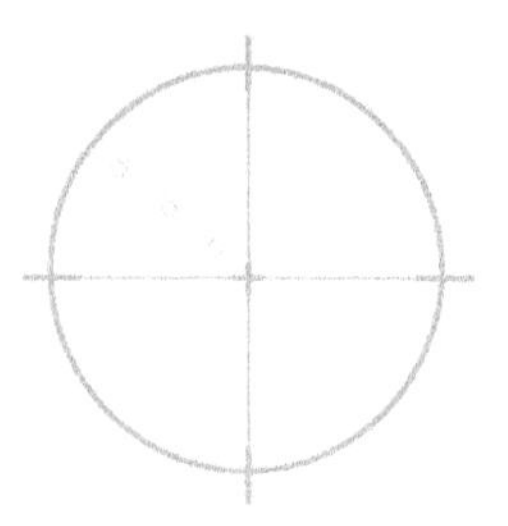

Chapter 76

Ahmed had not slept for well over 36 hours. He was being held at the same facility as Heather Lee. He sat on the mattress, rocking back and forth and holding his thigh. Contrary to their promise, the FBI had not provided him with any painkillers or medical attention. The bullet wound in his thigh had a constant pounding pain that allowed him no sleep.

No one had come to interrogate him yet. He was determined to give nothing to his captors. However, Ahmed had participated in enough torture to know that every man had a point at which he would break. Ahmed promised himself that he would hold out as long as he could so that Kamil could continue the attacks on America.

Ahmed did not hear the lock being turned but saw the door swing open. Two men enter the cell, grabbed him under the arms, and lifted him up. The pain shot through his thigh once again. He made no noise, determined not to give these men any sense of satisfaction that he was hurting. They dragged him down to a room at the end of the hallway. Ahmed was shoved roughly into a chair and both his arms and legs were strapped down so that he could not move.

A small, thin man entered the room, pulled up a chair, and sat down in front of Ahmed. He was wearing a plastic face guard and rubber gloves. He looked at the man seated before him and said, "Good morning, Ahmed."

With hatred in his eyes, Ahmed responded by spitting onto the man's face guard. The man took out an antiseptic cloth and slowly wiped off the spittle. Then, with lightning speed, he leaned forward and placed his thumb on the entry wound on Ahmed's thigh. He pushed his thumb deeply into the wound. Ahmed gave out a high-pitched scream, jerking back and forth trying to free himself from his restraints.

The man wiped off his thumb and looked at Ahmed. "Let's try this again, Ahmed. Good morning. I suggest you not spit on me again or you will simply feel additional pain."

Ahmed stared at the man and said, "Go to hell."

The man smiled and stated, "Now that's what I like—communication. You and I are going to have a lot of talks in the next few days. How comfortable those days are for you will depend solely on how you respond. You may be wondering where you are, so I will explain. Ahmed, a drug was administered that caused you to lose consciousness and have no recollection as to what had occurred. You are currently being held in Guantánamo Bay. I'm sure you are aware of that since many of your compatriots reside here. We have told no one of your capture and will not do so.

"As to your wound, expect no medical attention until such time as I believe you are cooperating with me. Since you have a wound that is obviously very painful, I see no other means to relieve that pain than your cooperation." He removed his glasses, pulled out a sheet of tissue, and began to clean them.

As Ahmed remained seated, struggling with his pain, the man walked out and into a room across the hall. As he sat down, an FBI agent who was also seated, stood and asked, "Are you just going to leave him in there like that?"

The man responded, "What would you have me do?"

"Feed him and give him medical attention before you question him."

"I suppose I could do that. Right now, this man is at his most vulnerable. I take no pleasure in causing him pain, but we need answers from him quickly, not in a month from now. I understand that your training says we should treat him appropriately. Your training may even say that we will get the most information out of him that way. However, I don't have the luxury of time."

The agent shouted, "That is not the way we treat people in this country."

The man gave the agent a hard look before responding. "Would you like to ask the thousands of people who are dying from the Ebola virus whether they think I'm being too rough with this gentleman. I wouldn't ask those thousands of people. You know why? They are already dead. We should ask the people who may die across the country about whether I'm being too rough.

"This is an age-old question. You violate your beliefs to save people? I answered that question long ago when I saw a little boy's body that had been shredded by a terrorist in the name of his religion. If you're having problems with my actions, I suggest you leave. I have been directed to do this by the highest authority in this country in order to save our people." He washed his face and hands, sat down, opened his lunch bag and began to eat.

After lunch, the man returned to speak with Ahmed. Each time, the terrorist refused to speak or told an untruth, the man once again inserted his finger into Ahmed's wound. Each time, the terrorist screamed until he passed out.

After six hours, Ahmed was a broken man. He answered every question put to him. His interrogator stood, put his hand on Ahmed's shoulder, and said, "You will be getting medical care immediately. We will talk again tomorrow."

As the man left the facility, he called Sam. "Ahmed has confirmed everything Chin-Sun told us, or at least as much as he knows. We will be having further discussions tomorrow."

Sam responded to the independent contractor. "Thanks. Please keep me informed."

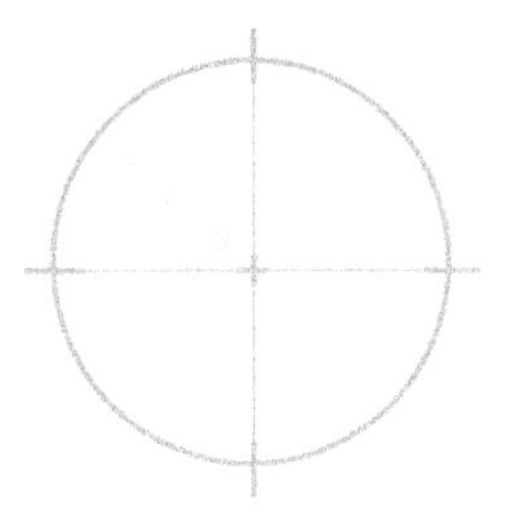

Chapter 77

Sandy and I checked out of our hotel in Philadelphia in the late morning. We walked through the lobby and out of the hotel. The lead agent for Philadelphia was waiting in his car. I put our luggage in the trunk and sat with Sandy in the back. I saw the agent looking at us in the review mirror and I said, "You're not still mad at me are you for going down to the warehouse?"

"No, Sam told me to lay off of you. He said you couldn't help yourself. So, are you going home now that your work here is finished?"

"No, Sandy and I are headed to Minneapolis to meet up with our friends Mac and Ann. They are part of the crew watching the warehouses in Minneapolis."

The agent pulled up in front of the airport and parked his car. The three of us got out and he helped me get our luggage out of the trunk. Sandy and I shook hands with him and headed into the airport. Our flight to Minneapolis seemed to pass quickly. After landing, we gathered our luggage and headed toward passenger pick-up. As we walked out the door, I saw Mac and Ann sitting in their car. He honked the horn, and I waved at him.

Ann got into the backseat, and I took her spot in the front seat. Soon we were headed for our hotel.

Mac smiled at me and said, "So, how are you doing?"

"Well, I could feed you a bunch of BS, but to be honest, I'm still a little shaken over what happened in Philadelphia. If it hadn't been for Sandy, I would be in a morgue somewhere. It was just a bit too close, I'd say."

Mac looked at me and grimaced, "I understand, my friend. I'm just glad you got Ahmed."

"We have Sandy to thank for that. It could've been much worse."

Ann asked, "Okay girl, where did you shoot him?"

"I got him in the thigh," answered Sandy. "DJ asked me why I did not hit him center mass. I told him I was trying to shoot his balls off." Laughter filled the car.

"Mac, what's happening here in the Twin Cities?"

"All of the warehouses except mine have been searched for the cylinders and nothing has been found. Mine was searched this morning, and I'll be damned if they didn't find the cylinder with the virus. Since Kamil has not been seen around my warehouse, he probably has moved on to a different city. We are scheduled, however, to keep our eye on it for a couple more days. After that, I suppose we head back to DC."

"We thought we would keep you company until we all can go back to DC. Hopefully, by then, Kamil will have been caught at one warehouse or another. When is your next shift?"

"Tonight, the graveyard shift," answered Mac. "I will drop you at the hotel, give you some time to get situated, and then we can go to dinner. How's that sound?"

"That works for us." A few moments later, Mac pulled up in front of the hotel. We got out, retrieved our luggage, checked in, and headed for our room.

Since we had agreed to meet downstairs at 5:00 PM, Sandy and I left the room and headed for the lobby.

We all walked to a restaurant close to the hotel that Mac had suggested. Once there, the hostess directed us to a booth in the back. I noticed the police officer in Mac pop out when he sat with his back to the wall and faced the door. I watched his eyes traversing the room looking for threats.

After we finished our meals, Mac ordered coffee and said, "A little caffeine to keep me awake tonight." Ann ordered some coffee also. Mac looked at her skeptically and asked, "Aren't you concerned that will keep you awake tonight?"

"I intend to be seated next to you, watching the warehouse. And don't even try to talk me out of it." Mac rolled his eyes in surrender.

Sandy spoke up next, "It seems to me that it would be a good idea for us to accompany you."

I responded to her, "I'm tired, and I think we should just sleep in the hotel."

"DJ, you can be tired tomorrow. Tonight will be our adventure. As I recall, Mac said that he would be surveilling from across the street. You also said that there would be four agents hidden within the warehouse itself?"

Mac responded, "I did indeed." Eyeing me, he continued, "You can sleep tomorrow, DJ. Besides that, they have a sofa where we will be. You can catch 40 winks there."

We kept drinking coffee until it was time to head for the warehouse.

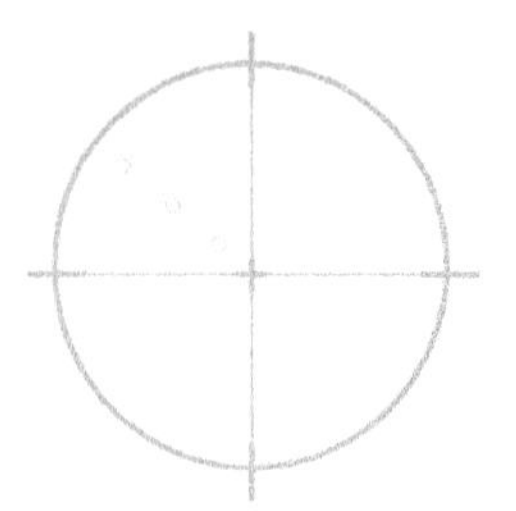

Chapter 78

Kamil was sitting on the bed at the dingy hotel. He was waiting for the time when he would leave to begin his attack. The terrorist had seen his likeness shown on the TV earlier. To change his appearance, he had shaved his head and placed cotton balls in his mouth to change the shape of his face. When he looked in the mirror, he didn't even recognize himself.

His first target that evening was the Fillmore Minneapolis. It was hosting a concert for a rock band he had never heard of. Previously, he had gone online and purchased a ticket to the event.

At 6:00 PM, he left his hotel room and walked to his car. Arriving at the Fillmore, he parked by 6:30 PM. It did not take long to be admitted to the concert venue. As he approached the security gate, he placed small tubes around his ears and the nose piece under his nose. This tube was attached to the small cylinder containing the virus. It looked just like an oxygen bottle. When he reached the gate, he placed his backpack on the metal shelf, opened it, and showed the cylinder to the security agent. The agent asked, "What is this for?"

Kamil responded, "I have asthma and it helps me breathe. I have a doctor's note explaining my condition and why I need it, if you would like to look at it." Without a second thought, the agent waved him through.

Once inside, Kamil walked around the venue, spraying in small amounts as he went. Slowly, the arena filled with people and Kamil kept up his attack. Just before the concert was scheduled to begin, he sprayed the last of the Ebola from that cylinder as he walked out into the street heading for his car.

Kamil had snuck into the warehouse the previous evening during a heavy rainstorm. He had spent a good hour watching the warehouse to see if it was under surveillance, but he had not noticed any. Kamil wanted to stop and have dinner because he did not want to arrive at the warehouse again before midnight to refill his cylinders. Kamil chose an all-night diner that was a 30-minute drive from the warehouse.

Since he was in no hurry, Kamil took his time ordering and eating. He ordered a salad with grilled chicken and some garlic bread. After completing his meal, the man walked toward his car. The clock on the dashboard read 11:45 PM. Kamil smiled to himself. Everything is going, once again, according to schedule. He started the car and headed for the warehouse.

Pulling the car to the side of the road, he stopped and got out. Previously, he had selected a point where he could observe the warehouse to see if it was being watched. Squatting down in a patch of bushes, Kamil began his observation of the warehouse. After an hour, he decided it was safe to move and walked along the chain-link fence that was the only protection from individuals who wanted to break into the warehouse. Coming to a place where he had previously cut away a section of the fence, Kamil walked silently to the building. On the side of the warehouse, there was a window approximately four feet off the ground. The window was still partially open, and he crawled through. Kamil walked to the door, which opened onto the warehouse floor.

Carefully, so as to make no noise, he opened the door and stepped into the warehouse. It was pitch black except for a little light coming through windows that were higher up on the wall. Kamil walked toward the container he knew contained the cylinder. For some reason, Kamil stopped, unable to explain why. He thought he heard a voice talking in low tones. Kamil silently crept forward toward the container. He was able to make out four men, two standing near and two sitting and leaning with their backs against the container.

Kamil had to decide whether to leave or risk taking on these four men. If he decided to attack these men, he would have the element of surprise. After much thought, Kamil decided to attack.

The terrorist jumped out of the darkness and fired a shot at each of the two men standing. They dropped without a sound. Kamil then swiveled to the two men seated and begin firing. One of the seated men was able to draw his weapon and fired in Kamil's direction. After two shots, the agent slumped to the floor. While he did not know if the four men were dead, it was clear to Kamil that they would cause him no trouble.

The terrorist opened the shipping container and began searching for the cylinder he had used the night before. It was nowhere to be found. Kamil had no way of knowing that earlier that day, a hazmat team had removed the cylinder and had taken it away.

I had been standing next to the window facing the warehouse. I heard the first two shots and saw the gun flashes for the second two.

Mac yelled, "Something bad is going on down there. Come on, DJ, let's go check this out." We ran down the stairs, out the door, and toward the door of the other warehouse. As we entered the building, we could hear someone shouting. We walked quietly toward the sound until we could make out an individual.

Mac screamed, "You're under arrest. Throw down your weapon!" Kamil fired two more shots in our direction and took off running. Mac and I followed after him. We saw him open a door, run through it, and slam it after him.

Kamil saw his chance to escape. He crawled through the window and jumped to the ground. He looked up and saw Ann and

Sandy pointing their weapons at him from ten feet away. He was not going to be stopped by these two infidel women.

He raised his weapon. Four shots rang out. The two women walked over and looked down at Kamil's body.

Ann said, "Damn, Sandy, you're getting to be a good shot. You double tapped him in the chest."

Sandy responded, "And you double tapped him in the forehead, but he still has his balls."

Ann replied, "He did, you mean," as she fired two shots into his groin.

Mac poked his head out the window and said, "What the hell happened?"

Ann smiled at him and said, "We were just backing you up."

While I ran back to check on the four agents inside the warehouse, Mac called the team leader and explained what had happened. Minutes later, the team leader was on the scene.

Someone had turned on the warehouse lights and now illuminated the four men near the open container. One man was deceased, but the other three were still alive. I called 911 and told them four officers were down and gave them the address. Within moments, we heard the sirens in the distance as they approached. By the time they arrived, the warehouse was swarming with FBI agents. After giving our statements to the lead agent, we were released to go back to our hotel. Both Mac and I had made a positive identification that the terrorist was, in fact, Kamil.

After a troubled sleep, the next morning the four of us flew back to Washington, DC.

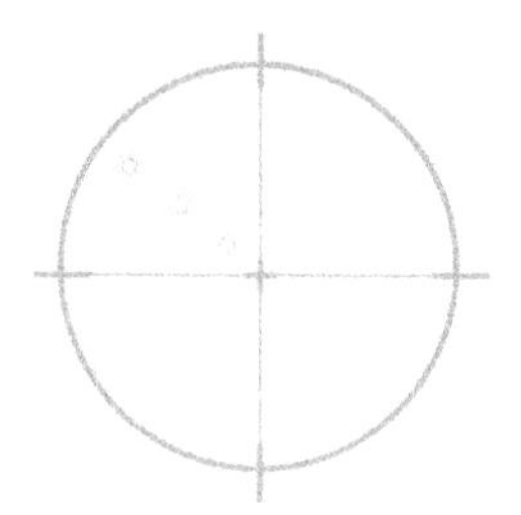

Chapter 79

Dr. Madelyn O'Hare, Director of the CDC, was sitting outside the Oval Office waiting to meet with the President. Layla Richards, the President's secretary, smiled at her and said, "I'm sure you've heard that the two terrorists have been captured or killed."

"Yes, I have heard that. Unfortunately, my work continues," replied O'Hare.

Understanding, the secretary nodded at her.

Soon, the door opened and Brad Nelson, Chief of Staff, walked out. "Good morning, Doctor O'Hare. Please come in."

She walked into the Oval Office and shook hands with President Bradford. The President, who was standing behind the Resolute desk, motioned for her to sit in one of the two chairs facing him. Brad Nelson took the second chair.

The President began the conversation by stating, "Well, Doctor O'Hare, what do you have for me today?"

"First, as you may have been briefed, we believe that we have found all of the Ebola cylinders. Each of the cylinders we found was in one of the target cities. Because of that, we are confident we have them all.

"Second, I have been coordinating with the labs around the country and have multiple teams trying to find a vaccine for this virus. However, we still could be many months away from developing and producing a vaccine.

"Third, it seems that most cases are around the target cities. Unfortunately, given the way people travel these days, we are seeing a spread of the virus throughout the country. In any state where Ebola cases have been found, the governors are enacting strict measures to prevent its spread. Unlike the Covid pandemic, there seems to be unanimity among the governors on the action that should be taken. I expect that is because this Ebola virus is so deadly.

"That brings me to my next point, Mr. President. We believe that there are over 25,000 people infected with the virus, most of whom will die. It would not surprise me if that number rose to 100,000 within a few days. Sir, if there is any way that we can find or develop a vaccine, we must do it now. If the virus continues to spread, we could be at a million deaths within a month or so. In all my years as a physician, I have not seen any virus as deadly as this one."

The President had been listening intently to Dr. O'Hare's briefing. He had been told and was mildly surprised that the Republican governors were following the recommendations of the CDC. It was clear to them that this virus was not a question of individual rights but of medical necessity. The President was concerned that some of the medical professionals would refuse to treat patients because of the deadly nature of this virus.

He was struggling with the number of deaths, potential deaths, and with the realization that this virus truly could end the human race. Bradford had, however, received information from the interrogation of those people captured that a vaccine may have been developed by North Korea. If so, he was determined to get that vaccine. In fact, his next meeting would be about what actions he could take to accomplish that goal.

Bradford had additional questions for Doctor O'Hare and spent the next half hour getting them answered. As the meeting ended, he told the doctor he might be able to help with finding a vaccine, but that's all he could tell her. As Dr. O'Hare and his Chief of Staff left, the President stood and looked out the windows. Unlike most days, the sidewalks were empty of pedestrian traffic. Fear of the virus had come to this country in a big way.

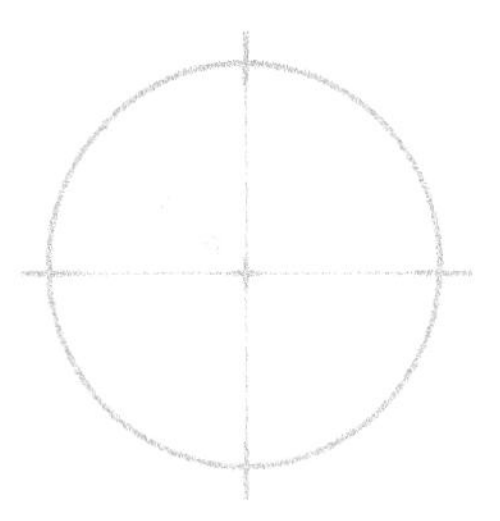

Chapter 80

Immediately after his meeting with Dr. O'Hare, the President had called for a meeting of his national security team. Present were the Secretary of Defense, Kyle Taylor; the Secretary of State, Toni McCrae; the Chairman of the Joint Chiefs of Staff, Gen. Pete Witkowski; the Secretary of Homeland Security, Brian Jenson; the Director of NSA, Bill Simpson; the Director of National Intelligence, Julianne Simmons; the President's Chief of Staff, Brad Nelson; the Vice Chair of the Joint Chiefs of Staff, Admiral Lara Williams; and the Director of the FBI, Ryan Tupper. Also present by secured video was Admiral David Miller, Commander of the US Indo-Pacific command. These individuals are responsible for protecting America from all enemies, both foreign and domestic.

Bradford began, "Ladies and gentlemen, thank you for being here for this most important meeting. What I'm going to tell you, you probably already know. However, I want to make sure that we are on the same page as we consider what action we are going to take. First, it appears that no further terrorist attacks involving the Ebola virus will occur. From what we know, only two male Mideastern terrorists were involved in spreading the virus in this country. The cities that were attacked were St. Louis, Kansas City, Minneapolis, and Boston. A terrorist also attacked Philadelphia but was captured before the virus could be released.

"In addition, we have captured two North Korean agents. Those individuals have been interrogated and have given us valuable information. Because of this, we were able to confirm that one agent was able to have a senator provide her with important national security information. That woman told us of another woman who is a North Korean agent living on the West Coast; she has been giving us tremendous amounts of information about this Ebola attack. Both of these agents revealed to us that this attack was planned, approved, and ordered by President Kim of North Korea.

"This meeting is convened to discuss what potential actions we should take against North Korea, determine the capabilities of our Armed Forces, and put our plan into action. From my perspective, the actions of Kim and North Korea constitute an act of war against this country. Does anyone disagree with that statement?"

The Secretary of Homeland Security spoke first, "How solid is the information that President Kim is behind these terrorist attacks?"

The President pointed to the Director of the FBI, who stated, "We have the highest confidence that Kim took the actions the President described. We have more than one person who has confirmed that to us. Both were in direct contact with Kim at some point."

"Does anyone else have any questions?" asked the President. Hearing none, the President asked, "Does anyone have any suggestions on how we should respond?"

The Secretary of State had been involved in the field of statecraft over many years. He stated, "Well, normally, we would say that our actions should be commensurate with the actions of North Korea. In my view, however, the potential deaths that will occur from this virus are so enormous that I believe we should strike North Korea as heavily as we can." There was a general murmur of agreement around the table.

The President spoke again, "I have given this situation a great deal of thought. Here's what I think we should do. We have reason to believe that North Korea may have an operational vaccine against this virus. I believe I should call Kim and tell him in no uncertain terms that we are sending an aircraft to their capital and demand that all vaccine for this virus be placed on that plane so we can take actions to stop it from spreading. Failing to do so, I will tell him that we will launch a nuclear attack on his country."

That statement brought many voices being raised in opposition. The President held up his hand to stop further discussion. "It would not be my intention, initially, to order such an attack. However, I want him to fear what our country will do. After we receive the vaccine, I believe that our military should strike North Korean military targets, command-and-control targets, and others recommended by the Joint Chiefs. I think we need to cut the little prick off at the knees."

After several hours of discussion, the meeting ended with every individual supporting the President's recommended action. The President asked the Chairman and Vice Chairman of Joint Chiefs of Staff and Admiral Miller to remain in the room while the others filed out of the room, still talking among themselves.

The President asked the three advisors still seated at the table. "I assume that our military has had plans to attack North Korea in place for some time. I would ask that the three of you provide me with a plan of action against North Korea by tomorrow evening. Is that feasible?"

General Witkowski answered the President, "Yes sir, we can be ready with a plan for you by tomorrow evening."

"Good, go to work and give Kim something he will always remember." The President watched the men leave and stated out loud, "Our best and brightest will show why the United States must be respected, if not feared."

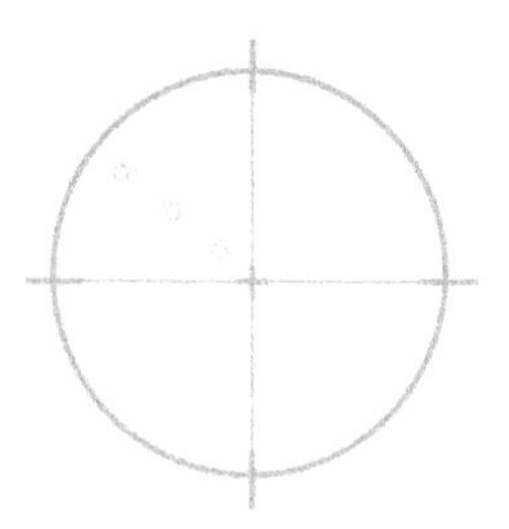

Chapter 81

Sam was returning from lunch. He had grabbed a tuna sandwich at a small sandwich shop down the street from his office. Leaving the office during some portion of his day had become a habit. Sometimes, the stress at his job was overwhelming, and just to get out for a few minutes helped clear his mind. Eating his sandwich, he sat alone but pondered what he should be doing with regard to the virus. Given all that had happened, Sam believed he should bring the French up to speed.

After the last bites were gone, Sam picked up his phone and dialed Mael's number. After several rings, Mael answered. "Hi, Sam, what's going on?"

"I wasn't sure I was going to find you in the office. I'm glad that I did though. I wanted to give you some information about what has happened here. First, regarding the terrorists, we have captured Ahmed and have killed Kamil."

"That's great news, Sam," responded Mael. "How did you manage that feat?"

"With some help of electronic surveillance, we were able to nail down which cities they planned to attack. After a lot of hard work and painstaking analysis, we were able to find each container arriving from China that was scheduled to be delivered to the target cities. At that point, we sent agents to those cities to watch all the warehouses that the containers had been destined for. However, Boston, St. Louis, Minneapolis and Kansas City were successfully attacked with the virus. We finally had sufficient resources to search every shipping container in every warehouse in every target city which might contain the virus. We were lucky enough to find that the virus was contained in a cylinder in each of those shipping containers and were able to secure these cylinders with hazmat teams. You have no idea how much manpower was involved."

"How did you get the terrorists?"

"You won't believe what I'm about to tell you. We had the three professors stationed at a warehouse in each of the target cities. Since they were not expected to see any action, their wives accompanied them. DJ Anderson was in Philadelphia watching a warehouse when he detected Ahmed there.

"To make a long story short, his wife, while backing up her husband, shot Ahmed in the thigh, and he was captured. In Minneapolis, DJ and Mac were watching a warehouse when Kamil entered. The two men confronted him, and he tried to escape. As he went out a window, who should be waiting for him, but the men's two wives. Each of the wives double-tapped Kamil. Can you believe that shit?"

"I hope I don't run into them in a dark alley! What kind of Ebola casualties are you having?"

"25,000+ and it's only going to get worse. To our knowledge, no vaccine is currently available. This virus travels through the air, and if you are infected, it is very likely that you will die. I've seen estimates that the number could reach a million in a few months. If no vaccine is found, this could be the deadliest pandemic the world has ever seen. However, all hope is not lost. There is the potential that a vaccine may be available. I can't tell you more than that, but I can assure you that the President will be launching new actions to find that vaccine. I will be able to tell you more later, but I suggest that you may want to follow the news coming from Washington."

Mael did not speak for a few seconds before he stated, "What you have related to me is terrifying. I've heard that we have identified a few cases in France. I know the government here has been in touch with your CDC and is looking for directions on how to proceed. These are certainly scary times for all of us."

Sam responded, "I couldn't agree with you more. Anyway, Mael, I wanted to let you know what I know. If I can be of any assistance, please give me a call."

"Thanks for all the information you've provided. Best of luck to you, my friend."

After hanging up, Mael spent several minutes reviewing what Sam had told him. He called Pierre and passed on the information he had received. After hanging up, Mael paused and said a short prayer for his country.

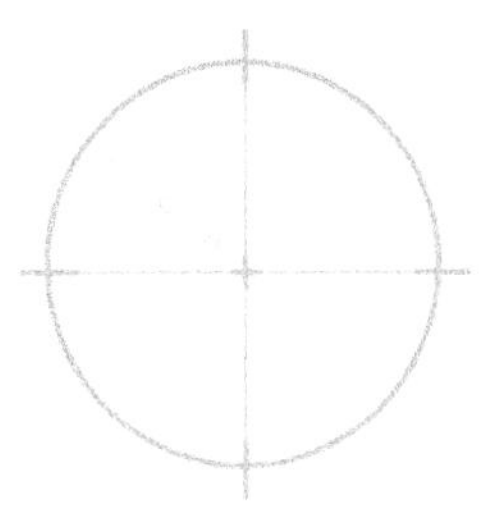

Chapter 82

The President's Chief of Staff, Brad Nelson, ushered Gen. Witkowski and Adm. Williams into the Oval Office. He informed both officers that the President was running a few minutes late and would be there shortly. Nelson left and returned to his office.

Witkowski stated, "Just another day at the office. We are here to advise the Commander-in-Chief as to his military options concerning North Korea. It is still hard to believe that the President is considering the use of nuclear weapons."

Admiral Williams responded, "If it's any comfort to you, North Korea is probably the only country that truly justifies being the target for nukes."

"I agree. When I became Chairman of the Joint Chiefs of Staff, I never really thought it was an actual possibility that I would advise the President to use nuclear weapons. I've known the President for quite a while. I have to give him credit for giving Kim an ultimatum. Even as governor, he was not averse to make hard decisions."

The door swung open, and in walked the President and Nelson. "Good evening. Please be seated. I'm sorry for running a bit late, but it couldn't be helped. I was meeting with some Boy Scouts from my home state. Now, to the more serious business. I presume you have an attack plan for me.

Gen. Witkowski responded, "Yes, sir, we do."

"Okay, let's hear it."

Admiral Williams took over the briefing. "We have a boomer currently stationed about 1,500 miles from North Korea. It is the USS *Henry M. Jackson* and carries 20 Trident II D5 missiles. Each missile carries a number of independently targeted nuclear warheads.

"Our non-nuclear force consists of two submarines, USS *Georgia* and the USS *Ohio*. Each of them has in excess of 150 Tomahawk missiles with conventional warheads. Each of those ships are within 750 miles of North Korea. The range of the Tomahawk is 1,000 miles. We have provided the captains of those ships with the targeting information necessary to take out various military targets in North Korea.

"The Air Force will have various aircraft on station to attack. Some of those planes will be carrying bunker-buster bombs.

"Finally, we have the USS *Ronald Reagan* stationed in Japan. That carrier and her group of supporting 12 ships are in the process of departing Japan to be on station to launch aircraft. Several of her group can also launch Tomahawk missiles. That would be in addition to the 75 planes that are available on the *Reagan* which can strike North Korea.

"In short, our plan would be to initially fire the Tomahawks to take out North Korea's nuclear program, missile sites, and air defense capabilities. Additional Tomahawks would then rain down on the command-and-control sites and various military installations, including her airfields. The attack would begin in the evening and continue until such time as we believe we have achieved our objectives."

The President stopped the admiral for a moment and asked, "If we attack, do you believe that we can destroy their missiles and nuclear program before they could order a counterattack?"

General Witkowski answered that question. "Mr. President, let me be frank. We expect to get most, if not all, of the targets we aim at. However, we cannot know whether their air defense system might be able to bring down some of our cruise missiles. It's not unheard of that there will be mechanical issues with the cruise missiles. And it is certainly possible that we do not know the locations of all their missiles that could be fired at us. All that I can tell you is that we will hit them with everything we have. We also have reconnaissance over their country to help us determine if we missed anything."

The President asked, "What kind of ordnance will you be using?"

"Most everything we have. We do have large bunker busters that will target certain missile facilities and nuclear facilities. These will be dropped by Air Force planes."

The President said, "Okay, I'm going to call Kim tomorrow. I want to be very straight with him on the weapons systems that are targeting him. I don't want him to be surprised by what we do. What is the plan on sending the plane to Pyongyang to get the vaccines?"

General Witkowski answered, "We have a C130 readied to make the trip. Once the vaccine arrives in Tokyo, we have jet aircraft ready to fly the vaccine directly to this country."

"Thank you. Please work with the Secretary of Defense and have the appropriate authorization orders ready for me to sign."

"Yes, sir."

As they were returning to the Pentagon, General Witkowski remarked, "I don't think he'll hesitate in using nuclear weapons if Kim does not agree to his demands."

The admiral commented, "it's a brand-new world, General. A brand-new world."

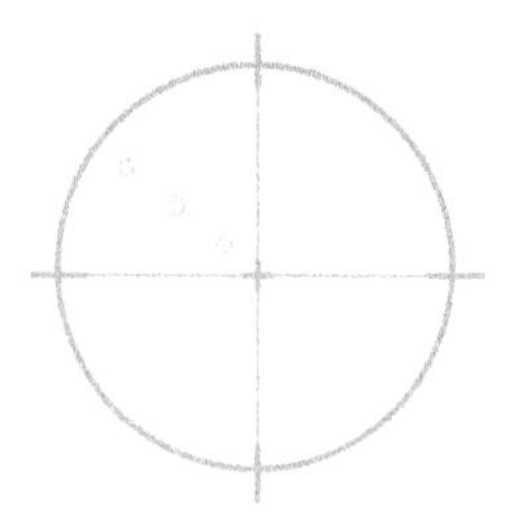

Chapter 83

Ty, Mac, and I, along with and our wives, were seated outside the Oval Office waiting to see the President. I had received a call from his Chief of Staff, telling us that the President would like us to come and see him. We were speculating why he would want us to come to the White House. The general consensus was that he probably was going to give us a medal for our work at the warehouses. It would be fun to meet the leader of the free world once again.

Arriving at the White House, we had been relieved of our weapons. It was made quite clear to us that no one got near the President of the United States with a weapon. We were escorted to the Oval Office by Renee, a young intern from Kentucky. She made small talk with us during our walk.

The door to the Oval Office opened and out walked General Witkowski. He told the President's secretary that from this point on the President did not want to be interrupted. The six of us looked at each other, wondering what that was all about.

The general stated, "Won't you come with me?" We followed him into the Oval Office and the President walked over and shook each of our hands.

We also greeted General Witkowski, Admiral Nelson, and several other individuals to whom the president introduced us. Some of these people we recognized and others, we did not.

Bradford spoke to us, "I asked you to be here for something special."

Mac leaned over and whispered to me, "It must be the medals."

The President continued, "I know about how you survived the attack in Paris. I've been briefed on your fight with Samir in this country. And finally, we've had your help in trying to find the terrorists, Ahmed and Kamil. You were hired by the FBI to be available to help identify these two men. But you did more than that, you captured Ahmed and eliminated Kamil.

"Those two men have caused the deaths of thousands of our countrymen and women already. What you may not know is this attack on the United States was the work of President Kim of North Korea. In just a few moments, I am going to be having a conversation with Kim and I wanted you to hear it for yourself."

As the President was speaking to us, the other individuals in the room looked at us and smiled.

Mac whispered to me once again, "I wasn't expecting this. Now it gets really interesting!"

The Chief of Staff stated, "The call should be going through in a moment, taking into account the time difference."

Bradford nodded and then the phone rang. "Mr. President, this is the President of the United States speaking."

Kim responded, "I am most happy to talk with you. I haven't spoken with anyone from your country since I talked with President Trump."

"Trump is a pussy. I am not."

"I don't understand this. What is pussy?" Everyone in the room could hear someone on the other end of the line explaining what the President had said. Kim continued, "What is this about?"

"I'm glad you asked," the President responded. "I have some things I want to say to you, and I would appreciate it if you would not interrupt me. Can you do that?"

"Yes, of course."

"As you know, the United States has been attacked with the Ebola virus. Many thousands of our countrymen and women have died already. We have arrested and interrogated two of your agents who have informed us, that based on conversations with you, and others in your country, that you planned and ordered this attack on the United States."

Kim started to speak but the President stopped him. "Please do not interrupt me. You'll have the chance to speak later. Your actions constitute an act of war. I've been assured by Congress that they are prepared to approve a declaration of war between North Korea and the United States.

"I assume that you would not want that to occur since both of us know that we can squash you like the bug you are.

"I want you to know what I have ordered so that you can carefully decide what you would like to do. First, the USS *Henry M. Jackson*, a ballistic missile submarine loaded with 20 missiles with multiple independently targeted nuclear warheads, is 1,500 miles off your coast. The captain of that submarine has orders from me to fire on your country 24 hours from now. If those orders are not countermanded by me, your country will be a nuclear wasteland within 20 minutes of launch.

"To avoid this attack, here is what must happen," the President continued. "We know you have a vaccine available to stop the spread of this virus. In 12 hours, a C-130 from Tokyo will proceed to your capital. You will have available at your airport all of the vaccine that you possess, which will then be loaded onto our plane. Furthermore, you will make available all of the scientists who are responsible for developing the vaccine. They will come to the United States to assist us with production of the vaccine. After the plane lands in Tokyo, and we verify that the vaccine and scientists are there, I will countermand the order I've given to the captain of the USS *Jackson*. Do you understand?"

Kim replied, shock and rage tightening his voice. "How dare you threaten me like this?"

The President answered, "Well, I just did what you called threatening you. However, I am telling you that this is not a threat, this is a promise!"

The President was speaking in a voice that hid his barely controlled anger. "If you think I'm bluffing, you simply do not know me. By the way, the crew of the C-130 are all volunteers. Because each of them is prepared to die during this mission, taking them as hostages will be of no benefit to you.

"Finally, the C-130 must be back in Tokyo one hour before the *Jackson* lights up your country. Also, President Kim, please understand that this matter is very personal to me. My best friend was killed by your virus. So, you little prick, you have a decision to make. I hope you have a good evening, sir." The President hung up.

Everyone sat there in stunned silence.

Mac spoke first, "Damn! Now that's what I call a President!"

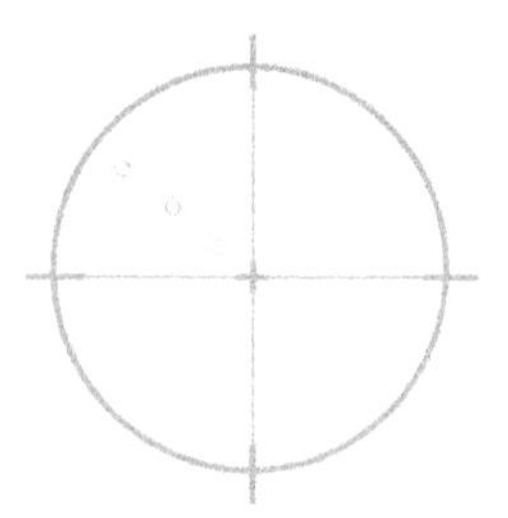

Chapter 84

President Kim and his sister, Kim Yo Jong, sat in stunned silence after the phone call ended. The other man in the room who listened to the call also said nothing. Finally, Kim stated, "Who in the hell did he think he was talking to? I am the President of North Korea and deserve the same respect as any other head of state.

Taking a deep breath, Kim screamed, "How did he find out?" stomping around the room, throwing epitaphs at the United States President.

His sister responded, "Dear brother, we must not look at this personally but rather logically. It is clear that the US president intended to inflame your passions. However, for us to determine the best course for our country, we must put his insults aside."

Kim seemed to calm down as he listened to his sister. She had been his most important advisor on relations with the United States. Looking at her, he asked, "How do you see this and what do you think we should do?" He sat down next to his sister and waited for her answer.

"My initial reaction is that we should meet his demands."

Kim exploded, "What are you talking about? How can we possibly lose such face?"

She responded, "Hear me out, brother. We can decide not to comply, but we risk a nuclear attack. That would end your rule and our control of the country as we know it. That is something we cannot risk. But the question remains, would he carry out such an attack? If you decide to do nothing, you must be absolutely sure that he will not attack using nuclear weapons.

She continued. "If you meet his demands, we do so in the name of humanity. You deny that we unleashed this virus, but you agreed to give him any vaccines we have. You deny that we caused this virus to spread in America. Also, you will send any scientists of ours who have knowledge of the Ebola virus to assist the United States in developing a vaccine. Doing that makes you appear to be the leader of a nation willing to help others as best as you can."

Kim then asked, "What about our agents? The US claims to have all of the specifics of our plan."

"You deny that you spoke to either of them. We also indicate that they were terminated from our employment some time ago. We consider them simply disgruntled former employees. As to the information they provided, we deny it all.

"If you think this sounds possible, we should respond to his demands immediately. Furthermore, you should assemble the vaccine and scientists at the airport and inform the US that they can send their C-130 whenever they wish. What do you think, brother?"

Kim was quiet for several moments as he thought about his sister's comments. Soon, he realized that her advice made the most sense. He will have achieved his goal of attacking the United States and causing great misery. Also, it will spread the message that the United States is vulnerable to attack. He looked at his sister and smiled, "I think your recommendations are very wise, sister. We can follow the lead of former President Trump. Never admit anything that is harmful to you, and simply deny everything in spite of the facts. As he showed in the United States, people were willing to follow the Big Lie.

"I want you, sister, to craft the reply to the United States and prepare to have our vaccine and scientists available." He smiled as he watched her walk away, confident that his wishes would be carried out.

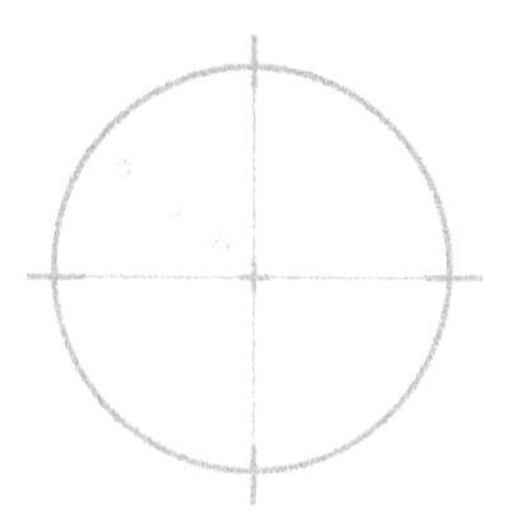

Chapter 85

The USS *Henry M. Jackson*, an Ohio-class ballistic missile submarine, is named after the late senator from the State of Washington. This boat carries up to 20 Trident II D–5 missiles. Each missile carries multiple, independently targeted nuclear warheads. It was currently at a depth of 500 feet, traveling in excess of 20 knots and was within 1,500 miles of the North Korean coast.

Commander Jonas Hardy was skipper of the blue crew currently stationed on the *Jackson,* Executive Officer Lieutenant Commander Sam Hill, told Hardy that an emergency action message was coming in. Hardy told Hill to bring it and two junior officers to his stateroom to authenticate the message.

When all the necessary officers had joined the captain in the stateroom, the four men, following protocol, authenticated the message. The captain dismissed the two junior officers to have a private conversation with his executive officer. The captain asked, "What do you make of this?"

"It obviously consists of an order to fire missiles at North Korea. It also provides us with the targeting information for each missile. Unlike other firing tests, it gives us 24 hours for missile launch. It tells us that unless we receive an order countermanding this order, we are to launch."

Captain Hardy responded, "Well, we have authenticated the message. Do you think it is possible that there is a potential error, or someone has figured out how to send this message outside the chain of command?"

"I assume that it is possible, but it is highly unlikely."

The captain continued, "Have you seen anything in the news or from other communications that would make this course of action possible? I certainly have not."

"Nor have I."

"Well, XO, what is your recommendation?"

"I suggest we prepare the crew for a potential launch. I do think we should ask Command Authority to verify the message."

The captain responded, "I agree. Get ready to follow through on those actions. I also believe we should check all of our newsfeeds to determine if we have missed something that would make sense of this order."

"I will, Captain. Are there any other words you have for me?"

"Not at this time, XO. Let's hope we find some answers before we have to start this madness. You know, since I've been captain of the *Jackson*, I never really believed I would have to launch these missiles."

XO Sam Hill left the captain's stateroom to carry out his orders.

Captain Hardy lay down on his bunk, closed his eyes, and felt the weight of his responsibilities. At least he had some time to figure this out. The idea he could initiate an action that could start World War III and kill millions of individuals shook him deeply. But his training told him that he had to trust those in command above him.

At the same time Hardy was lying in his bunk, the commanding officers of the USS *Ohio* and USS *Georgia* received similar orders. Their orders directed them to prepare to fire their cruise missiles at targets in North Korea.

The captain of the USS *Ohio*, Commander Jason Allen, called his XO into his state room to have a similar conversation. The difference in their orders from that of the *Jackson* was that they should be prepared to fire immediately. The two men talked at length about what preparations were needed to ensure a successful launch.

The captain of the USS *Georgia*, Commander Jessie Carter, did not initially talk to her XO. She sat and pondered what would be needed to carry out these orders. When she decided the appropriate course of action, she called in her XO to give him directions on how she wanted to proceed.

Admiral Wilson Turner, Commander of the Reagan carrier group, sat in his state room, reading the orders he had just been given. His orders were to the point. He was to get the *Reagan* ready to launch attacks against North Korea. He was informed that the actual targets would be given to him at a later time. The message Turner received indicated this was not a drill.

Turner and his people had a lot of work before them. He called in the captain of the *Reagan* and the commander of the air group. He laid out the tasks before them and was not surprised when they simply stated, "Yes, sir." These men were professionals and knew what they had to do.

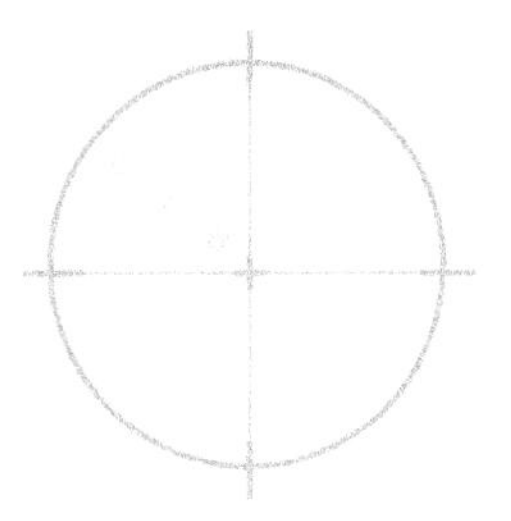

Chapter 86

At the Yakota Air Base in Tokyo, Capt. Shane Johanson and Lieutenant Donny Sherman were waiting in the ready room for word that their C-130 was ready to go. Of all the days you didn't want to have mechanical problems, today was that day. They were going to be the first US aircraft flying to Pyongyang, the North Korean capital, in decades. Both men had volunteered for this mission; neither had any family depending on them. The two load masters, Sergeant Jimmy O'Neil and Sergeant Wally Putnam, were already in the plane preparing for the flight.

This mission had just been scheduled that morning. Evidently, they were to fly to North Korea to load vaccine designed to stop the spread of the Ebola virus. Johanson did not know the quantity of the vaccine they were picking up. They were also informed that they would be bringing back the scientists who helped develop this vaccine. The two Americans had also been warned that this could be a trap and their lives could be in danger. To assist them would be 20 fully armed Marines who would guard the plane and crew while on the ground in Pyongyang.

The two aviators were called by airport officials and told that the plane was ready to take off. Lieutenant Sherman boarded the plane and went to the flight deck to begin the takeoff procedures. Captain Johanson walked around the plane checking to see if anything was visible that could cause a problem. Seeing none, he joined Lieutenant Sherman on the flight deck. Over the intercom, the captain informed Sergeant O'Neil to get the Marines on board.

O'Neil had direct radio contact with the captain in charge of the Marines. Without delay, the Marines were on board, seated, and ready for takeoff.

Sergeant O'Neil told the captain that they were ready to leave. The engines roared to life, the chocks were removed from the wheels, and the plane slowly began to move forward following the direction of the plane handler. They taxied to the end of their assigned runway and waited for clearance to take off. When the air traffic controller told him they were free to take off, Johnson held the controls and Sherman advanced the throttles. When the brakes were released, the plane slowly moved forward until it reached takeoff speed. Johanson pulled back on the controls and the plane lifted off.

The flight to the capital of North Korea was just over two hours. The flight crew and the Marines had been briefed on what to expect and what their jobs were. The flight was smooth with very few clouds as they headed toward North Korea. When they were 20 miles from the North Korean coastline, they began to circle, awaiting approval from the North Koreans to enter their airspace and land. Once requested, approval came back almost instantaneously. Johanson looked at Sherman and stated, "Well, here we go. Let's hope we all are operating from the same playbook."

Following the directions of the Korean air controller, the crew received final permission to land. Johanson had previously decided to show the North Koreans how Americans could fly. He brought the plane down with a soft touch that even made him smile. They followed the tower instructions on where to taxi and soon arrived outside of a large warehouse. Captain Johanson brought the plane to a stop, walked back into the cargo area, and ordered the ramp lowered. Behind Johanson were the 20 Marines.

Once the ramp hit the ground, Johanson and the marines walked down and came face to face with a North Korean officer.

Behind the officer were approximately 20 soldiers. Johanson introduced himself to the officer and they shook hands.

The officer asked Johanson to come with him as they entered the warehouse. The Marines stayed behind but within close proximity. The officer pointed out ten pallets that were to be loaded on the C-130. Johanson gave approval for the loading and watched as it commenced.

Once the last pallet was secured within the plane, four men wearing dark suits walked out of the warehouse. These were the scientists Johanson was expecting. He shook hands with the officer once again and led the scientists onto the plane. O'Neill raised the ramp while Putnam showed the scientists where to sit.

Once again, the crew prepared their aircraft for takeoff. They taxied to the end of the runway and waited for the approval of the North Koreans. Permission came after a long few minutes. There was no talking in the cargo area as the plane rolled down the runway. As they began to gain altitude and head toward the coast, the silence continued. As soon as they crossed the coast, Johanson provided that information to the Marines in the rear. There was sudden laughter as the tension cleared. Asked why they laughed, not one of the Marines believed that he would get out of North Korea without a fight.

The return flight to Tokyo seemed to fly by. In no time, Johanson performed another flawless landing and taxied to the warehouse that had been set aside for them. The captain ordered the ramp lowered, walked out, and was met by his commanding officer.

"No problem, sir, absolutely no problems," Johanson said.

"Good job, Johanson. You should expect a medal for this."

"Getting back without being shot at is better than any medal you could give me."

The pallets were removed from the plane. A soldier accompanied the Korean scientists. A few moments later, a C-17

Globemaster appeared. The pallets were carefully reloaded. The scientists were invited to proceed to their seats. The officer in charge of this part of the mission was Major Jack Elliott. Elliott had the plane in the air within 30 minutes heading to the US. The plane landed in Washington DC 13 hours after departing from Tokyo.

Employees from the CDC were waiting for the plane's arrival. After transferring the pallets and moving the scientists to waiting trucks, the convoy headed to the CDC labs.

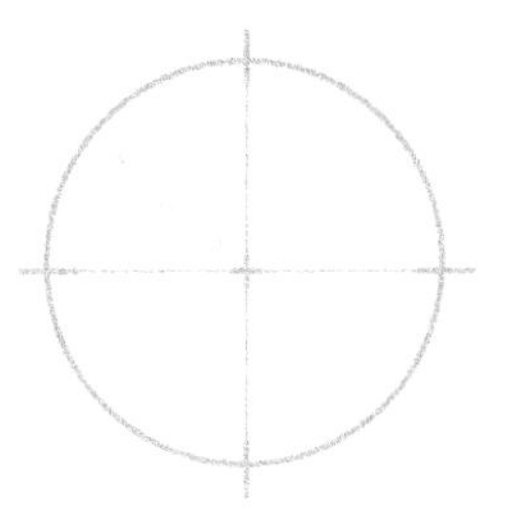

Chapter 87

President Bradford was seated in his rocking chair in the Oval Office. Sitting on the sofa to his left were the Speaker and the Minority Leader of the House of Representatives; to his right were the Senate Minority and Majority Leaders. Opposite him sat the Director of the CDC, Dr. Madelyn O'Hare.

The President stood and opened the meeting by stating, "Ladies and gentlemen, I have asked you to come here this evening so that I can brief you on the Ebola virus situation. First of all, I want to tell you that this was not a natural virus but was developed for the sole purpose of attacking this country."

All four members of Congress started to speak at once. The President held up his hand and asked them to let him finish. "We have proof that President Kim of North Korea ordered the development and distribution of this virus. Let me give you some background."

The President then began to explain all that had occurred. He began at the beginning and finished prior to his conversation with President Kim. "Before I go any further, I want Dr. O'Hare to give you some background on the virus."

Dr. O'Hare began, "First of all, the normal Ebola virus is transmitted by use of unclean needles, touching a contaminated surface, or by saliva transmission between people. This current virus, which, as I understand, has been engineered through 15 variations and is spread as an aerosol. Obviously, this makes the transmission much easier and results in more people contracting the virus. Initial symptoms include fever, headache, muscle pain, chills, and potentially internal bleeding. The most striking feature of this virus, aside from how fast it spreads, is how quickly it advances once in the body. We have had people come to the hospital for treatment and die within one or two days." Doctor O'Hare saw the members of Congress glance at each other.

She continued, "The numbers we are seeing in this country are hard to believe. In the last three weeks, we have identified over one half million individuals who contracted this virus. To date, over 100,000 Americans have died. If this virus continues to spread as it has, we can expect 4 to 5 million cases within several more months, which could result in at least as many additional deaths. However, at this time, I do not believe we can reduce the number of deaths."

The President interrupted O'Hare, "I want to tell you what steps I've taken. In a conversation with Kim, I told him we have proof that he attacked the United States with this virus. We also have learned that there may be a vaccine for this virus in North Korea. I gave Kim a choice. He could either provide the vaccine and the scientists who developed it to the United States or if he failed to do so, I would launch a nuclear attack on his country." Once again, the President raised his hand to silence the leaders of Congress.

The President continued, "I did not intend to authorize a nuclear strike without consultation with the members of Congress. That, however, is now off the table since Kim has provided us with the vaccine. I want to turn this meeting back over to Dr. O'Hare so that she can explain what is occurring with regard to the vaccine."

The director continued, "We have had the best virologists in this country meeting with the Korean scientists who developed this vaccine. It appears that the vaccine they brought with them does work in stopping the development of the virus at least in the short term. We believe we can develop a long-acting vaccine within a month. I know that this may sound amazing, given how difficult it was to develop a vaccine for the coronavirus. The difference is we have a complete history from the Korean scientists as to the development of the virus and the vaccine. We are working in partnerships with the companies who can make this vaccine. They too are comfortable in our belief that we can have a vaccine available within one month."

The President spoke again, "Now, I want to propose to you what actions I believe are appropriate. In my opinion, this attack by North Korea certainly constitutes an act of war, which warrants a vicious response. Given the threats that have been uttered by Kim, I believe that this country will be in grave danger in the future if he develops a missile that can be launched against United States. Furthermore, I think this country has been more than restrained in its dealings with North Korea.

"I am prepared, in consultation with members of Congress, to authorize a military strike of great significance against North Korea. That strike would include launching 300 cruise missiles aimed at military targets throughout North Korea. Also, I would direct the Navy to have the *Reagan* carrier group carry out strikes, as needed. The Air Force, using B-52s and other more modern aircraft, will carry out strikes, including using bunker buster bombs to lay waste to their nuclear and missile complexes.

"Through back channels, we will let the North Korean military know that if Kim and his family are removed from power, we would look favorably upon that. I know that you have many questions. Please ask them."

Surprisingly, there were no questions asked, but the Speaker of the House said, "I will support you in all of the actions you suggested. It's about time we take care of him." Each of the other members of Congress voiced their approval of the President's proposed actions.

The President rose and shook each of their hands. “I will keep you informed as to when these actions will take place. Because these actions may place American servicemen and women in jeopardy, I ask that you keep this information to yourselves and only yourselves.

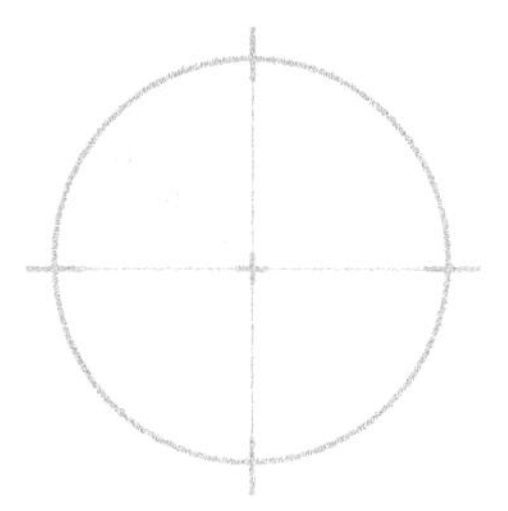

Chapter 88

Two days later, Captain Allen called his executive officer to his stateroom. One could see both the stress and the professionalism etched on both of the men's faces. He motioned for the XO to take a seat on his rack while he remained seated in his desk chair.

The captain began, "Has the targeting data been uploaded to each of the cruise missiles?"

"Yes, sir. As you know, we received the data yesterday afternoon. Our sailors completed uploading the targeting information early this morning. The birds are ready to fly."

"Okay, we have an order to launch at midnight. That gives us a little over an hour to make sure all things are prepared. At 2330 hours, I want you to bring the boat up to launch depth, and I want you to confirm with command authority that our order still stands to launch."

"No problem, sir, it will be done."

The captain changed topics for a moment, "I wonder if Rocket Man has any clue about what's going to happen to him and his country. It's been awfully quiet since they announced they were sending the vaccine to the US."

The XO smiled, "I hope it surprises the hell out of them."

A few hundred miles away, a similar conversation was taking place between Jessie Carter, captain of the USS *Georgia* and her executive officer. Like the USS *Ohio*, the USS *Georgia* had uploaded targeting information into their cruise missiles. At 2330 hours, both boats had made their way to their assigned launch depth. After asking the Command Authority whether their order to launch was still in effect, they were told to fire their missiles as ordered.

At midnight, each boat went through their firing protocols, sending their cruise missiles on the way to their assigned targets. After completing their launch sequences, both submarines headed back to base to reload.

Hours earlier at Whiteman Air Force Base in Missouri, several B-2 Spirit planes took off and began the long flight to North Korea. Each plane contained a huge bunker buster bomb. Those bombs were scheduled to be dropped on the North Korean nuclear and missile facilities shortly before the arrival of the cruise missiles.

Several B-52s based in Guam were scheduled to fly within 500 miles of North Korea and release their load of cruise missiles.

The USS *Ronald Reagan* and her carrier group were stationed within range of North Korea and would deliver any follow-up attacks deemed necessary.

Ty, Mac, and I, along with our wives had once again been invited to the White House. We were ushered into the situation room. Already there were various military officers. I asked one of the officers, "What's going on? Why are we here?"

He told us in a reserved voice the President would give us that information.

Shortly before 11:00 AM, President Bradford walked in and sat down. He looked up at us and said, "We need to quit meeting like this." After the chuckles died away, the President continued, "Since you've been involved in this since day one, I wanted to have you see how it was going to end. We have launched a massive attack on the military facilities in North Korea. We have a satellite over the area and hopefully we will see something."

An officer seated at a computer interrupted the President, "Mr. President, we can confirm launch of all missiles from the *Ohio* and

Georgia. Previously, the Air Force informed us that their forces were standing by and were ready to proceed. If the attack is going ahead as expected, we should be seeing the results from the satellite shortly."

The tension in the room was palpable as we waited for confirmation of the attack. The large screen at the end of the situation room suddenly lit up. It appeared that the whole country of North Korea had gone up in flames. The officer, using a pointer, showed the bunker busters that had been going off. Our cruise missiles had clearly overwhelmed the North Korean air defense system, which, along with the nuclear and missile facilities, were the first targets to be attacked.

We left the situation room in high spirits.

By that morning, there was very little left of the North Korean military. It was clear that North Korea would not be a threat to anyone for many years to come.

* * *

North Korea's President Kim was seated in his overstuffed recliner watching a favorite TV show with his sister. Neither of them had the chance to hear their defense system going off. A sole B-2 had dropped a targeted bunker buster that hit Kim's house and detonated in the room next to him. There was very little left of either of the Kims.

Chapter 89

It was 2:00 PM, and the President was in the Oval Office with several advisors. His plan was to speak to the nation at 6:00 PM. The advisors were gathered to discuss what to do and how he would craft his address. They spoke together for about one hour when the President ended the meeting and informed them that he was going to work with his speechwriter for the next two hours to finalize what he was going to say. The President instructed his Chief of Staff to clear his schedule for the rest of the day. Following that, the President and his speechwriter set about their task.

The President's communications office was working with the various television networks and others requesting time for the President's speech. Early that morning the communications staff had sent out press releases throughout the nation indicating the President would be speaking at 6:00 PM EST. Now, the time had come for the President to speak to his people.

The President, wearing a freshly pressed dark suit offset with a blue tie carrying the presidential seal, was sitting at the Resolute desk. His speech had been uploaded to the Teleprompter, and now, he was waiting to be told that he was live on television.

He began, "My fellow Americans. In this office and at this desk, presidents have come to you to explain what actions they had taken in response to any given crisis. I, too, come before you to speak of a matter of great importance to you and this country. Having occupied this chair and this office for some time, I can tell you that the weight of this country's security and safety weigh heavily on my mind every day. The actions I am going to describe to you were not taken lightly, but only after quiet deliberation with my advisors and members of Congress.

"Not too long ago, I came before you to describe the crisis we were facing involving the Ebola pandemic. We have discovered through various sources that President Kim of North Korea ordered the development of this virus and its spread throughout our country with one mission in mind—to kill Americans. Using two Mideastern terrorists, who were previously involved in strikes upon this country, he was able to spread the Ebola virus in various cities and subsequently throughout the country.

"When I received this information from my national security staff, I personally called President Kim. I had been informed that along with developing this virus, North Korea had also developed a vaccine for it. I told President Kim, as I'm telling you now, that his actions constituted an act of war against United States of America. Furthermore, I informed him that if he did not release the vaccine and the scientists who had developed it to this country, I would, in response, order a nuclear attack on his country. While this action, for many reasons, may be thought to be extreme, the CDC has estimated that our deaths could be as much as one million or more. Given that fact alone, a nuclear attack was warranted.

"Because he has repeatedly threatened this country with a nuclear attack, he should not be surprised that we would respond in such a manner. However, Kim responded to our demands in short order, and our nuclear response was removed from the table. I have been informed by the CDC that they expect to have a vaccine ready for use within one month. Until that time, every American is still at risk, and I urge that each of you follow the guidelines issued by the CDC for your protection.

"Now that Kim has provided us with the vaccine, the next question is how do we respond to his act of war. I can announce today that our response is currently taking place. The United States military, upon my order, has taken the following action. First, more than 300 cruise missiles have been launched targeting various military targets in North Korea. The United States Air Force has dropped bunker-busting bombs on the nuclear and missile facilities of North Korea. The USS *Ronald Reagan* and her carrier group are carrying out follow-up attacks. This will include more cruise missiles from ships in the carrier group. It will also include aircraft strikes on military targets.

"It is my intent that our attacks will destroy North Korea's ability to strike anyone. I have authorized the military to continue to carry out attacks to achieve our purpose. The only way for our attacks to cease will be for the Kim family to be immediately removed from office and be held accountable for their actions.

"To China, I say, we will not invade North Korea, but this country will not let North Korea's actions go unpunished.

"My friends, our country is not perfect. However, there is no country in the world that has so freely given of its people and its resources to others without asking anything in return. It is important that our allies and our enemies understand that this country will never allow such an attack like that of North Korea to go unpunished. To the terrorists who hide in the bushes, we are coming, and we will find you. To those terrorists' states that believe they can, as North Korea did, attack this country, I promise you that we will use the might of our military against you. With that being said, the United States will always hope that our former enemies can become our future friends.

"Finally, to our American family, we still face many dark days ahead as this virus continues to spread in this country. Too many deaths are still to occur. We will, I assure you, come out of this darkness stronger and with greater hope for our future. As we've seen in our history, this country can be knocked down, but we always get up and respond appropriately. Our actions against North Korea today are appropriate, strong, and devastating.

"To those countries who disagree with us because of their ideology, religion, or economic purpose, I say that we will respect our differences, but don't take that respect as a sign of weakness on our part. I suggest that you respect our strength of character, the nobleness of our purpose, and quite frankly, the professionalism of our military. Otherwise, you do that at your own peril.

"I have spoken at some length. I hope that my intentions have clearly been stated and understood. Thank you, my fellow Americans, and may God bless our country."

The television went blank, and the world sat stunned.

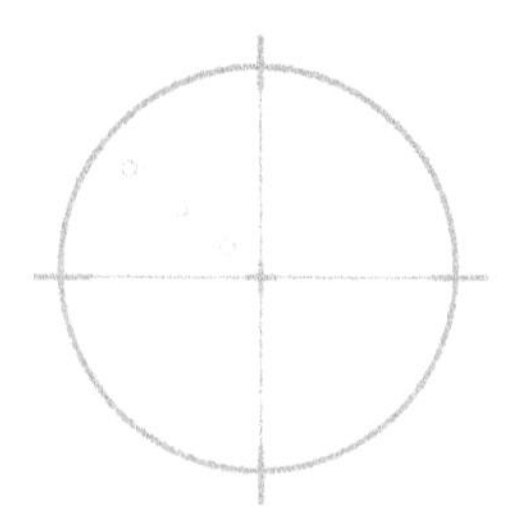

Chapter 90

While the world may have been stunned for a short period of time, the reactions to the President's speech came swiftly and furiously. As expected, our allies, with mostly unqualified support, stood by us. Both England and France, who had been the target of terrorism, supported without qualification the use of military force against North Korea. Some members of the European Union expressed concern about the possible use of nuclear force. However, they too understood the need to respond militarily to the attack by North Korea.

The fact that the United States had threatened the use of nuclear weapons shook many people to their core. While this was understandable, they had not been apprised of the President's intent not to use such force. But the threat of nuclear force had been necessary for the United States to obtain the vaccines and the scientists who developed it.

Many countries, specifically those in Africa and South America, felt that a diplomatic solution was better than military action. The President let these countries know via private message and in no uncertain terms that when their countries have been threatened with the scourge of AIDS, the United States had been there for them. The death toll from the Ebola virus could be so much larger than that of the AIDS epidemic.

Predictably, Russia and China raised serious objections to not only the threat of nuclear force, but also to the use of military force. One could read between the lines that China was not that concerned about President Kim. He had caused China innumerable problems. They were glad to be rid of him.

Various other countries reacted in different ways. Australia and New Zealand voiced their support for the military action the US had taken, but also expressed concern over the nuclear option. Several other nations chose not to react at all.

In the US, most members of Congress supported the President's action, given the number of deaths that were occurring as a result of Kim's attack. A few members of the extreme right and left criticized the President's action for a variety of reasons. Their ideology prevented them from understanding the concern of the average citizen for their safety and the safety of their children.

Almost all newspapers and television networks responded positively to President Bradford's action. Polls taken after the President's speech provided the best understanding of how people in this country viewed the President and his actions. His poll numbers jumped dramatically as the President and for his response to Kim's attack. It seemed clear that politicians opposed to the President's response risked the ire of their constituents on election day. A review of social media indicated a high degree of support for the President. All in all, it had been a good day for the President.

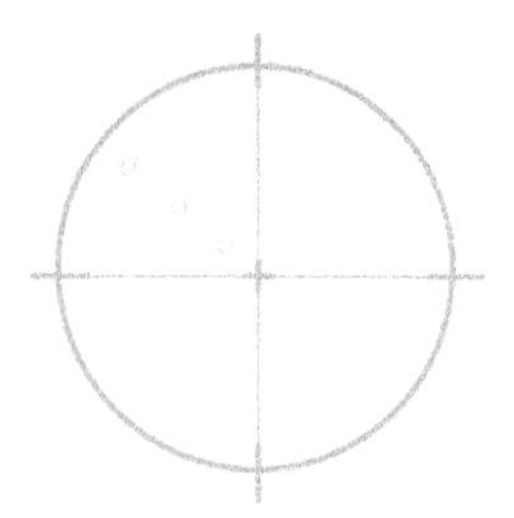

Chapter 91

Again, unexpectedly, the six of us were invited to the White House for what was called a very informal dinner. We were all concerned about what a very informal dinner required of us. Our wives decided that dresses would be appropriate attire for them.

Mac, Ty, and I also discussed what would be appropriate for us. Mac stated, "Well, informal is informal. I think that a Hawaiian shirt, jeans, and boots would fit in nicely."

I looked at Ty and he stated, "Mac, that's a little too informal for me. Why don't we wear nice slacks, a white shirt, and a sports jacket."

After some thought, I suggested, "Why don't we meet in the middle. I think that we can wear jeans as Mac suggested, and a sports jacket as Ty suggested. We pick our own shirts. How about that?"

Mac responded, "I believe that the Second Amendment preserves my right to wear whatever I want."

I laughed, "What are you talking about?"

"Frankly, I thought it sounded pretty good. You guys take this too seriously and have absolutely no sense of humor."

Ty looked at Mac and said, "You are one crazy SOB, you know that?"

Mac bowed to Ty and responded, "I take that as a compliment, my friend. DJ, do you also think that is a compliment?"

"No, I think you are crazy SOB too. I will admit, though, that you are colorful."

Following this conversation, we chose the compromise except Mac was adamant that he would wear cowboy boots. An hour later, the six of us walked outside and found a White House limousine waiting for us. In quick order, we were driven to the White House, where we were ushered up to the residence. The President and his wife were there to greet us.

The President was wearing jeans, a Western shirt, and cowboy boots. The First Lady, was wearing jeans, a cowboy shirt, and tennis shoes. As we walked to the dining room, the President looked at Mac and grinned. "Mac, I assume your mother was blind. I know of no other reason why someone would dress in jeans, cowboy boots, a Hawaiian shirt, and a sports jacket. Can you explain that for me?"

"Because I'm colorful, sir. What else can I say?"

The President looked Mac up and down, and said, "Well, I suggest you not come to Wyoming. We are real cowboys up there, and you may find yourself committed to a hospital for the criminally insane."

"I can see the wisdom of your comments. It's clear why you are the President of this great country," Mac smiled slyly.

The President laughingly replied, "Being full of shit isn't required to be a cowboy."

We sat down for dinner and soon we were chowing down on salad, meatloaf, and green beans. The conversation centered around our dealings with the terrorists. There was other polite talk until the President got down to business.

"I'm going to tell you something that you won't hear outside of this room. You probably have seen the reports of the international reaction to my speech and to the military action we commenced. Some of the responses were muted acceptance and others were not so good. I directed our State Department to respond to each country with the necessary diplomatic mumbo-jumbo and provided to the leader of each country by the respective ambassador. But what you will not hear and what I thought you might appreciate is the private message I gave to each leader. The message was, "Don't fuck with me on this."

Mac looked at me and whispered, "Now, that's what I call a President."

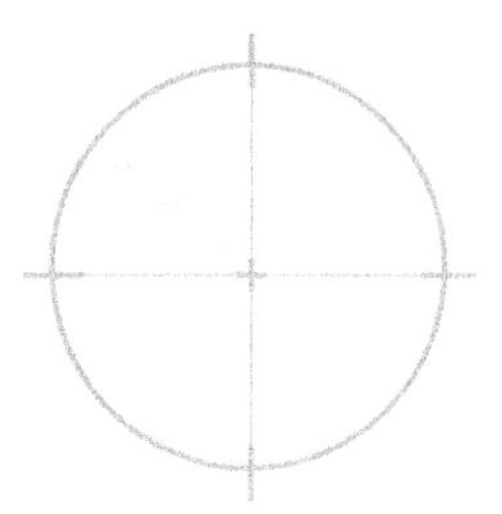

Chapter 92

Now that our service to the federal government was finished, it was time for the six of us to return home. The President was kind enough to provide a government plane to take us. Since we were the only passengers, the service provided by the crew was exceptional. As we discussed what had occurred in the last few weeks, it was all too clear that we were glad to have this terrorist business behind us. The worry and stress over the past years had taken a toll which was evident in each and every one of our faces.

The captain came on the intercom and informed us that we would be landing in a half hour. The smiles on our faces said it all—we were almost home. Through the windows, we watched the familiar landscape pass by. Except for a slight bump, the landing was perfect. The captain brought the plane to a halt in front of the small terminal that served our city. A stairway was brought to the plane, and we left the plane with thanks to our crew.

As my lovely wife and I walked into the terminal, I was surprised to see our four granddaughters waiting for us. They had balloons welcoming us home. Their parents were nowhere to be seen. Our grandchildren—Madelyn, Emma, Sophia, and Layla—surrounded us with hugs and kisses. All of a sudden, I realized how close I came to not being able to watch these young women grow up. Layla, Emma, and Sophia collected our bags while Madelyn retrieved her car. We hugged our friends goodbye and they left to return to their own homes.

It had been a long time since we had been with the "grand girls." We spent most of our time in the car talking about what they had been doing and how their school year was going. Neither Sandy nor I were watching where we were going until we soon pulled up to our house. As we walked in, waiting there for us were our children and our friends. Our kids had decided to throw a coming home party for us, which was just what we needed. Burgers were being barbecued in the backyard and there were plenty of drinks to be had. A table contained potato salad, baked beans, and chips.

It seemed like we had been gone for months, when in reality it was only several weeks. When we finished eating, everyone wanted to hear about our experiences working for the FBI. We gave them a general overview of what had occurred but left out items like the actual shootings. The discussion of our meetings with the President produced many questions about him and the White House.

By 8:00 PM, we were ready for bed. It had been a long day and a long flight. It seemed that our weeks in service to the FBI had tired us out. Our friends and family left for their own homes. Shortly thereafter, we were sound asleep.

Sandy and I slept in until almost 9:00 AM. We were enjoying our morning coffee when my phone beeped at me. I looked at my email and saw that it was from Art Rheingold. He asked if the six of us would have dinner on him, as he wanted to hear from all of us about our times as consultants to the Bureau. After phoning with Mac and Ty, we decided to meet the following evening at a local restaurant.

When Sandy and I arrived at the restaurant for dinner, we saw Mac and Ann's car already parked in the lot. For all the time that I had known Mac, he was always early to any dinner meeting. As I expected, we walked in and found Mac and Ann seated at a table with their drinks in front of them. After hugs all around, we sat down and ordered our drinks also. It didn't take long for Ty, Leanne, and Art to join us.

After we took turns relating much of what happened to Art, he asked, "And how is it that you got to meet with the President? What was it, three times?"

Mac responded first, "I hate to be the bearer of bad news Art, but some of us are held in such high regard that these perks come automatically."

Ty responded, "That's not quite true. The truth is that some of us are simply more important than others."

I spoke next, "Gentlemen, we are not here to demean the man who asked us to dinner regardless of how true your comments may be."

Art looked at our wives and asked, "Ladies, I must ask, how is it that three such smart and beautiful women ended up with these three guys who have such high and unwarranted views of themselves?"

After our laughter ended, we told Art of our visits with the President, both in his office and in the situation room. He asked a variety of questions, which we freely answered. Art finally stated, "All of you have served your country and the Bureau with great distinction. I must admit, however, that I'm glad my dealings with you are now concluded."

I looked up and saw a woman in a long black coat come through the doors to the restaurant. As I watched her, she pulled from under her coat what appeared to be an automatic weapon. Without thinking, I pulled Sandy to the floor, heard the weapon firing and returned fire with my revolver. I heard more than saw Ty and Mac firing their weapons, as well. This event, which felt like it took hours, was only minutes in duration. I jumped up and raced toward the woman and saw her lying on the floor. Ty kicked the weapon away.

The woman was obviously dead. She'd been hit multiple times. The blood from her wounds was pooling on the floor near her body.

I heard Sandy scream, and I rushed back to the table. I saw that Leanne had been shot in the throat and was trying to ask for help. Ann was lying on her side groaning, but there were no wounds visible. Glancing at Art, who was still sitting at the table, I saw that he'd been shot three times in the chest.

Within seconds, I was helping Ty place napkins on the entry and exit wounds on Leanne's neck in an effort to stop the bleeding. Mac had already placed Ann on the floor and was examining her. I came over to assist when Mac said, "She took a round in the shoulder, but she'll be all right. How is Leanne?"

I responded, "She was hit in the throat. We need to get her to a hospital as soon as possible. Sandy wasn't hit, thank God, but Art is dead. What is going on, Mac?"

Our eyes met, and he shook his head. We heard sirens in the distance.

Ty and Mac traveled to the hospital with Leanne and Ann. Sandy and I stood there covered in blood. I said, "I have to make a call." We walked outside. I took out my phone and dialed Sam's cell number. After the third ring, he answered. I said, "Sam, this is DJ. Art took us out to dinner tonight. A woman came into the restaurant with an automatic weapon and opened fired at us."

"Is everyone all right?"

"No, Leanne was hit in the throat, and we don't know if she will make it. Ann was hit in the shoulder but should be okay. Art did not make it. He was hit three times in the chest."

"And the shooter?"

"She is dead also."

"Maybe your involvement with the Bureau isn't over yet."

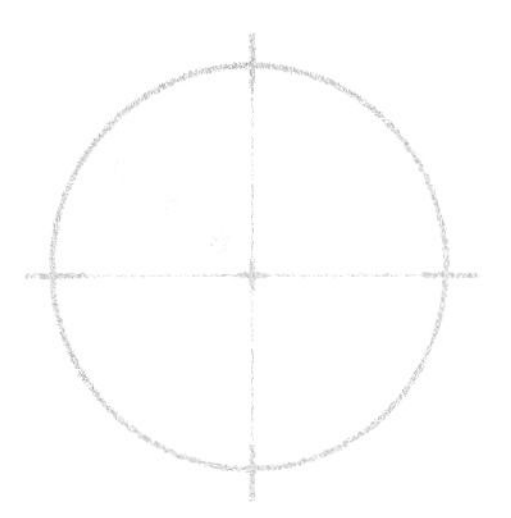

Epilogue

Sam flew into town from Washington to attend Art's funeral. The six of us sat in the back of a very crowded church. Obviously, Art was a man of many friends and a large family. Sam sat in the front as he was scheduled to give the eulogy.

Following the service, we were able to speak with Art's wife and family. It was very difficult talking with her since we felt some guilt for his death. Even though we knew we did not bear any responsibility, the guilt still remained.

We were standing outside of the church awash in the sunshine that tried to remove the clouds from our hearts. Sam walked up with a 30ish, heavily tanned woman. He smiled at us and said, "I wanted to introduce you to Emily Hassan. She was Art's deputy here and has been promoted to take his place."

She shook hands with each of us and we shared some memories of Art. After 20 minutes, she bid us goodbye and left.

Mac turned to Sam and asked, "Is she Muslim?"

Taken aback, as that would not be an appropriate question about an employee, Sam replied, "No, she is Catholic and goes to mass every day. She has been vetted many times. I would not place her in this position if there were any questions at all."

Mac let it go, and we moved onto another subject. I started the discussion, "Sam, we have been thinking about the recent attack. Have you identified the killer yet?"

He frowned as he looked at us. "You are not going to like what I am about to say. Her name is Amal Hakim. Her DNA is a direct match with Samir's."

"What do you mean, Sam?" asked Ty.

"She was Samir's sister."

"Well, I'll be damned," I replied.

"I don't like this," Mac stated. "Does he have any other sisters?"

Sam answered, "We are working on that."

Ty spoke up again, "Sam, I want you to hear me out. Samir and his family have tried to kill us in Paris and here, multiple times. I think it's time we take the fight to his family. If my guess is right, that would be in Europe. Keep us as consultants and let us go there. We can work with your French friends."

"That's a mighty big ask, Ty."

"You can send Derek to keep an eye on us and keep us out of trouble."

Mac clapped Ty on the shoulder and said, "Ty, my, friend, you are not as stupid as you look. Besides, I have always wanted to go to Paris in the springtime."

After much further discussion, the outlines of a plan grew to put Ty's suggestion into effect.

* * *

Emily Hassan drove to her church parking lot and turned her car off. Looking around and seeing no one, she pulled out a burner phone and punched in a number. When the person on the other end answered, there was the sound of the encryption software program coming online. "Yes," a robotic sounding voice answered.

Emily responded, "Tell our leader that I am in place." Emily hung up, started her car and drove off.

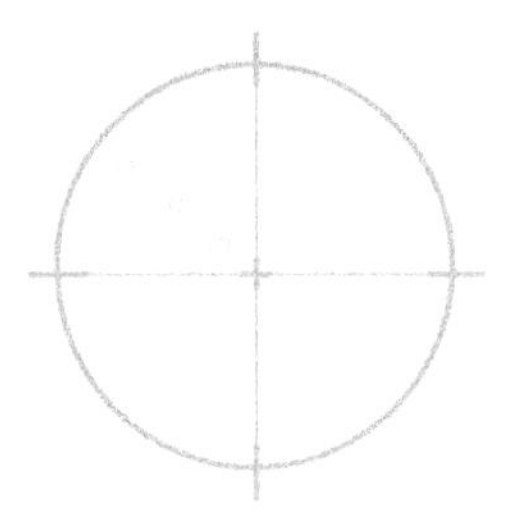

Acknowledgments

Many people are involved in the development and completion of a book such as this.

First, I want to thank Ron Flud and Daniel Swanson for their thoughts and insights into police operations and the reactions of police officers. Their review and comments about Mac and Ty brought these characters to life.

Several individuals reviewed this manuscript and provided helpful advice in the development of the final product. Those individuals include Sharyl Admire, Beverly Flud, and Madelyn Swanson.

Pivotal to a good book are great editors. I had three of the best in Sharyl Admire, Neal Smith, and Kira Henschel.

I also want to thank Ryan Allen for his talent and creativity in developing the book cover.

I want to extend my gratitude to Kira Henschel and Henschel-HAUS Publishing, Inc. for believing in this book and bringing it to you.

I want to extend special thanks to my wife, Sharyl, for her support, inspiration, and love. This book is as much hers as mine.

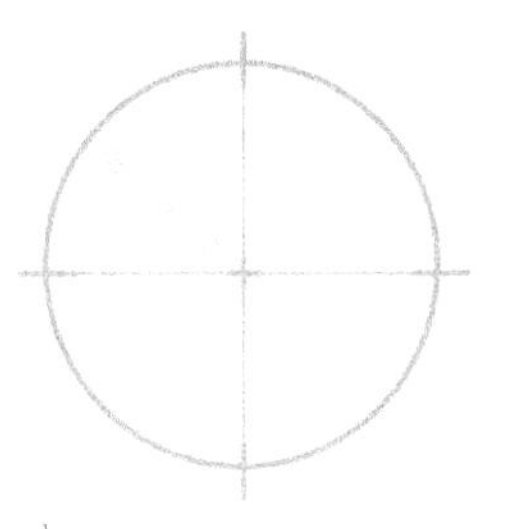

About the Author

Dave Admire received his law degree from the Catholic University of America. In his early career, he was both a prosecutor and defense attorney. At the age of 33, he was elected District Court Judge in the Seattle area. He served in this position for over 22 years. During his time of the bench, he developed a reputation for being creative and innovative in searching out alternatives to incarceration.

After retiring as a judge, Dave continued his work with young people by becoming a college professor. Before retiring, he was an adjunct professor at Seattle University for 20 years. He was chair of the Criminal Justice Department at Bethany College in Kansas. Subsequently, he became department chair of the Department of Political Science and Criminal Justice at Southern Utah University in Cedar City, Utah. In the summer of 2010, Dave served as a visiting professional at the International Criminal Court in The Hague, in the Netherlands, where he acted as a legal advisor to Judge Christine Van den Wingaert of Belgium.

Dave resides with his wife Sharyl in Cedar City, Utah.

Printed in the USA
CPSIA information can be obtained
at www.ICGtesting.com
CBHW051821050724
10941CB00012B/166